STEPHANIE PAIGE KING

FELLOWSHIP OF THE FRAZZLED MOMS

Stephanie Paige King

ISBN: 978-1-965352-15-1

Acknowledgments

Just as it takes a village to raise kids, it takes one to write a book. Thank you to everyone who inspired and encouraged me. I have the best church family and friends who pushed me to write. Because of you, I believed I could.

Tracee, Nelda, Kristen, Misty, and my mom Sharon, thanks for being brave enough to read my early version and still taking my calls afterward. A special shout out to Kristen for helping me write a better triplet family and for taking my first headshots. Thank you Melissa S. Your writerly gifts and your excited texts as you read the mostly-final copy kept me going when quitting would have been easier. Thank you, Cynthia Hickey for giving Dana and Josie a home and a future at Winged Publications and for being eternally patient with me. And to my English teacher friends Christina and Denise, who were a thousand times more helpful than the internet with my constant grammar and word questions, thank you. Why yes, I did just use 'and' at the front of a sentence. Please use your red pens accordingly.

I have only gratitude, love, and the utmost respect for my fellow writer and friend Brittnye Davis. You've been reading this story since day one and are the best critique buddy I could ask for. Please always edit for me.

Dear family, without you—and your shenanigans—there is no book. Brent, Collin, Kailyn, Carter, Alisha, and Mom, I love so you much. Thank you for letting me write, for believing in me, and for praying me through the journey. God is faithful and good, and He alone gets the glory for everything. Thank you for giving me words to write and for giving me Your Word.

Chapter 1

Dana

Executives in corner offices had nothing on housewives working at their kitchen counters. Nor did they have a handy roll of paper towels within arms' reach. Dana Harding had just uploaded her suspense story to her creative writing class's message board. She took a self-congratulatory sip of coffee when she eyed an embarrassing typo she had missed. What should have read, "She watched his chest rise and fall with each shallow, labored breath," instead said, "shallow, labeled breast." Dana gasped, spewing coffee on her keyboard. When her writing professor challenged her to put a body on the first page, she doubted he meant the kind with labeled breasts.

"No!" she coughed. The race was on to save her laptop from shorting out as she thrust a wad of paper towels on its keys, knocking over her coffee mug in the process. "Seriously?" Brown liquid baptized the computer and waterfalled over the edge of the counter. Harvey, the Bernese Mountain dog, all too happily lapped at the puddle on the tile floor while coffee continued to drip on his head.

Dana lunged for more paper towels, mentally apologizing to the planet for her wastefulness, just as the screen on her laptop flickered and went dark. No amount of random key tapping revived it.

Time of Death: 9:29 a.m.

She dropped onto a barstool and buried her head in her

hands. Why did everything have to be so hard? After years of sacrificing her career and dreams for her family, all she wanted was an activity of her own. Writing reminded her that she had talents beyond finding lost items and grilling the perfect cheese sandwich. It was proof she could be more than just a middle-aged mom of three kids. Dana secretly dreamt of writing crime novels, and she'd joined this class hoping it would be her steppingstone to literary greatness.

Before today, the longest thing she had written since becoming a mother was an apology letter to Adam's teacher when he presented his athletic cup from taekwondo for show-and-tell.

The short story she'd just submitted was the exact pivot she had been waiting for, a sinister tale with an undercurrent of wit. She'd been so proud of it too, right up until she hit send and realized her massive spell check fail. At least if her husband Will killed her for breaking the laptop, she wouldn't have to face her class tomorrow night.

Dana pulled her phone from her pocket to search nearby computer repair shops and noticed two missed texts.

The first was from the pastor's wife Serena. I have a proposition for you. Let's grab coffee asap

The second was from the pharmacy. Two prescriptions for Edward Johnson are ready for pick up.

Serena could wait. She probably needed a sub in the preschool department at church, and Dana didn't have the bandwidth for it right now.

She checked her phone again. There was one of those computer repair places near the pharmacy. Maybe after she ran her dad's errands, she would take him to lunch to get him out of the house. He hadn't been the same since they lost her mother to pancreatic cancer last year. Even though Dana's plans had taken an unexpected turn, maybe an outing would do them both some good. She wrapped the computer in a towel, grabbed her purse, and headed out.

The computer technician had at least been polite enough to stifle his chuckle at her dripping keyboard, but her cheeks were still flushed with embarrassment when she turned onto her dad's block. Her pulse quickened when she spotted a white-haired man up ahead wearing nothing but plaid boxer shorts and leather slippers. As if that weren't enough, he seemed to be herding ducks across the street. Dana recognized him and flinched. She overshot the turn into her dad's driveway and veered into his mailbox.

The ducks, spooked by the crash, flew off, and the mostly naked man jerked his head toward the noise. He looked horrified by the savage attack on his property, though not more so than Dana who squeezed her eyes closed to block out the image of her father in his boxers.

She didn't take time to assess the damage to her Tahoe or the mailbox. She needed to get her dad into the house before the neighbors came outside to investigate the commotion. Those who still had their hearing, anyway.

He tried to pry the box and its wooden post out from under the SUV like it was a fallen comrade he couldn't leave behind. "Why would you do such a thing?"

Dana put her arms on his shoulders and guided him toward the house. "It was an accident. Let's get you inside, I'll come back for the mailbox in a bit."

He didn't seem to even realize his state of undress or notice Dana. "I have to fix this before the mailman gets here, or he won't deliver my mail."

"Dad, if you don't get some clothes on, Miss Rita will call the cops and have you arrested for indecent exposure. Then you won't need a mailbox."

At that, he allowed Dana to lead him into the house.

What was it about the elderly and their fascination

with the mail? It seemed like all the retirees in this community had two jobs: keep tabs on the length of one another's grass and check the mail religiously.

Her dad reappeared in the living room dressed. "Now, young lady," he addressed her like she was still a child. "Do you mind telling me why you're driving recklessly and destroying property?"

"Dad," she said in her most soothing mom tone, "I came by to deliver your meds, but you distracted me by chasing ducks in your underwear."

"I can pick up my own medications just fine."

Dana took a breath to steady herself. She didn't know what was happening to her dad, but she was sure getting into an argument wouldn't help. "Do you remember we agreed after the flu catastrophe that Will or I would pick them up for you? In fact, after you slammed the door on the delivery guy, the pharmacy insisted on it."

He paced an antsy pattern, no doubt anxious to get back outside. Dana stepped in front of him and put her hands gently on his shoulders again. "Dad, stop. Can you tell me what you were doing outside?" She wasn't entirely sure she wanted to hear the answer, but it seemed necessary. As did electroshock therapy to erase the memory burned into her mind.

"I spilled apple juice down my clothes and went to my room and took them off. Then I noticed the blinds were open and didn't want Rita Brewer reporting me as a pervert."

Dana nodded. It was, after all, the same thought she'd had about her a few minutes ago.

"So, I went to close the blinds, and I saw a pair of ducks building a nest in your mom's flower bed. I didn't want them tearing up her petunias, so I ran outside to shoo them away." He said he'd hoped to corral them to the pond at the park, so they'd leave the petunias alone.

Dana pinched the bridge of her nose and closed her

eyes. It seemed unlikely ducks would be nesting in early March, but what did she know? She wasn't an ornithologist. The rest of his story seemed oddly feasible. Maybe in his haste to get rid of the ducks, he forgot he wasn't properly dressed.

Her dad pointed outside. "Now, would you get your car off my mailbox and help me remount it before the mail truck comes?"

Dana followed him outside and backed the Tahoe off the curb. A loud snap made her recoil. Hopefully it was the wooden post and not part of the car. She slid out of the driver's seat and peeped at the carnage through squinted eyes. The post was broken, and the metal box was mangled, much like the Tahoe's bumper. Will was going to be furious.

Her dad attempted to reshape the mailbox into a recognizable form while Dana stomped down the sod where the post was torn from its hole.

A petite woman in pink curlers marched up. "What on earth are you doing?"

"Hello, Miss Rita," Dana said. Before she could explain further, her dad interjected.

"What's it look like we're doing? My mailbox got run over."

She put her hands on her hips. "It looks like you've been having a frat party, Edward Johnson. What were you doing out here in your boxers earlier?"

"What business is it of yours, Peeping Tom?"

Dana knew she needed to intervene. "Dad, you never got to drink that juice, did you? I hope it's not still sitting out."

He seemed to forget his confrontation with Rita Brewer and went inside, giving Dana time to explain what happened. She could see why her dad got so irritated with the woman.

The busybody softened when Dana explained what

had occurred. "Without your mother, he's not himself, is he?"

Could grief really push a person so far that their memory slipped away? Once Rita was satisfied that no real mischief had occurred, Dana headed inside to check on her dad. He was eating a ham sandwich in front of *The People's Court* like nothing was amiss.

Her phone buzzed with a text from Will's sister, Julia.

Call me when you get a sec

Her stomach knotted. Julia was strictly a texter, so if she wanted to have an actual conversation, it was likely bad news. Or she needed a favor.

She kissed her dad on the head and trudged to her car. Her stomach clenched even tighter when she saw the Tahoe's crumpled bumper.

Julia picked up on the first ring. "Hey, sorry that was so dramatic, but I'm driving and can't text."

"No worries," Dana said as if the message hadn't just given her a peptic ulcer. "What's up?"

"I'm embarrassed to tell you this, but David and I are struggling to keep our marriage together. We're in therapy twice a week."

How bad did things have to be to sit through therapy that often? Double therapy must be outrageous. Probably still cheaper than a divorce.

"Anyway, we were wondering if the kids could stay with you during Spring Break, that is, if you don't have plans, so we can go to an intensive marriage retreat in New Mexico."

Dana had called it. Julia needed a *huge* favor, and she couldn't text it because Dana and Will would've had time to formulate an excuse. But how could they say no to saving a marriage?

Her nephews, Theo and Quinn Wallace, were good kids, as far as other people's teenagers went. At fourteen and thirteen, they were only sixteen months apart, so they had been wearing out their parents since birth. Dana thought their small age gap was ironic given that Julia was a physician's assistant for an obstetrician, and David was a pharmacist. If any two people could have planned their pregnancies at perfect times, it should have been them.

The Harding boys loved being with their cousins. Wherever the four of them were, they were easy to find. You only had to follow the trail of food wrappers, dirt, and noise. All the boys plus her daughter Leah for a whole week would be exhausting, expensive, and loud. In her current frazzled state, she wondered if she could even survive a week with all the kids. Was saving her in-laws' marriage worth the risk?

"Dana, are you still there?"

Tightness constricted her throat. She swallowed and tried to sound sincere. "We would be happy to watch the boys for you."

Dana avoided looking at the broken mailbox as she backed out of the driveway. Could this day get any worse?

A message from the computer repair shop lit up her phone screen informing her that the day could indeed get worse.

Chapter 2

After school, the boys dropped their backpacks by the door and made beelines for the pantry. Normally Dana would have monitored their snack choices and asked about homework, but she was too upset about her dad, the car, and the computer. She hadn't had time to process one catastrophe, let alone three.

Eight-year-old Adam hadn't noticed the damage to the Tahoe, but his big brother sure had. "Whoa, Mom. What happened to the car?"

"There's something wrong with the car? Are we gonna crash?" Adam had asked in a panic.

"Nah, Mom already did," said Nate. Kids could be so annoying.

She didn't want them to break the news of the wreck to Will before she could, so she sent them outside to play. Maybe they'd forget about the crumpled bumper by the time Will got home. Dana had called him earlier, but he had been in a meeting. He hadn't responded to her texts either. Work was starting to monopolize his time, and it was a problem.

When they met, Dana had just graduated college, and Will was in culinary school. He used the computers in the public library where she worked several times a week to research recipes because he couldn't afford a home computer. He was funny and handsome. His wavy light brown hair glinted in the sun and beckoned her to run her fingers through it.

They could talk for hours without noticing the time pass. She supported his epicurean aspirations by being his resident taste-tester, and they tied the knot in her parents' back yard the next year.

When Will's parents were killed in a collision with an eighteen-wheeler seven months later, he gave up the long nights in the kitchen for normal business hours. Will always put his family first. Though lately it felt like something was up. He hadn't made it home before dark in a week, and he'd missed two of Leah's soccer games. He wasn't his usual fun-loving self, and Dana was nervous about how he'd respond to her mishaps today.

He couldn't fault her for an accident her elderly father basically caused, could he? If this had been her first fender-bender, probably not, but it wasn't. Lubbock, Texas was home to a D-1 university and an inordinate number of retirement communities. Thus, every drive across town was a chance to stare death in the face. Yet somehow, none of Dana's previous accidents involved distracted college kids nor Moses's grandmother.

There was the time Harvey lost his ever-loving mind on the way to the vet and jumped into her lap. All she could see was fur, and it was a miracle she'd only sideswiped that Volkswagen instead of swerving into oncoming traffic.

Before that, there was the infamous garage door disaster. Unbeknownst to Dana, two-year-old Adam had found the lost garage door opener amid the shoes and snack wrappers in the rear floorboard of the Suburban. She realized it the instant she started to back out of the garage and collided with the closing door.

The deafening scrape of the metal muted her expletive, and the jolt sent Adam's sippy cup flying.

"Again, again." The toddler applauded and pressed the

garage door button with a sticky thumb.

Their insurance agent had shared Adam's amusement, but Will had not. It was sure to come up tonight when everyone learned of Dana's latest accident.

She tried calling Will again before she left to pick Leah up from soccer practice, but it went straight to voicemail.

Leah flung herself into the passenger seat in an exasperated huff. How did she manage to slump that far down without sliding into the floorboard? Dana wondered if there was a freshman elective where teens received formal training on how to be dramatic and simultaneously humiliated by the very existence of their parental units. That would explain Leah's high GPA.

"Hey Sweetie, how was-"

"Oh my gosh, Mom. What did you do to our car? Everyone is going to think you're day drinking or that we're poor."

"I appreciate your concern for my safety and well-being. It was a minor fender-bender, by the way, but since you care so much about what your friends think of my car, you should probably get out of it and walk home."

Dana put the car in park and waited.

Leah crouched even lower in her seat and covered her face. "Mom, drive. People are staring."

Dana looked around. The rest of the soccer team barely noticed their own parents' vehicles, let alone Dana's because their faces were glued to their phones. "I'm not driving away until you either exit or apologize for being so awful to me."

"Fine," Leah conceded. "I'm sorry. Can we go?"

"How about, 'Mom, I'm sorry for being rude and selfish. I'm sorry you had a wreck, and I'm sorry I made it worse by only caring about myself?'"

"Caring about myself and being selfish are the same things."

Dana turned off the engine and pointed at the passenger door.

"Okay, I'm sorry for being rude and selfish."

If her own mother were still alive, Dana would have called her to apologize for her fifteen-year-old self.

The doorbell rang as they walked in from the garage. Before Dana could get to it, Leah was already accepting a screaming baby from a tall redhead in an oversized sweatshirt and leggings. Josie Caraway was the mother of infant triplets. She and her husband Hunter were members of the same church as the Hardings, but they had never met before the Caraways bought the house across the cul-de-sac when they learned they were expecting.

When Josie was put on bedrest, Dana pitched in with errands, food, and entertainment to alleviate Josie's boredom. They watched Food Network together and consumed questionable amounts of Chinese food. They also ate enough Tums between the two of them to keep the company fully operational well into the next decade.

One time Dana brought over safety goggles. "These will protect you when the elastic on those maternity pants finally snaps. We wouldn't want you to lose an eye. Can you imagine how much harder it would be to parent three babies with no depth perception?"

Josie had laughed so hard she peed a little, which made Dana laugh so hard she did as well.

Dana called after Josie's swiftly-retreating back, "Thank you, sir. May I have another?"

Josie turned around with a furrowed brow and pursed lips. "Last I checked, I was not a 'sir.' And be careful what you wish for. I've got kids for days."

"It was an *Animal House* reference," Dana said. "Like the most famous quote from the movie."

"Before my time." she said flatly over her shoulder as she trekked back to her side of the cul-de-sac.

It was before Dana's too, but she thought everybody

knew that reference. She knew she was a decade older than Josie, but how was ten years an entire generation gap?

Josie frequented the Hardings' doorstep with crying babies who threatened to undo naptime for their siblings. Dana supposed other people would be mortified if their neighbors dropped off screaming babies and ran back home.

Leah bounced the infant on her hip and cooed to him until he was all smiles. It mystified Dana how her daughter could be so salty to her and so sweet to everyone else.

Dana's phone buzzed with a text.

Josie: Why does your Tahoe look like you hit a deer

Dana: Run in with my dad's mailbox. Will doesn't know yet

Josie: Yikes! Use Ben as a human shield when he gets home. He can't kill you while you're holding a baby

Dana: lol. In that case, I should put another one in a backpack carrier to prevent sneak attacks

Josie: Bahaha! Good luck, friend

Dana began to tidy up the living room, picking up random clothing items and an odd assortment of toys and electronics. A good mother would make her kids pick up their own filth, but sometimes efficiency took priority over stellar parenting. She could pick up the house faster by herself, and it was more peaceful than threatening the kids and pointing out every sock and Nerf dart they missed. It also gave her time to gather her thoughts before she had to break the news of the accident to Will.

Her phone dinged. She anticipated more ribbing from Josie. She would have preferred it over Will's message.

Dana, we have a problem.

Her stomach knotted. Did he already know about the accident? She tried to feel him out.

We do?

Will: We'll talk later.

"Hey Leah," she called. "Why don't you let me hold Ben for a while?" Josie might be onto something with her human shield idea.

Chapter 3

Josie

Josie folded the four hundredth onesie from the bottomless laundry basket and leaned back on the sofa. She rubbed her shoulder, concerned she was developing a hunchback from crouching all the time.

She pictured Dana wearing two of her babies to shield herself from Will and chuckled aloud. He was a chill guy, but she said a quick prayer for her friend, nonetheless. Her own mental health depended upon Dana's friendship. She'd been so lonely after she had to leave her university marketing job to go on bedrest. Now with her own sister Laurel ghosting her, she needed Dana as a lifeline more than ever.

Laurel was on sabbatical hiking the Appalachian trail with her granola friends who didn't wear deodorant or shave their armpits. She hadn't been responding to any of Josie's texts in the last month, and she had yet to meet her niece and nephews in person.

Her phone buzzed, but it took her a moment to locate it under a stack of burp cloths. It was her husband, Hunter. He told her he would be home late, and she tried to recall how much cash she had on hand to bribe Leah to come over later and help her. Whatever it cost, it would be worth every penny.

Hunter said, "Todd and Megan want us to go to some charity dinner with them next Friday night. What do you think?"

He began working for Todd Ferguson in college. When Todd decided to expand his business into residential construction, he made Hunter his business partner. He was the reason Hunter was becoming a well-respected home builder in West Texas. He was also a hoot at parties.

Josie shifted the phone against her ear and pondered a Friday night out as she inspected the ends of her auburn hair that had gone about a year too long without a trim and the frayed sleeve of her ancient Texas Tech sweatshirt. She leaned back against the sofa. "The attire wouldn't happen to be "postpartum grunge, would it?"

None of her pre-baby clothes fit anymore. Her old work friends used to tell her she looked like that Brazilian Instagram model, Flavia something. Now though she just looked tired and sloppy.

Dana had forced her to buy some new leggings last week after pointing out that she could see Josie's underwear through the threadbare ones she had on. They'd had a good laugh shopping online for them. Josie found a website advertising "buttery soft leggings."

"Is that supposed to be a good thing? How can you compare fabric to a dairy product?"

"I don't know why companies describe leggings that way," said Dana. "Butter seems more slick than soft. Kind of greasy."

"I think I need deep compression leggings instead of soft ones to keep my thighs from jiggling when I walk."

Dana had rolled her eyes. "There's nothing on you that jiggles. Buttery soft would feel better against baby skin."

"Unless they're slick and greasy like actual butter. Then babies would slip off my lap."

She chuckled to herself now remembering their exchange.

"I'll find out how we're supposed to dress," Hunter said, "if you can see about getting a sitter."

"I'll try, but…"

Josie heard a loud metallic crash and shouting. "Jos, I gotta go." The line went dead, and Josie prayed that whatever had just happened on the construction site was minor and that no one was hurt.

She stacked the folded baby clothes back in the basket atop the yet-to-be-folded clothes and hid the whole thing behind the recliner so she wouldn't have to look at it. Her babysitter options were limited by the fact that none of their family lived in town, and the Hardings were really the only people they knew with older kids. Leah was her best bet, but three infants were probably more than one fifteen-year-old could handle.

She was by nature an extrovert. While she was grateful for these babies she'd prayed so long for, being home alone with them all day every day was taking a toll on her psyche. She hoped she remembered how to interact with other adults. She and Hunter hadn't been on a real date out of the house in months, and it was long overdue.

Hunter and Josie met in Political Science sophomore year at Texas Tech. She took meticulous notes, while Hunter hardly took any at all. He sat behind her, and one afternoon he asked to borrow her notes, promising to give them back in the next lecture.

She shook her head and turned around. "I'm going to study them tonight."

She hadn't given the guy with the sweat-stained trucker cap more than a cursory glance before, but now that she had gotten a good look at his golden hazel eyes pleading with her in the most adorable, puppy dog way, Josie regretted turning him down. "What if instead you meet me at the library and you can *look* at my notes while I study?"

Hunter laughed. "Like a supervised visitation of the

notes?"

More like a date, she thought. "Sure, you can look at them, but I don't trust you to take them."

After graduation, he proposed to Josie on the steps of the campus library where they had their first unofficial date. Sometimes it felt like it all happened last week, and other times, the eight years since she said yes to Hunter's library proposal was a lifetime ago.

Josie glanced at the clock in the kitchen. There was just enough time to squeeze in a walk before the next feeding, which would make two days in a row, so that baby weight ought to fall right off.

She loaded Connor and Oliva and pushed the massive triple Peg Perego stroller she'd nicknamed Peg across the street to retrieve Ben.

Will answered the door holding Ben. He leaned down and buckled the baby into the open seat. "This is the best way to have babies. They come for a little while, but I get to sleep all night, and you can't beat the price."

"That's called being a grandparent, Will," Josie deadpanned.

He stood and shook a finger at her with mock anger. "Watch your mouth. We have a long way to go before anyone in this house becomes a grandparent."

She steered her enormous vessel back onto the sidewalk. "Thank you for entertaining my baby and for helping me keep all the tiny humans alive."

He waved off her gratitude. "It's nothing. We're always here for you guys."

Will seemed too chipper to have learned about Dana's wreck, so she paused to fire off a quick text to her friend.

I take it Will doesn't know yet?

Dana responded with a wide-eyed emoji and praying hands: no

Josie: Praying

After three blocks, Josie was already tired. At this rate,

the likelihood of fitting into a dress to wear next Friday night was going to be even slimmer than the likelihood of finding a sitter for her children. She needed to get her life together.

After wrestling Peg back into the house and changing a round of diapers, Josie commenced the circus feat necessary to get three babies fed simultaneously. Olivia happily gummed a teething toy that looked like it might have come from the dog section of PetSmart while Josie sat in the floor next to her and laid Connor on her folded legs. Then she propped Ben on a Boppy pillow so she could hold bottles for both boys. Again, she worried how her new lifestyle was damaging her posture.

Her phone vibrated near the edge of the coffee table, and she managed to answer it in speaker mode without dropping a bottle.

"Hey, Mom."

"*Mija,* is next weekend a good time for me to come for a couple of days? My friend from work is driving down to see her grandson play basketball, and she asked me to ride with her. I'd get in late Thursday night and leave Sunday after church if that works for you guys."

"Sure, you know we never say no to help." Her mother made the trip from Albuquerque every few weeks to stock the freezer, visit her grandbabies, and judge Josie's housekeeping skills.

Marie Saldana was a force of nature. Her larger-than-life personality was in stark contrast to her small stature. She moved with the speed and tenacity of a tornado, though she wouldn't dream of leaving a wake of debris like one. Her neatness bordered on obsessiveness, which was both a godsend and a curse for the new parents.

"Have you spoken to your sister?" asked Marie.

Josie hesitated. It would probably come across as tattling if she told the truth. "Uh, not lately. Why?"

"She has news, but I'll let her share it with you

herself."

Josie tried to imagine what her big sister's news might be. She hoped it was that she was finally coming to meet the babies. The sisters had been close all their lives, so Laurel's radio silence wounded Josie all the more. She couldn't tell her mom though.

Marie would tell her she was just pouty because she'd been couped up for too long, and maybe there was some truth to that. However, with her mom coming, she and Hunter could go to that dinner next Friday. Her mood brightened instantly.

It was after 8:00 p.m. when Hunter finally slipped in the door. Josie was lying on the sofa watching *Friends*. "Hey Babe, there's lasagna in the fridge," she said without getting up.

Hunter kissed her and apologized again for being so late. "You made lasagna?"

The incredulity she detected in her husband's voice was justified. Josie hadn't cooked many meals from scratch in the last year.

"I heated up one of my mom's frozen lasagnas."

He lifted his chin. "Ah."

Josie got up and followed him into the kitchen, took the plate from the fridge and warmed it. Hunter wrapped his arms around her and inhaled deeply into her neck.

She pulled away from him. "You're not gonna want to do that. My hair smells like sour milk."

Hunter pulled her back into his arms. "That's okay. I smell like dirt and sweat," he said. "We can reek of a hard day's work together."

She settled into his shirt. All felt right with the world when he held her. "What happened earlier when you had to hang up?"

"New guy dropped a copper sink."

The microwave dinged, and they pulled apart. Josie took the food out, while Hunter grabbed a water bottle from the fridge.

"Did the babies go down without a fight tonight?"

She shrugged and carried the plate to the coffee table in the living room. "I called in reinforcements."

"Leah?"

"Yep. I think Ben likes her better than me anyway."

Hunter sat down in the recliner and pulled the lever to lean back, but nothing happened. As he wrestled with the chair, Josie told him her mother was coming next weekend and that Leah agreed to come over to help the night of the fundraiser.

"Perfect." he said, pushing back against the recliner. "Is this thing broken?"

Josie reached behind it and pulled out the full laundry basket she had stashed that afternoon. Hunter flew backwards but managed to hold onto the plate of food so that none of it spilled. They both laughed.

"That was impressive," she said.

"I rode in the truck with Todd this morning, so I had some practice holding onto my coffee. He treats railroad tracks like bike ramps and potholes like extra lives in a video game."

Josie pictured flying over railroad tracks in her minivan. The doors would probably fall off.

"Remember when *you* used to drive like you were fleeing a crime scene?" she asked.

"That was before I had a pregnant wife or had three infants in car seats in the back."

"Mom said she's planning to leave after church on Sunday. We haven't been to church since I went on bedrest. What do we do?"

Hunter had a mouthful of lasagna, so Josie answered herself. "I guess we will have to go this Sunday to get the trial run out of the way before she comes so she'll think we go every week."

"This is bad, Babe. We tried like four weeks in a row

to get out the door, and every week there were too many obstacles stacked against us, remember?"

"I got puked on two weeks in a row. I remember. We are doing the best we can right now, and if Marie has something to say about us not raising her grandbabies in church, she's more than welcome to provide us with a weekend au pair to even the playing field. She'll need to hire someone who's also a body builder though since that stroller weighs sixty pounds."

Josie laughed. "Excuse me, Peg weighs sixty pounds *empty*. I thought I was going to die pushing it this afternoon. If I don't get ripped biceps out of this mom of multiples deal, I'm going to be ticked."

The stroller talk reminded Josie of the triplets' upcoming well check. "Peg won't even fit in the elevator, so I really need you to go with me."

"I'm planning to take the whole morning off for it. But maybe we think about a double umbrella stroller as an alternative. Could be a total game changer if we wear the third kid and push two. Elevators wouldn't be a problem anymore, but you'd lose out on the bicep workout though."

It was a worthy tradeoff. She beamed at her genius husband and started googling twin umbrella strollers on her phone when coughing erupted over the baby monitor.

Hunter's wild-eyed panic mirrored her own. He eased the recliner upright and set his plate on the coffee table. "It's probably nothing."

Sure, it was probably nothing. But what if it was something?

Chapter 4

Dana

Dana, do you mind coming fifteen minutes early tomorrow so we can talk before class?

Her stomach plummeted. Her writing instructor must have already read her story and planned to reprimand her for careless editing. At least he wasn't going to shame her in front of everyone.

"No phones at the table, Mom," Nate ever so helpfully announced. She shoved it in her back pocket and forced a smile.

Will had arrived home with her father in tow. His usual laugh lines were pulled taught by the pinched crease between his brows, and his only response when she asked him what the problem was he'd texted her about was a clipped, "Not now."

Dinner got off to a pleasant enough start until the conversation turned to the accident. Will had stopped by Edward's house and discovered the mangled mailbox upon arrival. He called the police and helped his father-in-law file a vandalism report.

Will fumed. "I can't believe vandals are perpetrating criminal mischief in Mesquite Village. It's shameful how people take advantage of the elderly."

Dana studied his face for any indication he was

messing with her. "Vandals? Really?"

"Either that or someone drove around the curve like a maniac. How else would they have splintered the post like that?"

"Well, I can assure you I wasn't driving like a maniac," she said.

Everyone stopped eating.

Will cocked his head to the side. "You carried out a hit-and-run in your dad's yard?" He seemed genuinely bewildered.

She narrowed her eyes. "Did you not see the crushed bumper in the garage?"

"*That's* how the car got smashed?" Adam shouted.

Dana ignored him. "Dad, don't you remember I brought you your pills, and you were trying to get ducks out of your flowerbed. Is any of this ringing a bell? Then Rita Brewer stomped outside with pink rollers in her hair, and you called her a Peeping Tom. She said she was glad I showed up when I did so she didn't have to call the cops on you for running around outside in your underwear."

If the family wasn't engrossed in the conversation yet, they sure were now.

Recognition dawned on Edward's face. "Oh yeah. That must've slipped my mind after the fall."

Dana's head swiveled to Will and then back to her dad. "What fall? Are you okay?"

He waved her off and took a bite of potatoes. "I'm fine."

Will interjected. "I want to circle back to the underwear thing in a minute, but if you hit your dad's mailbox, why didn't you say something sooner?"

"I tried. I couldn't reach you all day."

The kids' gazes shifted between their parents like Wimbledon spectators.

Dana nodded in their direction as she addressed Will. "Maybe we put a pin in this."

"Why was Pops outside in his underwear?" Adam asked.

Compassion for her father washed over Dana. Her eyes pleaded with Will. She knew he was curious about the underwear as well, but she didn't want to embarrass her dad in front of the whole family.

"How about some ice cream," Will said.

Dana scooted the Adirondack chair back from the firepit before sinking into it. The flames overpowered the chill of the March night air, but it wouldn't be long before summer's sweltering heat and mosquitos made evenings on the patio unbearable.

Will returned from taking her dad home. He handed her a glass of merlot and eased into the chair beside her. "We need to talk about your dad. I'll tell you about his fall, but hurry and tell me about the wreck while Adam is showering," he said.

"Then we have roughly a minute and a half before he runs out here asking about underwear again."

"Talk fast."

Dana recounted the duck-chasing boxer shorts fiasco for Will while he guffawed. If he fell out of his chair from laughing, it would serve him right. It was still too soon for her to see the humor in it.

"It's not funny. Hon, my dad didn't even recognize me at first. He yelled at me to get my car off his lawn like I was a delinquent. Then he didn't remember any of it tonight. What if he has something bad like Alzheimer's or a brain tumor?"

Will angled himself toward her. "You're saying your dad was running around the neighborhood in his boxers and nothing else *literally* chasing two ducks?"

She pressed her fingers against her temple. "Did you think I meant metaphorically? He was also wearing slippers. And he wasn't *chasing* them, per se. He was trying to herd them to the park."

Will pinched the bridge of his nose, her go to stress releasing move. If he was picking up her habits, what would be next, matching shirts? "He hasn't been the same without your mom. I'm worried this is the first sign of dementia." He took a sip from his glass and set it on the firepit. "That's what I wanted to talk to you about earlier. He called me at work because he fell."

"Yes, he told us at dinner. What happened?"

"He stood on a chair to change a lightbulb, and it toppled. He didn't want you to worry unnecessarily, which is why he called me. I checked him over. He's got a nice bruise across his lower back, but I think he's fine."

Dana wasn't so sure. Will was a chef and a CEO, not a medical professional. "Are you sure he didn't hit his head? What if he has a broken rib?"

"I brought him over here so we could see if he acted disoriented or in pain. He seemed fine though."

She had to agree that her dad seemed alright aside from forgetting about how his mailbox got damaged.

"I checked him again when I took him back home, and I'm sure he's okay."

She picked at a hangnail. "Falling off a chair could happen to anyone. That's not in itself a sign of dementia."

"Yes, but he was already in his pajamas and ready for bed by 5:00."

"Oh," she said for lack of a better response.

"So, what do we do about it?"

Dana raised her glass. "*That* is the $64,000 question."

She wanted to ask her husband why he'd taken her dad's phone call while sending hers to voicemail, but she'd had all the bad news she could handle today.

Then she remembered the phone call with Julia.

"There's something else. Your sister called and asked us to keep the boys over spring break so she and Dave can attend an intensive couple's retreat in New Mexico. It sounds like they're not doing well."

Will let out a long breath and ran his hand through his hair. "Ah man, I hate that for them. Did she say what was going on?"

"No, only that they've been in therapy twice a week for a while and that their counselor highly recommended this retreat. I didn't ask any questions."

"I guess it was divine intervention on their behalf that we didn't get around to making plans for that week." He promised to take the week off to help wrangle the masses.

"Great, it'll be you, me, *six* kids, and the giant dog."

He clinked his glass against hers. "Sounds like a party!"

Dana's phone indicated an incoming Facetime from Josie Caraway. She showed Will the screen. "Should I be worried? She never Facetimes me."

She answered and saw Josie and Hunter in the frame holding a baby monitor.

"Listen to Olivia's cough and tell us what's wrong with her."

The four adults listened intently to the silent monitor. Olivia coughed once, then more silence. Another cough.

"Did you hear it?" Josie whispered.

Dana and Will exchanged glances. "Why are you whispering?"

"So you can hear the cough," Josie whispered again.

"I'm not a doctor, but it doesn't sound deep. Is she breathing normally? Maybe she has a little allergy or some reflux, but I don't think it's croupe or RSV."

The new parents' foreheads relaxed.

"Thank you, Dana," Hunter said. "You put our minds at ease."

"Sure, but again, I'm not a doctor. If you're worried,

trust your instincts. But also, don't worry too much."

"It sure helps to have the reassurance of someone who's been there," said Josie. "It would be great if hospitals could send new parents home with a nanny to teach them everything about parenting for the first year."

Dana thought it would be great if a nanny could come teach her about teenagers too.

Hunter cleared his throat. "While we have you on the line, we have another problem." He told them about Marie's impending visit and how they were failing miserably at church attendance. He asked for their help.

Will laughed. "You want *our* advice? Have you met us?"

"What he means is that we struggle every Sunday, too," said Dana. "Thankfully we aren't getting pooped on anymore, but there's always drama. Half the time we're all mad by the time we get out of the car."

Hunter and Josie looked deflated. "Great, I guess we should just get used to watching via Facebook live for the next eighteen years because if y'all are floundering, then we will be *totally* hopeless," Hunter said.

Dana said, "Until Jesus comes back, there's hope for all of us. Keep trying. And we can help. We'll bribe the kids to get ready quickly this Sunday and then send them over to help with the babies."

"Uh, I'm not sure this circus will move any faster if the boys are helping dress and feed your three," said Will.

"Good point. It'll have to be an all-hands-on-deck thing," said Dana. "We can get up a little earlier and come over to help. And with all of us carrying babies and bags, you won't even need a stroller. It'll be fine."

"Just to be on the safe side, you might throw rain ponchos over your nice clothes before you get here," said Josie.

The new parents, satisfied that Olivia's cough wasn't indicative of a medical emergency, ended the call.

"Were we that intense when our kids were babies?" Will asked.

"I think we kind of were with Leah, but she was *one* baby, and she was born full-term. They're dealing with three preemies. They probably still have PTSD from their NICU days. Just looking at their giant stroller terrifies me. I have no idea how they go anywhere."

Will put his arm around her shoulder and drew her in for a kiss. "Thank you for not having all three of our kids at once."

Chapter 5

All the talk about going to church reminded Dana of Serena's text. At least if she had to help the Caraways with the triplets, she had a viable excuse to get out of subbing preschoolers. She picked up her phone. Hey friend, sorry it took so long to back to you. It's been a rough day. Let's meet up next week.

Will leaned over, pretending to read her screen. "Who are you texting?"

"Serena Pendleton. I'm dodging my Christian duty."

Will didn't get a chance to ask her to explain.

"Mom," Leah yelled. "Where are you? I need help with my Chemistry homework." Dana wondered how kids could sense when adults were enjoying time without them and ruin it.

"No, she can google Chemistry," Nate yelled. "I need you to proofread my essay."

Dana put her hand on Will's arm and whispered, "Shhh, let's sit very still, and maybe they won't find us."

"They're not T-rexes, and this isn't *Jurassic Park,*" he said.

"Are you sure?"

"Mom!"

Dana thew her head back. "I'm changing my name to 'Dad.' No one ever yells that," She pushed herself out of the chair and reached for Will's hand to pull him up.

"Rude," he replied. "How about I tackle Chemistry, and you can edit the essay. Sound fair?"

"Deal. Wait, do you even remember anything about high school Chemistry?"

"I was just gonna use Nate's suggestion and Google it."

Once the homework was done, all Dana wanted was to soak in a hot bath and forget this bad day. She trudged past Leah's open door and saw her daughter sprawled across her bed with Harvey lounging beside her. Dana entered and sat on the edge of the bed.

"Make yourself at home I guess," Leah huffed and scooted away. "Don't you ever knock?"

"The door wasn't even closed," Dana retorted. "It's cute though how you think you have rights in the room your dad and I furnished for you in the house we pay for. Did you finish all your homework?"

"Mm-hmm." Leah typed something into her phone. "Did they even teach Chemistry when y'all were in school because Dad seemed more confused by it than I was."

Dana chuckled. "They did. There was even a full periodic table and everything. But it's been a while since we've used it is all." Harvey laid his head in Dana's lap, so she scratched his ears and stroked his thick fur.

Leah gave them a cursory glance. "Don't get dog hair all over my bed."

Did she think he was keeping all his fur to himself prior to her arrival?

"Hey, Mom. Is Pops okay?"

Dana's hand froze on the dog's head. "Um, I think so. Why do you ask?"

"Well, he forgot about you hitting his mailbox. That's weird, right?"

Dana scrunched her forehead, but Leah would have had to look up to notice, which she did not. "I'm not sure."

Her throat constricted, and she fought to keep her tone light. "Sometimes that happens when people get older, but I don't want you to worry about Pops." She was worried enough for them both.

Leah didn't say anything else, so Dana sat up. "I'm going to take a bath and try to wash away the memory of seeing my father in his boxers."

"Gross, Mom. You need to pluck that chin hair too."

Dana ran her finger across her chin, feeling for the coarse, offending hair as she studied her daughter. Leah was beautiful. She had her dad's blue eyes framed by long eyelashes, the kind that women paid big money for, except hers were real. Her sun-streaked hair fell long and straight over her shoulders, and she had a self-confidence that Dana lacked at that age, or even now, for that matter.

Dana's own hips were always a tad too thick, and her eyes were a forgettable muddy brown. Her hair was limp and never seemed to grow past her shoulders. It was, however, a lovely shade of dark chocolate, thanks to faithful hair appointments.

Leah must have sensed her mother's gaze because she finally looked up at her. "What?"

"I'm wondering how you noticed my chin hair when your eyes haven't left your phone since I walked in here."

Leah shrugged. "It caught the light I guess."

Dana stood up. "And on that charming note, I'm leaving."

"Shut the door." Leah called.

Children were such gifts from the Lord.

Chapter 6

Will set out plates and opened takeout containers as
Dana slid her brand-new blue laptop into her tote.

"Carlos asked me to meet him before class, so I'm
taking off now."

"Carlos your writing instructor?" He raised his
eyebrows at Dana. "I bet he wants to declare his love for
you and beg you to run away with him." He made a goofy
kissy face at her.

She gave him a peck on the cheek and walked to the
garage. Without turning around, she said, "It would be
weird for him to do it two weeks in a row. Must be
something else." She smirked over her shoulder and left.

Despite his teasing, Will wasn't the jealous type. Not
that he had a reason to be jealous. She was attractive
enough, but no other man had looked twice at Dana in more
than a decade. They saw her for her labels—wife, mother,
homemaker. She was convinced the only moms in their
forties turning heads were either augmented and injected
far beyond Dana's budget and pain tolerance, or they
shunned carbs and lived at the gym.

Will, on the other hand, was still a total catch. Women
shamelessly flirted with him. He had a magnetic smile and
the faintest of laugh lines that alluded to his fun-loving
personality. They somehow made him better looking, more

rugged the more he aged. Yet another inequality of the sexes.

She sent a quick text to Serena before she backed out of the garage. Pray for me. I think I'm about to get in trouble in writing class

Dana arrived to find Carlos furiously typing on his laptop. He glanced up briefly to acknowledge her, then typed for several more seconds. He wore faded jeans with Sperry's Topsiders and a tan blazer over a chambray shirt. His outfit coupled with designer reading glasses made him look like an actor in an eyewear commercial.

She studied him, wondering what it was that reminded her of her twelve-year-old son, Nate. It must be the hair. It forever looked like it hadn't been combed in a week. Maybe messy hair was a sign of true genius, like Einstein, and not just the trademark of tween boys.

Finally, he closed the computer and took off his glasses. "Thanks for meeting me," he said.

"Sure," she said, dreading the lecture on careless writing she was sure was coming.

Carlos sat on the edge of one of the desks arranged in a semicircle and motioned for her to take a seat. "Why did you stop writing?"

That came out of nowhere. Didn't she have to *start* something before she could stop doing it? "What do you mean?"

He pointed knowingly with the earpiece of his glasses. "Your writing has a refined quality to it that novice writers simply do not possess."

She scratched her head and tried to keep her face from conveying the confusion she felt. Was this his way of addressing the typos in her story?

"Um, I was a double English and Library Science major in college and worked in a library for a few years. Maybe I absorbed something via osmosis?"

"So, you've never written *anything* before signing up

for this class?"

She wasn't about to tell him about the athletic cup apology letter even though she felt like it should count. She shook her head. "Not since college."

Carlos stared blankly into the distance. "Huh."

Dana followed his gaze. Did he see something she was missing?

"What have you been doing since then?" he asked at last.

She shrugged. "Cooking, cleaning, finding lost shoes, and laundry. *So* much laundry."

He seemed to be calculating something in his mind, and she started to squirm. If he was going to reprimand her for submitting her story before she'd properly edited it, then why didn't he just come out with it?

She folded her hands on the desk and leaned forward, a move she'd perfected through years of telepathically willing her children or husband to get to the point. "Did you want to talk to me about something specific?"

He set the glasses on the desk and crossed his arms. "You have an instinct for storytelling. I have a close friend who is a literary agent. I asked her to take a look at your story "Dying to Donate" after I read it yesterday to see if she shared my expert opinion.

That was the story Dana submitted for class right before she destroyed her laptop and her dad's mailbox. Dana's face got hot, and she thought she might get sick. She'd been bracing for whatever humiliation she was about to receive, but it still caught her off guard somehow.

"She was so impressed she responded almost immediately," he said.

Wait, what?

He stood up and paced slowly as he talked. "She thinks it would make a killer novel. Pun intended, of course."

Dana shifted in her seat. "Dying to Donate" was about

a mother desperate to save her son in need of a heart transplant. She takes matters into her own hands and stalks registered organ donors who are potential matches. How many victims would the mother have to kill to make a whole novel?

He stopped pacing and faced her. "Your story instincts are strong, and I think this would be a great one to cut your teeth on if a full-length manuscript is something that interests you."

Dana let out the breath she'd been holding. "So, this isn't about my inability to properly edit before hitting send?"

He looked down at a printout on his desk. "'Labelled breasts' wasn't what you meant to type?" he laughed. "Typos happen, but great storytelling outweighs them."

"Thank you, Carlos." She was so overwhelmed that she couldn't say anything else.

"You can see why I didn't want to tell you in front of the class. If Melissa got wind of an agent that I sent students' stories to, we'd never stop hearing about heaving bosoms."

Dana snickered. Her classmate was obsessed with writing bawdy romance, and no amount of criticism had deterred her. Then, as if they had summoned the devil herself, Melissa threw open the door with a flourish.

"Am I interrupting something? What are you two doing all by your lonesome?" She wagged her finger suggestively, and Dana rolled her eyes.

"We were right on the cusp of solving world hunger, but I guess now it'll have to wait." Dana sighed.

For the rest of the evening, she was so absorbed in thoughts about writing a novel that she got nothing out of the class. She smiled and nodded when others did, but mentally she was calculating the time investment required to write a novel. If her dad was in the early stages of a critical illness, he would need her more. She was the dependable one everybody else counted on, and following her dream might mean carving out time for herself that she didn't have.

On her way out of class she saw a text from Serena. How'd it go? I prayed.

She thanked her for praying and told Serena it went much better than expected.

Serena: so glad! Let's get together next week.

Dana replied with a thumbs up emoji. It was a polite, noncommittal agreement that would pacify Serena for a while.

Will also seemed interested in the outcome of her meeting because as soon as she walked in the door, he quickly ended a phone call to ask her about class. "What did Carl want to meet with you about?"

"His name is Carlos." She shrugged off her jacket and hung it in the foyer closet. "He had an interesting proposition for me, actually."

There was Will's goofy eyebrow thing again. Was he a little jealous after all? She told him about the meeting.

Will leaned back on the sofa and propped his feet on the coffee table. "That's cool about the book thing. Are you up for it?"

She eyed him from the doorway. "What do you mean?"

"It seems like a major time commitment is all. I didn't know you even wanted to be a writer."

She scratched her eyebrow and crossed the distance to sit next to him. "Why do you think I started taking a creative writing class if not to write?"

He raised his shoulders. "I guess I thought you just wanted to get away from the kids and me for a few hours and exercise your brain."

That too. "I want to write crime novels. Scary, suspenseful stuff that makes you check under your bed and sleep with a light on."

FELLOWSHIP OF THE FRAZZLED MOMS

He looked at her as if seeing her for the first time. "Should I be worried that the woman sleeping next to me wants to kill people for a living?"

"Fictional characters, not people. And yes. Always be afraid," she deadpanned.

He pulled her into a hug. "Well, I support you in whatever you do so long as you aren't picturing me as one of your victims."

She was glad her face was pressed into his shirt so he couldn't see it. She adored him, but what wife didn't occasionally want to get rid of her husband?

"Who were you talking to when I came home?" she asked, hoping she sounded casual and instead of nosy.

"Hmm?" He scratched his head and tucked his hands under his folded arms. "Just work stuff."

"And I guess work stuff is why you didn't take any of my calls or respond to my texts yesterday, even though you picked up when my dad called?"

Will stood up and paced. "Dana, come on. It's not like that."

"Not like what?"

He ran his hand through his hair. "Things aren't going well at work, and I spent the whole day in meetings. I should have responded to you, and I'm sorry. I took your dad's call because he never calls me, so I knew something had to be wrong."

Something was definitely wrong, and Dana had to get to the bottom of it, even if it meant she would never have another spare minute to write that novel.

Chapter 7

"Let's go, let's go, let's go!" Dana yelled up the stairs. She must have been out of her mind when she volunteered the family to help Josie and Hunter get their babies to church for the first time. Sunday was the most chaotic morning of the week, and something always went wrong.

Today Leah woke up in a snit and got even more unpleasant when Dana made her change out of her too-short skirt. Why were these kids always growing? It was ridiculously inconvenient. Adam put on athletic shorts with a long sleeve button down.

"Son, on what planet do basketball shorts go with dress shirts?" she asked.

Adam shrugged and continued to play his Nintendo Switch. "These are comfortable."

Dana pried the gaming device out of his hands. "I don't care about your comfort. I care about everyone at church judging me for letting you wear gym shorts in winter." Go put on pants that don't scream 'Trash-ket ball tournament in the foyer before the sermon.'"

"That would be sweet. We should really do that!" said Adam.

"Jeans, now," she shouted.

"Fine, but I'm not wearing a belt," he said as he

stomped up the stairs.

Nate was the only Harding who fully dressed himself without a fight today. His hair, on the other hand, was untamable. Dana decided to let it go this morning rather than waging another battle.

Will called Harvey in from the back yard and locked the door. "Are we ready?"

"Uh, I think so. Can you tell your daughter it's time to go? She's mean, and I can't deal with her right now."

Will laughed. "Why is she *my* daughter when she's mean?"

"It's the rule. When the kids are at their worst, the least affected parent must claim ownership."

At last, they were ready to walk across the street. Dana considered grabbing a raincoat, per Josie's suggestion, but decided to take the risk.

Hunter handed Connor to Dana before they crossed the threshold. "He's dry and fed, and his clothes are on the coffee table. Jos is getting ready, and Olivia and Ben still need to be changed. Do I need a tie? I should grab a tie." He was freaking out.

Will scooped Olivia out of the swing and gave orders. "Dude, chill out. We're going to church, not a wedding." He doled out orders to the boys on what to put in the diaper bag and sent Leah to dress Ben. Nothing was hotter than her man holding a baby bossing people around. Finally, the two dads loaded the babies into the van, and the Hardings headed to their own garage. All that was missing was Josie.

Dana knocked on the door frame as she entered the master suite. "Josie, I think everyone's ready to go. You okay in here?" She heard a soft sniffle.

"No."

"I'm coming in." Dana found Josie sitting on the edge of the bathtub. "What's wrong?"

Josie looked so young and scared. "I don't think I can do this. I *want* to be where the grownups are, but I'm too self-conscious. Everyone's going to stare at me to see if I'm stretched out or disfigured."

The resemblance between Josie's and Leah's insecurities was as remarkable as their enviable beauty. She didn't understand how someone who looked like that could be so self-conscious.

"I look hideous, and everyone's going to laugh at me," Leah would whine. Dana could usually placate the teenager, or if that didn't work, threaten her into compliance. She wasn't sure the same tactic would motivate a grown woman.

"Stand up and show me the outfit," she urged.

Josie obeyed. She was wearing a turquoise and purple shirt dress over black leggings and ankle boots. She was stunning, even six months postpartum. Suddenly Dana felt very uncomfortable in her own skin by comparison.

"You look great. Hold your head high and act like you parade into church with an entourage every week." She figured there was more going on in Josie's head than she was letting on, but they were on a time crunch, and Dana wasn't in the mood for an existential conversation right now. She led Josie out of the bathroom, careful not to spook her into bolting.

"Dana, what if I can't remember how to talk to adults anymore? I only talk to babies these days."

"Then we'll have a conversation later about the appropriateness of baby talking adults. But somehow, I think it'll come back to you." Dana made a mental note to revisit this with Josie when they weren't running late to church. She doubted Josie's apprehension was fleeting. She wondered if all women were worried how others perceived them. Her own mother never seemed to be, but it was a feeling she wrestled with often.

When they arrived, the boys raced to get to Sunday school. Leah hung back with her face in her phone, awaiting further instructions.

Dana checked her reflection in the sun visor. "Leah, you can head to class. Dad and I will help the Caraways." Leah walked away wordlessly.

Hunter unloaded the first baby and handed him off to Josie before unbuckling the next one. Will unbuckled Olivia from the other side of the minivan, and Dana grabbed the diaper bag. The four of them assessed one another like teammates about to take the field.

"Are you sure you want to carry Livvie?" asked Hunter. "She's the one most likely to spit up on you.

Will smiled at Olivia. "It's been a while since I've stared danger in the face. Let's do this."

Serena Pendleton greeted them in the preschool wing. She cooed over the babies and helped Hunter and Josie sign them in on the computer.

Dana and Serena had been foyer friends for years, exchanging pleasantries every week. However, when Dana's mother got sick, Serena had been a godsend bringing meals and checking on her dad. Since then, their friendship had blossomed into an off-site one. Serena's daughters were both in college, and she was a mentor mom of sorts to Dana.

"Dana, how's your dad?"

"I'm worried about him." She ignored the side eye Will was giving her. "He's having some issues that we aren't sure what to make of."

Serena squeezed her arm. "We must have coffee this week. I still need to run something by you." She affixed a nametag sticker to each triplet's back and handed claim tickets to Hunter who held them up for show.

"Just like luggage at the airport."

Dana looked around the nursery and was happy to see plenty of adults. That should ease Josie's nerves. Some of the volunteers were the same ladies who were the Harding children's first Sunday school teachers too.

"Now what?" asked Josie. Dana could hear the tension

in her voice.

"Uh, Sunday school," said Dana. It was like Josie had never done this before, even without children. "The new parents' class is upstairs, and it probably has a lot of the same people you knew before." She pointed to the ground. "Will and I are in the basement with the middle-aged adults. But you text me if you need anything, okay?"

What an offensive way to refer to parents of older kids and teenagers. Congratulations on reaching the middle of your life where your kids are halfway to adulthood, and you're halfway to the grave.

As they walked downstairs, Dana wondered to herself why the Sunday school classes were divided by the ages of their children. Sure, that arrangement helped people make friends in their same life stages, but Dana couldn't help but wonder if it limited them as well. She thought about her own relationship with women like her mom and Serena who had guided her through the hazards of raising kids. Now Josie seemed like she could use some guidance, but where would she find it if not at church?

The sermon was on the sin of envy. For the first five minutes, Dana couldn't help thinking it was good that Josie was here this morning to hear Pastor Gray's message. Poor Josie was really struggling with comparing herself to others. Then it hit her that she needed to pay attention and take stock of her own struggle with the green-eyed monster. Dana envied Josie. It wasn't fair that some women got to be tall, natural beauties while the rest were just average.

It also wasn't fair that she didn't have a mother or mother-in-law while Josie had a great relationship with both of hers. She was even jealous of Will and her own children for having siblings. A brother or sister would have kept her from growing up lonely and made life more fun. And it would ease the burden of dealing with her dad's issues now.

She could also add that she was jealous of everyone

who had ever written a novel to her growing list. She shifted in her seat and tried to pay attention, but the more she thought about jealousy, the more she realized it plagued her. Conviction was a funny thing. An hour ago, she would have said sarcasm was more her sin of choice.

Pastor Gray asked the congregation to turn in their Bibles to Proverbs 14:30. "A heart at peace gives life to the body, but envy rots the bones." He repeated it twice to drive the point home. Dana pictured her bones rotting from the inside out with all her jealousy.

She picked at her cuticles, a nervous habit that annoyed Will. He put his hand on top of hers to stop her. "You okay?" he whispered.

"I think I can feel my bones rotting," she whispered back.

Leah leaned forward, glaring at her parents, a look Dana had given her a thousand times before for talking in church. Dana mimed buttoning her lip and faced forward.

After they helped the Caraways retrieve the triplets and wrangle them in their car, Will asked again if she was okay.

"Yeah, I guess the sermon just hit me today. I was aggravated with Josie this morning for being self-conscious because she looks like a model even though she had three babies this year, and I miss my mom. All the things."

Will started the engine but didn't drive away. "It's not like you to get emotional from a sermon."

She assured him she was fine and suggested maybe it was hormones.

From the back seat, Leah shrieked. "Oh my gosh! Mom, are you pregnant?"

The boys joined her hysteria. "What? You're having another baby? But you're kind of old."

Will turned green.

These people were so annoying. She motioned for Will to start the car. "Can we go home, please? As much fun as geriatric pregnancy sounds, I am most definitely *not* pregnant."

"You said 'hormones,'" Leah said.

"What are hormones?" said Adam in a voice that was far too loud for the car.

Will backed out of the parking space as Dana glowered at him. "How about we go out to lunch?" he asked.

If there was one thing Dana was not the least bit envious of, it was having a new baby. She may not be young and look like a model, but at least her kids could wipe their own butts.

Chapter 8

Josie

The pediatrician's words stung. "Developmental delays are common among preemies."

In one breath he assured Josie and Hunter that the triplets were healthy, even agreeing with Dana's facetime diagnosis of Olivia's cough, but in the next he was referring them to Early Childhood Intervention for therapy assessments. For Josie it was like a personal attack on her maternal skills.

"While all three are still within the expected parameters for their age, their muscular development is a little on the low side." Dr. Swanson pulled Connor up by his hands into a seated tripod on the exam table. He held the baby by his hips, and Connor fell forward. He would have bumped his face on the table if Dr. Swanson hadn't had quick reflexes.

"Did you notice how his head slipped back slightly as I pulled him? His neck tonicity is good, but not quite where I'd hoped. I would also expect a six-month-old to try to control his upper body and put his hands down to stabilize himself in a sitting position. Connor did not. Nor did he try to catch himself when he folded forward."

Olivia's trunk control was noticeably more developed than her brother's. In fact, she readily held herself in a stable seated position for a couple of seconds before toppling forward. "This is more developmentally in line with full-term six-month-olds," said Dr. Swanson.

Ben's muscle tone mirrored Connor's. Josie had a hard time making her face maintain its composure as she absorbed the doctor's observations. What could she, or should she have done differently?

As if reading her mind, Dr. Swanson put his hand on her shoulder. "Let me assure you, there's nothing you could have done to cause this."

Josie clenched her fists and thighs to keep from crying. He recommended she join a group where she could talk about her concerns with other moms who understood her unique predicament. She didn't even know where to find a group like that, let alone the time to meet with them.

After more reassurances that the Caraways had in no way contributed to their sons falling behind the curve, they all agreed to the ECI referral and left with instructions to begin introducing solid foods.

Josie was quiet on the ride home. It was a lot of information to digest, and she was overwhelmed.

"You okay with all of this?" Hunter asked as they turned into their housing addition.

"I want what's best for our kids. Not super excited about someone coming into the house every week to tell me what I'm doing wrong though."

"Jos, that's not what they'll do. The babies are fine. They have no incentive to get up and get moving when their two best buddies are in the same place."

The rational part of her knew he was right, and it was better to get intervention now before they started missing milestones. The rest of her blamed herself and shame spiraled. Since she'd carelessly overlooked their delays, they might be late sitting up then fall even further behind with crawling and walking. Would they even be ready to start kindergarten on time? She should have worked harder to engage her babies.

By the time Hunter pulled into the garage, Josie's head throbbed, and her chest tightened so much she couldn't catch her breath. This was her first panic attack since the babies were newborns. Now a single thought suffocated her. She was a bad mother.

Hunter pulled her out of the minivan. "Look at me, Jos. Count to ten." He held her arms and counted aloud while she forced her breathing to match his.

Minutes passed until finally the pain subsided, and oxygen moved in and out of her body like it was supposed to.

"We're in this together, and our babies are healthy," he reassured her. "They hatched a little early is all."

Josie sniffled. "Hatched?"

"You know what I mean."

She wiped her nose with the cuff of her sleeve and chuckled. "Birds have it so easy, don't they?"

They unloaded the babies and ordered lunch to be delivered. While Hunter made bottles, Josie snapped a pic of the babies lined up in their bouncers to send to Laurel. She texted her that the doctor was worried about their development hoping her sister, who used to be her ride or die, would at least reply out of concern.

An hour and a half later, there was still no response from Laurel. The triplets were asleep, and Hunter had gone to work. Josie was alone with her negative thoughts and an internet full of horror stories of developmental delays because of neglectful parenting when Dana texted.

WRYD

Josie: not crying because my kids are never going to sit up or walk because their mother is the worst

Dana: ?

Josie: Nothing. What's up

Dana: I'm coming over

Dana let herself in quietly so as not to wake anyone

and parked herself next to Josie on the sofa. "Want to talk about it?"

Josie gave her the rundown on the pediatrician's visit and her own guilt-riddled delve into the internet's black hole of infant prematurity and physical therapy.

"Oh, Josie. I'm so sorry. I know this must be scary for you."

Dana had no idea. But she was glad to have a sympathetic ear.

"I did a deep dive into physical therapy exercises I can start at home so they won't fall even further behind before the Early Childhood Intervention visit."

Dana furrowed her brow but said nothing.

"What?" asked Josie. "Your face is saying things your mouth won't."

"It's a lot of pressure to put on yourself. I see them all the time, and I've never noticed any delays."

"But that's just it. We should have noticed," Josie countered. She picked up the laptop from the coffee table and angled the screen toward Dana. "I think if you or your kids were to come over and help do some of these balancing exercises with the triplets, then the boys might catch up to Olivia before ECI comes."

Dana set the computer back down. "I think it's great that you want to get a jump on helping them as long as you're doing it for the right reasons."

It took a lot of self-control for Josie to keep from telling Dana how condescending she sounded. She probably meant well, but she couldn't possibly understand. "What are the right reasons? Making sure my kids can sit up and walk?"

"Those are great, unlike trying to prove to the state agency that their services aren't needed. And this isn't like lifting weights or taking up running. You can't condition an infant to suddenly sit up or crawl. They move at their own pace. As a mother of kids who never stop moving or talking, let me tell you, it's not all it's cracked up to be. They'll do all the things soon enough, and then you'll be wishing for the good ol' days when they stayed where you put them and couldn't run away or say ugly things."

Dana's lecture only irritated Josie. What did she know about raising multiples? "Hey, Dana, remember that time you told me, 'If one more little old lady in the grocery store tells me to just enjoy this time, I'm gonna send my kids home with her?' Well, you've officially become one of those little old ladies."

Dana cringed, and Josie knew she'd stung her friend. "All I'm saying is that one minute you're all 'my kids aren't sitting up,' and the next, it'll be, 'my kids are in college and their empty rooms make me sad.' Just watch."

"How very *Cats in the Cradle* of you. Are you going to help me teach my kids to sit up, or not?"

"Of course, but don't come crying to me when they run in opposite directions in public."

Josie loved how easily she and Dana could transition from frustration to friendship again. If only her sister were that forgiving. She didn't even know what she'd done to Laurel, but she wanted to be forgiven so they could reconnect.

They agreed Dana and any Harding kid without homework would come over in the late afternoon for baby bootcamp. Having a plan made Josie feel a semblance of control. The anxiety she had felt over the impending early childhood evaluation subsided to a low rumble.

Olivia shrieked and giggled as Adam made faces and played peek-a-boo with her.

"Josie, watch. She sticks her tongue out when I stick mine out at her."

Josie smiled. "You're an excellent baby handler, Adam." She and Nate were each sitting in a straddle position with a baby seated between their legs. Josie demonstrated how to use her legs to break Ben's fall if he toppled to the side. If he fell backward, her body would catch him. Her hands supported his hips as she allowed him to wobble and flex his trunk muscles. Nate copied her movements with Connor.

The internet and a twelve-year-old kid were just as good as physical therapy. The boys were going to wow that early childhood interventionist, and he or she would quickly realize the Caraways needed to be crossed off the list of preterm babies with delays.

After a few minutes of wobbling, Connor and Ben began to fuss. Josie hugged Ben to her chest and patted him. He calmed right away in his mother's embrace.

"Alright, Adam, let's switch. See if you can get Ben to stick his tongue out at you, and I'll see if Miss Olivia wants to practice sitting up."

Olivia held a tripod for a few seconds unaided, as she had that morning for the pediatrician. Now that it had been brought to her attention, Josie wondered how she had missed the differences between Olivia and the boys.

"Josie, look." Adam's voice was perpetually louder than the situation called for. She and Nate turned to see Ben rolling over. Rolling wasn't a new accomplishment, but this time he rolled onto his tummy to reach for a toy, then he rolled again onto his back. He stopped a solid two feet away from his original position. Did this mean he was technically mobile now?

"Adam, you're supposed to make him laugh, not teach him how to get away."

He shrugged. "My mom said this was baby bootcamp. He's training for army crawls, I guess."

Josie googled, "where to meet other moms of young kids." The first suggestion was at the indoor playground of a shopping mall. She shuddered. Josie wasn't sure she could put her children on the mall floor, let alone become friends with other people who did that.

Another recommendation was to join a Mommy and Me class where the babies interacted with their parents in a circle of other parents with their one baby each. She could interact with all three at home without the stares or the trouble of transporting the kids somewhere else. What she needed was a group for multiples with curbside service to get everyone in and out of the car. Such a group didn't seem to exist. Dr. Swanson's recommendation that she find likeminded mothers was laughable. She had better odds of winning the lottery or finding a pot of gold at the end of a rainbow.

Chapter 9

Dana

Dana was the first to arrive at her writing class that night. She hadn't meant to be so early, but she was angry with Will and wanted to get out of the house before he got home.

Earlier in the week they'd made lunch plans for today, but when she arrived at his office to pick him up, his assistant said he was in a meeting and couldn't be interrupted. She waited for him in the lobby. When he finally stepped off the elevator, he was with a pretty, blonde woman in a business suit and did not look happy to see Dana.

His mouth was set in a grim line, as he approached her. "Dana, now's not a good time. I'm sorry." He exited the building with the woman, leaving Dana standing in the lobby.

She barely made it to her car before hot, angry tears blurred her vision.

If not for the kids, she would find any place other than home to go after class to avoid Will altogether tonight.

Carlos Ruiz, her instructor walked in next. "You know there's no extra credit for arriving early," he teased.

"I have three kids. I don't need extra credit, just solitude," she countered.

"How's the novel coming? It might be helpful to read an excerpt in front of the class to get some feedback."

Dana agreed to read the first few pages, leaving out that she'd only written a few pages.

The rest of the class trickled in, representing multiple generations and diverse backgrounds. The eldest members of the group intrigued her most. Paul was a Vietnam veteran who said he was keeping his mind sharp by writing war stories. Beverly, who looked to be approaching sixty, left a job in journalism to raise a family. Now that her children were grown and flown, she was free to pursue writing again. Raising a family seemed to table many a mother's dreams for themselves.

When Carlos called for volunteers to read their original pieces, Melissa raised her hand before Dana could muster the courage to do so. She was a self-proclaimed romance aficionado, and her stories made Dana uncomfortable. It wasn't that she hadn't read a bodice-ripper or two back in the day, but it was an entirely different thing when someone else read them aloud to a room of strangers.

Dana slumped in her seat. Paul looked equally uneasy as Melissa took the floor.

Just before she reached a graphic interlude, a voice from the back interrupted her. "I can't listen to it again. I'm sorry." A woman in her early twenties pushed her glasses up on her nose as the room collectively sighed in relief.

"The assignment was to write a mystery or suspenseful story. What's mysterious about what you wrote? In fact, I have serious doubts that you are abiding by the golden rule of writing to write what you know."

"Peyton," said Carlos, "*you're* currently violating the golden rule of my class. Melissa has the floor, and you're interrupting." He turned to Melissa. "On the other hand, we've been crafting suspense for the last few weeks, and you're sticking tightly to the romance genre."

She flipped her platinum hair. "I'm here to hone my craft, not to branch into areas of writing I have no intention of pursuing."

"I can appreciate that, but you signed up for Intro to Creative Writing. We explore many avenues of storytelling here," said Carlos.

"I for one would rather hear plainer terms when describing body parts." Everyone's attention was on Paul. "You write about so many members, it sounds like an Elks Lodge meeting."

"I have something I would like to read." Dana quickly interjected. She couldn't bear to listen to a man her father's age critique a steamy love scene. It might have scarred her for life.

"Great, let's hear from Dana," said Carlos with more enthusiasm than was warranted.

Melissa sat down with a huff.

Dana read without looking up and sat down quickly afterward.

"Intriguing," said a college-aged student from the back row. "A mother who will stoop to murder if it means saving her kid. It's edgy; I like it."

Dana ducked her chin.

"Hold on," said Melissa. "*I* got called out about writing what you know, she gestured with air quotes, "but, I'm sorry, what's your name? Deena?"

Hadn't Carlos literally said it when she offered to read? "Dana."

"Dana is supposedly qualified to write about murder committed by a mom with a sick kid?"

Dana bit the inside of her cheek. How dare this woman who couldn't even remember her name weigh in on her ability to write about a protective mother.

"I know *exactly* what it's like to helplessly hold my sick child while he cries in pain. I've also sat in the stands while a coach berated my kid and used all my self-control to suppress my rage at him. This character is no different except that she allows herself to do the thing none of us would go through with, even if we might consider it."

She took a breath. "Stephen King wrote some very disturbing characters in improbable situations. Do you think he had personal experience with an obsessed fan who kidnapped him and chopped off his foot? I also highly doubt that he had a demonic car that killed people, but it didn't stop him from writing *Christine.* Autobiographical experience is not necessary to tell a story. Background knowledge of a character's mindset or predicament is." Dana met Melissa's icy glare with one of her own as Carlos took the lead again.

The encounter left her with a bad taste in her mouth. She ducked out of class as soon as Carlos dismissed them, eager to put the whole thing behind her.

In her haste to escape, she forgot her anger at Will. He stood at the sink washing dishes when she arrived home.

She set her keys and tote bag on the breakfast bar. "You know we have a big appliance built right into the cabinet that washes the dishes."

"It's full."

Dana rubbed her forehead. "It's Nate's week to unload it. Then have Leah reload and start it."

Will's attention never left the sink. Was he avoiding eye contact with her on purpose? "Leah's studying at Kaitlyn's house. It was easier this way."

She grabbed a dish towel out of the drawer and wiped off a plate from the drying mat. "Everything okay at work today?" She labored to feign nonchalance.

"Fine."

Dana set the plate in the cabinet and reached for another. "They didn't seem fine when you stood me up to leave with another woman."

Will scrubbed vigorously at a glass. "She's the CFO of

Big Kitchen Supply. It was strictly a financial meeting if that's what you're wondering. I'm sorry I had to bail on lunch, but their president and some shareholders were expecting a tour of the warehouse, and I couldn't put them off. Things are tense right now."

His tight smile didn't reach his eyes. Dana studied him as he rinsed the glass and set it on the mat. He certainly looked stressed, but Dana couldn't ignore the sinking feeling in her gut that he was hiding something.

"You had a meeting with the CFO of your biggest competitor? And you're giving tours to their stakeholders?" She wasn't buying it.

He shrugged. "Let it go, alright? It's nothing to worry about." He pointed to the glass she was about to put away. "That still has water spots all over it."

Something was up. She couldn't force him to be honest about the woman at the office, and if she tried, they'd just get into a fight and upset the kids. Then she would have to face a new problem that she couldn't even put a name to right now. Instead of pressing the matter, she continued drying and changed the subject.

Dana recounted her confrontation with Melissa. "Can you believe that woman had the nerve to tell me I have no idea what I'm writing about?"

He contemplated for a beat too long while scrubbing a plate. "I mean, I can see her side. You haven't experienced a gravely ill child."

Dana narrowed her eyes at him. She picked up a clean plate he set on the drying mat and lowered it back into the soapy water. "This still has spots on it." She turned on her heel and left the room.

It was a petty move. Not her finest moment, but he didn't even have the decency to take her side out of guilt. She went upstairs to hang out with the boys, lest she regret her decision to even come home at all.

Chapter 10

Josie

Josie rifled through her closet looking for something to wear to the charity dinner while the babies bounced in their saucers. Nothing fit. She couldn't tug the red cocktail dress she'd bought for a university gala a couple of years ago over her hips. Even her stretchy black sheath betrayed her. Its zipper groaned and stopped dead at her waist. Her self-esteem was tanking with each garment she tried. She sat on the edge of her bed and texted Dana.

This is hopeless. What's a good excuse to get out of going to a fundraiser? I have nothing to wear, and I look hideous

A minute later, there was a knock at the front door, and Dana greeted her with a bag of Ghirardelli chocolates. Josie took the bag as she flopped into the recliner.

"This isn't going to help with the whole nothing fits me problem, but thanks." She unwrapped a chocolate square and told Dana how excited she'd been at the prospect of a night out with Hunter before she realized she had totally let herself go in the last year. She told Dana how she felt ugly and had nothing to wear, and she couldn't possibly sit at a table with Megan and other posh wives with whom she would have nothing in common. Besides, she would probably embarrass Hunter anyway.

Dana put up her hand to stop Josie's spiral. "First of

all, no one says 'posh' unless they're British or discussing the Spice Girls, who are also British. Second, you are a smoking hot mom, and everyone's going to be so jealous of you. Don't tell Pastor Gray I said that. Third, you've known about this for at least a week now, so why haven't you planned an outfit yet?"

Josie shrugged. Through a full mouth of chocolate, she said, "We were bithy." She really had been busy. Between caring for the triplets and cleaning house before her mom's arrival, she had more than enough on her plate to keep her from thinking about her lack of cocktail attire.

Dana reached down to retrieve a toy for Connor that had careened off his saucer tray. "You *are* going to that fancy dinner. You need a night out, and you should take it as a sign that your mother called and asked to come the same weekend that you needed a sitter. And you can't compare yourself to any other woman at the table because none of them have given birth to three babies within the year. Unless…wait, this isn't some event for families of multiples, is it?"

Josie swallowed the candy. "Doubt it, but Hunter didn't say. They get pressured to donate to so many charities that it could be for anything really."

"Maybe it's a gala to fund doghouses for underprivileged pets," Dana joked.

"With a silent auction of hand-knit dog sweaters. If there is, I'll let you know if they have anything in Harvey's size." Josie popped another chocolate square into her mouth. She should stop. Walking hadn't proved to be the miracle weight loss tool she had hoped it would be yet. But really, at this point, what harm would one more chocolate do?

"All you need is a dress and you'll be stunning." Dana pointed at Josie's messy bun. "Maybe a trip to the hairdresser too."

There was no way Josie could schedule that and find a

sitter in time, but her mouth was too full to say so.

Dana type something into her phone. "I have an appointment tomorrow morning to get my roots done, but I just texted Zola and asked her to see you in my place."

Josie swallowed. "No, I can't let you give up your hair appointment."

Dana waved her off. "I can Clairol my roots for now and reschedule." She insisted on watching the triplets and instructed Josie not to come home before getting a manicure too. "And I have a few cocktail dresses you can try. I know I'm bigger and shorter than you, but it's worth a shot. Some of them are from when I was young and thin, and if you don't find one in my closet, we'll load up the littles and run to the mall." Dana acted as if it was no trouble at all to load up and go.

"If by 'run,' you mean, 'walk at a slow clip,' I'm in." Josie didn't plan on running anywhere until she could walk a mile pushing Peg without passing out.

There was some deliberation over which would be easier, carting the children to Dana's house, or lugging an armload of dresses to Josie's. They opted for going to Dana's.

The two women gathered the babies, checked their diapers, and loaded them into the giant stroller that now lived in the entry way. It was both Josie's saving grace and the bane of her existence. She needed it to go anywhere with the babies by herself, but she could barely hoist it in and out of the minivan. She had taken to calling it Peg because "the giant stroller" seemed so negative and daunting. Peg was more of a member of the family that should have come with her own trailer.

As they eased Peg out the Caraways' front door, Dana said, "So uh, when you see my room, please know I wasn't planning on having guests when I didn't make the bed today."

Josie put her hand to her heart, feigning horror. "You

didn't make your bed? Barbarian."

"Will was still asleep when I got up. Common courtesy says I can't make it while he's in it. Besides, he should have to be the resident bed maker since he's always the last one up."

Josie detected resentment in Dana's tone. "Does he get up and help get the kids off to school?" She couldn't imagine how mornings in their house would work without Hunter. Both parents were needed to get babies changed and fed.

Dana scoffed. "Not lately. I wake the kids, toss some food on the table, and then yell at them every five minutes until they come downstairs. Will saunters in to make coffee and say goodbye to the kids. Then he does his own thing to get ready for the office while I make sure everyone has lunches, notes, library books, and whatever else."

"Wow," said Josie. "When do you have time to get yourself ready?"

"After I take them to school in my pajamas. Every flipping morning. It's infuriating."

Josie stopped short of the incline of the Hardings' driveway, took a deep breath, and heaved the stroller forward. The driveway wasn't steep. A wheelchair could have easily maneuvered it, but stopping first killed her momentum.

Dana got in front of the stroller and pulled.

"Thanks," Josie huffed. "I should have taken a running start at it. Are you and Will going through something? Your rundown on a typical morning was a little hostile."

"I don't know. He's been working late and missing Leah's games. And he blew me off for lunch last week while he was with a woman who looked like a walking Barbie doll."

Josie didn't think Will would ever cheat on Dana, and she told her so.

"Maybe. But I'm positive he's hiding something from

me. Also, everything has been so hectic lately that I'm completely stressed out. I need a break."

There was no way Josie was robbing Dana of her hair appointment now. She knew how an afternoon in the stylist's chair could transform a girl's mood. She told Dana as much.

"Oh no. Covering my grays and trimming some split ends aren't going to fix whatever's going on with Will or heal my dad's memory problem. You have a hot date and need it worse than I do."

Dana struggled to hold back Harvey the giant Mountain Dog while Josie pushed Peg through the front door.

She'd been beating herself up over her sons' developmental delays, but she couldn't imagine what Dana was feeling. "Are you stressed about the fender bender at your dad's house?"

Dana directed Josie toward her room. It took some effort to maneuver around the furniture, but they managed to get Peg and the triplets down the hall.

"Kind of. I'm sure not looking forward to paying the deductible or being in a rental car while the Tahoe is in the shop. More than that I'm worried about my dad, and between the worry and the guilt, I'm suffocating."

Josie could relate. "Why do you feel guilty?"

"He's been lonely since my mom passed away, but I've been too busy, too selfish even, to make more time for him."

Dana was genuine and selfless to a fault, even when she was running on fumes. Although she felt bad for her neighbor, knowing she wasn't the only one struggling encouraged Josie.

Dana flipped on the light in her room and yanked the comforter up to the pillows. "Do you really take the time to make your bed every morning? Because I'm going to feel really bad about myself if I'm getting outdone by a new mom with three babies."

Josie wiped a bead of sweat from her lip with the neckline of her shirt. How was she sweating in March just from pushing the stroller across the street? "Listen, my house may smell like one big dirty diaper, and I only bathe at most two babies on any given day, but I make the bed come hell or high water. If I didn't, I think my mother would sense it telepathically and ground me."

She believed this too. She was raised by a clean freak, and the beds were made religiously. It was the only meticulous habit her mother had instilled in her daughters that stuck with Josie after she left home.

"Wait, you only bathe two-thirds of your children? And you called *me* barbaric?"

Josie burst out laughing. "What, I'm outnumbered. They're squirmy and slippery, and they splash a *lot*. I can't hold them up without getting soaked, even in their little bath seats. Which, by the way, aren't little. There's only room for one of them in the tub, so on nights when Hunter is working late, I'm freezing, and my back is killing me by the time I get the second kid bathed. I would have a dislocated spine and hypothermia if all three got bathed."

"Do you at least have a system so no one gets left behind?"

"Yeah, the system is called whoever smells the worst gets bathed first." Josie suddenly felt judged for her survival-mode parenting.

Dana pulled some dresses from her closet and hung them on the door. "I don't want you to even look at the sizes. It might depress you. I also don't want you to think I'm making a judgment call about *your* size. I'm just showing you what I have. It also won't hurt my feelings if you decide these aren't for you. I can accept that you don't want to dress like a forty-three-year-old."

Josie rolled her eyes. "Just show them to me. I'd rather dress like a forty-three-year-old with impeccable taste than a thirty-three-year-old with a collection of worn-out yoga pants and shirts covered in spit up stains."

"Impeccable taste might be a stretch." Dana extended her arms. "This sweater was on clearance at the Banana Republic factory outlet, and the left sleeve is longer than the right."

Josie laughed.

The first dress was a shimmery purple sheath with a deep V neck. It wouldn't zip all the way up.

Dana offered reassurance. "The good thing is it's just your breasts."

Josie's hands flew to her chest. "How is that a good thing?"

"They'll go down when you stop nursing. My postpartum body stayed big all over." Dana waved her hands over her midsection. "This is all baby weight from Adam."

While Josie tried on the next dress in the walk-in closet, she could hear Dana admonishing Harvey to be gentle. The giant dog was fascinated by the infants. When they came over, he would sniff them and try to lick them while they giggled and flinched. Since they were constantly held by bigger humans at the Harding house, she never worried about him hurting them.

"Stop it, Harvey. Go find your ball. Hey Jos, sign Benny up for bath night. Harvey just baptized him in slobber."

"Meh, dog mouths are cleaner than humans, right?" She would google that later. "Let them all get a tongue bath, and I'll take the night off," she called.

"Gross."

She stepped out of the closet and turned so Dana could zip her.

Dana gasped when she caught Josie's reflection in the full-length mirror. "Wow!"

She studied herself from every angle. The black dress

had delicate beading at the empire waist, which disguised her belly. The neckline covered her ample chest and accentuated her collarbone and trim shoulders. Carrying around multiple babies all day was proving to be good for toning the arms. The hemline was about midway between her fingertips and knees, so she would have to remember not to bend over.

"I think this is the one." She pulled out her messy bun and shook out her hair. She didn't hate her appearance for a change.

"Josie, you're so beautiful. I really do have impeccable taste in clothes," Dana joked.

She didn't look like the mom who almost passed out pushing a stroller up the driveway. She looked like a younger, less burdened version of herself. The social version who loved being in the company of others and could carry on dazzling conversation with anyone. Her eyes filled with tears.

"What's wrong? We can go shopping if you don't like it. It really won't hurt my feelings."

Josie wiped her eyes and sniffed. "I'm crying because I look pretty. And because I'm so nervous about having to talk to other grownups."

Dana seemed confused. "Those are good things. Don't cry."

"Unzip me so I don't ruin it before I get to wear it Friday. I love it." She turned her back to Dana and swept her hair off her neck. "It's been so long since I've dressed up. I think I forgot what it felt like. And I *know* I've forgotten how to make small talk at a party."

Dana hugged her. "Ah, I'm sorry. I know it's hard to be a new mom and not recognize yourself in the mirror. But I think the talking stuff is like riding a bike. You never really forget how to do it."

Josie wasn't so sure. "How do I know if I'm being awkward and saying all the wrong things?"

"I think if people stare into their glasses instead of making eye contact after you say something you thought would kill. Or if they make excuses to walk away. Not that I would know from experience."

Josie went into the closet to change back into her own clothes. When she went on bedrest, it was like the old Josie ceased to exist, and she morphed into an incubator. From the first ultrasound where Hunter passed out, she changed everything about her life to be a mom.

She stepped out in her sweatshirt and yoga pants. "I'd do anything for these guys. They're my whole world, but I miss the good parts of myself I left behind, you know? Like being able to see my feet. And wearing nice clothes to the office every day."

She waved her hand over her outfit. "Now *this* is my work uniform. It's like a reverse Cinderella story."

Dana picked up Olivia who had gotten grumpy in her seat and bounced her on her hip. "I get it. That's why I joined the writing class I'm taking. I need something in my life that doesn't revolve around my family. I sacrificed my career and my body for my kids, and they just keep taking and taking."

Josie sat on the edge of the bed and took her fussy daughter out of Dana's arms. "I'm torn between hoping my husband is still attracted to me, despite the stretchmarks that make me look like Freddy Kreuger got a hold of me and hoping he's not because I *never* want to be pregnant again."

"I pushed out three watermelon-sized humans and nursed them each for a year, so I pee a little when I sneeze, and have to strap my breasts down like a death row inmate being executed to run on the treadmill. It's quite the glamourous life we lead."

Josie laughed. "There's an image for you. But I guess if we don't laugh at ourselves, we would cry all the time."

"Uh-hmm," Dana nodded. "Or hide in the closet and

gorge ourselves on chocolate." She got up and led Harvey by the collar to the hallway and closed the door. "Do you think any of those little parasites appreciate the sacrifices I've made for them? No, last week Leah made fun of my old lady clothes and asked me why I don't get Botox. And Adam told me it was a good thing I have their dad to take care of me since I don't have a job." She plopped down on the bed.

Josie nudged her with her shoulder. "You're really giving me something to look forward to."

"I'm nothing if not encouraging. I think all moms are torn between feeling invisible and wishing we were, just for a little while. The world stops seeing us, you know? We are our job, nothing else. I need to believe though that I'm still worth seeing."

Josie could totally relate, and it was relief to hear someone else say it. She wanted desperately to be seen as something other than a mom, even though she wouldn't give up anything for that chance. It was an impossible dilemma.

"She really said you needed Botox?" Josie would have gotten the business end of a wooden spoon to her rear if she'd talked to her mother that way.

Dana tucked a loose strand of hair behind her ear and batted her lashes. "You know *Kaitlyn's* mom looks like she's twenty-five, so I look ancient by comparison. The thing is, even if I were completely wrinkle-free, Leah would be embarrassed by me for something else. That's one of the curses of motherhood."

It really was the best and worst job on the planet. For months Josie thought she was doing something wrong or at a disadvantage because she had multiples, but to hear Dana talk, it didn't seem like any mother had it easy.

Connor began to fuss, and Dana picked him up. Olivia shrieked happily and reached for her brother.

"I can't get over how mouthy Leah is to you when

she's so sweet to us."

"Sure," said Dana. "You're not the one ruining her life daily. It doesn't make it okay, but she was mad at me for not letting her go to a party when she said that."

"What kind of party?"

Dana gave her a cutting look. "Does it matter?"

Josie thought back to the parties she went to in high school. Most of them were harmless. "Yeah, I can see keeping her home if she'd been asking to go to an unsupervised party where you know there's going to be alcohol, but you have to give teenagers opportunities to make the right choices in the face of peer pressure so they won't rebel at the first taste of freedom, like my sister did."

She knew she wasn't a parent of teens yet, but she remembered what it was like to be one. Maybe Dana and Will had forgotten. "You're depriving her of making memories with her friends. That's what being a teenager is all about." She missed hanging out with friends. Maybe if she weren't so extroverted, staying home with the triplets wouldn't feel like prison sometimes. "I know what it's like to grow up with a mother who tries to control every aspect of her daughters' lives, and it's a recipe for rebellion."

"Let me guess," Dana said, "whenever you and your friends laugh about getting in trouble back in the day, you say, 'I'm never letting my kids out of the house.'"

How did she know? "Well yeah. So, what's the alternative?"

"We give our kids a better yes. When I was a senior, my parents took me and my cousin Tracy to Costa Rica. These were the parents, mind you, who didn't let me date unless it was in a big group, and they grounded me for a month for catching me trying to sneak out *one time*. But they let us try all kinds of things on that trip. We went cliff diving and parasailing.

"So maybe I missed out on some stories with my friends about things we would never let our kids do, but instead, I had adventures that my grandkids can hear about and say, 'I want to be as cool as my grandma,' except I hope no one ever calls me that. I think I'm more of a 'Nana.'"

Josie thought letting a teenager go to a party with friends seemed far less risky than letting them jump off a cliff, but she kept that to herself. Instead, she pondered the idea of a better yes. She eyed Dana as if seeing her for the first time.

"What? Why are you staring at me?"

"I'm trying to picture *you* cliff diving, Nana Dana. Who knew the librarian was secretly an adrenaline junkie?"

Dana visibly flinched. "Note to self, cross Nana off the list of potential grandmother names. I think all the adventure drained out of me with the onset of motherhood."

Josie's heart swelled with gratitude. She may not see eye-to-eye with her neighbor on every issue, but the time they spent together made her feel valuable. "Thank you for all your help. You brought me chocolate, solved my dress problem, and gave up your hair appointment for me. I really appreciate your friendship."

"It's what we do. We moms have to stick together and be each other's village."

"I don't know what I'd do without you." Especially since her own big sister seemed to want nothing to do with her. She didn't voice that though. Instead, she asked, "How is it you always know what to do in every situation? You solved all my problems today when I couldn't even see the forest for the trees."

Dana adjusted Connor's sock. "It's easier to fix things for other people than for myself. I don't have a clue what's going on with my husband or my dad, and I'd almost rather not know. I'm not sure which would be worse, getting a divorce or having to put my dad in a nursing home. I wouldn't survive both."

Josie didn't even know how to respond other than to

hug her friend and promise to pray for her.

They loaded up the babies to head home. Josie backed the stroller out of the room and down the hall. Dana attempted to hold Harvey back with one hand while protecting the dress from dog hair with the other as Josie struggled to open the front door and pull the stroller outside. It would have been so much easier to have carried an armload of dresses to the Caraway house.

"How is it such a chore just to walk across the street?" Dana asked. "I think I need a nap."

"Welcome to my life. It's why we never leave the house. We went to Costco one time for diapers and formula, and we were sore for two days from hauling the stroller, babies, *and* pushing a flatbed cart all over the store."

"I'm sure that was a sight," laughed Dana.

"Oh yeah. The cashier asked us if our day care center had a tax exemption code. That's the day we fell in love with online ordering and delivery. They bring the diapers to the door, and no one puts our family circus on Instagram."

Dana held open Josie's front door for her. "Have you heard from ECI yet about the triplets' evaluations?"

"Not yet, but I've decided not to worry about it," she lied. She couldn't help but obsessively worry about her sons' muscular development. "I'm working with them, and they're eating solid foods, so that's enough for now." Dana helped unload the babies and offered to stay and feed them, but Josie waved her off. It wasn't quite time, and she was trying to keep them on a schedule.

Dana pointed to the dress that was now carefully draped over the back of Hunter's recliner. "Make sure you send me pics when you're all dolled up. I'll come over a half hour before your hair appointment tomorrow."

This thing was really happening. She was going on a real date. She was going to have conversations with adults, and she was going to look good doing it.

FELLOWSHIP OF THE FRAZZLED MOMS

Chapter 11

Dana

Josie returned from her day of pampering looking radiant and refreshed. Her hair was several inches shorter with subtle highlights, her toes were painted hot pink, and her hands no longer looked like they belonged on a restaurant dishwasher.

Dana whistled. "You look like a new woman."

"I feel like one too." Josie pointed to the redness above her nose. "Check this out. I have two eyebrows separate now. I've been too tired to even look in a mirror in months, and I hadn't realized how much I resembled a *Survivor* contestant on day 35."

Dana laughed. "I haven't noticed you having a unibrow, or I would have come at you with tweezers." She thought for a second and added hesitantly, "You at least occasionally shave your legs and armpits, right?"

Josie shrugged. "One time, I was so tired, I fell asleep in the bathtub mid-shave. When the water got cold enough to wake me up, I couldn't even muster the wherewithal to finish the job, so my leg looked like Mr. T's head for days."

Dana couldn't remember ever being that tired, but she had a glimpse into Josie's extreme exhaustion after her morning of babysitting. She returned home and faceplanted on her bed. How did Josie do it twenty-four seven? They weren't even difficult babies, just plentiful. And babies. She had grown accustomed to living with people who wiped their own faces and behinds and could dress and feed themselves. She was used to sitting on furniture instead of on the floor, and she was not as quick to get off it as she had once been.

Still, it had been worth the trouble and the soreness she would feel tomorrow to see Josie's transformation.

She forced her head off her pillow and pushed up onto her elbows. As much as she wanted to nap, she had things to do this afternoon. She still hadn't made plans with Serena, and she had a goal of writing at least two thousand words of her manuscript--if she could even call it that yet-- by the end of the day. She trudged to the kitchen counter and opened her computer. How was pursuing her dream turning into such a chore? Transforming a doting mother into a believable serial killer was much harder than she had anticipated. While it booted up, she called Serena. She couldn't put if off forever.

"I was beginning to think you were avoiding me," Serena said in lieu of a hello. Dana usually appreciated Serena's no-nonsense direct approach, but it was intimidating when she was in the hot seat.

Dana apologized. "I'm meeting myself coming and going."

"Well, what are you doing right now?"

Now? Dana shifted to hold the phone with her shoulder so she could type in her password on the laptop. She couldn't tell Serena she was about to work on her manuscript in progress because then she'd have to explain what she was writing from the beginning. "Nothing at the moment," she lied.

"Perfect. Can you meet me at that coffee place across the street from the church in fifteen minutes? It's central to both of us."

Dana cringed. She pressed a fist to her forehead, cursing herself for thinking she was going to get away with a polite five-minute phone call. "Of course," she said, her voice a little too high.

It was a blustery day, and Dana had to fight the wind to open the coffee house door. Backpacks littered the floor, and earbud-clad college students on their laptops occupied every table. Did no one study in the campus library anymore?

She scanned the room and located Serena waving in a far corner. She was seated in one of two club chairs flanking an end table so small it barely held the plate of scones and two mugs of black coffee resting on it.

"Come sit." Serena patted the arm of the empty chair. "How is everyone?"

"Oh, hanging in there. You know how it goes when everyone is busy."

Serena blew over the top of her mug. "You mentioned your dad was having some issues?"

Part of her wanted to protect him by keeping his condition private, but the rest of her needed guidance, so Dana told her the whole awful duck story. "Have you experienced Alzheimer's or dementia with your parents?"

"Sure." Serena seemed to be examining something deep in her coffee cup. "Gray's mother was in a memory care facility when she passed. It's the kind of place that makes a true believer question the goodness of God."

Those words hung in the air between them. Dana said a silent prayer that her dad wouldn't suffer that fate.

Finally, Serena cleared her throat and donned a thin smile. "On that happy note, let me tell you why we're here." It sounded like a multilevel marketing shpiel or a summons to the principal's office. "The deacons want to start a grief support group at the church, but some of the widows have complained that these groups tend to turn into meat markets."

Dana had trouble imagining that scenario. Her dad certainly wasn't trolling for a new lady, she hoped. "Are you sure that's what's happening?"

Serena flicked her wrist. "Far be it from me to correct Mrs. Hoffman if she says she's getting asked on dates every time she goes to meetings. That's not the point though. Gray has the idea that maybe we start two separate support groups. One for men and one for women so there's less pressure in that arena."

"I'm not sure I could drag my dad to a grief support group regardless of whether it was coed or not," said Dana.

"What about you?"

Dana set down her coffee mug. "What about me?"

Serena leaned in and clasped her hands in her lap. "Would you be willing to facilitate a women's only grief group on Wednesday nights?"

She was serious, but why would anyone want Dana to lead a grief group? Her husband was very much alive. She suddenly understood. "Oh. Because of my mom."

Serena nodded almost imperceptibly but said nothing. Her silence made Dana squirm.

"I'm doing fine. I know my mom's not suffering anymore, and I will see her again."

"Which is why you would make a great leader. You have a healthy handle on your grief. You're an example that others need to see in their time of sorrow."

That was one way to try and guilt a girl into something. Had Serena not been listening on the phone when she told her how busy she'd been? Immediately she thought of her lonely, mostly-unwritten manuscript on the screen of her sleek new laptop. It was already in dire jeopardy of never being completed without adding to her commitments.

"Can I think about it?" Translation: buy some time to think up plausible reasons to turn down the request.

"Of course," said Serena. "But don't take too long. We're hoping to launch the program at the start of the new quarter next month."

The conversation turned to less somber topics. Dana learned that the elder Pendleton daughter was studying for the LSAT.

"If anyone should be arguing for a living, it's her," said Serena. She's been looking for loopholes in every rule we've made since she was old enough to talk."

Dana could relate. Leah was quite the arguer herself. The two traded war stories of life in the trenches with daughters until Dana was at risk of being late getting to Adam's school.

She couldn't bear Mrs. Bilson's judgment again. "Mrs. Harding, all students are expected to be picked up by 3:25. If you can't make it on time, you need to secure afterschool daycare."

She'd arrived at 3:27 *once* because she had to detour around a broken water main.

The women hugged goodbye, promising to get together again soon. No decision had been made about the grief group, and no parenting problems had been solved, but somehow, Dana left feeling a little less burdened.

It was a short-lived feeling squelched by a phone call from her dad's nosy neighbor, Rita Brewer. Rita had never called to chat, so it couldn't be good news.

"Hi, Miss Rita. How are things? Is my dad keeping his clothes on this week?" She crossed her fingers for luck and said a quick silent prayer.

"I'm not sure, dear. That's why I called you." She sounded worried. "Your dad hasn't been answering his phone today."

"He's probably just being difficult." She figured her dad saw Rita's name on his caller I.D. and declined her calls.

"Well, there's more." Rita went on to explain that his lawn mower and some tools were in the front yard, and Edward's side gate that led to his back yard was open. "It's been a couple of hours, and it's not like him to leave everything like that. I've even banged on the front *and* back doors. Nothing."

That was odd, even by her father's standards. He would not leave tools or lawn equipment in the front yard because he was wary of thieves. She tried to call him herself and got no answer. Even the device locator app on her phone was no help.

She called Will and relayed Rita's concerns.

"Why would he work on the mower now?" Will asked. "The grass hasn't grown all winter."

"You know I don't know the answer to that. Can you go check on him, please?'"

He sounded put out about having to drop everything, but at least he agreed to go. Will called back a half hour later as Dana waited at the middle school for Nate. "Did you find him?"

"Not yet. His car is here. Can you track him on your phone?"

Dana tried to stay calm for Adam's sake. "It says 'no location found.'" She got out of the car and shut the door so Adam couldn't hear. "Will? Did you check *everywhere*? Inside the car, the bathroom floor. What if he-?" She couldn't bring herself to finish her question, and she tried desperately not to picture her father lying somewhere unconscious.

"Honey, he's not here. I've gone over every square inch of the house and yard. He probably wandered off. Maybe something got his attention like the ducks in his flowerbed did. We'll find him."

Adam spotted friends from his class. "There's Landon and Ethan. I'm going to play football, okay?" He hopped out of the car without waiting for a reply.

"Watch for cars and stay out of the street."

Adam's and Nate's school dismissal times were twenty minutes apart. This left younger siblings to do homework in the car or start pick-up games on the school lawn. Without having to put on a brave face for her son, Dana sat back in the car and rested her forehead on the steering wheel. If her mom were alive, she would know where to find him. In fact, she would be keeping him on his toes and thereby keeping his mind sharp, and he wouldn't have wandered off at all.

Her mother was the best, the quintessential caregiver. She could do everything. She cooked, crafted, and played games with her grandchildren, making sure each child felt uniquely special. She was the yard stick by which Dana measured her own parenting abilities, and she always felt like she came up short next to her.

Dana couldn't remember ever buying socks or winter coats for herself or her kids while her mom was alive because Carolyn Johnson kept everyone fully outfitted for the cold. She had taken Dana coat shopping every October for as long as she could remember. This was an excursion Dana dreaded growing up because Octobers in Texas were usually warm, often still in the 80s. Her mom didn't care. She insisted they not wait until the selection was picked over.

Now Dana would give anything for another fall shopping spree with her mom. In fact, she'd noticed this morning that Nate's arms were an inch too long for his jacket. She hadn't been able to bring herself to buy him a new one last fall without her mom. Maybe she wasn't handling her grief as well as Serena thought.

Mom, where is dad? She bolted upright. "Hey Siri, call William," she commanded.

Dana didn't wait for Will to speak. "Check the cemetery. When he gets frustrated, he says, 'if Carolyn were here, she would know what to do.' Maybe trying to fix the lawn mower made him think about Mom."

Will's doubt was loud and clear in his silence. Finally, he spoke. "Hon, the cemetery is miles from here. If he wanted to visit your mother's grave, wouldn't he have driven?"

"Sure, if he was lucid. But if he had another episode, I don't know what he might do."

Will agreed to go to Carolyn's grave, and they said a prayer together that Edward would be found safe and soon before hanging up. Dana had to push her terrified what ifs to the back of her mind and put on a happy face for her boys who were both breathlessly hopping in and slamming car doors.

"I win," Nate gloated.

"That's not fair," Adam whined. "Your legs are longer."

"But I had my heavy backpack on, so that made it even. Mom, I'm starving. Can we go get something to eat?"

"Sure," she said as she pulled onto the street. "At home."

Her sons groaned in unison.

"Why can't we go to Sonic?" asked Nate.

"Because we have to get to Leah's soccer game in an hour." That is if they located her dad safe and sound before then.

Nate, the master negotiator said, "All the more reason to go to Sonic. We can grab drinks and a snack without getting distracted by the TV or Harvey. That way we won't risk showing up late and missing Leah scoring a goal."

She knew she was being manipulated, but the kid made sense. A Sonic trip would be a good diversion while her husband was on a wild goose chase for her missing father. The boys slurped ocean waters, oblivious to their mother's worry, as Dana pulled into her father's driveway. She left the car running and told them to stay put while she let herself in the front door. Dana wasn't sure what she would find inside, but she wanted to shield her sons from knowing their grandfather was in trouble. In hindsight, they would have been better shielded in the house.

Chapter 12

She called out for Edward as she walked room-to-room. Through the living room window, she saw a police cruiser pull into the driveway next to her Tahoe. She ran outside as an officer opened the back seat and helped her father to his feet.

"Dad!"

The boys hopped out of the car to find out what was going on. "Pops, did you get arrested?" asked Adam in his outside voice.

The officer explained, "No one was arrested. We found Mr. Johnson here sitting on a porch two streets over. He was trying to get inside, and the homeowner called us."

"I thought it was my house, but my key wasn't working. Sat down to call you when these gentlemen pulled up," said Edward.

Dana shuddered to think what might have happened if he'd gotten into the house. Some Texans were fans of the "shoot first, then ask questions" approach to home security. "Dad, Miss Rita called us because she was so worried about you." She hugged him and whispered into his neck as she held onto him. "You scared us."

Edward chuckled. "But I scared Rita too, so that's fun." He seemed awfully cheery under the circumstances.

"Ma'am," said the police officer who stepped out of

the passenger seat. "Elder care is a serious matter. I trust that you're going to get a better handle on your father's whereabouts in the future."

She started to defend herself, but her dad beat her to the punch. "I'll have you know I don't need my daughter to babysit me."

"The fact that you tried to gain entry to a stranger's residence believing it to be your own says otherwise," the first officer said.

Will pulled up as the cruiser drove away. "Ed, I've been looking everywhere for you. Why were the cops here?"

He scratched his head. "They picked me up for attempted B and E. Well, technically just entering. I was trying to come in the front door, so not breaking."

"Boys," said Dana. "Why don't you run inside and use the bathroom before we head to Leah's game?" When Nate and Adam were safely out of ear shot, she turned to her father. "Dad, this is the second time you've had a strange episode." She didn't know what else to call it. "Memory lapse" seemed harsh. "I don't know what to make of them, but I'm worried about you getting behind the wheel and getting lost or hurt."

He waved off her concerns. "Don't be ridiculous. I'm fine. All these cookie cutter houses look alike, and I got a little turned around is all."

Will caught Dana's eye. She could tell he was wondering the same thing she was. "But you were in the middle of working on your lawn mower. Why did you go on a walk?"

"I needed an Allen wrench, and Howard Perkins borrowed my set a while back. He lives over on Denton Avenue, so I walked over to get my wrenches." He pulled a metal thing that resembled a thick pocketknife from his pocket and held it up. "See?"

The boys emerged from the house. "It's game time,"

shouted Adam.

"Dude," said Nate. "We're right here."

Will convinced Edward to join them for the soccer game and dinner afterward. They all helped move the tools and mower to the back yard and then piled into the Tahoe.

Edward pointed to the mangled bumper. "What happened here?"

After the kids had scarfed down pizza, Will sent them to shower and work on homework. "Ed, we have to talk about your memory issues. I think it might be a good idea for you to stay with us for a while until you can get checked out by a physician."

Dana rewarded Will's proposal with an icy glare. He hadn't bothered discussing it with her before suggesting it to her dad. They didn't even have room for him unless they moved the kids around, which would be a lot of work, especially for her.

"We can put the boys in the same room and move Leah upstairs so you can have a downstairs bathroom and bedroom all to yourself," he added.

Leah was sure to love this idea as much as Dana did.

Edward put down his slice and wiped his hands on a paper towel. "Absolutely not. I know you mean well, but I'm not moving in here so you can babysit me. Besides, this place is a circus." He jutted his chin in the direction of the stairs. "Now don't get me wrong, I love those grandkids of mine more than anything, but you've got chaos zooming in one door and flying out the other. And *loud*. All the energy sure comes with volume, doesn't it? I love coming over for visits, but staying here would only stress all of us out."

Dana folded her arms across her chest. "You know what, Dad? It may be a circus, but you should see it when we're trying to be the ringmasters *and* juggle *your* shenanigans. Yours is the center ring of this three-ring show."

Will came around the counter and laced his fingers with Dana's. He squeezed her hand. "What she means, Edward, is that we love you, and we thought having you live here might help combat some of your memory lapses."

That wasn't what she meant at all. She didn't need Will putting words in her mouth any more than she needed her dad criticizing her wild household.

Edward stood up, dropped his napkin on his plate, and planted his own palms on the counter. "Well, this is a fine how do you do from my only child. I'm seventy-four. Of course, my mind isn't what it used to be. You've got your own aging issues, too. Can you still do a backflip like you could when you were a kid?" He paused and waited for her to answer.

Dana felt like a teenager in trouble and shook her head almost imperceptibly.

"No, you can't. You're in your forties. And let's not forget who crashed into my mailbox, young lady. So let any of you who are without aging problems be the first to cast a stone at me."

Now he remembered the mailbox incident. Dana gazed at her feet. She wasn't about to argue with the man twisting scripture against her. How was the same person who three hours ago mistook a stranger's house for his own now as coherent and quick-witted as he had always been? It made no sense.

"Now if the two of you are done weighing in on my mental state, I would like to go home. If you aren't up to driving me, I'll use that app Leah put on my phone." He pulled his phone from his pocket. "Leah, honey, come show your Pops how to get a ride home from the internet."

"That won't be necessary," said Will. "But this conversation is far from over. We're family, and we look out for each other. I left the office to search for you, which I'm happy to do, but it's not fair for you to scare Dana when you have these lapses." Will tapped his cheek and stared into the distance as though he were trying to recall some forgotten detail.

Ordinarily, his lectures irritated Dana, but now that he was chastising her father, she thought her husband had never looked hotter.

"I just remembered something. We may be overlooking a simple solution here," Will continued.

Edward pointed his thumb at Will. "See? Everyone forgets things. Are we moving him somewhere else too?"

Will ignored him. "I read that some simple medical conditions can cause dementia symptoms."

"Nobody said anything about dementia," Edward said.

"I'm just trying to help you get back to your old self again."

Her dad threw up his hands. "I thought the *old* part of myself is why we're even having this conversation."

Neither of them reacted to his attempt at lightening the mood, but Edward conceded to contact his doctor.

"Great," said Will. "I would feel better if you didn't drive until then. I need you to agree to give up your keys temporarily until we get some answers."

Dana held her breath and braced for a verbal firestorm. Thankfully, all the fight had drained out of him for the time being.

"Whatever." He walked toward the living room. "As long as *you* feel better about it. Now I really will need Leah's help with that taxi app." He mumbled something about ankle monitors and prison. "Are you two satisfied that I can go home without a babysitter tonight?"

Will and Dana nodded.

"Great, then I will tell my grandchildren goodnight, and one of you can drive me home."

"Can I drive Pops home?" asked Leah. She had come

out of her room when her grandfather called for her and had been silently listening from her doorway.

"No!" the three adults answered in unison.

Edward crossed the room and patted Leah's arm. "I'm sure you're an excellent driver, sweetie. I promise I'll let you drive me soon, but I already rode in the back of a cop car, and that's about all the excitement I can take for today." He pointed between Dana and Will. "I'm going to need a chauffeur since the wardens here think I shouldn't drive, so I promise to be your guinea pig, uh, I mean driving coach soon, okay?"

Leah hugged him and skipped back to her room.

Dana grabbed her bag. "I'll drive you home, Dad."

She didn't feel any resolution, but at least she would have a little peace of mind knowing he wouldn't be a danger behind the wheel for a while. He would be endangered by his fifteen-year-old chauffeur with a learners permit instead.

On the drive, she tried to imagine herself as an elderly widow. Would her kids come visit her? Would she have friends to hang out with? "Dad, do you think women have an easier time adjusting after the death of a spouse than men do?"

"Hard to say. I only know the one perspective. But it does seem like the widows at church and in my neighborhood have a lot more going on than the widowers. They take trips together, have their sewing circles, and who knows what else."

Dana shot him a skeptical half-smile. "Sewing circles? Are you sure? I mean, it's not the nineteen fifties."

"Maybe sewing circle is code for something else. How would I know? They just seem busier. Maybe it has to do with finding ways to fill the void after raising kids, whereas men lose a little of their identities after retirement. We are used to being defined by what we do."

That wasn't unlike how she felt as a mom. She tried to

think of activities her dad had participated in since his retirement. He had joined a men's group that did repairs and odd jobs for elderly shut-ins and single mothers, but when her mother got sick, he invested all his energy into caring for her.

"You used to volunteer with the men from church. You could call them up," she suggested.

"The group fell apart after Teddy and Ellen moved to San Antonio to be near their kids and Martin had a stroke. It was time to pass the torch to the younger men."

Dana laughed. "The younger retired men?"

"Getting old stinks. I don't recommend it."

She pulled into her dad's driveway. "I know I've been preoccupied with the kids and Will, and I haven't been the best daughter since Mom passed. I'm really sorry about that."

"Nonsense, I see you all the time. I haven't felt neglected or like you haven't been there for me at all. Besides, I'm your dad. It's *my* job to be there for *you.*" They both opened their doors to go inside. "You don't have to walk me in, daughter. I'm not going anywhere else."

She continued to get out and followed him to the front door. "Right, but you told Will you would hand over your car keys until we talk to the doctor, so…"

Edward shook his head, but he held the door open for her with one hand and pulled the keys from the lock with the other. He handed her the set. "Do I get to keep my house key, or do you want that too?"

Dana twisted the car fob off the ring and gave the keys back to him. He dropped it into the bowl on the entry table and crossed his arms. "Are we finished, Warden?"

"Stop calling me that. The spare set, please." she ordered. He walked to his room and returned a moment later with them in hand. "Do I need a pat down too? There's a metal detector in the garage if you want to wand me. Might be easier to just boot the car though."

"I'm glad your sarcasm hasn't suffered with your memory. Do you think it brings me joy to take your keys away like you did to me when I got caught sneaking out in high school?"

He shrugged. "That would make sense. Revenge of the teenage drama queen."

She maintained a neutral expression. "Yes, I've been stewing over that for twenty-five years, just waiting for the right moment to get even." She softened. "It's just what's best, for now. Okay?"

He hugged her. "I love you, kiddo. You are always taking care of all of us. I hope you're taking care of yourself too."

They parted and she tried to read his face. "What do you mean?"

"I see the strain of keeping up with the kids, Will, and me in your smile. You squeeze your eyes shut and pinch your nose and rub your forehead like you're sealing in the stress, keeping it from leaking out. You've lost your sparkle, that lightheartedness you and your mom always shared. Yours and her laughter used to fill every room of the house, but it's been ages since I've seen that side of you."

"Hey, I still laugh." In truth, she couldn't remember when the last time was. Maybe her identity was so tied to being a caregiver for her family, even sometimes for the Caraways, that she forgot to let loose and have fun. Maybe she did shove all the stress down so she could get to and through the next thing on the schedule. Or maybe her father was turning the tables on her to make her feel guilty for taking his keys.

She hugged him. "Well, on that happy note, I'm going to go. Have a lovely night."

"I would say 'see you soon,' but I guess that depends upon whenever you come back to get me," he said and shut the door behind her.

"Hilarious. See? I'm laughing now." she said to the closed door.

At home, she found Will sitting at the counter, in her office space, typing on her laptop. He had his own computer, so what was he up to?

"I found something," he said without looking up. She wondered what she would find on *his* computer. Emails from the woman he was with when he bailed on their lunch date? She stood behind him and read the screen over his shoulder. It was an article on illnesses that cause dementia-like symptoms.

"This says he needs to have a urinalysis, blood panel, and a cardiac referral. Decreased blood circulation contributes to memory loss and confusion. A bacterial infection can even cause disorientation. Dana, there's a whole list of potential medical issues that could be his problem. It's possible his symptoms are curable, and if not, they could be slowed by medications."

He went on to list activities that would help her dad exercise his body and his mind. None of it was revolutionary, but Will read it as if the answer to all their problems were contained in a few easy steps.

She lowered the screen and closed the laptop. "We aren't going to fix my dad tonight. It's been a long day, and we haven't spent much time with the kids." Dana tugged him away from the counter and nudged him up the stairs. "Go see what the boys are up to. Let them smoke you in Fortnite." She headed toward Leah's room when Will yelped. She looked in time to see him stumble forward and then slide down a step before he caught himself in a clamor worthy of *America's Funniest Videos.*

"Are you okay?" she tried unsuccessfully to stifle a giggle.

"Fine," he mumbled. "Adam," he yelled. "You left Legos on the stairs."

A fit of laughter consumed her until she couldn't

breathe.

"Glad I could amuse you, milady," Will said with a bow and scurried up.

What was it about other people falling that cracked her up? She snapped a selfie of her watering eyes and hysterical grin and sent it to her dad.

Proof I still laugh

Chapter 13

Dana struggled to hoist five canvas grocery bags onto the kitchen counter. She chided herself for not just ordering online instead of pacing up and down the aisles with her kids. Kids who asked to buy everything, wrote notes in the condensation of the doors in the frozen food section, and morphed into the most obnoxious humans on the planet every time they entered a store. She couldn't do grocery pick-up though because she was a control freak.

The only time she ordered her groceries, she waited for forty minutes in the parking lot only to realize after she got home the store made a nonsensical substitution. Instead of chili without beans, she got cilantro lime chili marinade. Those weren't even on the same aisle. She could spend the same amount of time pushing a cart and waiting in a checkout lane as ordering online and waiting in the car for items she wouldn't use. Plus, she got in more steps that way.

Dana had offered to pick up groceries for her dad too, but he was still sulking about handing over his keys and refused her help. She hoped talking to Will would reassure her that they'd made the right decision and maybe even cheer her up, but once again he had been out of the office when she called. The receptionist even seemed cagey about when he could be expected to return. His cell phone went straight to voicemail. The more she thought about it, the angrier she got.

She finished putting away everything but the eggs, which she was saving for last to examine for casualties after the boys used the shopping cart as their real-life *Gran Prix II* game in the parking lot. Shockingly enough, they were all intact. Maybe she should check with the body shop and see if the Tahoe's bumper could be replaced with egg carton foam.

She began transferring them from the carton into the egg holder at the top of the fridge door when Nate zoomed past on his skateboard. Before she could scold him for riding it in the house, Harvey, the world's clumsiest 120-pound dog, barreled after him and skidded into the refrigerator door, slamming the carton against Dana's chest.

Nate saw his mom dripping in raw eggs and snickered.

"Hey, Mom. You've got a little something on your shirt." The fire in his mother's eyes was the only response to his ill-timed quip.

Clutching the dripping egg carton to her chest, Dana fumed.

"Are you freaking kidding me? I've told you a thousand times not to ride your skateboard in the house."

Harvey proceeded to lick egg off her shirt, eliciting a second wave of shouting. "Get this horse outside and put your skateboard in the garage. If I ever see it in this house again, and I do mean EVER, I will throw it in the dumpster. Have I made myself clear?"

The preteen froze, his eyes saucers.

"I SAID, have I made myself clear?"

Leah and Adam stood in the doorway, their mouths hanging open. Meanwhile, Harvey continued to dutifully squeegee egg off the tile with his massive tongue.

"Whoa, Mom. What happened?" asked Adam.

It was not unusual for her youngest child to forget he was eating a popsicle and leave it to melt wherever he set it down. He couldn't brush his teeth without squeezing half a tube of paste all over the sink. The kid produced a wake of chaos everywhere he went, oblivious to his own carelessness. Yet, here he stood, marveling at dripping egg like it was the first time he'd ever seen a mess.

"Read the room, bro," Leah said as she pulled him out of the kitchen while offering to help her mom.

"Just get the dog out of here and give me some space," Dana ordered. When the kids had cleared out, she removed her shirt, careful to avoid getting egg in her hair, and dropped it into the sink. Next, she tackled the inside of the fridge and used a dustpan and paper towels to scoop as much of the mess off the floor as possible before mopping. Finally, after cleaning egg goo for a small eternity, Dana stood in the doorway to check for any missed eggshell.

Will chose that exact moment to burst in from the garage with flowers in one hand and guiding her father by the elbow with the other.

"Surprise," he said, "I thought your dad could..." There was nothing left to say when he saw his wife in her bra holding a mop.

"Should I have brought wine instead of flowers?" he asked.

Dana dropped the mop handle and dashed from the room.

She was donning a clean T-shirt when he walked in and leaned against the closet door. "Do I want to know what happened in the kitchen?"

"Do I want to know why you came in with a bouquet of flowers after you were out of the office all afternoon with your phone turned off?"

He folded his arms across his chest. "I just felt like doing something nice for my wife. I thought you needed a reminder that I still think you're hot and awesome. Is that a crime?"

"I just spent a half hour cleaning raw egg, and my dad saw me in my bra. Thank you for that, by the way, and you haven't explained why you were MIA today. So, I'm not impressed by your hollow gesture."

"Why did it take you so long to clean up a broken egg?"

If Dana could have shot literal daggers with her eyes, he'd have been blinded, and she would be on her way to prison.

Without offering a reply, Dana grabbed her purse and keys and headed to the garage. Nate chased after her. "Mom, wait."

She turned with her hand on the door handle.

"I'm sorry about the skateboard, and I'm sorry I didn't obey you." He stared at the floor. "I didn't mean for all the eggs to break."

Dana softened and pulled him into a tight hug. She sniffed his messy hair and savored the rare embrace. She was lucky these days if she got a half-second side hug from him. At last, she pulled away from him and lifted his chin.

"Hey, look at me," she said softly. "It's okay. I forgive you for riding in the house, and I'm sorry for yelling at you." They hugged again, and Nate disappeared from the kitchen.

Will asked, "Are you going to pick up dinner?"

She pulled her purse strap up higher on her shoulder. "Are we going to talk about what happened with you today?"

He rubbed the back of his neck. "I can't right now."

She waved her keys over him, over the room in general. "Then I can't do this right now." Dana left and turned off her phone.

She drove around listening to the radio. Usually this calmed her down after a fight with Will, but tonight was different. She didn't want to face him at all. She passed by a nice hotel near the university campus. Will had taken her to dinner there when it first opened, and she'd had the most delicious crème brulée for dessert. Her stomach growled and her mouth watered thinking about it now. So, she parked and went inside.

"I can put your name on the waiting list for a table," the hostess informed her. "But there's open seating at the bar, and the entire menu is available there as well."

Dana scoped out the bar seating. At one end, a couple sat with their knees touching and their heads close together. They looked happy and in love. Dana didn't want to sit anywhere near them. She hopped onto an empty stool as far from the love birds as she could get. A basketball game was on the screen over the bar, and she halfheartedly watched it as the bartender set a menu and glass of water in front of her.

"You a Sooners fan?" asked the man on her left. He nodded toward the screen.

"Only when they're playing the Longhorns," she replied.

The waiter took her order, and she and the stranger exchanged college basketball small talk. They high fived when Oklahoma scored a three pointer. She about jumped out of her skin when a hand tapped her arm.

"Dana Harding, as I live and breathe, what are you doing here?"

She swiveled on the bar stool and came face-to-face with Serena Pendleton. "Enjoying crème brulée for dinner. What about you?"

"Employee banquet for my company," said Serena. "Between ginning and planting season, of course." She worked in some kind of cotton production, but Dana couldn't remember what exactly.

Serena cut her eyes to the man on the other side of Dana. "Where's William?"

Dana shrugged. She rotated her stool back to its bar-

95

facing position and fixed her attention on the basketball game. If she had to look Serena Pendleton in the eyes for one more second, she would burst into tears.

Serena squeezed herself into the gap between Dana and the man on her left. She stared at Dana's profile until her gaze finally penetrated Dana's façade.

"What?" Dana hissed.

Serena leaned in and whispered so fiercely that she might as well have been yelling, "What are you doing in a hotel bar with another man?"

The stranger must have heard her because he stood and carried his plate to an open seat further away. Serena slid onto the newly vacated stool. "Okay, you're not together."

Dana laughed. It was ironic that the pastor's wife thought she was having an illicit encounter in a hotel when her husband was the one keeping secrets. "Serena, there's nothing nefarious going on. I just needed to get out of the house, and the temptation of a decadent dessert to soothe my soul lured me in."

Serena watched her but said nothing.

Finally, Dana cracked. "You want to know what's really going on with me?" Serena nodded. "I'm a failure at everything, and my family is in trouble."

"Come with me." Serena pulled some bills out of her beaded bag and slapped them on the counter and led Dana by the wrist to a secluded seating alcove in the lobby. They were a sight, what with Serena in her evening attire and Dana in ripped jeans and a tee shirt that read, "867 FIVE 309." "First of all, you are *not* a failure. But why do *you* think you are?"

Dana recounted the egg disaster and how she'd yelled at Nate. Serena bowed her head and put her hand to her mouth, perhaps trying to cover her dismay over her complete overreaction.

"Remember how I told you about my dad chasing ducks? Well, right before that, I startled myself and spilled coffee all over my keyboard. Ended up completely destroying the laptop all because I turned in my homework with a typo that said 'breasts' instead of 'breaths.'"

Serena kept her head down.

Dana told her about her dad's run-in with the cops the day before. Serena shoulders began to tremble. Soon her whole body quaked with laughter. Dana waited for her to pull herself together.

"I'm so sorry," was all Serena managed to sputter between guffaws. Her laughter was contagious. Before long, neither of them could catch her breath, and Dana's sides hurt.

"My goodness, you've had a rough few days, haven't you?" said Serena when she finally caught her breath.

Dana had laughed so hard she slid to the edge of her seat. Now she sat up properly and wiped the tears that streaked her cheeks. "That's not even the worst of it." She described Will's evasive behavior. "Tonight, I asked him to be straightforward with me, and he wouldn't. So, I left. And now all I want to do is check into a suite in this fine establishment, soak my weary body in a bath, and fall asleep on clean sheets without having to have another conversation with Will or anyone else in my house."

"I ran away from home once," said Serena.

"*You?*" Dana's mouth hung open.

"Oh yeah. And not just to a hotel in town. I packed a bag and took a cab to the airport. I got a stand-by ticket to New York and went sightseeing in the Big Apple for three days all by myself." Serena beamed at the recollection. "I was a new woman when I came home, but my family walked on eggshells for weeks like they were afraid I would bolt again at any moment. That earned us a few months of marriage counseling."

"But your girls are angels, and you're married to a minister."

"Yeah, and that minister can be a real pain in the rear.

His kids too. We've had plenty of days over the years when I prayed for the strength to stay married. To get through one more day even. I can't tell you how often I would get up and ask God to show me what He loved about Gray and beg for the patience to endure my dramatic teenagers. Families are wonderful, but they're hard."

"So hard."

Serena leaned forward and took Dana's hand. "I'm gonna pray for you. Not only right now, but you'll be on my list until you tell me otherwise."

"Well at least keep me on there until Adam moves out."

The women bowed in prayer together. Serena asked the Lord to cover Dana in peace and grace to get through the challenges in her marriage and with her dad. Dana silently added a request for Will to feel compelled to tell her the truth about whatever he was hiding. Afterward, Serena asked her if she'd had a chance to think about the grief group.

Ah yes, the grief group. Dana could think of a million things she'd rather do than moderate a grief support group. Remove her own appendix, for example. She implored Serena to find someone else. Surely there was a lady already involved in the group who would be more suited to lead it than she was. She'd even done some research and discovered that there were no less than eight other churches in town that hosted Grief Share. Why couldn't a few of them be persuaded to host separate men's and women's groups?

"Maybe you're right," said Serena. "Since Mrs. Hoffman is the one who seems to be having the most difficulty with the current group, maybe she should lead the women's only group. I only thought of you because you seemed to have it so together after dealing with your mother's passing, and because I know I can count on you."

Dependable Dana. She grimaced. "I'm sure bumping

into me tonight cleared that up for you. I have nothing together."

"I think you're selling yourself short. You're not like those women at church who dress up and fake it until they're safely in the car again. You're genuine, and people see that in you."

The Hardings did their fair share of faking it on Sunday mornings. Chaos had a way of getting the better of them on the Lord's Day, but it felt like a moot point. Everyone faked it to some degree at church. However, it reminded her of the thought she'd had when Josie and Hunter dropped their kids off in the nursery for the first time.

"There is something that's been weighing on me though. Why does the church segregate adult Sunday School classes by the age of the children?"

Serena shrugged. "Simple. It allows people to make friends with the parents of their kids' friends and build a network of support."

It didn't feel so simple when Dana was a new mom. She'd quit her job to stay home with Leah while the other women in class compared notes on daycares and the woes of working while breastfeeding. It didn't feel like community a few years later when everyone was extolling the benefits of private school and home school over public school. Their class had split into camps, covertly judging the families who had chosen foolishly.

"I wish there were older women in my class I could turn to when I feel like I'm drowning and know that there's light at the end of the tunnel. I would have appreciated a more seasoned mom holding my hand and praying over me like you just did when I dropped my tiny baby off in the nursery for the first time. And if someone like Mrs. Steen, who's been married almost as long as I've been alive, had marital advice for those tough times, I think I'd feel buoyed up. Able to weather any storm."

Serena gave a slight nod. "Mm-hmm, I know what you mean. If I'd had someone like Mrs. Steen to mentor me, maybe I wouldn't have had to fly all the way to New York to get some perspective."

"I'd give anything to get a pep talk from a former stay-at-home mom who went on to be successful in another field after raising awesome kids. I need to believe I can become more than just the soccer mom and a housewife."

The two spent a few more minutes lauding the virtues of mentorship and having veterans reassuring rookies in the trenches before Serena's phone vibrated. "Oh my. I better get back before Gray thinks I've run away again. Are you gonna be okay, Dana?"

She was. She even felt good enough to head home and face Will again, thanks to Serena's wise counsel. She stood and hugged her friend. "Thanks for being my Mrs. Steen tonight."

"I guess that means you won't be trying to catch a plane then?" Serena squeezed her hand.

"Maybe tomorrow." Dana winked.

The family was seated around the dining table devouring a bucket of fried chicken when she got home. Will's bouquet of flowers was arranged in a crystal vase that rarely saw the light of day, likely thanks to Leah. She wordlessly kissed each child on the head and hugged her dad from behind and went to soak in the jacuzzi tub. No one had asked her where she was or why her phone had been turned off, and she wasn't sure what to make of that.

She stayed in the tub long after her skin had pruned. Will didn't tell her goodbye when he left to take her dad home. She put the boys to bed alone, and by the time she'd finished helping Leah with a Geometry problem, Will was asleep. Apparently, he didn't yet feel any conviction to tell her what was going on with him. Maybe she should have explored that jet-setting to New York option after all.

Chapter 14

Josie

Josie inspected her reflection from all angles in the full-length mirror. She didn't mind what she saw for a change. She smoothed down the front of her borrowed dress, took a deep breath, and blew it out slowly. She may have been radiant on the outside, but inside she was a bundle of nerves. She double-checked the nursing pads in her bra, praying they held. The only thing more mortifying than leaking down the front of her dress would be leaking down the front of someone else's dress.

Josie entered the living room where her mother was giving a bottle to Ben while Leah sat on the floor playing with Olivia. Hunter came down the hallway wearing a slim fitting suit with a black tie holding Connor at arm's length.

Josie felt their stares as she crossed the room. "What? It's not like I've never worn a dress before."

Hunter whistled. "Wow! Babe, you're gorgeous."

She put her hand on her hip and did a runway turn. "Thank you. You're pretty hot yourself."

"Ew," interjected the disgusted teenager. "But yeah, Josie, you're stunning."

Josie pointed at Connor, still dangling by his armpits. "What's happening here?"

Hunter bent down and handed him off to Leah. "I

changed his diaper, and I was sweating bullets the whole time. I did not want pee on this suit. Once we got through that, I wasn't taking any chances with spit up or drool on the way back in here."

Josie laughed. "And now you see why I dress like I do every day."

He lightly planted a kiss on her lips, careful not to mess up her lipstick and sniffed her hair. "You smell good too."

She squeezed his hand. "Thank you. Now let's get out of here before our kids mess that up."

The banquet was held in a historical building downtown that had been converted into an event venue. It had stamped metal ceiling tiles and opulent detailing on the wood columns that separated the space into a large dining area with elaborately decorated round tables and an entertainment area with the stage and dance floor. The sandwich board at the door welcomed them to the High Plains Homes for Change Gala to raise money to build homes for indigent families.

Josie made a note to report back to Dana that they were attending a legitimate fundraising event that was indeed *not* a thing for families of multiples nor a dog sweater auction.

High top tables flanked a bar on the right side of the room, where Todd and Megan sipped cocktails while chatting with another couple. Todd waved them over, and the confidence Josie had felt about her appearance began to wane.

Megan was of course a knockout. It wasn't just her looks; her easy-going personality and infectious laugh spellbound everyone in the room. Todd was fun to be around, but Josie couldn't figure out why she would shackle herself to a man old enough to be her father when she could easily attract any man she wanted. Josie side-eyed Hunter to see if he was checking out Megan, but he didn't seem to see anyone but her.

"What? Why are you staring at me?"

He put his hand on the small of her back and whispered in her ear, "You're the hottest woman in this place, and I'm proud to be here with you."

Hunter's declaration did something to her stomach that she hadn't felt since before they found out they were expecting triplets.

She spun to face him, squeezing his hand that was still on her waist. "You wanna get out of here and go make out in the car?"

"Alright you two, don't make me separate you," said a jovial dad voice.

"Hey, Todd." Josie and Hunter parted, and she hugged his business partner. "Thanks for inviting us."

"I'm glad you could make it. We buy a table every year, but we usually fill it with clients and contractors. This year we ended up with tickets we couldn't give away."

Hunter clapped him on the back. "Well, it's good to know we were your last resort," he joked. Josie wondered why he had no knowledge of this arrangement and made a mental note to ask him about it later.

The cocktail hour felt more like three hours. Every conversation began with, "What do you do for a living?" When she said she was a stay-at-home mom, some people made placating remarks like, "Well, that's a noble profession," while others were downright condescending. "It must be nice to get to sleep in and wear whatever you want all the time."

Clearly none of them had been around children. She just smiled politely and held in her sarcastic rebuttals to avoid embarrassing Hunter. She didn't want his colleagues and clients to think he was married to a shrew.

Megan grabbed two colorful cocktails off a passing waiter's tray. "Here, Jos. You're empty-handed, and these events are way more fun after a round or two." Josie waved off the proffered glass.

"I can't but thank you."

"Why can't you drink?"

"I'm still nursing." She bit the inside of her lip and prayed this would be the end of the conversation. She didn't think she could stand to hear Megan weigh in on her parenting choices when her only maternal experience included two college-aged stepchildren.

Megan clinked the two glasses together. "More for me then."

They made their way to their assigned tables which were adorned with tall vases filled with tropical arrangements and twinkle lights. Josie gaped at the extravagance and wondered how many homes for the needy could have been constructed for the price of these decorations alone. They were far more lavish than any wedding she had ever attended, that's for sure.

Her own wedding had been an understated yet elegant affair. Her mother's family from Albuquerque did all the food and decorations themselves. There were over two hundred guests, and a three-course meal served at round tables covered in ivory brocade tablecloths with elaborate, albeit low, centerpieces. Her aunts insisted that the guests should be able to talk across the table and still make eye contact over the flowers.

Now Josie wished tonight's event planners had heeded the same advice because Josie couldn't see the couple across from her at all.

She checked her phone and was glad to see her mom hadn't texted because it meant the babies were fine. Or did it mean that something terrible had happened? Josie shook off the thought. Leah was there, and Dana and Will were right across the street. Everything was fine.

Over a delicious meal of mushroom chicken and risotto, Hunter and Todd told jokes and made small talk with the other couples at the table. Josie laughed and added comments occasionally, but she was a fish out of water. This was the most people she had been around at one time in at least a year. Her extroverted personality that had thrived in the admissions department of a large university now felt broken and rusty.

Megan thumbed at Josie and told the couple on the other side of her, "They have triplets. Can you believe it?"

The other woman's eyebrows shot up. "You really have your hands full. You must be thrilled to be out of the house."

By 10:00, Josie's feet hurt, her breasts were swelling, and she had made all the polite conversation she could stand for one night.

She sidled up to Hunter while he was talking shop with his cabinet supplier and slipped her arm into his. "How much longer?" she whispered.

He excused himself from the conversation and led Josie out of earshot. "What's wrong?"

"Nothing, I just thought we might try to get home before—" She looked down at her engorged chest, willing Hunter to understand.

Hunter followed her gaze, and his eyes got big. "Good call, we don't want you to spring a leak."

In the car, Hunter asked, "What was with you tonight? It seemed like you didn't want to be there."

His irritation blindsided her. "What are you even talking about? I had a good time, and I was nice to everyone."

"You had that plastered on smile that you give your mom when she makes comments about your housekeeping. You were fake friendly, not like you used to be at these things. Lord knows we went to plenty of them for the university when it was for *your* work. I had hoped you could make a little more effort when it's something for *my* job."

Heat rose up her neck. Where did he get off accusing

her of not trying?

"This is the first real event I've been to in a year, so yeah, maybe I was a little bit like an injured hawk being reintroduced into the wild for the first time," she said defensively. "But I wasn't the problem. Your colleagues and their trophy wives are the ones who treated *me* like a social pariah for having triplets."

Hunter kept his eyes on the road, but his neck muscles tightened, and Josie thought she saw him roll his eyes. "Nobody treated you like a pariah, Jos. The last time I checked, the triplets belonged to both of us. You act like you're the only one raising them."

"That's right, *both* of us were on bedrest for almost three months. And *both* of us have stretch marks and swelling breasts that are about to erupt all over this dress, which, by the way, *we* had to borrow because *both* of us are carrying a ton of baby weight." She was fully prepared to continue her tirade, but Hunter interrupted.

"Now you're just taking cheap shots."

"Am I, Hunter? You're the one who got bent out of shape at the end of a perfectly good date night because I didn't act like a party girl. I've been under house arrest for ten months. You, Dana, and my mom are the only adults I talk to regularly. All my friends my own age are busy with their own families, and it's not like I can just meet up for a quick play date. Besides, no one wants to hang out with the weird lady with too many babies."

"Josie, stop being a martyr. Other people manage to go in public with their children, and lots of them have *more* than three kids. You *can* go out, but you choose not to. You've been miserable for months, and I can't fix that for you. You have to figure out what it is you want and go after it."

Josie folded her arms over her aching chest. Then she uncrossed them because she was afraid the pressure would unleash the flood she was hoping to avoid. "What I want is for you to get home before dark once in a while so I can have a free evening to go out with friends." Did she just say that out loud? Josie had to think for a second whether she meant that or if she was just trying to get back at Hunter for criticizing her. He was a good dad, very involved. Sure, his business sometimes lent itself to twelve-hour workdays and some weekends, but he really did try to guard his family time. She started to apologize for her low blow, but before she could get a word out, Hunter retorted.

"One of us has to make the money that pays for diapers and formula and keeps a roof over their heads. We could swap roles, but it would be a little tougher to provide on an admissions clerk salary."

If he was hoping to hurt her feelings, it worked. "Yeah? Well, speaking of your job that makes all the money, if you and Todd are business partners, why does *he* buy the tables for these fundraisers and fill them with other people? How is it a partnership when he told us we were last resort invites?" It had not set well with her that Todd said she and Hunter were invited because they had leftover tickets.

"Todd's the business manager, and he uses these events to schmooze vendors and clients. It's a business move. Besides, there's no way we could have ventured out to a gala before tonight, so what would have been the point? There's not a conspiracy to cut me out if that's what you're thinking."

It was exactly what Josie was thinking, but she wasn't going to admit it. They didn't speak the rest of the way home.

When they arrived, Marie was on the sofa watching a *CSI* rerun. Hunter lingered in the kitchen, rummaging in the fridge. Marie hit the pause button on the remote and sat up. "Well? How was it, *mija*?"

"It was great. We had fun, and the food was delicious." She looked around at the clean but quiet house.

"Did Leah leave?"

"Once the babies were asleep, I paid her and sent her home. Was fifty dollars enough? She said it was, but I think she was just being polite."

Josie nodded. It was a good thing they didn't go out often or else they might need to take out a home equity loan to pay the sitter bills.

"Why is Hunter eating again if the food was so delicious," Marie asked.

She rolled her eyes and shrugged. "Ask him, but could you unzip me first? I need to pump." She turned her back and raised her hair out of the way. Her breasts practically heaved a sigh of relief at being released from the dress. She grabbed the pump from the side of the sofa and retreated from the room.

She returned a while later in pajamas and settled onto the sofa next to her mom. Hunter was reclining in his chair with his arm over his head, his tie and jacket long gone.

Marie nudged Josie with her shoulder. "Mr. Chatty Cathy here said it was great, but I got no details. I need more."

Josie described the food and centerpieces.

Marie shook her head. "Large centerpieces make a statement, but they impede conversation."

"That's what I said."

"What did Megan wear?"

Hunter sat up. "I think centerpiece and fashion talk is my cue to call it a night. Ladies." He leaned over and hugged Marie and kissed Josie on the cheek and exited.

Marie turned to face Josie. "Spill it. What happened tonight?"

Josie avoided eye contact by adjusting the throw pillow beside her. "What makes you think something happened, Mom? We both told you it was great."

"A mother knows. You rolled your eyes when I asked why Hunter was eating again, and you two didn't say a word to each other. Did you guys have a fight?"

Josie shrugged. She really didn't know what had gone so wrong. "Hunter said I acted like I didn't want to be there tonight. Then I got defensive because I had a perfectly lovely time despite feeling totally out of place. I also didn't know anyone but Todd and Megan while Hunter seemed to know everyone there. He worked the room while I stood off to the side and smiled like a dork."

It might have been a bit of an overstatement, but she didn't care.

"Were you jealous, *mija*?"

"Of Hunter being in his element? No. Of the beautiful women who didn't have to leave three babies at home and stuff their bras with maxi pads to be there? Definitely. When people hear I have triplets, the expressions on their faces are always the same." She raised one eyebrow, tilted her head, and smiled toothily. "It's like I'm the weird kid who eats glue at recess."

"Josefina Camille Saldana Caraway, that's enough of that. Do not compare yourself to others around you. Your path is not their path, and you don't know what challenges each of those women may have had to overcome to be there. Just because someone manages to look nice and put on a smile in public doesn't mean she has it altogether and isn't struggling. You don't know whose marriage is in trouble, whose kid is an addict, who's hiding a cancer diagnosis or has a dying parent. There are a thousand things that are harder to deal with than triplets."

"Yeah, well, Hunter called a martyr. I guess I make everyone around me miserable or something to that affect."

"He's right, you know."

Josie's eyebrows shot up, but before she could defend herself, her mom put her hand on her arm and shushed her.

"I don't mean about making everyone miserable, but about feeling sorry for yourself because no one understands what it's like to be in your shoes. You're the only one who can shut down your pity party."

Josie laid her head back against the sofa. She didn't have the energy to protest, and there might have been some truth to Hunter's and her mom's statements.

"Mom, thank you for being here. And for doing laundry and everything else. You're like a tiny, Latina Mr. Clean. With more hair, of course."

Marie wrapped her arms around Josie and kissed the side of her head. "I'm happy to help. Cleaning is my love language. But more than that, I love getting to spend time with you and Hunter and my sweet *nietos*."

"I have to go talk to Hunter." She patted her mom's leg and left her alone in the living room. Hunter was lying on the bed channel surfing in his plaid pajama pants. Josie smiled. The only time he slept in pajamas was when they had guests.

She sat on the bed next to him. "You were right, and I'm sorry," she said.

He looked up from the television. "What am I right about?"

"I was faking it tonight. I should have made more of an effort."

He reached for her hand. "I'm sorry for not realizing you were uncomfortable. I should have stuck closer to you instead of leaving you with Megan and the Second Wives Club."

Josie snickered. "Maybe your next wife will fit in with them. She might be the baby of the group though."

Hunter wrapped his arm around her waist and pulled her down beside him. "You're the only wife I ever want." He kissed her mouth. "Besides, who's going to marry a guy with three kids."

She laughed and then cleared her throat. "I'm sorry I've been so miserable."

"I was a jerk to say that. You do seem unhappy lately, but it's understandable. Your whole world was upended this past year, and you're constantly outnumbered by small, smelly people who scream at you all day."

She touched his cheek. "So, we're good?"

"We're good," he said as he kissed her again. "I heard your mom call you by your full name. Did she find a stash of laundry or dirty dishes somewhere, Josefina Camille Saldana Caraway?"

"Ugh, no. She reminded me in that special way of hers that there are harder things than having triplets, and I need to stop comparing myself to other people. She's not going to find a laundry stash because I may or may not have sent a heaping basket full across the street yesterday and paid Leah ten bucks to wash and fold it. Between babysitting and doing our excess laundry, we'll have her college tuition covered by the time she graduates high school."

Hunter nuzzled her neck. "At some point our kids are going to be able to help with the chores instead of creating more of them, right?"

"Theoretically, yes. But I've seen what chaos the Harding kids create, so I wouldn't hold your breath. Oh hey, I totally forgot to tell you, Laurel got engaged."

His eyebrows practically touched his hairline. "Your sister?"

"Do you know any other Laurels?"

"To a *guy*?" he asked. She elbowed him in the ribs. "Ow! It's a legit question."

"I asked Mom the same thing, and she yelled at me in Spanish and smacked me with a dish towel. Apparently, he's a river guide or something like that. They met in Colorado last year when she hiked Mt. Elbert."

"How did he propose if she's still out on the Appalachian Trail?"

Josie shrugged. "I don't know. Knowing Laurel, they went on the trip together, and she didn't share that detail with Mom."

"Does this mean we have to attend a family wedding

with both of your parents? The last time we saw them in the same room was at our own wedding, and your aunts were like the state police keeping the peace."

Josie covered her face with a pillow and groaned. "Don't remind me."

Javier Saldana was a successful corporate attorney, but not such a great dad. He moved to Los Angeles when Josie was in middle school and married Alana as soon as the ink on his divorce papers was dry.

He flew the girls out to spend that summer with him, but they were left in their stepmother's care while he worked long hours. Alana was very into fitness and her appearance and less keen on hanging out with two teenagers. Thus, the summer in L.A. only lasted two weeks before the girls begged to go back to Albuquerque. Eventually, their relationship with their dad dwindled to sporadic calls or texts.

Javier had come to meet his grandbabies after they came home from the hospital, but he had only stayed one night, in a hotel, of course. He was never going to be a hands-on grandparent.

She propped herself on an arm and pushed the pillow away. "We could freak everyone out at the wedding and beg the grandparents for a group photo with each of them holding a baby. Can you imagine Alana holding a baby?"

Now Hunter laughed. "Definitely not. That vein in your mom's forehead would pop if she had to pose with the two of them. Besides, I doubt your stepmother can even get her arms in front of her to hold a baby with all that silicone in her chest."

Josie put her hand on Hunter's mouth. "Shhh. We can't talk about you-know-who with my mother in the house. She will sense a disturbance in the force. You know how she feels about the walking Malibu Barbie doll."

"Maybe Laurel and Whatshisname will elope or have a destination wedding, and we can just watch it online. No one will expect us to travel with the babies," he said.

Josie wondered if they would even be invited to the wedding since Laurel hadn't even responded to her in months. She got up to brush her teeth, thinking about how families simultaneously complicated life and made it worth living.

Hunter's parents had moved to Oklahoma City weeks before Josie had gotten pregnant to care for his mother's aging parents. His younger brother was overseas in the Marine Corp, and his older brother had recently been laid off and moved into the family home as well. Hunter's parents had come down to see the triplets three times and Facetimed at least once a week.

She walked to the doorway, still holding her toothbrush, and sporting a foamy outline on her lips. "Do you think we should plan a trip to OKC so your grandparents can meet the babies?"

Hunter slipped under the covers and laid back down. "How did you get from *not* being expected to travel with the babies to "let's take a road trip" in the two minutes you've been in the bathroom?"

She shrugged. "This is different. Your parents and grandparents can't come here. My dad and sister haven't made any effort to visit us, whereas your parents have done their best to support us and get to know their grandchildren while caring for your grandparents."

He yawned and said, "I could ask them. Maybe we could take Marie with us to be extra hands."

Josie shook her head and whispered, "You want to put the clean freak in the minivan with the five of us for road trip? I thought you loved me."

"But at least we'd have a one-to-one ratio of adults to babies. And she might be able to whip my brother into shape."

"Or at least scare him out of the house," Josie called over her shoulder as she returned to the sink. By the time she came back to bed, she had already made a mental list of all the provisions they would have to pack to travel with the babies. "Do we even have enough luggage to take a trip with our kids?"

Hunter turned off the lamp and pulled her to him. He kissed her and said, "Maybe we should sleep on it."

Chapter 15

Dana

Dana and the kids spent hours Saturday morning cleaning the house for their cousins' arrival. She wished they'd gotten a jump on it sooner, but then the fight to keep their rooms clean would have been unbearable.

Adam's feet poked out from beneath his bed where he pulled out an alarming amount of lost clothing, toys, and trash. "It smells bad under here."

"I see now why you never have socks for school. They're what's holding up your mattress," she said.

Leah's room was no better. Her bathroom counter had amassed a stash of makeup and moisturizers that rivaled a Sephora.

"You can't even see the sink. How do you live like this?" Dana chastised.

Leah sorted and grouped products at a snail's pace. "I just need a better storage system."

What she needed was a garbage bag and a shovel.

"I don't see why Aunt Julia and Uncle Dave have to stay in my room. Why can't they sleep in the living room? It's so unfair." Leah whined.

"You have the best room for guests. It has a queen bed and its own bathroom."

"What about *your* room? I don't see you giving up

your sanctuary for company," Leah complained.

Dana patted her on the head. "Poor baby, her *sanctuary* is being ripped away from her for the *one* night. I'm shocked child welfare hasn't swooped in to right this atrocity."

She left Leah to her organizing and saw a missed call and voicemail from Serena. Before she could even listen to it, Will poked his head around the corner and patted the wall.

"Since you did the hard work of getting the house ready, why don't I take the kids and we'll do the weekly Costco run while you write or relax for a while?"

That was suspicious. Will only voluntarily ran errands on the weekends when he could escape by himself. He viewed staying home with the kids and their friends as drawing the short straw over pushing a cart full of toilet paper through a crowded box store.

"Why? What's the catch?" she asked.

"I know you won't have much time to yourself, so I thought you might appreciate a little solitude before the craziness starts."

She stared him down as if he were a kid with chocolate on his face, denying eating a cookie. Finally, Will cracked.

"Okay, there's a catch. I can't take off all week to help you entertain the kids."

"Oh," she replied, masking her disappointment. "That's alright. How much time *will* you be off?"

"I have to work Monday through Thursday for sure, and I might have to work half a day on Friday."

"So, the answer to my question was 'none.'" Dana continued to stare him down. She hadn't asked him to take off work when his nephews were coming; he had offered. Then her dad scheduled a doctor's appointment for Monday, and she was thankful Will would be available to keep the kids from reducing the house to rubble while she was out.

She shrugged. "You're the CEO. If you can't take off, you can't."

"Some big wigs are coming in from the Metroplex to tour the facilities and review the financials for the shareholders." He swallowed. Was swallowing a sign of lying? A tour was the excuse he'd given the day he blew her off for lunch.

"Is that blonde lady from Big Kitchen Supply the reason you have to work?"

He ran his hands through his hair. "This again? Dana, there's nothing going on between us. I told you; work is just intense right now."

He rounded up the kids and headed to Costco. Dana figured she might as well use the last few minutes of quiet she would have for a week to work on her book project. When she sat at the kitchen counter and opened her laptop, she noticed Will's phone sitting nearby. It was common for him to forget it. She picked it up and saw a text alert from an Helena Shaffer. She'd never heard him mention someone by that name. She looked over her shoulder as if someone might catch her before trying to unlock Will's phone.

She hesitated. Snooping was wrong, but so was keeping secrets from one's spouse. If Will wouldn't talk to her, then what choice did she have?

The first number she tried worked. It was the same four-digit code as his bank PIN and their garage door keycode. She let out a breath. Will was a simple man, and if he'd been hiding a secret relationship, wouldn't he have at least locked his phone better?

My plane lands at 9:10 Monday. Will be in your office shortly after

Dana's heart pounded. There was no text thread between Will and Helena Shaffer. He had this woman's name saved in his contacts, and the only exchange between them was her expected arrival time. Had he deleted previous texts? Usually when someone texted for the first time, the person included their name. There had to have been prior messages between the two of them.

She looked up Helena Shaffer on Facebook, but there were too many to narrow down which one was texting Will.

She had an idea. Her dad's appointment was scheduled for 10:30 Monday. She could swing by Will's office before she picked up her dad and find out for herself if this Helena character was the same woman she'd seen before. She just needed to come up with a believable story. How hard could it be?

Dana tried to write, but her mind raced. She tapped her fingernails on the counter. She could confront Will today. Clear the air. But she'd have no way to know if he was being honest or not. Besides, the in-laws would arrive in a few hours. She would distract herself by returning Serena's call. Maybe she'd even confide in her friend and get her take on Will's behavior.

"Hey lady." Dispensing with small talk, Serena cut to the chase. "Thought you'd be interested to know that Gray loved your suggestion so much that effective immediately we will have a Wednesday night women's group." Dana was certain she had lobbied *against* the women's only grief support group.

"Y'all aren't even going to wait for the new quarter?"

"Gray said the ministry staff has heard rumblings that there's a whole slew of women who feel like they're drowning under the weight of motherhood." Serena chuckled. "I think the men on staff are afraid their wives are going to take off and leave them home alone with their offspring. This is a tangible way the church can make a positive impact on weary mothers."

Gradually Dana realized they weren't on the same page. "You're not talking about a women's only grief group, are you?"

"What? No. The deacons agreed to reach out to one of those eight other churches about their programs instead. The day after I ran into you at the bar," Serena giggled at her own joke, "I showed Gray an article that talked about how the cultural shift of moving away from extended family has weakened our support systems and left parents feeling more isolated than in the past. It leads to depression and mental exhaustion and a whole slew of preventable problems."

Dana held the phone with her shoulder and typed into her laptop's search bar "How distance from extended family impacts isolation" and confirmed Serena's information.

"When I showed Gray, I told him how you wished we had a mentoring group for mothers of all ages. Turns out that in our whole city, the only groups like that are for moms of preschoolers."

Dana already knew this to be true. She'd been part of a mothers of preschoolers group back when Leah was a toddler.

"I even contacted Anita Steen myself this morning and secured her as our veteran mentor mom. I am going to assume I can count on you to be a part of the group since it was your brainchild."

She didn't really see how it was her brainchild when she'd only asked about desegregating the Sunday school classes by age and said as much to Serena.

"You know how diehard folks can get about their Sunday School classes. Some people have been in the same one for decades, and they're not going to be open to switching things around. But Wednesday nights are more fluid, and when we put the idea out there, we are going to find like-minded women in need of an adopted village."

Dana envisioned a grass hut village in Africa. "We need to adopt a village?" She had to pull the phone away from her ear to keep Serena's laughter from piercing her eardrum.

"We *are* the village, silly. You know the 'it takes a village' thing? Well, when parents don't have a built-in support system to help them raise kids, pick them up on time, etcetera, they improvise by adopting a village of other adults to help them survive this phase of life and carry them through the next one."

Serena had clearly been giving this mentorship idea a lot more thought than Dana had. It was a solid concept though, and she was pleased to have put the bug in her friend's ear. If Anita Steen was on board, Dana was too. "What are we calling this group?"

"I don't guess we could get away with putting up signs in the foyer for "The Village People," could we?"

They threw out ideas like The Village Advocates, and Survivalist Resources for Moms. "Maybe we better sleep on the name and come up with a curriculum instead," suggested Serena.

Dana thought they should have assigned seating so there would be an even distribution of moms in various stages at each table. "What if we have a drop box where women can submit questions for a moderator to pose to the group for table discussions?"

Serena asked for an example.

"Well, what would you do if your husband promised to take off work to take care of his own nephews and three kids for a few days and then broke the news that he couldn't do that after all? Then right after that, you saw a text message from a woman you've never heard of telling him when her plane will land. Hypothetically of course."

"That's probably weightier than what the Village People could handle in a one-hour discussion, but hypothetically, I would snoop until I got to the bottom of things while still giving him the benefit of the doubt, of course."

"So, I shouldn't confront him outright until I do some

digging on my own?"

"Look friend, this isn't the godliest advice you could get, but generally, if you confront someone for suspicious behavior, they'll deny and cover their tracks. Better to know what you're dealing with before you give the other person a reason to destroy evidence."

"While giving him the benefit of the doubt, of course," Dana parroted.

"Naturally."

Dana shifted the conversation back to the Wednesday night group. "What should we do the first week and any time the drop box is empty?"

Together they came up with a list of discussion questions and icebreakers. When they finally hung up, Dana decided to walk across the street and tell Josie about the new group. She opened the front door and was startled to see Josie on her doorstep, knuckles poised to knock with a crying Connor on her hip.

"Please tell me you have a minute," Josie said. Without waiting for a reply, she placed a burp cloth on Dana's shoulder and handed her Connor and a bottle.

His cries were replaced with ravenous slurping as soon as Dana cradled him and put the bottle to his lips.

"Of course," said Dana. "Want me to go with you?"

"Uh, sure," Josie said as she rushed back to her own side of the cul-de-sac. "But you're doing it at your own risk."

Dana followed, not bothering to keep up with Josie. She recoiled at the stench as soon as she entered the Caraway house. "Goodness, have y'all acquired livestock since my last visit?" She walked down the hall toting a now-content Connor and found Josie changing Olivia's diaper on the nursery floor. The changing table resembled a crime scene.

Across the hall, Hunter knelt in front of the bathtub. "Hey Dana," he called over the sounds of running water and a screaming infant.

"Rough morning?" she asked.

Josie looked up with pursed lips and flattened eyebrows. "What do you think, Captain Obvious?"

"Sorry," said Dana. "How can I help?"

"You're helping plenty just by feeding Loudy."

Dana settled onto the sofa where the odor emanating from the nursery was slightly less pronounced. Josie placed Olivia in a bouncer in front of Dana and disappeared to clean the mess. After a while, she dropped into the recliner. She thanked Dana for her help and apologized for imposing on her. "Where were you headed when I hijacked your plans?"

"Over here, actually." She told Josie about the women's group Serena was spearheading. She told her childcare would be available and invited Josie to come.

At first Josie seemed to balk at the idea of dragging the babies out of the house in the evening.

"I know you must be drowning just as much as I am. Ever since my mom passed away, I feel like I've lost my support system. Husbands are great, but sometimes they don't understand."

Hunter carried in Ben with his wet red hair sticking up in all directions. He must have overheard Dana, but he didn't seem offended by her comment about husbands. "Josie and I were talking last week about how she should get out more, weren't we?" Dana caught the pointed look he shot Josie. "I'll even come home in time to take over. You won't have to take the kids."

Josie glared back at him, leaving Dana to wonder what she'd stepped in the middle of.

"Fine," said Josie with a forced smile that didn't reach her eyes. "I'll go as long as I get to tell my mother our church is hosting The Village People."

Chapter 16

The Wallaces arrived shortly after lunch.

"Wow, y'all made excellent time," said Will as he helped bring in luggage from their car.

"That's because your sister treats speed limits as suggestions," said his brother-in-law, David.

The four boys decided to bunk together in one room, which meant it would smell like a gym bag by next weekend. As they barreled upstairs with Theo and Quinn's bags, the adults migrated onto the back patio with glasses of sweet tea.

Spring weather in West Texas could be more dramatic than a teenage girl, but today was perfect for soaking up the afternoon sun without sweltering nor freezing. The wind wasn't even blowing for a change.

"Can you believe we had ice last week in the Metroplex?" asked David.

"God was preparing you for your week in the mountains," Will said.

"Wait, what?"

Dana and Will both eyed David. Surely, he wasn't serious.

"Dude," said Will. "It's the last week of ski season up there. You knew that, right?"

"I tried to tell him," Julia said. "But he doesn't listen

to me these days."

David's responding glower caught Dana off guard.

"You *did* pack for winter, didn't you?" asked Will.

"The forecast said the high would be in the fifties, so no." David pulled out his phone. "Well, this is great. Now it says the lows will be in the twenties with a chance of snow. I swear none of this was on there when I packed."

Dana could see the "I told you so" written on Julia's face.

Will stood and motioned for his brother-in-law to follow him. "Come inside. I'll loan you some outerwear so you don't get frostbite."

Dana wasted no time accosting Julia as soon as the guys went inside. "Spill it. What's going on with you two?"

Julia confided that she and David fought all the time. She said he openly called her a control freak in front of the boys, and neither of them missed an opportunity to make a snide remark directed at the other. She resented him and wanted to separate. David convinced her to try counseling first insisting that God hates divorce, and she would be setting her kids up for failure by modeling that for them.

"I agreed to go hoping I'd be vindicated when a therapist took my side, but that hasn't exactly happened yet."

"I guess counseling is helping if you're going on this trip together?" Dana asked.

She shrugged. "Depends on the day. We are working through some tough issues we let build up for too long. It's like picking at a scab. Then the therapist also has us do homework assignments to help us rediscover the things we loved about each other in the beginning, build intimacy, all of that. It's been the hardest process I've ever gone through, including childbirth.

"I'll be honest, Dana. I'm dreading everything about this retreat. It feels like going to the hospital for a painful procedure, but in a makeshift war hospital in nineteenth century Siberia, and instead of pain meds, you bite on a stick."

Dana searched for something wise or encouraging to say, but her own fears overtook her ability to comfort Julia. What if whatever was going on with Will turned out to be more than just a work thing? They might end up in the same boat as the Wallaces. Or worse.

"Do the kids know what's going on?"

Julia took a sip of her iced tea and stared out into the yard. "They know we go to counseling twice a week to learn to communicate better and that this is a marriage-building retreat, but we haven't told them how close we are to splitting up."

"I'm proud of you for doing the hard work to save your family."

Julia reached for Dana's hand and gave it a squeeze. "Thanks. I'm sorry for dropping extra kids on you. David's parents are in Italy, and his siblings are too unstable or too far away. I appreciate you taking one for the team."

"No worries. But don't forget to swing back by on your way home to pick them up."

That evening, the boys made several semi-clandestine trips through the living room. Their parents didn't ask questions when Quinn and Nate passed by with a poorly concealed strand of Christmas lights in a pillowcase, but when the end of a set of jumper cables poked out from under Adam's shirt, they mounted an investigation into the smuggling operation.

Dana was first up the stairs. She could hear muffled giggles and shuffling behind Adam's closed door. "Boys?"

"Don't come in!" said four voices in unison.

Will edged past Dana. "That's not suspicious at all." He opened the door halfway because that's as far as it would go and poked his head inside.

"Just give us two more minutes," begged Theo.

Will closed the door with a smile but said nothing to

the other waiting adults.

When they were given the signal, the parents squeezed single file through the small opening.

"Don't let Harvey in," warned Nate.

The kids had constructed a massive blanket fort decorated with twinkle lights and held together by an assortment of binder clips, hair scrunchies, and the jumper cable clamps.

Dana crouched at the opening to check out the interior. Two air mattresses and what looked to be every pillow in the house comprised the floor of the fort. She grinned at Leah who was seated on a throw pillow adjusting one of the fleece walls.

"I figured I might as well help them do it right since they borrowed half my stuff to build it," she said. Spoken like a true firstborn.

The fort collaboration set the tone for the week. The cousins played games, watched movies, and showed off their skateboard tricks. A minor kickflip mishap that resulted in a badly skinned elbow for Quinn, but it was nothing Dana couldn't handle. Her dad and Will were another story.

Monday morning, Dana still hadn't come up with a reason to visit Will's office to investigate this thing with Helena So-and-So. She didn't have a devious mind, but the main character in her crime novel did. Dana channeled her. "What would Kelsey do?"

She finally decided to let a little air out of one of her tires. That would give her a believable reason to need Will's car without raising suspicion. She thought her plan was solid, until Will poked holes in it.

She arrived at his office building at 9:40. Hopefully Helena's plane was on time, and a half hour would give her enough time to get there from the airport. If Dana waited any longer, she would be late getting her dad to the doctor. Will was standing in the lobby looking at his phone when she walked in. His eyebrows shot up and his jaw hung slack when he spotted Dana but quickly recovered and kissed her cheek.

"Hey, Hon. Everything okay? Where's your dad?"

Dana told him her tire light came on, and she wanted to switch cars with him rather than risk driving her father on a flat tire. "I can come back this afternoon and take mine to the shop," she said.

Will rubbed his forehead. "Wouldn't it have made more sense for you to take your dad's car instead?"

Obviously, it would have. She did some quick thinking. "Sure, if the light had come on at home, where both sets of his keys are stashed. It was easier to come here than go back." That sounded reasonable enough, and technically it wasn't a lie since the warning light didn't come on before she pulled away from the house.

He reached into his pocket and produced his key fob. As he handed it to Dana, he brushed past her to shake hands with someone coming in. "Helena," was all he said by way of greeting. He did not introduce Dana, but turned to her and said, "Let me know how the appointment goes," and led Helena to the elevator bank.

Dana rushed to her car. She was so flustered that she forgot to drive away in Will's car. She had confirmed that the blonde beauty was indeed the woman who had flown in to meet her husband in his office. What wasn't clear was the nature of their relationship. On the one hand, wouldn't he have introduced them if Helena was a simple colleague from a competing company? On the other, he didn't have the look of a man caught with his pants down, so to speak.

She tried to put her worry aside and focus on her dad. Regardless of whether her marriage was in trouble, her father's memory was.

"I think I can put a rush on the cardiology referral since the dementia symptoms could be caused by a blockage that makes a stroke more likely," said Dr. Barton.

"Neurology might be another story, I'm afraid. They're backed up for months."

Edward inquired about getting back his driving privileges.

"From what you've told me today, you're one episode away from a Silver Alert on the overpass. I'm not comfortable allowing you to drive without further testing first. I'll see what strings I can pull to get you seen sooner, but just know, every doctor in town is doing the same thing for their patients, and there aren't enough specialists to go around."

The thought of waiting for months to find out if her dad's symptoms were reversible was disheartening. No less so for him, she assumed, as he was the one who couldn't drive himself in the meantime.

After the appointment, Dana invited Edward back to her house. "I was looking forward to checking out that blanket fort Leah texted me pictures of, but I have plans already. Maybe tomorrow?"

"Plans?" To her knowledge, he hadn't made plans without her or her family since her mom passed.

"It's no big deal. I'm just going across the street to have lunch with Rita Brewer." He held up his hand. "And before you say anything, it's not a date. It's taco soup. She made your mother's recipe and offered to share."

Dana thought it best to keep quiet, but she was thrilled that her dad was getting out of the house and making friends.

"Besides," said Edward, "she thinks I'm half off my nut like the rest of you do, so I'm sure she sees it as her Christian duty to keep an eye on me."

Dana just shook her head. Some people confused their Christian duty with prying.

Chapter 17

Wednesday evening, Will wasn't home from work before it was time to leave for the first meeting of the yet-to-be-named mentoring moms' group. Josie came over to catch a ride, and the seven of them crammed into the Tahoe.

"Aren't they a little old to need childcare?" Josie asked.

"There are midweek classes for all ages. We always go to youth group on Wednesdays," said Leah with only the slightest hint of indignation in her voice.

"Unless we have to watch you play soccer," Adam replied in his signature stage voice.

When Josie asked which Wednesday night class Dana attended, she kept her eyes on the road hoping to avoid admitting she usually dropped the kids off and left.

Adam announced her shame on her behalf. "Mom doesn't stay very often."

"Hey, that's not fair. Wednesdays are hard." She did her best to get the kids fed and out the door early, by which time, she was drained and sometimes needed an hour to herself.

The sign pointing Dana and Josie to the right room was a graphic of a ship's life preserver with the words "Grab a Hold of Your Motherhood Lifeline."

Dana pointed her thumb at it. "Why not just say 'Drowning Moms Meet Here?'"

"I still think Serena should have stuck with The Village People," whispered Josie.

Serena, Anita Steen, and a woman Dana didn't know were chatting by a snack table when they entered. There were several round tables set up, but the room was otherwise empty. Dana hoped the crowd would pick up after spring break, but it was hard to say considering her own sporadic Wednesday night participation.

A young mother leading her toddler by the hand dropped her purse onto a chair and left in the direction of the preschool drop off.

Serena welcomed everyone. "We'll wait for Yvette to return before we get started. Grab some cookies and let's all sit at one table." She introduced Dana and Josie to Kathy, the mother of a fourth grader and a twenty-year-old. Dana's eyes widened before she could conceal her surprise. She estimated Kathy to be a few years younger than she was, so she hadn't expected her to be the mother of a twenty-year-old.

Kathy chuckled. "I get that a lot. I had my daughter when I was still in high school and waited until I got married and had a career before I had my son. They're surprisingly close for being ten years apart in age though."

"That must be nice to have a built-in babysitter," said Josie.

Kathy bobbed her head noncommittally and said something about her older child's busy social calendar when Yvette blew back in and flopped into her seat in a huff. Dana noticed she was pregnant, so she was likely worn out more so than exasperated. Serena asked her if she got her little one dropped off okay.

"Just great." Yvette described her three-year-old's antics from the car to the building and how she had to wrestle her down the hall. "I don't know what I'm going to do if this next one is as strong-willed as her big sister."

Dana caught Josie's eye and smiled. Josie, on the other hand, looked horrified. She must have been imagining dragging three three-year-olds into church against their wills.

Serena had each woman tell the group about herself and her most recent "drowning mom" moment. Dana recounted the skateboard-induced egg explosion in the kitchen and her subsequent escape to eat crème brulée for dinner. "If I hadn't run into Serena that night, I might not have gone home."

Serena squeezed Dana's hand. "We also wouldn't be here tonight if not for Dana's bad day. That's when she came up with the idea for us to establish a connection point for moms to pour into one another. Proof that God uses all things for good."

Serena may have been overstating Dana's role, but she didn't correct her.

Josie told them about last Saturday morning. "I actually feel like I'm drowning pretty regularly, but it was a high stress instance where my husband and I didn't have enough hands to deal with the situation. I ended up running a baby across the street to Dana so we could run man-to-man coverage." The women all giggled.

Serena described a phone call with her youngest where she needed her shot record for a study abroad application but couldn't access it. Serena couldn't either because her daughter was legally an adult. "She acted like it was my fault. As if I somehow control the medical privacy laws. She made me feel like I couldn't do anything right."

Mrs. Steen's drowning mom anecdote was the most shocking to Dana because she had been under the mistaken impression that when one's kids were grown and flown, her parenting days became smooth sailing.

She confided to the table that her son was going through a divorce. His wife had left him and their three children to be with another man. Now her son was struggling to work and care for the kids without a partner, so the four of them moved back home until their legal and financial mess was resolved. "My house is back to being loud and messy again. I guess this is where the mentor becomes the mentee," she said with a weary smile.

After they had shared a recent struggle, they encouraged one another by talking about the ways they saw motherhood, and grandmotherhood, molding their character for the better. Mrs. Steen closed out the evening by suggesting self-care tips like taking a bath to relax and escape, and the two moms of the youngest kids laughed about the unlikelihood of staying awake long enough to enjoy a soothing soak. Their motley group was off to a good start. Except for the name, which still needed work.

On Thursday, Dana's dad called. "You're never going to believe this," he said in lieu of a greeting. "At lunch on Monday I told Rita about my appointment. Thought it might give her some peace of mind that her mentally unstable neighbor was under medical supervision. She asked all kinds of questions about my primary care doctor and the referrals. And guess what?"

Unlike one of her children who would have made Dana throw out guesses until she lost her patience, he kept going without pause. "Rita's niece is a neurologist. Her office just called, and I have an appointment with the doctor two weeks from today. They apologized that they couldn't get me in sooner, but I figured two weeks was nothing compared to what Dr. Barton estimated. And get this, they've already scheduled me for an MRI next week."

Dana thought he sounded awfully excited about medical tests and appointments and told him as much.

"I would like to get my life back," he said. "If going to a bunch of doctors and being hooked up to machines is what it takes to drive again, then let's do this."

That was fair. Dana shifted to speaker mode so she could add the appointment to her phone's calendar and prayed for a favorable outcome. "Are you sure they put a rush on your appointment because Auntie Rita insisted?"

He chuckled. "You question whether or not Miss Buttinsky has more pull than Dr. Barton?"

She leaned against the counter and gazed out the window at nothing in particular. "Good point. By the way, how was the taco soup?"

"Not bad, but Mom's was better."

Her mother had been a better cook and housekeeper than Dana would ever be. "She did everything so well."

"Except for pot roast," he said.

She laughed "Except for that."

Carolyn Johnson's pot roasts were constant disappointments. They were over or under seasoned and always tough. No matter how bad or mediocre the roast turned out, she kept trying, determined to get it right. She never quite succeeded.

"Remember the birthday cake she made you that was supposed to be a unicorn?"

"The hippo with rainbow dreads?" They laughed at the memory. Dana had forgotten her mother had any flaws at all. Though to be fair, one dish and a cake decorating fail were minor weaknesses.

"Listen, kiddo, I better go. And if we end up with food poisoning later today, we'll know your mother can hear us making fun of her cooking, and she pulled some strings to make us pay for it."

Dana reflexively looked up, as if expecting to be smote

on the spot. A loud thud overhead almost scared her heart right out of her chest.

"I'm okay," yelled Adam.

She threw her head back and dragged herself to the stairs. "Lord," she called aloud. "My mother heard me laughing at her cake, didn't she?"

Chapter 18

Julia and David returned from their marriage retreat Friday evening. They seemed happier together than they had at the beginning of the week, but Dana couldn't be sure. After all, she never would have guessed they were teetering on the edge of divorce then either.

"Was it the war hospital you were expecting?" Dana asked when she and Julia were alone in the kitchen after dinner.

She shrugged. "We did a ropes course that ended in a huge zip line. We hiked, played games like kids at camp, and we went to group sessions and couples therapy every day. It was fun and awful at the same time."

"Did you have an epiphany about your future with David?"

Julia was quiet for so long that Dana was about to apologize for her nosiness. "I didn't necessarily get the clarity I'd hoped for. Instead, I felt convicted of my unforgiveness and realized I must let go of the fairy tale version of marriage that doesn't exist and trust God to build a new version of our marriage in its place."

Dana wiped a serving bowl with a dish towel. "I don't think any of us lives 'happily ever after' this side of Heaven. All of life is a series of highs and lows, good and bad, heartache and happiness."

Julia flicked dish water at Dana with her wet fingers. "You would make a great shrink."

"I'll keep that in mind when this writing thing runs its course." She reached up to place the bowl in the cabinet. "Do you think your negativity toward David is displaced anger at God for what happened to your parents? He could have saved them but didn't."

Julia pinched her thumb and index finger an inch apart. "Maybe dial back the therapy just a hair."

"Okay, but it's a fair question. Grief is a heavy burden for a marriage to carry." She thought about her dad's growing memory problems and her own inability to measure up to her mom's picture-perfect motherhood example.

Julia admitted that she was sometimes still furious with God for taking her parents too soon. "But it's been sixteen years. I get sad that my boys never got to meet them, but no, my anger with David isn't misplaced at all." She lowered her voice to a whisper. "He cheated on me with a twenty-five-year-old, and I can't seem to move past it."

The baking sheet Dana was drying slipped from her hands and clattered on the tile. Boy, had she been off base.

"When? But also, Eew! He's old enough to be her father." Her shock made whispering impossible, so she handed Julia the towel to dry her hands and pulled her toward the patio where they would have more privacy.

Once they were seated by the firepit and out of earshot of everyone, Julia answered. "It was two years ago. She was his pharmacy tech, and according to Dave, the relationship never progressed beyond kissing. Shortly afterward, he took the hospital job and didn't see her anymore."

"How did you find out?" Even though she asked, Dana wasn't sure she really wanted to know the answer.

"He confessed after another coworker caught them

making out and threatened to tell me if Dave didn't. After my initial rage, I completely withdrew and wanted a divorce."

"What made you change your mind?" Dana asked.

"The boys. The life we had built. Leaving wouldn't erase the pain of what had already been done. Instead, it would cause even more pain to my sons that would stretch for generations. I'd get them on half the holidays. Then I'd still be miserable, and it would get worse when eventually I'd get half the visitation time with my grandkids than if we stayed together."

A lump formed in Dana's throat. She hadn't even thought about what the future would look like with her kids if Will was having an affair.

"Besides," added Julia. "Dave was trying so hard to be sweet to me and attentive to the boys. He even changed jobs. It seemed like he was genuinely sorry for what had happened and tried to make amends. Truth be told, things hadn't been great between us in a long time, so while he was trying to earn my forgiveness, I was beating myself up for being a bad wife. I mean, happy husbands don't usually fall for co-eds with daddy complexes, do they?"

Dana wasn't sure. She figured most middle-aged men would be so flattered by the attention of a much younger woman that they'd fall hook, line, and sinker, no matter the complex. She shifted uncomfortably in the Adirondack chair.

Was she doing something to push Will into the arms of another, more attentive woman? After all, she had been very preoccupied with her dad and trying to write lately. "What happened recently to make you change your mind about sticking it out?"

Julia was thoughtful and then shrugged. "We fell back into the same old routines. We fought about all the same old stuff again. Only now I had new fuel to put the blame on him. I became blind to my faults and focused on his one big one. I also told myself he would run to someone else like he did before since things weren't going well between us. I reasoned that our boys would be better off in two peaceful homes than in one with constant tension. I'm still wrestling with that."

Dana didn't know what else to say. Julia and David's marriage had seemed so rock solid, and to find out otherwise stung. It meant no marriage was impervious to potential infidelity.

She continued to wrestle with her thoughts while lying in bed later that night.

Will turned on the lamp on his nightstand and rolled toward her. "What happened?"

"Huh?"

"I can tell something's bothering you. You've been off for days, but it got worse after you and my sister went outside. Did she say something to upset you tonight?"

Dana relayed the conversation in hushed tones. "Did David say anything to you?"

"No, but he and I don't talk about much other than sports. I can't believe Jules never told me though."

"She was probably too ashamed to admit it or afraid you'd go into protective brother mode and confront Dave. You can't let either of them know I told you."

He slipped his arm around her waist and nuzzled her neck. "I won't, but you have to promise me that you won't leave me for your writing instructor Carl."

She pushed him away so she could see his face. "You're worried about me and Carlos? What about you and that woman at your office?"

He reminded her that Helena was his competitor's CEO. When she asked why he hadn't introduced her either time she saw them together, he said he needed to keep up the appearance that he ran the company with topnotch professionalism. "She'd have pounced on any indication that my family comes by to hang out whenever they want."

Dana started to ask him if he'd deleted text messages between himself and Helena, but she wasn't ready to explain how she knew about the texts in the first place.

He pulled her close again. "You're the only woman I want," he said as he settled into his pillow and yawned. "Besides, I've never had a thing for blondes or for women trying to take my job." He drifted off to sleep without elaborating further.

How was Helena Shaffer gunning for Will's job?

As his even breaths morphed into soft snoring, Dana gave up on trying to fall asleep and crept out of bed. She went hunting for her laptop.

She'd moved it several times over the course of the week because two extra kids had overtaken her usual space at the counter. She remembered stashing it in her tote this morning before she drove everyone to the trampoline park.

Her plan to write in the coffee shop across the street while the kids wore themselves out jumping was thwarted when she ran into some weary moms she knew from church and school. So instead of writing, she chatted. She'd talked up the new mentor group.

The computer wasn't in her tote.

When they'd gotten home, she'd thought the kids would be tired and watch a movie while she eked out a chapter or two. But no. Their energy from the jump park sparked the skateboard showdown that led to blood. Aha! She found her laptop on top of the dryer where she'd set it when she grabbed the first aid kit from the laundry room.

She plugged it into the charger at the counter and checked to be sure that Leah, who was on the sofa a few yards away, was asleep. She doubted the light from the screen and the clicking of the keys would rouse the girl who slept through chirping smoke detectors and thunderstorms.

Dana typed fervently for the first time all week. She wrote until her body was stiff and the clock at the bottom of her screen showed 3:30 am. She stood to stretch and was met with a sharp crick in her neck. She guessed she wouldn't be turning her head to the left for a few days. Lane changes were about to get dicey. She decided to call it a night while there were still a few hours left of it and made a mental note to look at office chairs and desks online tomorrow. Today, actually.

Something shook her, and the room was too bright.

"Dana, wake up. Breakfast is ready, and Julia and the guys will be heading out in a little while."

How was breakfast ready when she wasn't up to make it?

"What time is it?" she mumbled.

"Almost 9:30. I started to put a mirror under your nose to make sure you were breathing."

Dana never slept this late, so Will was right to be concerned. She also never stayed up through the wee hours to write suspense fiction. Maybe she was too old to start something new that was so painful and time-consuming.

Her left arm ached as she dragged herself out of bed. Wasn't that a sign of a heart attack? Turning to look at her arm brought back the sharp pain in her neck, and she remembered she was only injured from slumping over her keyboard and was not having an acute medical episode. Leah shouted for her in a blood-curdling pitch.

"It's Pops." Leah thrust her phone at Dana.

Her heart raced. Why had he called Leah instead of her? "Hi, Dad."

"Maybe answer your phone once in a while," he barked. "I need you to pick me up. I called an Uber to take me to the store, and the driver got a flat tire on the way. The kid had no idea how to change it, so I helped him, but his ancient spare won't get me to the grocery store. I sent him on to the tire store and told him not to go above thirty, and I'm in the parking lot where that pizza buffet used to be across from the mall."

Of course he was. Leave it to Edward Johnson to end up changing a tire for his driver the very first time he ordered a rideshare.

Dana threw on clothes and bribed Leah with a Starbucks run to tag along. She hoped the teenager could reverse the charges her dad had spent on his failed ride. She padded to the kitchen in flip flops looking for her keys and purse.

"What's going on with Ed today?" asked Will.

She shook her head. "He's fine. Mayhem seems to find him even when he's not the cause of it. I'll be back as soon as I can."

She turned to David, who was setting the table. "Are y'all in a rush, or will you still be here?"

"We'll wait," said Julia.

When Dana pulled into the parking lot of the defunct restaurant, she spotted her dad sitting on a parking curb looking down at his phone. She was impressed he could still lower himself like that but wondered if she should get out and help him stand. He rose and walked over before she could put the car in park. His mind might be slipping, but he was remarkably spry.

"Ladies," he said as he tipped an invisible hat.

Dana leaned across the center console and kissed his cheek. "Morning, Dad. Where to?"

He decided to complete the errand as intended. "I'll call you when I'm about to head to checkout, and you can pick me up, alright?"

Dana tried to calculate how long it would take a single man who didn't cook to buy groceries. He would probably be ready to leave right about the time she pulled into her driveway.

"Any chance I could persuade you to grab coffee with us and head to my house first? The Wallaces are about to leave, and I'd like to see them off."

He agreed to put off his shopping trip and go home with her. He glanced at Leah in the back seat. "I see you both survived being outnumbered by boys all week."

"We're always outnumbered," said Leah. "We've had to watch every *Die Hard* and *Rocky* movie at least a thousand times."

"Don't forget *Rudy*," Dana added.

"You ladies have been through a lot," Edward responded with mock sympathy. After a beat, he added, "How can you not love *Rudy*? It's the greatest story ever."

"So help me, Dad, I will drop you back on the side of the road."

He laughed. "You think I didn't watch more than my fair share of rom coms when you were growing up? I didn't get to watch any of the great guy movies of the last several decades until Will came into the family. I just assumed all movies ended with kissing in the rain or at an airport until Will saved me from chick flick cinematic torment."

Leah giggled.

"Well thank goodness you survived that," Dana said. She liked seeing this version of her dad. When Leah handed her the phone this morning, she'd braced herself for another hairbrained misadventure. She pictured him lost in an underground cave somewhere in New Mexico after getting into the wrong car while attempting to hitchhike to a flower shop. There was no telling with him lately. She said a silent prayer for that scenario to never come to fruition.

She told him she was glad he was able to help his Uber driver. Not everyone would have changed his tire for him.

"Nice kid. Probably raised by video games though. Leah, do you know how to change a tire and check your oil?"

"We watched a video in driver's ed, but I haven't done it yet. Dad said I can't get my license until I can change a tire by myself and check all the fluids. But my birthday's a long way off anyway, so I'm not worried about it."

"Nonsense," he said. "You need to practice more than once. You can't depend on strangers to help you when you're by yourself on the road."

Leah held up her phone. "What strangers? I would just call triple A or my dad."

Edward turned around in his seat to face her. "Granddaughter, what if that phone of yours didn't have a signal or the battery was dead, and you forgot your charger? What if you *had* your charger, but the car wouldn't start, so you couldn't even charge your phone? What would you do then?"

Dana caught Leah's pleading eye in the rearview mirror, but she just smiled and looked ahead. She was curious how her fifteen-year-old who had an answer for everything would respond.

"Pops, if my car won't start, what good will changing the tire do?"

Dana burst out laughing. Edward was undeterred. "After your aunt and cousins leave, you'll come home with me. I'll let you drive me to the store and teach you how to change a tire and check under the hood." He turned to Dana. "Is that agreeable with you, sweetheart? I may not be allowed to drive myself, but I'm still technically a qualified licensed driver."

Dana left the decision to the sassy one in the back seat who was wholeheartedly on board with the plan.

Leah's tune changed by the time Dana picked her up that afternoon. She was covered in dirt and oil, wearing a man's flannel button down over her tee shirt and slumped in a lawn chair on the porch when Dana arrived.

"Why are you sitting outside?" Dana asked as she approached.

"Because Pops said I'm too dirty to sit on any furniture in the house. He offered to put a shower curtain on a chair for me, but I said I'd rather sit out here."

Dana snickered but regained her composure quickly under her daughter's glower. "I take it your day wasn't what you expected."

"It was freaking fantastic. Can we just go?"

Leah was always happy to hang out with her grandfather, especially if it meant she got to drive, so Dana was concerned. "What happened?"

"Your *dad* made me rotate the tires *and* check the oil pan on his car. I had to lay on the ground *under* a car."

Dana maintained a straight face with great difficulty. She was amused to see the practice of placing ownership of a relative on someone else wasn't limited to one's offspring.

"How in the world did you rotate the tires with only one jack?" she asked.

"Let's just say there were cinderblocks involved."

Dana stepped into the house to find her dad and Rita Brewer sipping iced tea at the kitchen table.

"Hello, Dana," said Rita. "I just stopped by to investigate the child labor operation Edward's running over here and to offer refreshments."

Dana acknowledged her and addressed her dad. "You made her rotate the tires? Really?"

He held his palms up and exaggerated a shrug. "It's the same way I taught you to change a tire."

Dana held up her index finger. "*A* tire is *one*."

"Four times the practice," he replied with zero remorse. "Now there's no way the kid will ever forget what to do if she's stranded on the side of the road. She won't hesitate, and she won't have to worry about creeps."

Dana thought that was debatable, but she didn't argue. "Well, you should be worried how she feels about *you* right now, because she's never been angry with you before. Do you remember mad fifteen-year-olds, Dad? They're terrifying. You better check the garage and be sure she didn't booby trap something in there."

He dismissed her with a wave of his hand. "She'll get over it, and she'll thank me the first time she has a flat tire."

"Yeah well, while you're at it, you should get rid of that shower curtain you offered her. It would be poetic justice if she used it to wrap up evidence should you have an 'unfortunate accident.'" She made air quotes. "Morbid but poetic."

Rita spat out her tea and grabbed a napkin. Edward flinched. "You've been spending too much time writing that crime fiction."

The Tahoe door slammed shut outside. "I dunno, Dad. True crime has been the bread and butter of prime-time TV and podcasts since their inception. Text your granddaughter and make up with her." She kissed his cheek, said goodbye to Rita Brewer, and braced herself for the drive home.

Chapter 19

Josie

Josie admired her spotless kitchen and contemplated snapping a photo to send her mom as proof she did occasionally have a clean home between her visits. Hunter and Josie had cleaned the house last night in anticipation of the early childhood interventionist's home visit this morning.

The assessment went well, and the interventionist was very complimentary of the babies' progress. "The doctor's notes mention that Ben and Connor were only slightly below the developmental curve, but they're even further along than I expected." He repeated the same trunk exercises Josie had learned online and noted how the boys held themselves. He first held Connor's hands and pulled him from a supine to a seated position. This time Connor held his neck in line with his shoulders. Both boys had already come a long way from that checkup three weeks ago.

After several minutes of working with each boy while Josie mirrored the exercises with Olivia, the therapist said, "They're really taking to the exercises like fish to water."

Josie smiled, never letting on that they were already well-versed in them thanks to her Baby Bootcamp, as Adam called it.

The triplets were napping now, and Josie took a moment to send a group text to two of her former coworkers who had kids. I know I've been the worst at keeping in touch (she added three baby face emojis) But I wanted to invite you to this new mom group at my church. It's a safe place to talk about the hard parts of the job and feel uplifted.

She included the time and place and fielded a couple of questions about how she was holding up at home full-time and whether the group was a cult. She assured them it was not and that she was surviving to the best of her abilities, although she missed human interaction deeply.

Then she sent a photo of her kitchen to Laurel. I need someone to be amazed with me that this happened when I'm not even expecting a visit from Mom

Per the new and dismal norm with Laurel Saldana, there was no response.

That evening she walked across the street to hitch a ride to church with the Hardings. Their garage door was up, so she hopped into the passenger seat of Dana's Tahoe and came face-to-face with Leah in the driver's seat. She looked behind her where Dana and Nate waved.

"Hi Josie," Adam called from the third row.

"Uh, hey everyone."

"Put your seatbelt on," Leah instructed.

"Wait," protested Josie. "Don't you have to have an instructor in this seat?" Did Leah just roll her eyes?

Dana waved off her concerns. She was typing something on her iPhone. "You'll be fine. I need to finish this short story for class. It was due yesterday, so if I don't get it in by tonight, it'll be a failing grade."

If it was that important, Josie guessed she could take one for the team. She gripped the door handle and cinched her seatbelt nice and tight. She could do this. And if not, well, maybe her mother could move to Texas and help Hunter raise the babies in her absence.

She needn't have worried so much. Leah's driving skills were solid. She told her so as they pulled into the church parking lot.

"Thanks. I've been getting a lot of practice with my Pops."

As they walked inside, Josie asked Dana about her story.

"It's about a war veteran who tries to live a worthy life after his buddy dies saving him."

It sounded intriguing. And a tad dark.

"Sometimes I wonder if taking this class was a mistake," confided Dana.

"But you love writing."

"I can't keep up with my kids and my dad and whatever William Harding has going on right now *and* write. My brain is being pulled in too many directions."

Josie sympathized with that feeling. Since the triplets were born, her brain operated like a computer with too many programs running at once.

The sign by the door to their meeting room said, "Keep Calm and Mom On."

"What happened to the life preserver?" asked Josie.

Dana shrugged. "I guess we aren't drowning this week."

There were several new faces, including one of the ladies she'd texted today from the admissions office. "Zooey, you made it."

Zooey put the cookie she was eating on a napkin and leaned in to hug Josie. "Girl, today was rough, so I just told my husband I had to check out your support group and make sure it wasn't a cult. He can bathe those little heathens on his own tonight."

Serena called everyone to order. "Welcome to our no-judgment tribe. You are seen here. Lean on one another and allow us to be each other's lifelines in what is by far the hardest, most beautiful career God created." She asked them to find a table with women in a variety of stages.

Josie saw that Dana was about to sit at a table between Yvette and an older lady she didn't recognize. Dana gave her an encouraging wave. She and Zooey sat at Mrs. Steen's table. The class had tripled in size since last week.

Once they'd completed introductions around the table, Serena told them to share a dream they put on hold for their families. Josie thought of Dana typing in the car. Tenderness washed over her. She hoped her friend would find the success she sought in writing.

She hesitated when it was her turn. The truth sounded far too self-involved, but the pressure of everyone's eyes trained on her proved too much. She ripped off the band-aid and blurted, "I never wanted to be a stay-at-home mom. I loved working and dressing up. I loved feeling like I made a difference in the world. So, I guess the dream I put on hold was wearing heels and makeup every day."

"I wanted to be a college women's basketball coach," said Zooey. "I was already an assistant coach at the junior college when I had my son. But the hours were tough. I had to travel with the team, and the job paid almost nothing. We were losing money by paying for daycare and after-hours sitters, so I did the responsible thing and quit coaching. Then we moved here, and I took a job at the university where there was an on-site daycare and health benefits."

Josie looked at her old friend as if she was seeing her for the first time. She'd never known Zooey had done that. "Do you think you'll go back to coaching?"

Zooey shrugged. "When the kids are older, maybe, but if I don't ever make it to a D-1 program, I'll be okay with that. I coached my son's first pee wee team this year. It's not the same, but maybe more rewarding. These kids, tough as they are, make me a better person, and I'm willing to give up my old dream for that kind of growth."

Zooey had gotten wise in the past year. Or maybe she always was, and Josie hadn't realized it because she'd been too wrapped up in her own life to notice.

The next table exercise was to share a piece of advice that had come at exactly the right time. Not someone admonishing her that she'd understand in time, but a useful morsel of information she was able to savor and put into immediate practice. Josie made a mental note to find out where Serena was getting all these inciteful questions.

"The timeliest advice I ever got was to invite people over, even when my house was a disaster," said Anita Steen. "I used to get so anxious about the state of my house, and this was back in the day where husbands sometimes brought their bosses home for dinner or invited the pastor and his wife for lunch after church. I would get so mad at him for not giving me at least a day's warning."

Josie could identify with that. If her mother ever showed up unannounced, she didn't know what she'd do.

"Then one day I vented to my friend about how angry it made me when my husband would invite people over, and she just laughed at me. She said 'tell 'em to give ya a ten-minute head start to make sure there aren't any unmentionables out in the open, and don't worry about the rest of it. People feel special when you let them see your real life, and they'll give you grace for the dirty dishes and laundry. And if they're appalled, well they won't likely say yes to the next invite, and you win either way.' So, I quit worrying about it, and you know what? I boosted many a mother's self-confidence over the years because she stepped into my house and felt better about how her own house might have looked."

The women at the table all laughed.

Josie tried to recall any advice that had changed her life in the moment. Nothing stood out right away, but she remembered the thing printed in every parenting magazine and at least a dozen people must have said to her in the past year. "I guess mine would be to nap when the babies nap." Heads nodded. "I'll let you know if I get to try it out," she joked.

Mrs. Steen patted her hand. "Hang in there, sweetie. Even if you napped every day, you'd still never be well-rested again. You're a mom now."

By the end of the hour, Josie had both laughed and shed a few tears. She'd gotten to hug a colleague she hadn't seen in ages. And she felt lighter somehow.

"Well girlfriend, this might not be a cult, but I definitely drank the Kool-Aid," said Zooey. "At first, I just needed an excuse to get a break from my kids this evening, but it made me feel better to talk to people who know what it's like. I'll be back."

Dana didn't speak on the walk to the car. Her face gave away nothing, but Josie sensed her friend was troubled.

"What's wrong?" Josie asked.

"Did you know it took Alice Whitten twelve years to complete her bachelor's degree?"

Josie didn't even know who Alice Whitten was.

"Her youngest daughter is on Leah's soccer team, and she was at my table. She had four kids and took care of a husband with cancer while trying to finish school. Now she runs the entire marketing department for some big corporation."

Josie didn't know if she had that kind of determination. Really, she just wanted to have a social circle that understood her. Friends who didn't judge her or make the pity face when she told them about her family. She'd felt that connection tonight.

They sat in the car waiting for the kids. Josie was glad that Dana jumped in behind the wheel and invited her to ride shotgun because even though Leah had driven fine, she wasn't ready to brave being the passenger of a fifteen-year-old after dark. Dana broke the thoughtful silence. "I don't want to give up writing."

Josie turned to face her and studied her profile while Dana stared out the windshield.

"Things have gotten so hard in the last couple of weeks that I felt like God was telling me to ignore my selfish desires and focus on my family."

That did sound like spiritually wise counsel. But did God tell people to give up on their dreams and just be content with mediocrity?

Josie tugged at the seatbelt that dug into her shoulder. "Do you think God told Alice Whitten to give up on her dream of finishing college?"

Dana shrugged and mumbled something incoherent.

"Do you think God thinks writers and artists are more selfish than everyone else?"

"Sometimes."

Fair enough. Many probably were. But not Dana. She was the most giving person she knew. "You are anything but selfish, Dana. God gave you a gift in your ability to write stories. I don't think he expects you to squelch the creative part of yourself He designed just because it's hard to do it while also taking care of your family."

Dana turned and smiled at Josie. "What do you mean '*anything* but selfish?'" she asked with a mischievous smirk.

"You might have just a hair more snark than the Lord adores, but you use it to make me laugh, so it's probably fine," she teased. "Oh, I wanted to ask you, is the pastor's wife just a naturally insightful woman, or do you think she got all those questions from a website?"

"We came up with them together and decided to take turns each week moderating." She faked a cough and felt her forehead. "I think I feel the flu coming on next week."

Dana and Serena talked about being in the trenches

just trying to survive, but here they were light years ahead of Josie in their understanding of the complexities of motherhood. These women amazed her.

The kids piled into the back. "How were your classes?" Dana asked.

They all told stories about their lessons and the kids in their classes while Josie soaked it up. What a change from being in the car with three kids who couldn't talk. Maybe when the triplets were older, she wouldn't feel so lonely.

The following week the signage was replaced with printout of a teepee welcoming them into the Tribe of the Perpetually Tired. The room was mostly full. Josie hoped the children's ministry had enough staff to handle childcare for this many families.

"Look, Dana, people must have heard it was your night to moderate and turned out in droves," said Josie.

Dana looked a little green, but she seemed to recover from her case of nerves once it was time to get started. "Last week we invited you to pose your own questions to the group anonymously in our little box by the door. There are only a few, but let's start with those." She pulled a slip of paper from the box. "Oh, here's a great question. How do I get my preschooler to quit getting in my bed in the middle of the night?" She reminded the women that they were in a no judgement zone, and no one should presume her parenting style was the only right way or that someone else's was wrong.

Even so, Josie thought if you didn't let a kid climb into your bed in the first place, then they wouldn't keep trying. She certainly hoped this were true since she would have to deal with three toddlers at once.

By the end of the hour, the discussion around her table

left her with the overwhelming realization that no method worked on every child, even siblings. She wasn't sure she and Hunter would be able to come up with enough parenting strategies to get the triplets raised, but for now at least, she had a community to help her through it.

Chapter 20

Dana

Dana tapped her foot and drummed her fingers on her leg.

"Don't you have something to entertain yourself, like a book or a game on your phone?" her dad asked.

She glared at him. "I finished my book twenty minutes ago, and my battery is too low to play anymore games because we've been here all day." she hissed.

"It hasn't been all day. You're just grumpy because you're hungry and bored."

Dana hated being treated like a petulant child. She crossed her arms as her stomach growled.

The lobby of the neurology clinic was full, mostly with senior citizens, some with their adult children impatiently checking phones and periodically huffing up to the receptionist's desk to ask how much longer. The last couple of weeks had been a blur of appointments and tests including an ECG, MRI, and a battery of cognitive tests, for which they were waiting to hear results.

"Edward Johnson?" At long last it was their turn. They followed the nurse through the corridor to Dr. Leyva's private office rather than to an exam room. They sat in two club chairs across from the desk and waited.

Dana's palms began to sweat, and the only sound she

could hear was the pounding of her own pulse. She gave her dad a thin smile and squeezed his hand, hoping he wouldn't notice the clamminess of her nerves betraying her. Dr. Leyva did not keep them waiting long. She shook both their hands before taking her seat at the stark maple desk.

Not so much as a sticky note or pen cap littered the surface, leaving Dana to wonder if this was a real office at all or nothing more than the room for delivering bad news. Her parents had been led into a similar office to receive the news of her mother's pancreatic cancer diagnosis.

The doctor typed on a keyboard stashed beneath the desktop. "I understand you're a good friend of my Aunt Rita."

Edward nodded and gave Dana an "I told you so" nudge. "We've been neighbors for several years."

The doctor checked the computer monitor. "Oh, you're the white house across the street. Lovely yard, by the way. I remember meeting your wife a couple of years ago."

"Your aunt must have some dirt on you to have gotten me an appointment so quickly," he teased.

She chuckled. "No dirt, I'm afraid. One of my brothers maybe, but not me. We try to keep a little wiggle room in the schedule for critical needs or assertive relatives."

Dana considered the two and a half hour wait in a room full of agitated people in the same boat and wondered if "wiggle room" meant something different in clinical terms.

"Rita is indeed assertive. Her concern about living across from a crazy person probably classifies me as a critical need," said Edward.

"With your quick wit, Mr. Johnson, I wouldn't say your case is quite that dire yet." She returned to the notes on her screen. "Your test results do not indicate vascular dementia or Alzheimer's. Of course, the only definitive way to rule out Alzheimer's is to do a PET scan or a lumbar puncture, but I don't think we need to do either. At this time, what I am seeing is mild degenerative cognition that's common for your age and likely exacerbated by grief and isolation. I see this a lot in retired widowers. It says here that you are not a smoker and do not drink alcohol. That's great because both factors can significantly impact dementia. Your calcium and vitamin D are a bit low, which can contribute to confusion and memory fog."

Dana exhaled slowly. The terrible news she had been bracing for did not come. Her dad's grip on her hand loosened slightly. She smiled at him.

Dr. Leyva continued, "I would like to prescribe a mild antidepressant and some vitamin supplements that you can get over the counter. If you want to maintain your independence, Mr. Johnson, you will have to take your nutrition and exercise more seriously. I can't promise you that the decline you're experiencing will reverse itself, and if it does, the improvement may only be a temporary stopgap. However, if you take better care of your body, your mind will stay sharper. Engage with people and find activities that give you purpose, preferably ones that also require you to problem solve and use your brain. You must face your grief over losing Mrs. Johnson rather than pushing it down."

There would be no living with Will when he found out his internet assessment was spot on.

"Am I allowed to start driving again?" Edward asked.

Dr. Leyva furrowed her brow and consulted the notes on her screen. "Did you have your license revoked?" she asked.

"No, ma'am." He shook his thumb in Dana's direction. "The warden here took my keys away."

Dana shifted in her seat. Leave it to her father to throw her under the bus. "I told you to stop calling me that." She sighed.

"What precipitated that decision?" asked the doctor.

Dana described the event that ended with his ride in the back of a squad car.

"A wise decision under those circumstances. I would like you to start the medication and supplements and join a fitness class or other group activity and give yourself a few days to adjust to all of it before you start driving again, but I think it's probably alright for you to drive to places you frequent around town for now. I do *not* recommend that you take a road trip by yourself though. That would most certainly increase your confusion and likelihood of having an accident."

Dr. Leyva's diagnosis and instructions seemed easy enough to follow. Dana was relieved and hopeful that they would see a reduction in her dad's memory lapses if he did as she recommended. Unfortunately, no sooner than they had reached the car, he became irritable and defiant.

"There's no way I'm taking antidepressants. I'm not one of those head cases who needs to pop pills to keep from being sad. I also don't see how going to water aerobics at the senior center is going to help me one bit. If anything, it might make me gouge out my own eyes."

Dana started the SUV. "No one called you a head case. You've been bottling your grief over losing Mom for too long. You disconnected yourself from your friends and from community in general. If the neurologist who deals with this sort of thing daily thinks your symptoms can be helped with an antidepressant, then trust her and take the pill.

"Also, nobody said anything about water aerobics. There are other ways to exercise and engage without having to gaze at elderly people in swimwear. But I'm telling you, you're going to do everything on Dr. Leyva's list if you expect to get your keys back."

He crossed his arms and fixed his attention out the passenger window. "Whatever."

What did he have to be mad about when the prognosis

was much better than they'd expected? "Dad, everything the doctor said was good news. What are you upset about?"

He huffed. "Good news? You're not the one who has to change your whole lifestyle to stave off old age."

She had changed her life to accommodate *his* devolving mental health. She had tabled her writing plans repeatedly over the last few weeks to rescue him from scrapes. If he didn't start trying to stave off old age at least a little, she was the one who was going to lose it.

"Dad, you're not unique." She propped her arm on the window and rubbed the tension from her temple. "We all make choices that affect our health and aging. Eating better, exercising, and confronting grief are helpful for everyone. The changes Dr. Leyva recommended aren't all that difficult." She crossed a busy intersection and turned into the local deli parking lot.

"Why are we stopping here? Just take me home."

Dana switched off the ignition and turned to face him. "We've been at that clinic for hours, and we're both irritable and hungry. Come inside with me and order lunch, or so help me, I will drop you off at the nearest nursing home with no I.D. and claim I found you wandering the neighborhood."

He got out of the Tahoe, and Dana did her best to hide her self-satisfied smirk. When it was their turn to order, he mumbled that he'd lost his appetite and wasn't hungry. Exactly something Leah or Nate would do if they were pouting because she yelled at them. She smiled sweetly to the youth at the counter. "We'll take two chopped salad and club combos, please."

"And two sweet teas." Apparently, his appetite wasn't as lost as he had thought.

Dana paid while he took their number and located a table.

"Will did some checking," Dana said as she handed him his tea and sat down. "That community center down the street from you has a whole calendar of activities."

He glared at her. "If I wanted to play Bingo or sit and stretch with the rest of the old folks, I would, but it sounds even more torturous to me than it does to you."

Dana laughed. It did sound awful.

"Well, what about Tai Chi in the park? There's an 8:00 class on Mondays and Thursdays when the weather is nice. When it gets too cold to meet outside, they work out in the community center. That might be interesting. You wouldn't have to make awkward conversation, and everyone is fully dressed, so it's a step up from water aerobics."

Edward made no effort to reply. Dana decided she would show up Thursday morning to drag him to Tai Chi, even if it meant she had to participate as well.

"There's also an after-school robotics club at Adam's school, and the teacher who leads it has been asking for parent volunteers with experience in circuits and engineering to help build robots. That would be fun for you and Adam to do together. You'd be great at that."

Edward said nothing, but Dana saw a faint twinkle in his eyes like he was recalling a happy memory. She played on his sympathies. "There are lots of kids with the same curiosity as Adam who don't have anyone to foster that desire to create. It's sad really. I would volunteer myself, but I don't know the first thing about robotics or circuits."

"Adam is in the robotics club? Seems a little late in the year to be asking for volunteers," he said.

"It started back in January, but one of the sponsors is on maternity leave. They meet in the cafeteria after school on Mondays." Dana carefully avoided answering the question about Adam's involvement because, for all she knew, he had no idea the club even existed. Like she needed another place to be between soccer for Leah, football for Nate in the fall, and whatever other extracurriculars they decided to sign up for. She was sure he would happily join though if his Pops were volunteering, and the teacher would likely welcome a latecomer in exchange for the help.

Both their phones indicated a new message. It was Rita Brewer, so it couldn't be good.

Not urgent, but I could use a hand at earliest convenience. Limb broke off, and it's wedged against my back door. Too heavy for me to move.

"Shouldn't be too hard to get a limb out of the way. I've got a chainsaw and some loppers that'll turn it into firewood in no time," he said.

Dana texted a reply just as her battery was about to die: We'll be there in about a half hour

Rita sent a thumbs-up emoji. Edward chuckled. "Does she think using the cartoon pictures makes her seem younger?"

"They're emojis, Dad. Are you saying your grandkids have never taught you how to use them? I'm sure they've sent them to you because it's basically the language of the youth."

"It's different with the kids. You're supposed to goof around and act young with your grandkids. Rita is too old to send emojis to her fellow senior citizens."

Dana scoffed. "Hey! She sent it to me too, and I have at least a couple of decades before you can lump me in that category."

"I'm sorry, sweetie. You're right. I bet you still get carded when you buy wine."

Just then, the server, who appeared to be a teenager, arrived with their meals. He stifled a snicker. Dana stifled the urge to kick him.

Rita Brewer met them in her driveway and led them through the side gate where the fallen branch was indeed

wedged against the door. It was as large as the courtyard itself, so even with the three of them tugging it away from the door, there was nowhere for the limb to go.

Dana surveyed the damage while her dad went home to grab his saws. She marveled that the massive limb landed in just the right place where it didn't break a window or crash through the roof. "Miss Rita, God was watching out for you. That limb could have really torn up your house if it had fallen even an inch more this direction. The wood is a bit scraped up on the door, but that's an easy fix compared to what could have happened."

"Well, I hope the Lord was protecting my heart too because I thought it was going to shoot right out of my chest when that thing fell. All I heard was a loud crack. I didn't know if it was the apocalypse or if we were being invaded, but I was thankful I had just gone to the bathroom, or else my heart wouldn't have been the only thing shooting out of me."

Dana burst out laughing. Who knew the prim busybody could be so crass?

She used loppers to chop off the smaller portions of the limb and stack them for firewood while her dad made easy work of the fattest portion with the chainsaw. At first, she had worried that he might not have the strength to wield the saw, but he certainly seemed to be in his element.

Dana could see contentment on her father's face, even as half of it was covered in safety goggles. He had found a purpose, and it made him appear younger and more alive. He would be too sore to lift his arms tomorrow though.

She headed home as Miss Rita and her dad were sweeping the patio and discussing the best way to repair the door. He volunteered to sand and re-stain it for her, and Dana was glad he'd found an activity for the time being to keep his mind and body active.

Will's car was in the garage when she pulled in. Had she lost track of time and forgotten to pick up the kids? She checked the car's clock. Why was Will home at 2:30 in the afternoon?

He flung open the door. "Where have you been, and why is your phone turned off?" he demanded. He was awfully combative for someone who ignored her calls frequently as of late.

"You know I was at the neurologist with Dad all morning. My phone died at lunch."

"You don't keep a charger in your car? Moms always have a backup plan."

"You borrowed that charger last week and didn't give it back. And I *thought* my phone charged overnight, but *someone* unplugged it to use the outlet for his new sound machine." Honestly, husbands were as bad as children sometimes. She paused to allow him the opportunity to apologize, but he didn't. "Now that we have solved the mystery of why I'm a terrible mother with a dead phone battery, please tell me why you're home so early and what you're mad about."

"Adam's sick. The school sent him home, and since you weren't available, I had to leave my meeting to deal with it."

"Is he okay?' she asked, worried about her child and angry that Will hadn't led with that information.

"He threw up after P.E., and the nurse said he had a low-grade fever, but he seems better now. He's resting."

Dana nodded. Adam vomited every time he had a fever, so it was probably an ear infection or strep.

"Did he make it to a trash can when he threw up?'

"How should I know?" Will exploded. "I handled it. I did not launch an inquisition."

Dana's neck grew hot, and she pinched the bridge of her nose. Holding in her stress was better than going to prison for unleashing it, she reasoned. She took a deep breath before she lowered her hands and spoke.

"First of all, Adam would be mortified if he vomited in

front of his class. Kids get teased for less. Second, he's our son, and 'dealing with it' and 'handling it' is in the job description. Third, you would have had to walk out of your meeting regardless of my battery status because I couldn't leave my dad's appointment to pick him up."

"So, you're telling me you *just now* dropped off your dad?" Will's incredulity was not endearing him to Dana in the least.

"No, Your Honor. Following the interminable appointment, the witness and her father ate lunch at a nearby eatery, and subsequently helped his neighbor with a tree situation." Sarcasm fueled her eloquence.

"Since when do trees have situations?" he asked.

"Since they tend to get dead limbs, which occasionally break off, trapping elderly women in their homes. Now if there are no further questions, move so I can see my son." She edged past Will and into the house, dropped her purse on the counter, and darted up the stairs to check on Adam. She had to step over Harvey to get into the room. The giant beast raised his head and whimpered, worried for his boy.

Adam's eyes were closed, and there was a trash can by the head of the bed and a washcloth on his forehead. She put her hand gently on the side of Adam's neck. He was warm.

"Hey, Mama," he whispered.

"Hey, sweet boy. You threw up, huh?" She wanted to kneel and cradle her son to help him feel better, but she knew she couldn't afford to get sick. Moms didn't get to take sick days. Instead, she stood beside him and prayed the air up higher above his head wasn't swirling with germs.

"Yeah, but I made it to the toilet, so no one saw me."

She smiled. The fear of every kid was public puking. "I'm sorry I wasn't there to pick you up. I was helping Pops and didn't get the message."

He tried to sit up, but Dana eased his shoulders back onto the mattress. "My head hurts a lot. There's pounding back here, and this one stings." He indicated his left ear. A non-contagious, easily treated illness. Totally doable. She sat on the edge of the bed and rubbed his arm.

"I'll get you some medicine and call the doctor while you try to rest. Stay in this bed, got it?" The thing with sick children was that they tended to feel better and get a burst of energy in between bouts of fever and vomiting. Moving children were more likely to feel sick again quickly, and it all pretty much went downhill after that.

She was still fuming at Will when she came downstairs, but she had lost some of her fire. She went to the master bathroom to locate the Tylenol and found him donning a tie and sport coat in their bedroom.

"What are you doing, Will?"

"What does it look like? I'm going back to the office. It's not a good day for me to skip out."

She felt the niggle of worry in the pit of her stomach again.

He threw his arms up. "What do you want from me, Dana? You can take care of Adam now, and I have to go. I did your job for two hours, and now I need to go do mine."

She took a breath before responding. "Adam has an ear infection, and he's going to need antibiotics, which our pediatrician won't prescribe over the phone. Therefore, one of us has to take him to the doctor while the other picks up Nate and then drives to the high school to get our daughter. The middle school science fair is also tonight, and in case you forgot during your all-important *work,* Nate entered a project about how lizards regrow their tails. So, you either need to pick up the kids or take Adam to the clinic. Then we can have Leah stay with Adam while we *both* go to the science fair to support Nate because he needs us to be his fans."

Will glared at her in silence as he yanked his tie off again. Dana wondered if his eagerness to get back to the office had anything to do with Helena, but she didn't ask.

She wasn't in the mood to fight anymore.

Dana called the pediatrician's office as she gave Adam pain meds. She asked to speak to a nurse, hoping that they would make an exception and prescribe the antibiotic over the phone, but no such luck.

The patronizing receptionist informed her they could not schedule Adam that day. "Ma'am, you really should have called earlier to make an appointment."

"I'll take that under advisement and make sure my children know that all fevers and infections must take place before lunch from now on," Dana snapped and hung up without saying goodbye.

Using an app on her phone, she was able to get Adam an appointment for 3:30 at an urgent care clinic. With any luck, she would still make it to the science fair on time. Dana debated for about a minute what to do between now and then, but with Adam resting and Will fuming, she made the easy decision to slip out and pay Josie a visit.

Chapter 21

Josie

There was a soft knock at her door at the same time her phone buzzed in her back pocket. Her arms were full as she bounced Olivia on one hip and Ben in the other. Only one person would knock so politely, so she simply shouted, "Use the code and let yourself in." No sooner had Dana stepped in the door than Josie unloaded a crying Ben into her neighbor's arms.

"What if I had been a serial killer, and you let me walk right in?"

"Unless *you* are a serial killer, I think I'm in the clear." She was so grateful to see another adult that she might have given the door code to a stranger. What were the odds it would have been a serial killer? "No one else has the key code." She shifted Olivia to a swing and calmed her with a pacifier before retreating down the hall toward the sound of more crying. "Did you hear us from across the street?" she called over her shoulder.

Dana patted Ben and shouted over the noise, "No, I'm just here avoiding Will."

"It's the middle of the workday. Is he sick?" What was it about men and their inability to act like grownups when they felt bad? When they were newlyweds, Hunter had a bout with abdominal pain and insisted Josie take him to the

ER, lest his appendix rupture and leave her a widow. After a four-hour wait and a thorough examination, the doctor assured Hunter he did not in fact have appendicitis but instead was experiencing moderate constipation. It took all of Josie's willpower not to leave him in the parking lot.

"No, but Adam is, and Will had to take off to pick him up. Now he's in a royal snit, and I can't be in the same room with him."

Josie nodded. "Well, that bites, but I've never been so happy to see another adult in my whole life." She paused to consider her statement. "Since yesterday anyway."

"Everything okay?" Dana asked over the noise.

"Just the usual. Ben is teething, and Olivia has tummy troubles. Connor doesn't like to be left out, so he's crying because his brother and sister are crying. If you hadn't gotten here when you did, I'd be crying too."

It had been a long day already that began at 5:00 this morning when Olivia woke up the whole house. No two babies had napped at the same time today, and the only time Josie had had to herself was using the bathroom.

Now Hunter had a final walk-through on a new home with a client this evening, so he likely wouldn't be home before the triplets went to bed.

She eased into the recliner and rocked Connor as her eyelids drooped. Just once Josie would love to get a consecutive eight hours of sleep. The crying finally subsided. "What happened with Will?"

Dana paced the living room as she patted Ben's back and told Josie about her morning with her dad and about the fight she'd had with Will. She lamented about having too many things to do with a sick child to boot, and how Will complained about having to put his own schedule on hold this afternoon.

"He was weird about spring break, too. When we found out his nephews were coming, he said he'd take the week off and help entertain the kids. Then the day they were set to arrive, he told me he had to work all week. It's one more layer in his sketchy behavior, but I don't even have the energy to figure out what's up. Between my dad, a sick kid, the science fair tonight, and a soccer game, I'm already meeting myself coming and going."

Josie imagined what it must be like trying to get three older kids to various events while also juggling an elderly parent who kept getting himself into jams. She giggled aloud.

"What's so funny over there?" Dana asked.

"I'm sorry for laughing at your misery. But I was just thinking that this is the first time since becoming a parent that I've tried to put myself in someone else's shoes and thought their life was harder than mine."

Dana shook her head. "You're not thinking clearly because of sleep deprivation. *Nothing* is harder than triplets. Except quadruplets. Also, how do you carry two babies? My arm is getting tired from just the one."

She shrugged. "Gradual increase as opposed to starting with heavy weight. They were only four pounds in the beginning, and my strength grew with them. You're bouncing fifteen pounds that you haven't been training for."

"Benny, your mama is calling you a chunk. Do you hear her?" Dana baby talked to Ben who rewarded her with a gummy smile.

He'd been fussy all day, so this was a surprising change. "Maybe you and your family could help Hunter raise the triplets, while I sneak away to a tropical paradise where dirty diapers and 3:00 a.m. feedings don't exist." Josie lost herself in a daydream about lying in a hammock on the beach sipping frozen concoctions and listening to the waves pound the shore.

Dana laughed. "Well considering the current Harding family dynamic, your kiddos are better off with you than they would be with us. Between my dad, the novel, and our usual upheaval, we're barely hanging on by a thread."

It took Josie a second to register what Dana said. "What novel?" She would kill to be in a book club right now. Unless they expected her to read. She didn't have time for that.

Dana told her about her professor urging her to expand her story into a novel.

"Wow! That's so exciting." she exclaimed, startling Connor in her lap. "Sorry, Baby. Tell me all about it." She listened as Dana described the plot and the character of the mother who shops for a heart among potential matches who are terrible people.

"She has a *Dexter*-esque quality in only wanting to harm bad people but wrestles with the dilemma of not wanting her child to live with an evil heart."

It was no small feat to be able to take an idea and turn it into a whole story that entertained other people. Josie longed to feel her own sense of purpose outside of being a wife and a mother, labels by which she would be defined for the next eighteen years.

"What's wrong?" Dana asked. "Your face is doing something weird."

"Maybe I'm a little envious of you. When you ask a kid what they want to be when they grow up, they always say something life-affirming, world changing. Firefighter, doctor, racecar driver. No kid says, 'when I grow up, I want to change eighteen diapers a day, get puked on, and clean other people's messes. And I want to never shower or brush my teeth again.'"

Dana tilted her head. "Adam would be thrilled to never shower or brush his teeth. I get what you're saying though. The mom thing is thankless on its best day, and the whole goal is to do such a good job that they don't even need you eventually. There's no identity in 'I used to raise kids, but they all grew up, so now I wait for them to call me.' It's depressing."

Josie lowered herself onto the floor and placed Connor on his belly. "Look at you though. You're out there in the world doing something incredible."

"I'm having trouble wrapping my mind around the time commitment." Dana admitted. "There's a good chance I'm wasting time that I should have been investing in my family."

Josie thought about that. Wasn't every investment a gamble? You could be the best mom on the planet and still have a kid who made bad choices. There were no guarantees. "The only thing that's certain is that you will never be a writer if you don't write."

She congratulated herself for imparting wisdom to Dana instead of being the recipient of her older, wiser neighbor's sage advice for a change.

"What about you?" Dana asked. "If you didn't have these cuties who need you twenty-four seven, what would you want to be when you grow up?"

The answer came to her at once. She'd been thinking about it nonstop since the second meeting of the Village People. "Hairdresser." Then she quickly added, "but don't tell my mom."

Josie spent her childhood playing beauty shop with her dolls and her friends. Laurel played too, until the time Josie used real scissors on her. The family had gotten very bent out of shape over it.

In high school, Josie wanted to sign up for a cosmetology class that would let her enter the workforce with a license after graduation, but Marie wouldn't hear of it. She was determined that her daughters would both get college degrees before they set out to do anything else. "That way," she said, "you will never have to depend on a man to support you."

Josie never understood her mother's logic. People supported themselves with cosmetology careers every day, but there was no chance of swaying Marie once she had her mind made up. Josie planned to appease her mom and pursue cosmetology in night school during college, but it didn't work out. Besides, college had been a great experience after all, and she was happy to land a good job with benefits in the admissions office. Childhood fantasies sometimes were best left in childhood.

"Hold up," said Dana. "You can cut hair?"

"Uh, no. I said I *wanted* to cut hair. My mom wouldn't let me pursue cosmetology, and after I supposedly butchered Laurel's hair, I was forbidden from using scissors, so I guess it's for the best."

Dana laughed. "What did you do to it?"

Josie rolled her eyes. "I barely trimmed it, but everyone flipped out like I'd shaved her head."

"A trim doesn't sound so bad. If it was basically even, why was it such a big deal?"

She grinned sheepishly. "I mean, I was only seven, so maybe it wasn't basically anything, but whatever."

Dana laughed so hard Ben began to whimper, and Josie reached up to take him.

"I'm sorry for breaking your kid and leaving, but I better get back and check on Adam before Will accuses me of abandoning the family again. Can I hand you anything before I go?"

Josie positioned Ben opposite Connor. They exchanged drooly grins and shrieked like they hadn't seen each other in ages.

"Will you toss me the remote? I'll be good down here for a while, especially if they're all content. I sure hope I didn't just jinx myself."

As Dana left, Josie got a call from Zooey, her former coworker who had come to the mentor group.

"Hey girl. I wanted to thank you again for inviting me to your church thing. I didn't realize how much I had been missing having people to talk to about that stuff."

Josie muted the television. "What about the girls in the

office? Y'all don't hang out and vent about your home lives?" It was the part of the job she'd been missing most.

"Sometimes, but it's hectic since the new dean implemented recruitment quotas. I've been at a different high school every day for the past month. Can you believe some seniors still don't know where they're headed in the fall? Anyway, I also wanted to apologize for not keeping in touch after you left. I thought you needed to rest and that you had your hands too full to bother with an old coworker, but I should have been a better friend."

Josie considered this. She'd let most of her relationships fall by the wayside since her pregnancy. She attributed it to exhaustion and laziness on her part but hadn't thought that her friends were giving her space because they thought she was too busy for them. Hunter had pointed out as much after the gala.

"You don't need to apologize. It's hard to know what a friend needs when she doesn't speak up. I haven't done a good job of maintaining friendships either. This mom thing is all-consuming, isn't it?"

"For sure. And my single friends don't get it. They— ugh. Speaking of hard. The daycare is calling. I'm gonna have to go."

They said their goodbyes, and Josie ended the call. The screen indicated a new message from her mom as well as the message from when Dana arrived.

I'm at your door. Don't want to wake anyone.

Josie chuckled at Dana's politeness. The new message said,

Hey Sweetie. Laurel and Jefferson (yes, that's his first name, not Jeff) are having their engagement party in Denver on Mother's Day so all the families can meet before the wedding. I know it's a long way with babies, but what do you think?

She had thoughts alright, but she couldn't share them with her mother. Laurel and Jefferson-not-Jeff had a lot of nerve. Her sister hadn't spoken to her since Christmas, let alone contacted her to say she was engaged. Mother's Day was less than a month away, and they were just getting around to planning a big family get-together? Was Laurel so self-absorbed that she expected everyone to commit to out of state plans on short notice? On Mother's Day, no less.

A question mark appeared on the screen. She realized she had been staring at the text with her keyboard open, so her mom saw three dots and was expecting a response.

IDK, mom. That's an 8.5 hr drive WO kids! Would prob take 3 days with. And on my first Mother's Day?

She didn't add what she was really thinking, which was, "That's a long way to travel for someone who clearly wants nothing to do with me."

A new text from Dana appeared. I think you should chase your dream. I'll even let you practice on my hair...AFTER you start classes

Why couldn't Laurel be more like Dana? The neighbor who had known her less than a year was supportive and caring, a much better big sister than her selfish, free-spirited actual sister.

She replied to Dana with a pink heart emoji and set her phone on the coffee table. She would face her mother's chastening later, but now she played with the boys and watched Olivia drift off to sleep in the swing. Josie moved the boys to their bouncy seats and shushed them to sleep, imagining what it would be like to have her own booth in a cool salon. Envisioning having a job again where she got to dress in cute clothes and talk to new people every day excited her.

As the boys' eyelids drooped, she eased herself onto the sofa, careful not to wake them. If Dana could pursue her dream while juggling her dad's issues and three kids with all their activities, maybe she could as well. She googled the cost of cosmetology school, local salon booth rental costs, and childcare. Maybe it wasn't feasible right now after all, but in a few years when the kids were in school and their NICU stays were paid off, she could.

"Josie, wake up." A strong hand shook her shoulder. A baby cooed.

She lunged off the sofa. "This is why moms shouldn't nap when their babies are napping. Did I sleep through the entire afternoon?" Josie's breasts ached. It was past time to pump, but sun still shone through the window, so it couldn't be that late. Olivia and Ben were both still asleep where she had placed them earlier.

Hunter cradled Connor in his arms and grinned. "Babe, relax. It's only 4:00. Rough day?"

She put her hands on her hips and stretched her stiff back. "We survived. I'm confused. You're supposed to have a walk-through, and you usually work late after those." Her eyes got big. "You didn't get fired, did you?"

"I own half the company. How would I get fired?" Hunter told her that the walk-through had been moved up and went great. The client was very easy to please, and there were no last-minute issues to fix in the house before closing. The other homes he had under construction didn't require his on-site supervision today, which was fortunate since he too had been up since 5:00.

"That's amazing," said Josie.

"What, that I got home before dark or that everything is running smoothly today?" he asked.

"Both."

Hunter fed Connor while Josie pumped and filled him in on his children's difficult day, her mom's text, and her conversation with Dana. "What would you think if I got my cosmetology license when the babies are a little older? Is that something we could afford?"

He was quiet for a moment, and Josie's stomach

dropped. It had taken several years and countless prayers to even get pregnant. It was the thing she had wanted most in the world. She was ashamed of herself for wanting anything else so soon after receiving their miracles.

"I think it's a great idea, Babe. Your mom will flip out, but you'd make a great hairdresser. Think of all the money we will save when these little guys all need haircuts."

"My mom has been worried about Laurel or me having to depend on a man financially since the day my dad left. But I know you'll never leave me for a younger woman like my dad did, so she has nothing to worry about."

Hunter grinned. "You're right, but are you saying I couldn't get a younger girlfriend if I wanted one?"

"That's exactly what I'm saying because guys with three babies and a minivan aren't hot commodities to anyone else but their baby mamas." She winked and blew him a kiss.

"Fact. What got you thinking about cosmetology? It's been years since you've talked about it."

She told him about the discussion in the mentor group about putting dreams on hold for their families and about Dana's writing endeavor. "I didn't give up on it because of our family. My mom gets all the blame for that one, but when Dana asked me today about *my* dream career, I realized I never really wanted to be anything else except a hairdresser and a mother."

Hunter sat Connor upright and patted his back. "And you feel like this is the thing that's missing from your life?"

Josie knew she would still have joy even if she never got to practice cosmetology. What she couldn't live without were people. "The thing that's missing is connection. I'm isolated on an island of babies, and I want to interact with grownups. But the icing on the cake would be getting to do that while designing hairstyles for people that give them confidence and make them feel like I did when Dana gave up her hair appointment for me."

After a beat, she added, "I think I need to invest more into self-care. I'm sure I would feel better if I tried harder to look nice. Then I might have the energy to get out of the house more." Hunter had said as much the night of the gala, but she couldn't understand it then. She still wasn't sure she could, but Dana and the moms' group had inspired her to at least consider that her life could be more than diapers and bottles.

Hunter grinned. "I think that's great, but for the record, you're smoking hot in whatever you wear." Olivia wailed as if in protest. "Don't listen to her. She thinks her toes are delicious, so what does she know?"

Chapter 22

Dana

Harvey snoozed in a sunspot on the kitchen tile. The only sounds in the house were the hum of the refrigerator and the rapid clicks of Dana typing on her keyboard. Her anger toward Will had inspired an entire chapter about the serial killer mom she'd created. She paused to consider what that said about her.

Will's bad attitude was taking a toll on everyone. He snapped at the kids about their chores and griped about the growing mound of clean laundry that needed to be folded and put away. He himself hadn't folded a single towel or even put away his own underwear from the stack though.

The last straw happened Thursday night during Leah's soccer game. Her dad had called Will asking him to come over and jump start his Buick. Apparently, he had left the car door open when he was unloading groceries the day before and forgotten about it. Will blew up in the middle of the stands. After he scolded Edward and hung up on him, he berated Dana for returning her dad's keys to him. His outburst caused her to miss Leah's game-winning goal, and they didn't speak for the rest of the evening.

Her dad had been cleared to drive by his neurologist, but even so, Will was out of line. In a few weeks, he'd gone from working long hours and missing games to having meetings with a mysterious beautiful woman and humiliating his wife in public. She needed to get to the bottom of his weird behavior or at least clear the air.

She called him, and it went straight to voicemail. She fired off an angry text. Seriously? You're ignoring my calls after the fit you threw over my dead phone battery when Adam was sick?

He responded: not a good time

He hadn't even asked if there was an emergency. Her dad might have been in trouble or one of the kids hurt for all he knew.

Are you having a mid-life crisis? Because you could just buy a sports car and leave the rest of us out of it

She returned to her laptop. Her keystrokes grew so fierce she was afraid she would stab her thumb straight through the space bar. Rather than cause irreparable damage to her new computer, she called Serena.

She vented about Will's reaction to her dad, and her friend prayed over her and her family.

Dana's heart rate slowed, and the heat drained out of her face. "What would I do without you?"

"You'd lead our new little project by yourself," Serena teased. "I've been thinking though. For the women to build connection like you and I have, we should establish permanent table groups with lead mentors."

Dana liked where the idea was going. "Maybe the most experienced mom serves as a table host and even invites her group to get together outside of Wednesday night."

After some discussion about the time commitments associated with older kids in sports and a dozen other activities, they decided to let each table elect a host instead of designating the one who might be the most frazzled at the table.

"We also need to come up with a name before long. Our announcement in the church bulletin simply says, 'come fellowship and connect with other moms,'" said Serena.

She laughed. "Why do church folk love the word 'fellowship' so much?"

"It's biblical."

They hung up promising to give it some thought before the next meeting.

Her phone buzzed. Will had either come to his senses or thought of a comeback to her sports car comment. The text was not from Will though, but Rita Brewer.

Your dad is tromping through my back yard with a metal detector. Thought you'd want to know. Tried asking him why, but he shushed me.

Dana laughed aloud at the mental image. Hilarious, sure, but also alarming. She grabbed her purse and headed out. She parked in her father's driveway and noticed the side gate to Mrs. Brewer's backyard was ajar, so she made her way across the street. Per the text message, Dana found her father methodically sweeping a metal detector over the yard in straight lines.

"Dad? What are you doing?"

He shushed her without looking up. She stood in front of him. "Stop and talk to me for a sec. What are you doing?"

He waved his hand over the metal detector. "Baking a cake. What does it look like I'm doing?"

"I can see *what* you're doing. What I fail to see is *why* you're using a metal detector in your neighbor's back yard. Dad," she hissed. "You're trespassing."

"Oh relax." He began swiping the metal detector over the ground again.

Dana put her hand on it to stop him. "It's not like beachcombing on the National Seashore. You can't go looking for buried treasure on other people's property."

Edward held up his left hand to Dana. "I've lost my wedding ring," he said. "I've searched everywhere, and I don't even remember when I last had it. I thought maybe it fell off the other day when we were cutting the tree limb."

Dana huffed. "Why didn't you just tell Rita that and

save me the trip over here?" He shrugged in answer and returned to his task. She knew it was useless to press the matter further, so she went to the back door to explain to Mrs. Brewer.

Rita handed Dana a glass of iced tea. "I heard the whole thing, hon. Come on inside. I was about to offer the tea to Ed, but he's a man on a mission, and you look like you could use it more."

Dana sniffed the glass. "Why, is this spiked?"

Rita chuckled. "No, just plain old sweet tea." She motioned to her flowered sofa. "Have a seat. I'm sorry I got all worked up over something so silly. But I never know if that man is in his right mind or not, and I was concerned."

Dana nodded. "Same. I mean, people in their right minds don't barge into their neighbor's yards without explaining themselves. They use their words."

The two women sipped their tea and made small talk as they watched Edward scan the yard. Dana wondered how long etiquette required her to stay here. He could be at this for hours, and she didn't have that kind of time to waste on a school day. The ring could be anywhere.

She remembered the last time she saw it. It was the day she took him for his MRI. She leapt out of her seat and made a beeline for the back door. "Dad!" She waved her arms to get his attention. "I think I have your ring."

Edward stopped and took his headphones off. "What'd you say?"

"I think I have your ring in my purse. You had to take it off when you got your MRI, and I don't remember giving it back to you. Come inside and I'll check." She grabbed his arm and whispered, "and you better apologize to Rita for being so weird."

He nodded and placed his headset and metal detector on a lawn chair and followed her into the house.

Dana rummaged through her oversized bag. "Here it is." Dana handed him the ring. "Dad, I'm sorry. I should have given it back to you as soon as your MRI ended."

"That's okay, sweetie. I didn't even think to ask for it. How did I not notice it was missing for a whole three weeks? What does that say about me?" He looked at his hand and rotated the band on his finger.

Dana put her hands on his. "It says you have been living your life. I think Mom would want that."

His eyes misted. "Ladies, I'm sorry for inconveniencing you and for my intrusion. I guess I went off the rails again."

"Oh, that's alright, Ed," said Rita. "I don't know what I'd do if I lost this old wedding ring. My Harry gave it to me in 1965, and he's been with Jesus for fifteen years. They had to butter my hand to get it off for my hip surgery a few years back."

Dana exhaled relief at Rita's understanding. She halfway expected her to read him the riot act.

Rita got up from the table and opened the fridge. "I made a roast yesterday, and I have leftovers with potatoes and gravy. Why don't I heat us some for lunch?"

Dana left her dad and his neighbor to their lunch, anxious to get back to writing before the kids got out of school. On the drive, she thought about how Rita seemed less nosey than she'd always thought. Maybe she was just lonely. She would text her and invite her to come to the mentor group.

Back in her kitchen, Dana returned to work finding an unwitting organ donor for her main character's dying teenage son. She was deep into stalking her next victim when the loud hum of the Hardings' garage door spooked Dana. Why was Will home in the middle of the day again? He lumbered into the kitchen and dropped his keys onto the counter. Dana closed her laptop but stayed silently planted on the barstool. She hadn't forgiven him for blowing her off earlier.

Will walked around the counter and hugged her from

behind, resting his head on top of hers. "How do you feel about Fiji?" he asked.

"Place or brand of water?"

"Place." Was this his roundabout way of apologizing, or was it a segway into a big announcement?

She shrugged. "I hear the beaches are nice and that you can stay in one of those huts over the water and watch fish swim through windows in the floor."

"Mmm. So if there's wifi, you could finish your novel, the kids could do school online, and I could fish for our meals right off the porch."

She put her hands on his arms that were still wrapped around her. "Sure, but we can't even drag the kids to Red Lobster, so I hope there's also an endless supply of chicken nuggets and a microwave in our new island paradise."

Will dropped his arms and rotated the bar stool so Dana was facing him. "I just lost my job," he said. "I wanted to tell you in person while the kids were gone."

"But you're the CEO. How can they fire you?"

"Big Kitchen Supply has been trying to buy us out for months. They put an offer on the company, and the investors voted to take it. They already have their own executive staff, so my team and I have become redundant."

That meant he wasn't kidding before about that Helena woman wanting to take his job. No wonder Will had been a beast lately. It didn't quite explain the deleted text thread between them though.

"If she is nothing more than the woman who put you out of a job, why would you delete text messages from her?"

Will's eyes widened and he pursed his lips. "What are you talking about?"

She bit back the urge to yell, "Don't play dumb with me." She stared at him with her arms crossed. "You left your phone next to my computer when she texted to tell you when her flight would land. I found it odd that there was nothing preceding that little announcement."

After a moment, his deer-in-the-headlights expression shifted. He laughed. "You little snoop. Somebody was jealous." He playfully poked his fingers at her ribs.

Dana squirmed and batted his hands away. "Don't tickle me to avoid answering the question. Why did you delete the thread?"

He straightened up. "There were no texts to delete. We'd only communicated in person and via phone calls and email before that. I'm sure you would have seen proof in my call log and email when you went through my phone."

Her eyes narrowed. She studied his face for signs he might be lying and found none. The corners of his mouth twitched out of amusement rather than duplicity. She believed him.

She began to think about the implications of losing Will's income. They had a mortgage to pay and three kids to feed and clothe. She could get a job, but what was a stay-at-home mom/former librarian qualified to do that would support a family of five? What if they had to move to another city or state? What would happen to her dad? Her breath quickened with every new question.

Will placed his hands on the sides of her face and tilted it to his. "It'll work out, I promise. God has always taken care of us, and He's not going to stop. I got a good severance package, which should give us plenty of time to figure out our next steps. I'll find something, even if it means starting over as a line cook."

His last statement offered Dana no comfort. She remembered the early days of their marriage when he worked long hours as a chef. She would be a single mother while Will worked nights and weekends again.

She tried to keep a brave face for his sake. "Is this why you've been a total grouch for the last few weeks?"

"Yeah, I'm sorry I've been on edge. I guess I did a poor job of masking my stress, but I didn't want to worry you until I knew for sure what was coming. I've been meeting with their CEO to try and save as many jobs as possible before the buyout became official. But I couldn't save my own."

Dana forced a smile that she hoped expressed reassurance. "Things were starting to get boring around here, so this new challenge might be the thing we need to energize us," she lied. Helping Serena coordinate the Wednesday group was a new challenge already. Trying to write a book while dealing with her dad's issues caused more excitement than she knew how to handle already. And on a slow day, she could count on Josie's triplets to spice things up. Starting new careers and possibly moving to a new city weren't even on her radar.

Will pulled her into another hug. "I'm so glad I have you," he murmured into her hair. "I know we can get through anything as long as we are doing it together."

She was glad he thought so because she wasn't so sure.

Chapter 23

Josie

Hunter couldn't make it home in time to watch the triplets tonight, but Serena had already assured Josie that there was plenty of space in the nursery for them. The Harding crew helped her drop them off before dispersing to their own classes.

A new sign pointed the way for Josie and Dana. It was a picture of a glass of lemonade adorned with a straw and a lemon slice on the rim offering "Refreshment for the Frazzled Mom." She blinked at Dana, expressionless. "One of you is having way too much fun with these."

"It's not me." As they made their way inside, Dana whispered, "I think the signs are Serena's way of pressuring me to name the group."

Josie put her hand to her heart and feigned disappointment. "So, we definitely aren't going with The Village People then."

"Welcome, welcome," Serena sang. "As you're finding your seat tonight, I want to advise you that these are going to become your permanent seats for the rest of the semester. The ladies at your table will become your tribe, your found family of motherhood, if you will."

Josie and Dana exchanged glances. Serena's banter was a little corny, but she meant well. Josie scanned the tables. A hand grabbed her by the wrist from behind and

187

pulled her sideways into a seat. "Zooey!"

"Girl, you have to be in my tribe."

Dana took the last chair at the table across from Josie. "We're each other's village already, so it just makes sense, right?"

Josie nudged Zooey. "Oh hey, what happened with the preschool the other day?"

"Azira got bit by a kid in her class. Don't feel too sorry for her though. She's suspended from childcare at the gym for biting other kids. Maybe being the victim will teach her not to bite."

The other moms at the table included everyone from the first meeting, minus Serena who was standing at a table across the way making sure everyone had a place before she sat. Mrs. Steen, Kathy with the kids ten years apart, and Yvette whose belly looked like it had grown several inches since then.

When it came time to select a table host, Josie noticed Dana had her eyes fixed squarely on the table. Poor girl already had a full plate. Seven months of motherhood hardly qualified her to lead, but Josie was willing to sacrifice herself to save Dana. She cleared her throat to speak.

"I'll do it, unless someone else would rather," said Kathy.

Josie exhaled a sigh of relief. Thank goodness.

Everyone unanimously endorsed Kathy for table host.

"That would be lovely, thank you, Kathy," Anita Steen said.

Kathy started a group text so they'd all have each other's contact info and suggested they plan a meet up soon.

"What about brunch at my house on Saturday?" Josie was almost as shocked to hear herself extend the invitation as Dana appeared to be at hearing it. Her house was full of small humans and their smells. It was never quite clean enough.

Mrs. Steen clapped her hands together. "Oh, this is lovely. I think the best get-togethers are the ones that happen with the least notice. I'll bring muffins."

They all volunteered to bring items, and Josie congratulated herself on getting back out there socially. She hoped Hunter would feel the same way when he found out he'd have to help get the house ready for guests.

"I'm proud of you," Dana said as they buckled babies into their car seats. "I know you've been going stir crazy for months, but it's a lot of work having guests over when you have babies to care for."

Josie told her what Mrs. Steen had said a couple of weeks ago about inviting friends to come over despite the mess. She took Ben from Leah and put him in the van. "It's going to be years before the chaos in my house subsides, and I need to be with people. I can't wait until things are calm and clean before that happens." She climbed into the driver's seat and talked through the open door. "Besides, we've been keeping the front of the house neater since the ECI therapist started coming. How hard can it be?"

"Are we sure about this?" Hunter asked as he stooped over a highchair and cleaned spit up out of Olivia's neck folds. He pulled the soiled dress over her head and tossed it in the direction of the laundry room.

"Not at all," said Josie. Olivia hadn't stopped crying for more than a minute since she'd awakened at 6:30. She wasn't running a fever, so they'd decided to soldier on instead of cancelling the brunch. But now that the guests were set to arrive at any moment, Olivia had an upset stomach, and Josie realized she was in over her head.

It was a shame too because she was ready to host. The

kitchen, otherwise clean except for Olivia's highchair, sported matching spring plates and napkins next to mugs and an assortment of flavored creamers.

Dana and Leah knocked softly and entered without waiting for an invitation. "Knock, knock. Thought you might need a hand before everyone arrives." She set a fruit tray on the counter and turned to Josie. "You look cute."

She had donned an oversized sweater and her newest leggings with a cute pair of ankle boots. "Thanks. Maybe between my cuteness and the delicious food, no one will notice my screaming baby."

Leah held her hands out to Olivia who reached for her. "Come on, sweet girl. Let's get you changed." The teenager whisked the baby, whose screams were already waning, to the nursery.

Hunter wiped down the highchair tray. "I've heard Jos call the Harding kids baby whisperers, but you don't appreciate the gift until you witness it firsthand."

Josie pulled a teether out of the freezer and took it to Leah. When she returned, she asked Dana, "Did your kids get sick when they were teething?"

"Sometimes. I've read that they don't run a fever or vomit from teething, but our pediatrician said it can happen. Cutting teeth can be very irritating and stressful."

Josie prayed that's all that was wrong with Olivia and not something worse. The doorbell rang. She raised her eyebrows at Dana and smoothed down the front of her sweater. "Showtime!"

The get together was a success. Zooey brought her six-year-old son, Darius, so Adam came over to entertain him while the women shared embarrassing stories about raising their children. It had been a while since Josie had laughed as hard as she did when Kathy recounted the time her toddler son crawled out of the dressing room stall and ran off while she was trying on pants.

"I took off after him while hopping into my jeans at

the same time. I'm sure the security footage kept the staff entertained for days."

Josie couldn't wait to relay their tales to Hunter, who had suddenly found important things to do in the garage upon their arrival. They were going to be in for a real doozy in the coming years.

Yvette rubbed her burgeoning belly. "I can relate. The three-year-old can unbuckle the stroller seatbelt now, and she tried to bolt during my last doctor's appointment. Please tell me it's all downhill after three."

Kathy and Mrs. Steen shared a knowing smile. "Hang in there. Parenting toddlers is rough. It gets easier after age four," said Kathy.

"And then it gets worse for a while when they approach puberty," added Mrs. Steen.

"I have another year of this?" Yvette moaned.

"Two, three tops," Anita Steen said.

Dana set down her coffee mug. In a hushed tone she asked, "Wait, how long after puberty before they get easy again?"

The moms of grown children laughed. "Eighteen-ish," said Kathy. It came out more like a question than a statement.

Mrs. Steen cooed at Ben. "Eighteen-ish sounds about right. They're for sure tolerable again by twenty-four."

Dana, Yvette, and Zooey groaned in unison.

Mrs. Steen held Ben on her hip and ate a muffin with the other hand. Her bright beaded necklace held his attention, so he wasn't attempting to grab her food. Josie would have to invest in some of that teether-friendly jewelry for herself so she could hold her children without them knocking her food or drink out of her hands.

She posed a question to the group. "If you could go back and change one thing about how you parented with the knowledge you have now, what would it be?"

After a moment, Mrs. Steen said, "I would have had

more patience and not sweated the inevitable minor disasters."

"I would have taken more time to recharge my own battery," said Dana.

After their recent conversation about how Dana felt selfish for trying to write when she thought her family was coming apart at the seams, Josie imagined she was still wrestling with how to recharge. She said a silent prayer that God would give Dana the time and rest she needed to chase her dream.

Kathy stood and carried her mug to the sink. "I wish I had been more present with my daughter. I was so young when I had her that I was always leaving her with my parents to go to school and work and to go out with my friends. It took a few years for me to start acting like a mother instead of a cool aunt to her."

The women all helped clear the kitchen and promised to get together again soon. Yvette and Zooey got Leah's contact information so they could call her to babysit, which only slightly worried Josie. She wasn't comfortable with the teen watching all the babies on her own, but she was a huge help to Josie, and she wasn't prepared to compete for her availability. She was already wondering about moving Leah into their guest room and hiring her as a full-time nanny when the triplets started walking.

"Yvette," said Dana as they were all walking out. "Why don't you let me watch your daughter when you go to your next appointment?"

Yvette put her hand to her heart. "Oh my goodness, that would be amazing. We don't have any family nearby, and it's been a struggle since we moved here." She fanned her face to keep from crying.

Josie understood. She wouldn't have made it this long without the Hardings stepping in to fill the role of found family. She hugged her new friend. "I get it. And you have us now, so speak up and let us be there for you." Her sudden boldness caught her off guard. As the newbie mother of their group, she couldn't offer much in the way of maternal advice, but she was learning the value of a tribe. If she could convince Yvette to lean on her new friends the way she had been able to with Dana's family, then maybe she could make a difference for another mom.

The following Sunday, there was a graphic of an army helmet in the church bulletin inviting "weary moms in the trenches to join the Wednesday Warriors at 6:00."

Josie snapped a picture and sent it to Dana. Did we accidentally enlist?

Dana leaned forward in the pew and saluted her.

Chapter 24

The Caraways were a week away from their first road trip as a family of five. Josie wanted to be sure no necessities for the triplets were left behind. She'd been piling baby items on the dining table all day, and it could not hold any more. Several bibs tumbled off the mountain of baby supplies. At this rate, they'd have to rent a U-Haul trailer for their three-day trip to Oklahoma.

After some discussion and phone calls between Hunter and his parents, Josie agreed to share her first Mother's Day with Hunter's mother and grandmother. They longed to be more involved with their grandbabies, but the reality of caring for elderly parents made it difficult to travel. It seemed only fitting to introduce the triplets to their great-grandmother on a weekend meant to celebrate moms.

Her own mother was not pleased. While she hated disappointing her mom, Josie refused to give up her first Mother's Day for Granola Girl and Not-Jeff. Laurel had still not bothered to contact her little sister to share her good news or to personally invite her to their engagement soiree.

Hunter's parents had fully embraced their new daughter-in-law when Josie joined the family. After raising three boys, Emmaline Caraway told everyone she was excited to finally have some estrogen in the house. For years, they had family dinners together once a week and even sat together in church.

When she and Hunter announced they were trying to have a baby, Emmaline, in her excitement, began buying diapers and necessities to stock the nursery. Before long, Hunter and Josie's spare room looked like the baby section of Target. After a few months though, she stopped shopping, and Josie couldn't help but feel like Emmaline had given up on her daughter-in-law's ability to produce the highly anticipated grandchild. In hindsight, Josie realized that she'd quit shopping for a non-existent child so as not to add to the pressure Hunter and Josie had placed on themselves. It was an act of love really.

Then around the time that Hunter and Josie began seeking fertility help, Emmaline's mother had a stroke while her father was recovering from knee replacement surgery. Peter and Emmaline moved to Oklahoma City to become their caregivers.

Josie knew it pained them to leave, but there wasn't a better solution. As she thought about it now, it reminded her of Dana and Will's current predicament with her dad. At least they lived in the same town as Edward.

There was no way this mountain of baby supplies would fit in the minivan, at least not if they expected to bring the babies too. Josie pondered the dilemma as her phone vibrated with a text at the same time someone tapped softly on the front door. Dana's calling card.

"What brings you to the west side of the cul-de-sac, neighbor?"

"I know why Will has been so testy lately," Dana said. She told Josie how his company was bought out by their competitor, and all the executives had been let go.

Josie's heart sank for her friends. It must be terrifying to lose a job with a family to support. Then her heart sank for herself as well. What if they moved away or Dana got a full-time job and wasn't just a few yards away when she needed her? Who would take her screaming infant when the others were asleep?

"Oh my gosh, Dana. I'm so sorry." She wrapped her arms around Dana and hugged her for a good ten seconds. "Let's go to the kitchen and drown our sorrows in coffee." Josie saw her friend gaping at the pile on the kitchen table.

"Are your kids moving out?"

"Very funny. I'm trying to pack for Oklahoma," Josie said.

"Oh, did y'all decide to extend the trip?"

Josie busied herself with the coffee cups and Keurig so Dana wouldn't see her roll her eyes. She knew it was a lot of stuff, but no one understood what it was like to leave the house with so many infants. "I don't want to leave behind something we will need. That's all."

"You know they have stores in OKC, right?"

Josie turned to see her friend picking at the pile. "You sound like Hunter. You don't remember the pain of the middle of the night diaper run, do you? I don't even know how to get to a store in Oklahoma. I'm being proactive."

"But you have six pacifiers. Isn't Connor the only one who still takes a pacifier?"

"Who knows what the other two will need to soothe themselves away from home?" Josie was trying to plan for all contingencies.

"You have...1...2...3..." Dana trailed off as she counted. "I've lost count of the pajamas. You're bringing two of everything, per kid, per day, aren't you?"

Josie crossed the kitchen with coffee mugs in hand. She had to admit, watching Dana fish for pajamas was giving off rummage sale vibes. There was too much stuff.

She sighed. "I've been speaking to this mountain of stuff like the book of Matthew says, but it won't move. I guess I don't have the faith of a mustard seed."

Dana snorted. "Maybe it's not a lack of faith. You just need an outside perspective on the mountain. What if you consolidate your contingencies? For instance, take two pacifiers for the one baby who needs them. Hook one on his car seat and toss a backup in the diaper bag. If you lose both, you can probably find one under the van seat or something. Nate found an old pacifier in the seat pocket a year after we finally got him off the thing. They tend to turn up everywhere."

"You're probably right," Josie chuckled. "There's no telling what all has fallen out of diaper bags back there. One day a bottle of milk rolled out from under the passenger seat, totally solidified."

"I've been there," Dana said. "Toddlers with sippy cups and goldfish crackers will ruin a good family car faster than anything."

Some days, the thing that kept Josie going was the knowledge that eventually the babies would be able to walk themselves to the van and climb into their own seats but imagining the impending messes they would create made her cringe.

She moved four of the pacifiers from the table onto the kitchen counter. "What else could we eliminate that we won't miss when we get there?"

Dana scanned the table. "What if you packed *one* outfit per kid per day and then a few, as in *three*, gender-neutral onesies with pants for emergencies? Plan for each baby to re-wear the same pajamas all three nights and take an extra set or two." She held up three packages of baby wipes. "Do you go through a whole package of wipes in a day?"

Josie took one of the packages and set it next to the offloaded pacifiers. "Sometimes. They were slow to sit up, but they can spit pureed carrots like the fate of the world rests on their distance record. Hence the multiple outfits."

Dana responded by holding up eight bibs. "Do the grandparents not have running water? Just wash them off between meals."

Josie yanked four of them from her hand and tossed them onto the counter.

They continued whittling the stack until everything but a large box of diapers fit into a suitcase, albeit the largest suitcase in the house. The women exchanged triumphant high fives.

Dana pushed the suitcase underneath the table. "Where are the babies going to sleep? And will this giant suitcase fit in the van with that locomotive of a stroller?"

Emmaline had assured her they had portable cribs as well as saucers and highchairs, which would free up a ton of cargo space.

"We bought two umbrella strollers, so poor Peg will stay home alone."

Dana put her finger under her chin like she was thinking through a problem. "I want to come back to the fact that you have named and personified your triple stroller, but don't *two* umbrella strollers still leave you a seat short?"

"A double and a single. The twin umbrella stroller weighs like fifty pounds less than Peg. Granted, it's too wide for a regular doorway, but whatever. We just won't go inside anywhere. As for naming the sixty-pound transport vehicle, it's short for the brand name." Josie indicated the wallflower parked in the corner with a game show model's flourish. "I can't help it if she has taken on a life of her own."

The expression on Dana's face was unreadable. Perhaps she thought Josie had lost some of her marbles. Maybe she had. Nevertheless, Josie silently prayed the Hardings would not have to move away. This friendship was essential to her very existence.

Josie refreshed their coffee mugs that had been ignored until now. "Since you've sorted out my packing crisis, can you help me repair my relationship with my sister?" Josie asked.

Dana scooted a highchair out of the way and sat at the kitchen counter. "Sorry. Only child, remember? All I know about sisters is what I saw at my friends' houses growing up. The older ones get mad when you borrow their clothes, and the younger ones rat you out when you break a rule."

Josie snorted. "That checks out. I just don't understand why Laurel's ghosting me. And even though she never comes to visit, she expects everyone to travel out of state to her engagement party on short notice. Now my mom's feelings are hurt that we are going to OKC instead."

Her complaint didn't elicit the sympathy from Dana she had hoped it would.

"I can understand why you'd feel hurt, but how is planning a different trip for the same weekend going to teach her a lesson? It's only going to intensify the rift between the two of you and cause one with your mother."

Josie crossed her arms. "Oh, what do you know? You're an only child," she snipped.

Dana laughed. "You know I'm right. I'm not saying you should cancel your trip, but you need to talk to your sister and your mom. It's understandable that their feelings would be hurt that you're choosing to go to OKC instead of Albuquerque."

"The party is in Denver, actually. That's at least three hours further than OKC, more depending on traffic. Hunter and I even talked about me going up there by myself or only taking one baby, but I don't want to be separated from any of them on Mother's Day. I *earned* the right to be celebrated this year."

"There are direct flights out of Lubbock to Denver, you know. If you all flew, that would be easier than driving," Dana suggested.

Was she serious? Could Dana hear how entitled she sounded? Like hopping a plane was the easier, more convenient mode of travel, and anyone could do it.

Josie tilted her head and scratched her eyebrow. "Sure.

You know only one lap child is allowed to sit in a row, so we would have to buy *three* tickets, check *three* car seats *and* the sixty-pound stroller because car seats don't snap onto umbrella strollers, and we wouldn't have enough hands to carry them." She could see Dana putting the pieces together.

"I guess you'd have to rent a large vehicle once you got there too, wouldn't you?"

Josie gave her a thumbs up. " So, flying's not at all easier than driving. At least not for a few years." No one understood life with multiples except other parents of multiples, she supposed. "Your heart is in the right place, and I'm not intentionally trying to hurt my mom, but the truth is, I'm crushed by Laurel's behavior toward me. I don't want to go out of my way to celebrate the engagement she still hasn't even told me about."

She went on to justify how boycotting Laurel's party was to her mom's benefit as well.

"When my mom comes here, she's extremely helpful and focused on us. If we made that trip, she would feel like she had to help *us* whenever she should be focused on the bride-to-be and meeting Jefferson's family. She doesn't *feel* like we're doing her a favor, but we are."

Dana rubbed her temples, and Josie braced for the rebuttal she could see brewing in her eyes. "I know my understanding of family dynamics is somewhat limited, but you're rationalizing your decision to make yourself feel better. I'd give anything to spend another Mother's Day with my mom, and I know she would have chosen to have my rowdy kids be with her instead of getting to 'focus' on other people any day." Dana made air quotes with her fingers.

She checked her watch and took her cup to the sink. "I've gotta go. You're free to spend Mother's Day with whomever you want, but don't believe your own lie. This is about *you* and how Laurel made *you* feel. You're not doing your mother any favors by staying away."

With that, she gave a small wave and left.

Josie's eyes stung with tears as she sagged into Hunter's recliner. She'd grown so accustomed to Dana's support that it had never occurred to her they might not see eye-to-eye on her predicament. She wished she'd kept the conversation superficial so Dana wouldn't have judged her for being a bad sister or daughter.

Her phone buzzed. She grabbed it, hoping to find an olive branch from Dana.

Mija, enjoy your trip. Give Em and Peter hugs from me XO

She may be on the outs with Dana, but at least her mom had forgiven her. She typed, You're not mad?

Her mom sent a shrugging girl emoji. I don't really want to spend my Mother's Day at an engagement party with strangers either. Even if the party's for my kid. (winking emoji) But you better not miss the wedding

Depends, typed Josie. Are we even sure I'll be invited?

Her response was an eye roll emoji.

What was with her and the emojis today? Somehow having her mom's absolution inspired her to make amends with Dana right away. She slipped her phone into her back pocket and grabbed the baby monitor. She checked that everyone was still napping, locked the front door behind her, and jogged across the street.

Dana answered the door, eyes the size of saucers. "What's wrong?"

"You were right, and I'm sorry," panted Josie. "It bugs me that my relatives will go to Colorado for Laurel but not come here for me. And I am sort of punishing my whole family because of my sister, but I'm still not going to Denver, and I am taking my kids to Oklahoma." She bent over and put her hands on her knees to catch her breath and to avoid eye contact with Dana. "You've become like a sister to me. But better because you don't ignore my texts." The words spilled out in a rush. "I love you, and I really hope y'all don't move away."

Dana pulled her up and into a hug. "I love you too, and I'm sorry, too. I don't know what you're going through, and I have no right to judge your decision or to try and dissuade you from going to Oklahoma."

Josie backed off the porch. "Are we good?"

"We're good."

Josie waved the baby monitor as she walked away. Why couldn't things with Laurel be this easy?

Chapter 25

Dana

Dana checked her phone again. Still nothing. Today was Will's first day of unemployment, and he had gone to the office to deal with paperwork for human resources. It was also the first day of robotics club for Adam and her dad, and she expected to hear from someone, anyone, by now. No news was good news, she reminded herself.

Harvey barked and darted to the front door seconds before it flew open.

"Mom, did you know Pops knows how to connect wires and stuff?" Adam dropped his backpack in the middle of the floor and ruffled the fur on the dog's head. "Show her the pictures we took, Pops."

He hadn't made it to the porch yet. "Pops, come *on!*" Adam bounced on the balls of his feet.

Dana worried that robotics club might be too much for her dad after all. "You weren't this tired when you sawed that giant limb or when you went over Rita's whole yard with a metal detector," she said as she hugged him.

"Rita doesn't have twelve kids in her back yard."

"Pops, show mom the pictures on your phone." Adam's volume was several decibels louder than necessary.

"Alright, alright. By the way, I'm forgetful, not hard of

hearing. Take it down a notch." He unlocked his phone and handed it to Adam.

"Look at our robot, Mom. Isn't it cool? It can scoop up ping pong balls and drop them in a box." He had not lowered his voice even a little.

Dana scrolled through the many photos of feet, ping pong balls, and a robot. The angle and quantity indicated Adam's handiwork.

"I take it y'all had a fun afternoon at robotics club." She caught her dad's eye as he sagged into a chair. The hint of a grin played at the corners of his mouth as Adam regaled her with stories about his first day. After several minutes, Adam finally took a breath.

"Hey, buddy," said Dana, "why don't you go grab a snack? A *small one*. It's close to dinnertime." She watched him charge into the kitchen and turned back to her dad. "So, was it everything you thought it would be?"

He chuckled. "If you mean, did my daughter hustle me into volunteering for a club under the guise of spending time with my grandson, a grandson who had no knowledge of this club before today, then yes. Yes, she did."

Dana smirked without an ounce of remorse. "But did you have fun?"

"Probably not as much as Adam had, but I enjoyed it. That poor Miss Simms was so happy I came that she hugged me afterward and made me swear I would be back next week."

"I bet she did. She's brand-new this year, and she was roped into leading an afterschool club with a pregnant co-leader. I'm sure she is grateful for the help."

He propped his feet on an ottoman. "I'm staying for dinner. You owe me."

She laughed. "Well don't get your hopes too high for the meal, but you're always welcome. I made Cajun taco casserole."

"Never heard of it." Edward stuffed a throw pillow

behind his back and adjusted in his seat. "Is that one of those fusion dishes made up by a celebrity chef?"

She laughed. "No, more like the chef forgot to set a timer, and the casserole is slightly blackened. 'Cajun' sounds more appetizing than 'burnt.'"

Dana watched her dad. His weary countenance resembled someone who had done manual labor for hours rather than supervise a few kids for one. "I'm sorry I didn't tell you that Adam was a robotics newbie, but this is good for both of you. He needs more STEM implementation, and you get to interact with the youth, which will get your brain back in top form."

"You should have said more Stimulation," said Edward.

"Exactly!" She was happy her dad understood the benefit of robotics club for the two of them.

"S-T-E-M-ulation. You missed a great pun," he said.

"Your dad jokes are STEMulating," she deadpanned.

Edward told Dana how Adam's enthusiasm had won the other kids over after their initial reluctance to let in a new kid so late in the semester. "He didn't mind fetching and cleaning up, so they accepted him and let him help set up the obstacle course."

Dana remarked that it seemed a bit advanced for a group of third through fifth graders. "Maybe I forced the two of you into something above Adam's competency level."

"Meh, the kit is basically fool proof if the kids follow instructions and work together, according to Miss Simms. The competition gets fiercer, and the robots more complex as the kids get older."

The door to the garage flung open.

"Hi Dad," said Adam.

Dana poked her head in the kitchen in time to see Will set carryout bags on the counter. "You were already writing off my cajun casserole?"

"No, didn't know you made one. I always bring home dinner on Thursdays."

She smacked her forehead. "Oh no, I totally forgot."

"How did you forget it's Thursday?"

Dana checked her watch and gathered her laptop and purse. "I spent half the day updating my resumé and applying for jobs online. I guess I was so preoccupied that it slipped my mind." She realized what she had said aloud and froze. She and Will hadn't told her dad and the kids about his layoff yet, and she hadn't discussed job hunting with Will.

"Wow, Mom, you're finally going to get a real job?" asked Nate who slipped in to assess the takeout.

She had an urge to thump him. "At the rate you keep outgrowing shoes, one of us needs to, and since you're underage, I guess it has to be me," she replied.

Will glared at her. "Mom's just looking for ways to procrastinate finishing her novel," he said. "She's not really getting another job, *are* you, Honey?"

His tone had an edge to it that she hoped the children and her father hadn't noticed.

"Sure," she said. "But you should stop growing, to be on the safe side," she told Nate.

Dana took her usual seat in the front row and nodded hello to Carlos. She hoped he wouldn't call on her to read tonight because she had nothing new to contribute. Next week was their final class of the semester. If she could fly under the radar until then, she wouldn't have to tell Carlos she couldn't cut it as a real writer. There weren't enough hours in the day to fix everyone's problems, clean up their messes, *and* create fascinating characters and edge-of-your-seat plot twists.

At the end of class, Carlos stopped her at the door. "How's the extended version of 'Dying to Donate' coming along?"

Dana pressed her lips into a thin line. "It's coming. I don't know how much I will be able to accomplish this summer when the kids are out of school, but I'm plugging along." She almost crossed her fingers behind her back as she told the lie.

He smiled. "Great, if you want me to proofread it, let me know. I don't mind. I also think once you have the first five chapters polished, you should submit them to my agent Elise. She did love your story, you know. She could give you feedback and might even offer you representation."

"Why would she do that for me, an unknown author?" she asked.

Carlos told her Elise owed him a favor and offered nothing further.

She squirmed under his gaze. "Carlos, to be honest, I keep running into snags. With all the family issues we have going on, I can barely keep up, and I'm not sure I'm cut out for this." She left out the specifics. Her dad seemed to be improving, and she now knew that her husband wasn't having an affair, but it was still almost impossible to find time in her schedule to write.

He wagged his index finger at her. "Don't sell yourself short. You have the soul of a writer. I see it in you. I hope you can see it in yourself." He tapped the edge of her desk thoughtfully. "I'll see you next week."

Her dad's car was still parked in front of the house when she got home. Robotics club must have energized him more than it wore him out.

She entered through the garage to a quiet house. Will was working on his laptop at the coffee table. Through the glow of the screen, she saw her father dozing in the same chair he'd sat in before she left. Will looked up to acknowledge her.

"Where are the kids?" she whispered. "It's unnaturally quiet down here."

"The boys are getting ready for bed, and her royal highness is doing homework."

Dana angled her head toward her dad and raised her eyebrows.

"He drifted off after dinner while Adam was showing us the pictures he took at robotics. We should probably wake him and send him home though."

That was concerning. No one could sleep through Adam telling a story. She gently shook Edward's shoulder. "Dad, the coast is clear. You can sneak away now." She shook him harder. "Dad, wakey wakey."

He slumped sideways.

"Dad!" She shrieked and pressed the side of his neck. His skin was warm, but she couldn't feel a pulse.

Will jumped up from the sofa and leaned over Edward. "Help me get him to the floor. I'll start compressions, and you call 911."

Will and Dana grabbed hold of Edward's arms and legs to lower him to the floor, which woke him with a start.

"What the heck are you doing to me?" He flailed to right himself and gripped the arms of the chair.

"I thought you were dead. I couldn't wake you, and then I couldn't find your pulse."

He put his own fingers to the side of his neck. "Blood's pumping fine."

Dana slid to the floor beside the chair, and Will put his hands on his thighs. She hadn't panicked like that in…she couldn't remember ever panicking like that. It took her a minute to catch her breath.

Leah appeared in the doorway. "Why is mom yelling? And why is she on the floor?"

Edward stood. "Everything's fine, Granddaughter. Your mom just scares easily." He kissed the top of her head. "I'm heading home now. Thank you for a lovely evening, everyone."

Leah returned to her room. Dana was still crouched on the floor with her head on her knees.

Her dad bent over and put his hand on her shoulder. "I appreciate you trying to resuscitate this old man."

She covered his hand with hers. "I love you, Dad. I don't know what I would do without you."

He kissed her head, waved to Will, and left.

Will, who had said nothing since her dad awoke, stared at Dana.

"What? You saw how he fell over when I shook him. What was I supposed to think?"

He pulled her off the floor and into a hug. She felt his body quiver with stifled laughter.

She freed herself from the embrace. "You're laughing at me now? I thought my father had passed away in our living room."

"I'm sorry, honey. I imagined I was Edward, and I awoke to two people trying to wrestle me to the ground. We're lucky he didn't slug us."

She chuckled too. "I bet he never falls asleep over here again."

Will led her to the sofa. "Poor Ed. He's had quite the day. First, he kept a dozen kids from electrocuting themselves, and then we tried to give him CPR."

She confessed to Will that sometimes she thought she was selfishly pushing her dad to take care of himself not for his sake, but for hers. She wasn't ready to lose another parent. "I practically forced him to help the robotics club, and he was so wrung out afterward that I thought it killed him. What kind of daughter does that?"

He tried to soothe her. "You only want what's best for him, and he knows that."

She slumped against him. "I don't know. I haven't been my best self lately. I've been trying to control things that aren't mine to control and making things worse. I misled my dad into believing Adam was in robotics. I even lied to you about my tire that day because I saw the text on your phone that Helena was meeting you at your office, and I wanted to see if there was something going on between you two."

He laughed again. She elbowed him in the ribs. "Why is that so funny?"

"You were jealous of the woman who took over my company and put me out of a job. And also, I kind of figured that out when I saw you leave in your own car."

"Will, I don't even know who I am. And I don't mean in the way my dad sometimes doesn't recognize us. I mean, who am I besides your wife, the mother of our kids, and my dad's daughter and part-time caregiver?" She didn't wait for him to answer. "Obviously I'm *not* a writer because I'm too busy to write. I even forgot about my writing class tonight. It feels like every day around here is pure chaos and damage control. I'm having an identity crisis because I don't have time to *be* anyone other than the fixer."

Will shushed her. "You've had a wild night, and you're not speaking truth over yourself. You're never going to find your identity in titles and accomplishments because who you are rests in being a child of the Most High King. Anything else you do will always pale in comparison. Got it?" He kissed her nose.

Dana nodded.

"Besides, I think being the wife of Will Harding kind of makes you a rock star," he teased.

Harvey licked her hand.

"I'm already getting stalked by my number one fan."

Chapter 26

Josie

The Harding kids had a student holiday, so Josie had handy childcare for her lunch date with Zooey. She couldn't remember ever being this excited about meeting a friend in the middle of a weekday. One of the perks of staying home with babies was how thankful it made her for adult interaction.

She and Zooey had been talking and texting often since they'd reconnected on Wednesday nights. She'd learned that her former coworker was up for a promotion. Zooey was such an engaging person who made others feel important in her presence. She would be a wonderful supervisor, and Josie prayed she would get the position. This was to be their pre-celebratory lunch.

A knock on the front door preceded Leah's announcement. "We're here."

Josie checked the time on her phone. "You're early."

"Mom was about to make us do chores, so we told her you needed time to get ready," said Nate. Smart kid.

"That's great, actually. The babies had food and will be ready for bottles and naps in about half an hour. In the meantime, they're excited to play."

She checked her reflection in the bathroom mirror and slipped her favorite gold hoops into her ears. Nothing could make a girl feel pretty with less effort than a good pair of hoops. They were weapons in the hands of grabby infants, though, so she hadn't gotten to wear them in months. Satisfied with her appearance, Josie grabbed her keys and wallet.

"Josie, your phone's ringing," called Leah from the living room.

She hadn't even remembered setting it down. Zooey's name lit up the screen, and her heart sank. What were the odds this *wasn't* a last-minute cancellation call?

"Zooey, what's up?" Disappointment crept over her, even as she kept her tone light.

"Girl, I'm so sorry, but the school just called. Darius needs stitches. Can we take a raincheck."

She heard the fear in Zooey's voice. "Is he alright?"

"Uh, I don't know. They said he cut his hand on the playground."

Josie urged her to keep her posted and to let her know if she could help her somehow. She ended the call and flashed a tight smile at the Harding kids.

"Ah man, we have to go home and clean house now, don't we?" Nate lamented.

He sounded as disappointed as she felt, but Darius needed his mom worse than Josie needed a lunch date with an old friend. Inspiration struck her. "Not necessarily. What were your favorite foods and treats when you were six?"

She made a note of the suggestions Leah and Nate gave her and went to the store. There wasn't much she could do to help Zooey, but at least she could ease her evening stress a little. Josie would make a kid-approved dinner and pick up some get well soon treats for Darius. She made sure to get two of everything so his little sister wouldn't be left out.

She came home with arms loaded with more groceries than hers and Zooey's families could possibly eat in a week. The Harding kids had gotten the triplets down for naps and reluctantly trudged home to do their chores. Josie promised to send over any criers to interrupt their work. Then she set about preparing two pans of her mom's famous chicken enchilada recipe, one to deliver to Zooey, and one to surprise Hunter tonight. She'd even had the forethought to buy disposable metal pans so no one had to worry about washing and returning dishes.

By 3:00, the enchiladas were ready to come out of the oven, and a pan of brownie batter was ready to go in. She set the timer on her phone and saw a message from Zooey. She'd sent a photo of Darius holding up his hand with four black sutures poking out of his palm like spider legs.

Josie needed both her hands to finish her meal prepping, so she called Zooey and set the phone on the counter in speaker mode.

"How did it go? Was it awful?" She couldn't imagine holding one of her kids while a doctor stitched a wound closed.

"He was a trooper. The worst part was when she injected lidocaine into his hand. I had to put my head between my legs to keep from passing out."

She pulled out a cutting board and began chopping vegetables for a garden salad. "What did he get cut on? I thought school playgrounds were supposed to be kid friendly."

"Right? Darius said there was broken glass in the area where he and some other boys were playing football. The nurse told me they've had a problem with homeless people using the playground after hours. She said the staff walks the grounds every morning to pick up trash and chase off the occasional person sleeping in a doorway, but pieces of broken beer bottles are easily overlooked." Zooey paused for the briefest of moments. "What in the world is going on at your house? It sounds like you're busy."

"I'm being productive. And don't even think about a dinner plan because I've got it covered."

Zooey conveyed her surprise and gratitude. Before they hung up, they planned for Josie to stop by in a couple of hours.

Josie shot a text to Dana requesting the big kids to come back over so she could deliver dinner. Then she looked around her kitchen wondering what to do next. With the babies still asleep, making dinner for two families hadn't taken nearly as long as she'd anticipated. She had even prepared dinosaur shaped chicken nuggets and boxed macaroni—the name brand, per Leah's emphatic instructions. Maybe she would do this more often.

Zooey met Josie as she was coming up the walk and took a large grocery bag from her hands. "You did *not* have to do all this."

"I wanted to cheer up Darius and give you one less thing to have to think about tonight," Josie said. "I remember when I fell off the monkey bars and broke my wrist. Getting x-rayed was so scary. And then that awful cast made me miserable for weeks."

The women unloaded their wares in the kitchen. "It smells divine. Maybe we should get injured around here more often."

Zooey's two-year-old jumped from the arm of the sofa to the coffee table.

"Be careful what you wish for." Josie nodded in her direction. "I think that one might be a daredevil in training."

Zooey shouted at her daughter to get down using her first, middle, and last names. "We're going to have to find a school with a padded playground for her."

"Speaking of school, why didn't Darius have a holiday like Dana's kids did today?"

Zooey snagged a brownie. Her eyes rolled back as she savored it. "Private school. They don't get out when the other kids do. This is heaven, Jos."

"Why don't they have a barrier fence to protect the playground like every other school in town?" Josie asked.

"They do, but it's falling apart. Some of the parents are demanding that it get fixed, but the headmaster said they can either fix the fence or retain the dual language program, but at the current tuition rate, they can't do both. It's a great school, and Darius loves it, but the location is not the best."

Josie thought back to her own childhood playground in Albuquerque. It had little more than a small blacktop with weeds growing through the cracks and three swings on a gravel island. The grass around it had served as a ball field, running track, and infinite magical kingdoms in make believe realms. That scant playground had been central to the most exciting part of each school day. Every kid deserved a recess that ended in long water breaks and a smelly classroom full of worn-out kids, not one that landed them in urgent care.

On her way home, she detoured by Darius's elementary campus. Not only was the gate leading to the playground rusty and broken, but there were several places in the six-foot chain-link fence that needed repairs. Anyone could slip through without bothering to walk around to the gate. She snapped some photos of the disrepair and formulated a plan.

Hunter moaned and closed his eyes while he chewed. "Babe, don't tell your mom, but I think your enchiladas might be even better than hers."

She laughed. "I might tell her the next time she criticizes my housekeeping." Josie showed him the photos she'd taken of the school yard. "How much do you think it would cost to redo a fence like that to keep out people who don't belong there?"

He swallowed a bite of his dinner. "Cyclone fencing is cheap and easy to install. That's why we use it to secure construction sites."

Josie warmed a brownie and scooped vanilla ice cream on top. She set the bowl on the table, just out of Hunter's reach. "I don't suppose you and your business partner could scrounge up the funds and manpower to fix this fence?"

He reached for the bowl, but she pulled it back. Her raised eyebrows let him know she would hand over the dessert when she got the answer to her question.

"I don't see why not. We probably spent more on the table at that charity dinner than we would replacing the gate and repairing that fence. I'll work it out with Todd if you can get the school to sign off on it."

"It shouldn't be too difficult since it's a private school with no red tape." Her mind was already working overtime. After dinner she set a reminder on her phone to contact the school tomorrow. Once they were on board, she would talk to Serena and Dana and see about organizing the Wednesday moms to clean up the playground. Having a goal was energizing. She hadn't even realized she was smiling as she typed notes into her phone until Hunter pointed it out.

"What are you grinning at? You're not texting some guy who drives a sports car instead of a minivan on the weekends, are you?"

She rolled her eyes at him. "I had a good day is all. It's nice to be the one helping instead of depending on other people to help me for a change."

The headmaster at Brighton Academy jumped at the opportunity to have the fence professionally repaired and the grounds cleaned up. Serena and Dana were easy sells. By Wednesday, the moms were on standby to plan a Saturday morning service project as soon as the work on the fence was completed.

Chapter 27

Dana

Dana held her breath when Harvey licked Yvette's daughter CiCi in the face. He outweighed her by a solid one hundred pounds, but the toddler only giggled and wrapped her arms around his furry neck. "Dis puppy yikes me."

After a few minutes, Harvey grew weary of CiCi's overzealous affection and tried to hide from her under the coffee table.

"We have a cat and an elderly leopard gecko at our house," said Yvette. "They're both terrified of her right now."

Dana wondered what was considered elderly for a leopard gecko.

"My husband Matt got it for his fifteenth birthday. Apparently, they can live up to twenty years."

"Wow!" said Dana. "Who knew?"

"Certainly not I when I married a man with a terrarium in his living room."

Dana had brought a tub of Legos down from Adam's room. When CiCi finally gave up trying to coax Harvey from beneath the table, she asked Dana to help her build a princess Lego house.

Yvette watched them from the sofa. "So as a veteran mom, tell me how long it will take realistically once the new baby arrives to establish a good routine with her and CiCi?"

"Uh, how long did it take when CiCi was born?" Routines were not Dana's strong suit. She couldn't even remember how she kept three kids alive when Adam was a newborn. "My guess is about that long. Give or take a few weeks."

Yvette laughed. "I thought I was going to learn all the secrets of motherhood when I joined the Wednesday night group."

"Same," said Dana. "Turns out, the real secret is that no one knows what they're doing in this job. We're all winging it."

"And I suspect we all believe we are failing miserably at it."

Dana handed a pink brick to CiCi. "I think that about sums up the heart of motherhood right there. We give it everything we have and still worry we aren't right for the job."

Yvette scratched the side of her baby bump. Dana remembered how itchy growing humans could be. One of the many parts of pregnancy she didn't miss. In fact, the only part she enjoyed was feeling her babies moving and getting to park near the door at the supermarket.

She asked Yvette what her family was like growing up.

"I'm the middle child of five, only girl, so basically loud. We lived on a farm, and everyone showed sheep or pigs in 4-H and ag."

"Are you close with your brothers now?" She thought of Josie and the turmoil she was experiencing with her sister.

"Some more than others. The youngest is kind of the black sheep, and he's worrying our mom to death right now. The oldest is a workaholic and doesn't come to family holidays much, but we keep in touch." She pointed at CiCi and at her belly. "I hope these two have a good relationship. It makes life easier and more fun when you're friends with your siblings."

Dana tucked her hair behind her ear. Yvette couldn't have known she'd struck a nerve. Having a sister to walk with her through her mother's illness surely would have eased the burden. Unless of course, they were at odds like Josie and her sister were.

Yvette hoisted herself off the sofa. "Cecilia, it's time for us to get out of Miss Dana's hair. Let's clean up now."

CiCi obediently dropped the bricks back into the bin. "Bye, Harvey." She ducked under the table to snuggle the dog.

Yvette reached for her purse. "So, you're good with watching her next week when I go to my appointment?"

"Of course. But I don't mind coming to your house if that would be easier. I'm sure CiCi would be more comfortable in her own home where there are more toys for kids her age." Harvey would probably appreciate it if Dana babysat CiCi at her own house too.

"That would be great. I'll send you our address."

When they left, Dana reviewed her list of questions for the Wednesday night group. The ever-changing name, or lack thereof was getting old.

She texted Serena. We need to come up with a fitting name once and for all.

Serena replied within seconds. I have a million ideas… The Edification Station, Mission: Connect, The Fellowship of the Moms (like Lord of the Ring)

Dana rubbed her forehead. She dialed Serena's number. "Why is this so complicated?"

"Everything about motherhood is complicated, so it stands to reason that naming a group for moms would be too."

Serena was right. Momming was hard, important work, and there was no title that could rightfully encompass all of that. "We all attend because we need an extra measure of grace for the journey from likeminded people who understand."

Serena replied, "So, Embracing Grace?"

It wasn't worse than any of the other suggestions she'd had. Her screen lit up with her dad's name.

"My dad's calling me."

Serena told her she hoped everything was alright with Edward and ended the call.

"Hey, Dad." She about jumped when a woman's voice replied.

"Dana, it's Rita Brewer." This couldn't be good.

Her stomach twisted into a knot. "Is everything alright?"

"Sure. He's driving, and we were on our way to your house and took a wrong turn, so I need to type your address into my map. That's why I called from Edward's phone. I'm gonna put you on speaker so I can type it in."

Rita sounded so casual, like it was a normal occurrence for her dad to bring his neighbor to her house and forget where she lived. And neither senior citizen realized they could talk on the phone and use their map app at the same time. Dana tried to keep her own tone light to mask her worry. She gave Rita her address and pulled up the device locator app to see how far off course he'd gotten.

He was close and had probably turned a block too soon, cutting off access to her cul-de-sac. She'd done it herself a few times when they first moved in.

"Okay, Dana, I'm hanging up so I can tell Edward where to turn. See you in a sec."

The line went dead before she could reply. Why on earth were they coming to her house, and why hadn't her dad given her any warning?

She put Harvey in the back yard and waited on the front porch for them to pull up. When they arrived, she met them in the driveway. The back seat of the car was full of boxes and clothes.

Her dad popped the trunk and stepped out. "Before you say anything, I didn't get lost because I'm forgetful. Well not *just* because of that. Rita distracted me."

"Dad, what is all this?" The scent of her mother's perfume flooded her nostrils as she peered into the trunk at her mother's belongings.

"What does it look like? We cleaned out your mother's closet and dresser."

Dana looked around. For what, she wasn't sure, but she needed help from somewhere. She put her hands on her hips. "You're not unloading all of Mom's stuff here. I have a full house already. What was wrong with your house?"

"Well, that's just it," he said. "It's time for me to move on and let her go. I've kept a few sentimental items and her jewelry for you at my house. This is what's left to donate to the church benevolence center, but I thought you should take a look first and make sure I didn't get rid of anything you wanted to keep."

It would take hours to go through every item in this car.

Rita appeared next to her. "I've categorized everything so you can look through it all quickly. We don't even need to take anything in the house."

Dana sighed. She wasn't going to get out of this, but at least Rita had the forethought to sort her mother's life into manageable pieces that all fit into the back of one car. She leaned into the trunk and flipped through the boxes of shirts and pants.

Carolyn Johnson dressed well for a woman of her age. Her idea of dressing down was a sweater set over dark, creased jeans. Dana's taste leaned more heavily toward faded jeans and joggers, never ever creased. Even if she wanted to dress like a woman in her seventies, her mother was taller and two sizes smaller than she was. Neither did they share the same shoe size. This was doomed to be an exercise in futility. A waste of all their time.

She was about to pull the trunk lid down and comment on Rita's careful organization when she eyed the sleeve of a denim button down. She tugged the shirt out of the stack, careful to keep the rest of the pile in its box. It had a rose embroidered on the breast pocket with the words "Grow Joy" in cursive script above it. The sleeves were ragged and stained from years of gardening, and one of the elbows was patched with plaid flannel.

Dana hugged the shirt to her chest and inhaled her mother's scent. The tears spilled over her cheeks before she realized they'd even left her eyes. Rather than temper her emotions, she leaned against the car and wept into the fabric that had protected her mother's arms from rose thorns and sunburn. It could not, however, protect her from her own pain.

"Oh, sweetheart." Her father wrapped his arms around her and crushed her to his chest. He held her until her sobs ebbed. "I'm sorry. I didn't mean to upset you."

"I miss her so much," she whispered through sniffles. Finally, she wiped her face on her sleeve and wrapped her mom's gardening shirt around her shoulders. "Show me the back seat."

She ran her fingers over a red and white sequined snowflake sweater that her mom had worn every Christmas day. She pulled it out and draped it over her shoulder. Maybe she could talk the family into a silly Christmas sweater photo. That would honor her mom and embarrass her kids at the same time. Double win.

She kept another oversized sweater that her mom had deemed her "rainy day cozy sweater" and pronounced the rest ready to be donated.

She invited Rita and her dad to come in, but they declined. "We better get this stuff to the church before our bodies realize how hard we worked packing it all up," Rita said. "We'll be stiff once we sit for a spell."

"You sure you remember how to get out of the neighborhood?" She razzed her dad.

Rita held up her phone. "I still have the map pulled up."

Dana waved as they pulled away, taking her mother's worldly possessions with them.

Josie stepped onto her porch. "Everything okay? I wasn't spying, but I saw you crying and hugging your dad when I was washing bottles."

Dana crossed the street hugging her mother's shirts to her chest. She smiled tightly and forced her grief to retreat into the depths of her soul. "Yeah, Dad and his neighbor finally cleaned out my mom's personal effects. They wanted me to give my blessing over the stuff to be donated."

"That's good for him, right?"

She squeezed herself tighter and nodded. "It's just so final. And weird that he had another woman helping him do it. A few weeks ago, he called her a busybody. Now she's helping him get rid of my mom's belongings." As she spoke it, she realized the ridiculousness in her own words. Her mom wasn't coming back for any of it. "I'll be fine. I assumed the day would come when my dad would ask me to help him go through her things, and I would be strong for him while we did that. Having them show up with everything he planned to get rid of caught me off guard."

Josie thumbed at the door behind her. "Do you want to come in for coffee or tea?"

All she wanted to do was hide from the world, but maybe Josie invited her in because she needed adult interaction. She studied Josie's face. She was different today. She looked happy, well rested even. Maybe some of Josie's new outlook would be contagious.

"That would be great, thanks."

Josie told Dana about the fence replacement at Darius's school, and they talked over the plans for the upcoming cleanup project on Saturday morning.

"I'm bringing Will and the kids. I don't see any reason we shouldn't get the whole thing knocked out in record time." She hoped that was true because she needed to spend the afternoon alone with her manuscript. She was so far behind in writing her novel that she'd be a great grandmother by the time she finished it.

Chapter 28

Josie

What should have been a six-hour drive from Lubbock to Oklahoma City had now surpassed eight, thanks to the triplets.

Hunter had to pull off the highway three times for diaper changes because the babies wouldn't coordinate their bodily functions with fuel stops. A garbage bag of dirty diapers was stashed in the furthest corner of the van and needed to be removed as soon as possible. Josie was sure the poop smell would never fully come out of the upholstery, but the stench of sour spit up masked it somewhat.

The screaming from the back seat subsided as Hunter pulled off the congested interstate and zig-zagged through the suburban neighborhoods. By the time they arrived in the driveway of the large, single-story home shared by Hunter's parents, grandparents, and older brother Stephen, all three babies were asleep.

Hunter killed the engine and turned around. "Of course. They're exhausted from tormenting us for hours, so the grandparents will think they're perfect angels."

Before Josie and Hunter could unbuckle a single car seat, Emmaline and Peter rushed out to meet them in the driveway.

"You made it!" said Emmaline. "I couldn't wait one more second to get my hands on my grandbabies." She took Ben from Hunter and cradled his head to her chest. "Oh goodness. You have grown so much since I saw you last, my sweet Ben."

The boys weren't identical, but Josie marveled that Emmaline could tell them apart when she hadn't seen them in person in months.

She passed Ben to Peter and repeated the same showering of affection on Olivia. "Everyone, come inside. Dinner will be here in twenty minutes."

Hunter climbed into the minivan to get Connor. "You didn't cook, Ma?"

"And take time away from my babies?"

Stephen and Grandpa appeared on the porch waiting to greet the family as they filed in carrying babies and bags.

Hunter handed the garbage bag of dirty diapers to his brother. "Happy early birthday, bro."

"Nice, I actually thought that sewage smell was you." Stephen punched Hunter in the arm before hauling the diapers to the garbage bin on the side of the garage.

Josie had come to accept their ribbing as brotherly affection, but she hoped her own boys would behave more maturely.

The interior of the house looked a little different than Josie remembered it. Hunter's grandparents had the home built in the late eighties, but gone were the brass doorknobs and the grapevine wallpaper of the past. She took in all the changes and caught Emmaline's eye.

"I've been doing some updating. When Mama feels good, I keep busy with projects around here."

"It looks great." said Josie. She pointed to three portable highchairs and an infant swing and bouncy seat. "You bought baby gear for three days?"

Emmaline waived her off. "These belong to the ladies in my Bible study group. We all hit up the church garage sales and children's resale shops and then pass things around to whomever has visiting grandbabies. Between the six of us, we could stock a day care center. I set up the portable cribs in your room already. It's a little tight, but you can store your luggage on the top bunk to save floor space."

Behind Emmaline's back, Josie mouthed to Hunter, *Bunk beds?* When they had come to visit for holidays in years past, the bunk bedroom had been occupied by the unmarried brothers. Josie should have guessed that Stephen would have moved into the room with the queen bed.

When they were planning the trip, Hunter and Josie had intended to get a hotel room nearby to limit the stress on his grandparents, but the elder Caraways wouldn't hear of it.

"We built this house to fill with family," Grandpa had said. How were they to argue with that? But as she dropped the diaper bag on the full-size lower bunk and side-stepped the three portable cribs, she wondered if staying here was the right call.

After she finished pumping and headed to the kitchen with two bottles of breast milk, she caught Hunter and his grandmother sharing a moment. Hunter helped Grandma hold Olivia on her lap. Her speech was limited after her stroke, but her pride and love were written on her face. That was all the reassurance Josie needed that going to a hotel would have been a mistake.

A few hours later when the triplets refused to sleep in the Pack 'n Plays, she second guessed herself again. Emmaline and Peter had rocked babies to sleep, but they awoke as soon as they were put down. After several attempts, Josie and Hunter sent his parents to bed to contend with the criers on their own.

"I don't get it," said Hunter as he bounced Connor on his shoulder. "Are there invisible needles in the cribs or something?"

Maybe the cribs smelled funny, or the mesh walls scared them. Josie's back hurt from leaning over with her hands on Olivia's and Ben's chests in a fruitless effort to soothe them to sleep. Her patience was at its breaking point. "This isn't working. We're going to have to put them in the car and drive around until they fall asleep."

"And then what? They'll just wake up again when we stop."

Josie stood to stretch the soreness out of her lower back, but Olivia's whimper morphed into a wail as soon as her mother's hand left her.

"What if we try rocking them in their car seats?"

"Isn't that dangerous?"

She glared at her husband through the dim light. "What's dangerous is these little punks keeping all of us awake all night. And I don't see how sleeping next to us in car seats is any different from them sleeping in a moving vehicle."

Hunter put his hand over Connor's ear and turned sideways as if shielding him against his mother's words. "You called our babies punks."

"Not sorry. If they go to sleep, I'll apologize tomorrow."

Josie took Connor from Hunter so he could fetch the car seats from the van. Seconds later, the burglar alarm blared. Josie ran out of the room, pressing the baby's head to her chest to muffle the sound. She reached the hallway at the same time as Stephen did wearing only boxer shorts and wielding a baseball bat.

"Hunter went out the front door," she explained while keeping her gaze fixed on the ceiling.

Stephen ran to the keypad and disarmed the system as Peter raced in similarly dressed. Josie backed quickly into the bunk room and left Stephen to explain. Moments later, she heard Hunter come back inside.

"What are you doing sneaking out in the middle of the

night, son?" she heard Peter ask.

"Dad, it's 10:40 on a Friday night, and I don't have school tomorrow."

Josie's idea paid off, and all of the babies nodded off within minutes of being buckled into their seats.

"You loosened the straps so they can move around some, right?" she whispered.

"Yeah. Now let's try to sleep while they sleep." He eased himself onto the bottom bunk, but the mattress creaked anyway. Both parents flinched. The full-size bed was considerably more cramped than their king-size bed at home. Facing one another, Josie could feel Hunter's breath.

"This was a bad idea, wasn't it?" she whispered.

"Roll the other way then. But don't make a sound."

She meant the trip itself. Staying in the family home, doubling its typical occupancy, and disrupting everyone. "Maybe tomorrow we should check into the hotel after all. I'm worried we're going to give your grandmother another stroke. I almost had one myself when the alarm went off."

Hunter put his arm over her. "Let's not worry about it right now."

He drifted off while Josie lay awake listening to the soft breath of her children in the dark. Families were so complicated. They were the people you loved the most and the ones who could drive you to the brink of insanity the quickest.

The next morning, Emmaline and Grandpa made a huge breakfast, and everyone gathered around the dining table.

Hunter looked up from feeding Ben to tease his brother and dad. "It's good to see you both in pants for a change."

Stephen thumped him on the back of the head and shoveled a fork full of eggs into his mouth. "I was trying to protect the family. I wasn't thinking about my wardrobe."

"Too bad you weren't. I had to stop my wife from

gouging out her eyes last night."

"Boys, knock it off. Stephen, don't talk with food in your mouth," scolded Emmaline.

After breakfast, Josie read the paper beside Grandpa while her children were doted on and entertained. She couldn't even remember the last time she had held a newspaper, let alone read one. It made her feel more grown up somehow, more so than being a wife and mother in her thirties even.

A little while later, her mom texted. It was a group selfie of her mother, two of her aunts, and Laurel. Wish you were here, mija

Her gut ached. Part of her wished she were there too. She would have been in the back of a family selfie because she was a good four inches taller than all the women in her family.

"Everything okay, Josie?" asked Emmaline who was on the floor with Olivia and Ben. "You look like you got bad news."

She turned her phone around and showed her mother-in-law the photo. "My mom's trying to make me feel bad for not being in Denver for my sister's engagement party."

"Why didn't you go?"

Josie told her Laurel hadn't contacted her at all since meeting her new fiancé, and she felt unsupported as a new mom by most of her relatives. As she explained it though, the whole thing sounded ridiculous and juvenile in her own head. If in the future Connor refused to show up for Ben, even if Ben wasn't acting like a good brother at the time, she would be upset, like her mother was with her.

"I guess I feel a little guilty about not being there, but I still don't want to go, you know?"

Emmaline nodded. "I do. My own sister is a self-absorbed know-it-all."

Grandpa pulled down the newspaper to give her a disapproving look.

"Well, she is. One time, she Facetimed Daddy and saw that I had redone the kitchen and went ballistic about how I had no right to change something in a house that didn't belong to me." She lifted Olivia into a standing position and kissed her cheek. "Well anyway, I'm sorry about your family situation, but I'm very glad you're here. This was the best Mother's Day gift you and Hunter could have given to me or Mama."

Tension drained from Josie. Emmaline got it. What's more, she didn't lecture Josie or try to convince her to make amends. Instead, she took a cute photo of the babies with Josie's phone and told her to send it to her mom.

When the triplets went down for an afternoon nap, Emmaline took Josie to a nearby craft fair. They strolled up and down the rows of booths perusing each vendor's wares at a leisurely pace. Josie stopped in front of a textured painting of a sunflower. It looked like each individual petal had been applied to the canvas with cake frosting. The detail captivated her, and she longed to run her fingers over it.

She checked the price tag and balked. "I wish I could paint like this." The only way she'd be able to own it would be to replicate it herself.

"Did you ever take art classes?" asked Emmaline.

Josie shook her head. "Nope. Marie Saldana didn't believe in us wasting our educations on frivolous pursuits, and she considered art frivolous." She surveyed the other paintings in the same booth.

"But aren't you supposed to take fine art classes in school? What electives did you take?" asked Emmaline.

Josie picked up a small, bright abstract. It would look great in her guest bathroom. "Orchestra." She tapped her chest. "Third chair viola."

Emmaline's eyebrows arched. "How did I not know this? And why did your mom allow you to be in orchestra but not take art?"

"Hold on." Josie bought the little painting., and they moved on to the next booth.

"My mom didn't *allow* us to be in orchestra; she insisted on it. Laurel played the cello for one year before she revolted. She refused to practice, so she got kicked out of the orchestra. Her senior year she was still missing a fine art credit, so Mom's hand was pretty much forced at that point. Laurel got to take a photography class and be on the yearbook staff." Josie's brow furrowed at the memory.

"I could never openly defy my mom like that, so I stuck it out until graduation."

Emmaline touched Josie's arm. "Art was my passion when I was in school. I wanted to be a sculptor."

Josie's jaw dropped. She'd only known Emmaline as a stay-at-home mom. It never occurred to her that she might've aspired to be anything else.

"You know that big painting over the mantle at my parents' house?"

The impressionist seascape. Josie knew it because she had admired it for years. "I love that painting, but I never knew you painted it."

Emmaline told her she'd finished her degree in studio art four months before marrying Peter. She taught classes at a community center until she got pregnant with Stephen, but then she had to quit because the smell of the paints made her sick.

"After the boys came along, I got too busy with life to get back to it."

Her story reminded Josie of Dana. They both left pieces of themselves in the past as they sacrificed on behalf of their loved ones.

Emmaline nudged her shoulder. "What about you? What was your dream when you were younger?"

Josie recounted her cosmetology aspirations and how her parents pressured her to get a business degree. "Ever the compliant child, I did what they wanted me to. I'm thinking when the babies are older, I might try to go back to school and get a cosmetology license."

Emmaline put her arm around her. "Oh Jos, that would be incredible! You have beautiful hair, and you always style it so gorgeously. I'm so sorry you didn't get to do that sooner, but there's still time."

Josie touched the side of her ponytail. Messy buns and ponytails were the only way to keep tiny fingers from grabbing fistfuls of it. Emmaline's sincerity moved her, though.

She smiled. "Thank you for bringing me here. I'm having a great time with you."

They spent another hour wandering the booths. Emmaline bought matching sun hats with rubber duckies on them for the triplets, and they split a funnel cake.

Emmaline moaned. "I love a good cholesterol frisbee. They remind me of happy childhood memories."

Josie pinched off a bite, savoring it. She couldn't remember the last time she'd had funnel cake, but she'd never be able to eat it again without remembering this happy memory. Or without calling it a cholesterol frisbee.

Chapter 29

That evening, Marie Facetimed from Laurel's engagement party. Her phone panned the crowd. and Josie estimated there were close to fifty guests.

"See the guy in the gray suit standing next to your sister? That's Jefferson." She spoke to someone in the room. "Laurel, Jefferson, come say hi to Josie and Hunter."

Laurel and her fiancé briefly turned from their conversation with another guest to wave from a distance, but neither of them moved closer to speak on camera. Josie held her breath and waited for her mom to react. Sure, her sister had ignored her for months, but she was doing so now blatantly in front of their mom.

She turned the camera back on herself and brought it in close. "It's just as well. He's a bit of a drip. I wasn't expecting a rocket scientist out of a river guide, but he should really move to a lower altitude where some oxygen gets to his brain cells."

Hunter's mouth gaped. "Goodness, Marie, what did you say about me the first time we met?"

Josie cleared her throat and changed the subject before her mother could embarrass her in front of the in-laws. "Where are Dad and Alana?"

Her mom shrugged. "Not here. Laurel said he couldn't get away. Maybe the trophy wife's behind was getting a little low, so she's in the shop for a nip and tuck.'"

"Mom!"

"What?" She brushed off Josie's admonishment with the swipe of her hand. "The woman ran out of original parts fifteen years ago. She's probably due for some resurfacing."

Her mother's bitterness at being replaced with a much younger, albeit higher maintenance wife hadn't subsided after all these years. Josie wondered though if her mother envied the longevity of her dad and Alana's marriage, which had thus far lasted five years longer than her mom's marriage to him.

She and her mom exchanged good-byes, and Josie plastered on a happy face to hide her hurt at Laurel's snub.

"Shake it off, sweetheart," said Emmaline. "If he's as dim as your mom says, then Laurel might have been trying to preserve her dignity by keeping him from saying something foolish." Her tone turned from soothing to playfully malevolent. "Or maybe he has a Nanny McPhee tooth and gnarly mole that she didn't want you to see."

Josie was sure her mother would have mentioned Jefferson having an incisor four times bigger than the rest of his teeth, but it was kind of funny. She smiled at Emmaline. "Thank you."

"Let's talk about tomorrow," said Emmaline, diplomatically changing the subject. "We take Mama and Daddy to the early service, and we would love for you all to join us. My Bible study friends will be so jealous when they see how much cuter my grandbabies are than theirs."

Josie and Hunter caught each other's eye across the room. She knew they were thinking the same thing. Early service would be a challenge, as they did well to roll into the late service on time, but it was Mother's Day. And how many more opportunities would they get for four generations of the family to sit on a pew together?

Rummaging through suitcases and bumping into cribs slowed down the process of getting ready for church. Negotiating their tight quarters was taking its toll on Hunter and Josie's moods.

"Why do the babies need to wear shoes?" Hunter griped. "Shoes are chew toys to them."

"You heard your mom. She wants to show off her grandbabies." Josie twisted her hair into a topknot. "We can't have her friends shaking their heads and judging what kind of mother sends her babies to church with cold, bare feet."

"There are no shoes in this suitcase, Jos. I've looked everywhere."

She squeezed past him and pulled out three tiny pairs of shoes from the inside pocket, the exact spot she had indicated to him. "They're right here. How did you miss them?"

"Maybe they would have been easier to spot if you hadn't crammed everything we own into that thing."

Hunter's dad poked his head around the open door. "What can I do to help?"

Hunter held up the shoes. "You can force their kicking feet into these things, I guess."

"Do they need shoes?" asked Peter. "They can't even walk yet."

Hunter shook his open hand in Josie's direction where she was donning earrings in front of the mirror.

"I saw that," she said.

The men loaded the babies into their car seats while Josie grabbed the diaper bag.

"Oh, Hunter," his mother gushed. "They're so precious. I can't get over their adorable little dress shoes."

Josie pursed her lips into a smug grin. Never underestimate the power of a cute pair of shoes. "We should snap family pics as soon as we get there because there's zero chance they'll look this good by the end of church."

"Or still have shoes on," mumbled Hunter.

When the whole clan arrived at church in two cars, Emmaline and Peter each took a baby and filed in behind Grandpa pushing Grandma in her wheelchair. Hunter tried to hand the third baby to Stephen who put up his hands.

"Dude, it's your kid."

"My son is not an 'it.' And why wouldn't you want to hold your nephew?" Hunter gestured toward his parents. "Keep up the pattern, doofus. The Okies carry the babies."

Josie hoped the brothers wouldn't sit next to one another in the sanctuary. She envisioned them picking on each other like the Harding boys often did in worship.

Despite their dad's and uncle's examples, the babies were on their best behavior for their Oklahoma church debut. They smiled and tolerated being passed around, that is when the grandparents were willing to hand them off. Grandma and Emmaline beamed over their family and made everyone pose for pictures in the foyer.

"My heart is so full," said Emmaline. "If only Kyle could be here too."

Josie hugged her and said a silent prayer for Hunter's little brother overseas.

Later that afternoon when Hunter and Josie were on their way home in the overloaded minivan, he asked Josie, "What about you? Is your heart full, too?"

She smiled and lied, "Completely." The only thing lacking was her relationship with her sister.

Chapter 30

Dana

Will had been unemployed for three weeks, and Dana was desperate for him to get out of her domain. The kids only had two more weeks of school before summer break, and she needed every moment to perfect her first five chapters before sending them to Carlos to edit.

Yet, Will disrupted her focus with his incessant pacing and his apparent disdain for silence. He turned on the television every time he walked into the room and asked her random questions that he could easily have looked up answers to on his own.

He asked her to proofread his cover letters and stood over her shoulder second guessing her edits as she did so. "Are you sure that should say '*an* M.B.A. instead of *a* M.B.A.? You only use A-N in front of vowels."

Dana wasn't the one who bought out his company and fired him, but she was the one being punished for it. She was ready to google the home addresses of Big Kitchen Supply's executives to drop Will off on one of their doorsteps for a few hours.

"I'm going to clean out the rain gutters," he announced. "Will you come help me?"

"William, I'm in the middle of something." She closed her laptop and loaded it into her tote and grabbed her purse.

"Where are you going?"

"To a coffee shop or the library. Or maybe Michigan. Somewhere that I can write in peace. Your nervous energy is wearing me out. If you need a buddy, call my dad, but *don't* let him get on a ladder."

She hadn't even stepped through the door of her favorite local coffee shop when he called. "Will, Honey, I love you, but you're *literally* driving me mad."

"Your dad isn't picking up. Should I go check on him?"

Dana lifted her face to the cloudless sky. It was another sign that she wasn't meant to write. The constant obstacles were forever stacked against her. She pinched the bridge of her nose and trudged back to the Tahoe. "I'm closer. I'll go."

At the entrance to Mesquite Village, an ambulance with lights and sirens blaring turned in behind Dana. She pulled over to let it pass. It wasn't unheard of to see first responder vehicles in the neighborhood. After all, it was a retirement community. However, because her dad wasn't answering his phone, its presence was even more ominous. Her own pulse pounded against her eardrums as she watched the ambulance turn onto Edward's block. She sped up and pulled in behind it as it stopped in front of his house.

Dana jumped out of the Tahoe without even killing the engine. Three paramedics got to the front door as she did. She tried the knob, realizing right away that her keys were in her car, and she couldn't unlock the door. But before she could retrieve them Edward opened the front door and disappeared back inside. "This way," he yelled.

Now Dana was confused. Medical personnel were entering her father's home, but he had opened the door for them, seemingly fine. The medics rushed past her, and the screen door to the back yard slammed. Dana followed them outside. Rita Brewer was lying face up on the grass. Her father knelt over her, rhythmically compressing her chest. He fell back on his haunches as the professionals took over.

Dana squatted next to him and helped him to his feet. "Come sit in a chair and catch your breath."

His words came out in staccato bursts. "We had lunch. Came out to admire. Petunias." He rubbed his hands over his hair. With wild eyes, he told Dana, "She said she thought she'd better sit down, but she didn't make it to the chair." His eyes misted, and he was shaking.

"Oh, Dad." Dana wrapped her arms around him.

At the first responders' request, Dana took Rita's keys and sprinted across the street to look for family contacts and prescription medications, any pertinent information. On the counter between the fridge and stove, Dana found Rita's cell phone and a neat row of pill bottles. She scooped them up and threw them into the purse she saw on the table. She also ripped a rectangle of bright yellow cardstock emblazoned with "IN CASE OF EMERGENCY" across the top from the fridge and ran back across the street.

The medical workers took the purse in the ambulance. Dana held up the yellow card and reached into her pocket for her phone to call Rita's emergency contacts, but it was empty. She ran to the Tahoe to retrieve her phone and realized it was still running. "Pull yourself together, Dana," she admonished herself aloud and inhaled a sharp breath. Dr. Leyva's name was at the top of the yellow card, but the call went to voicemail. Dana left a message and then sent the same text to every number on the list.

This is Dana Harding, daughter of neighbor to Rita Brewer. She collapsed.

Unresponsive, ambulance taking to University Medical Center

The ambulance pulled away with sirens blasting once again. She walked back through the house and found her dad in the same patio chair where she'd left him. Edward was a tall man, but for the first time in her life, he appeared to Dana withered and small.

"Someone should be with her," he said. A lump caught in Dana's throat, and she could only nod in reply.

Dr. Leyva ran toward them from another hall as they entered the emergency center. "Thank you for calling me about Aunt Rita," she called out as she used her badge to bypass the reception desk and enter the locked doors across the way.

They sat in silence for more than an hour. Dana texted Will to let him know what happened. She was of course worried for Rita, but she also couldn't help but feel relief that the ambulance hadn't been for her dad.

Dr. Leyva appeared from the back, her eyes puffy from crying, and she shook her head. She hugged Edward. "Thank you for being her friend. I know she could be a difficult person, but she meant well. I'm glad you were with her although I know that was hard for you."

The doctor stepped back and swiped her wet cheeks. "Aunt Rita had a myocardial infarction. This was her third, and they couldn't revive her. I've contacted my cousins. They also wanted me to convey their gratitude to you, Mr. Johnson for trying to save her, and to you Ms. Harding for contacting them. You guys have been a godsend to my family."

Keys rattled in Dana's pocket as they said uncomfortable goodbyes. She handed them to Sarah Leyva. "Oh yeah, these are Rita's. An EMT took them from her pocket and sent me to look for contact information and medications at her house."

Dr. Leyva chuckled. "I bet she had it all organized and easy to locate." Dana made a mental note to help her dad make a list of meds to keep with his emergency contact card.

The drive home was somber. Dana stole furtive glances at her father, but he was unreadable. The only time he spoke was to let her know he wasn't ready to go back to his house.

Will met them in the garage. "Is Rita alright?" Dana had forgotten to update him from the hospital.

"Technically speaking, she's perfect now," said Edward. "Gone to be with her Savior and to report to Carolyn all my misdeeds since she left us."

"Dad's going to hang out with us for a while," Dana said.

Will seemed to read her mind and understood that Edward needed a distraction. The men went into the living room to watch TV, and Dana perched on her usual barstool that doubled as her office chair. She thought she could take her mind off what just happened by working on her novel, but the words on the screen blurred as she saw only Rita's lifeless body on the lawn and watched her father and the paramedics performing CPR. No words would come to her, and even if they had, writing about a killer whose son needed a heart transplant felt calloused under the circumstances.

To clear her mind, Dana walked to the bedroom looking for something to clean or organize. She spotted her mother's sweaters draped over the treadmill in the corner of the room. She lifted the gray "rainy day cozy sweater" to her nose and breathed in her mother's lingering essence before pulling it on over her tee shirt. She sat on the side of the bed and pulled her Bible from her nightstand and onto her lap.

It fell open to Psalm 84. "How lovely is your dwelling place, O Lord Almighty. My soul yearns, even faints for the courts of the Lord; my heart and flesh cry out for the living God…better is one day in your courts than a thousand elsewhere."

Miss Rita, her mom, and Will's parents were experiencing the presence of the Almighty. Dana set the Bible on her pillow and hugged her knees to her chest. She rested her chin on them and tried to imagine what Heaven might be like. In her mind, it was Alaska, the Greek isles, and all the world's most spectacular landscapes rolled into one place with colors more vivid than the eye had ever seen. She envisioned a place where humans had the ability to do all the things that eluded them on earth.

She laughed to herself despite the sobering thoughts about death and her losing the people she cared for. "Maybe in Heaven I can be a published author," she said into her sleeve.

Chapter 31

CiCi, still dressed in her Disney princess night gown, was eating a dry waffle when Dana arrived to babysit. She pushed her messy curls out of her face with the palm of her little hand and waved.

Dana waved back and smiled. Entertaining her for a while would help get her mind off Rita Brewer's death. Snuggles and playtime would be good for her soul.

"I meant to have her dressed before you got here, but it's been a rough morning," the weary mom apologized.

"Is everything alright?" Dana asked. Rough mornings were a Harding specialty, so she could relate, even though it had been a while since her kids were that small.

Yvette hands shook as she attempted to smooth CiCi's hair into a ponytail. The girl thrashed her head to avoid her mother's grasp. "I don't know. I've had some spotting for a couple of hours. That never happened with CiCi. The doctor told me to go to labor and delivery at the hospital, instead of the clinic. Matt left for work at the crack of dawn, and he's not even in the county."

Yvette had told the table group that Matt was a game warden, and he travelled all over the region.

Dana's stomach knotted. "Let me drive you. You shouldn't be alone."

"No, that's okay." She nodded toward CiCi and

mouthed over the top of her daughter's head, "I don't want her to know."

Dana pulled out her phone and googled reasons for third trimester spotting and grew even more concerned. "I'd feel better if you let me drop you off at least. Should I drive your car, or would you rather I move CiCi's car seat to my Tahoe?"

Yvette gave up trying to tame her daughter's hair. She opened her mouth to argue with Dana, but her face contorted. Her hand flew to her belly.

Adrenaline pulsed through Dana's veins. She lifted CiCi up and shifted her to her hip and guided Yvette by the elbow with her free hand. "Everyone to the car," she ordered.

She tried to stay calm on the drive so as not to alarm CiCi and studied Yvette out of the corner of her eye. "Do we need to go faster?" Dana asked.

Yvette shook her head. "I don't know," she whispered. "My due date is still a month away."

Dana reached across the armrest and took her hand. She said a silent prayer for both the mother and baby.

Yvette's phone rang, and she let go of Dana's hand to find it in her purse. "It's Matt," she said as she swiped to answer the call. "I'm on my way now. Dana is driving me." Her eyes widened as she listened to him. "I don't care how you do it. Just get there, okay?" She ended the call and turned to Dana. "His truck broke down in the middle of nowhere, and he doesn't know how long it'll be before someone can get to him."

Dana's stomach soured as she pulled up to the hospital's circle drive. It had only been a few days since she'd been here with her dad after Rita's heart attack. The thought that this trip could potentially have a devastating ending like the last one did niggled at the back of her mind. She ran around to the passenger side to help Yvette out of the vehicle and watched her disappear inside. Helplessness filled her once again.

Back at the house, Dana tried to convince the toddler to get dressed, but CiCi wasn't having it. She shook her head, wild hair sticking to her cheeks. "No. It's gajama day, and I wearing my gajamas. See?"

Dana smiled to herself remembering how Adam used to insist on pajama days too. Instead of arguing with a three-year-old, she opted to let CiCi have her pajama day and spent the rest of the morning playing with what was surely every toy the child owned. They stacked blocks together and fed baby dolls before CiCi pulled several books off her low shelf and asked Dana to read.

They were on the last page of *Five Little Monkeys Jumping on the Bed* when Yvette texted. Placental abruption. C-section today

Dana swallowed the lump rising in her throat. What can I do to help you?

Pray. I'm freaking out. My mom is driving in from Abilene to take care of CiCi, and Matt is trying to get a ride.

As if on cue, the little girl whined. "Where's my mama?"

Dana stroked her hair. "She's taking care of your baby sister." She stared at her phone trying to conjure the right words to comfort Yvette, but they wouldn't come. God had this in the palm of his hand, but what if it didn't have a happy ending? She pushed the thought out of her mind.

Dana instructed Yvette to send her Matt's number and a list of anything she needed from the house. Then she got to work. She turned on the television and distracted CiCi with a preschool show while she sent a text to the Wednesday women's table group, plus Serena, to fill them in. Then she called Yvette's husband, Matt, whose frame of mind was no better than his wife's.

"Parks and Wildlife are sending someone, but it could take a couple of hours. I can't just call a cab down here in Terry County to get me to the hospital. Yvette needs me, and I may miss our daughter's birth."

"Let me see what I can do."

Dana tried to call Will. Since he wasn't working, maybe he could pick up Matt. He texted back that he'd have to call her later. He'd found her dad in another of his harebrained schemes, but he was alright. He'd fill her in on the specifics after his interview. She didn't even want to know what Edward Johnson had gotten himself into right now. If Will had told her about an interview, she sure couldn't remember, but her current focus was on helping Yvette.

The Wednesday moms came through in spades. Serena volunteered to sit with Yvette at the hospital so she wouldn't be alone. Kathy's husband was making a farm supply delivery about six miles from where Matt's truck was stuck. He would pick up the expectant dad and bring him to the hospital. Anita Steen organized a meal train for Matt and Yvette. Dana wondered how anyone got through a crisis without a community to rally around them and hoped she never had to find out.

Time stood still while Dana waited. She and CiCi played outside, ate lunch, and read more books until CiCi finally went down for a nap. For hours, the only new information Dana received was that Matt had been delivered to the hospital before Yvette was taken to the operating room.

Her phone finally buzzed with a call from Will. "Sorry I couldn't talk when you called this morning, but I was about to walk into a job interview."

She asked him for more details, as much out of a need to take her mind off Yvette as out of genuine interest.

He told her it went well. He met with a holding company that owned four restaurants. "They're looking for a sous chef and an executive director, but neither position pays anywhere near what I was making."

Dana said a silent prayer that he would find the right

job, even if it meant scaling back. She also prayed it wouldn't involve late nights and weekends. "What did my dad get up to this morning?" She chewed her lip hoping it didn't involve the police again.

Will chuckled. "He locked his keys in his trunk at the grocery store."

"That's not so bad. It could happen to anyone." She'd done the same thing a time or two back in her pre-SUV days.

"Yeah, so he walked back to the building and saw a shuttle to Mesquite Manor Assisted Living Center at the door. It's just up the road from him in Mesquite Village, so he thought he'd just hitch a ride back with them and pick up his spare keys."

It sounded logical to Dana, and she mentally applauded his resourcefulness. "Did the driver let him on?"

"Yes, but the staff at the assisted living center held him until I could get there. They were worried about his lucidity. Their shuttle wasn't heading back to the store anyway, so he needed a ride to his car."

She pinched the bridge of her nose and closed her eyes. "And was he lucid?"

"As far as I could tell. I didn't see any reason to keep him from driving himself home."

Will would have been the first one to take her dad's keys if he thought something was off, so she breathed a sigh of relief.

When they ended the call, Dana sank into the sofa. A few hours ago, her problems seemed insurmountable. Losing a job, having a low-key identity crisis, and a father with memory problems had seemed like a heavy load this morning. However, those things didn't hold a candle to Matt and Yvette's current situation. Her heart ached for them.

Her spiraling what ifs would have buried her if not for her phone. Matt texted a photo of Yvette smiling at her tiny infant. Tears clouded Dana's vision, and she struggled to read his message.

They're both doing great. Baby Talia was checked out by neonatologist-all good. She's breathing on her own and won't need to stay in ICU.

Dana raised her eyes heavenward and thanked God.

By the time CiCi's grandmother arrived to take over, Dana's reserves were spent. She trudged in the garage door and caught a whiff of the most tantalizing scent wafting from the oven and spotted a plate of brownies on the counter. A note beside the plate contained rewarming instructions for chicken and green chilis casserole in Josie's handwriting.

She dialed Josie's number. "You baked brownies, *and* you made dinner for us?"

"Well, I baked from a mix, and I donated one of my mom's meals from my freezer stash. Will should have put it in the oven before he left to get the kids."

"He did, but to what do we owe this act of kindness?"

"There was nothing I could do to help Yvette today, but I could show *you* my appreciation for helping her by taking dinner off your plate. No pun intended."

Dana tried to express her gratitude. "You don't know the gift you've given me after such an exhausting day."

"My mom used to tell us there was healing power in a good meal."

Dana pinched the corner off a brownie and felt the stress of the day melt away as she savored its chocolatey goodness. "I feel healed already."

Chapter 32

The Wednesday moms had their final gathering of the school year. Serena and Dana's pilot project gained so much momentum in only a couple of months that their little church group was bursting at the seams. They would reconvene in September, hopefully in a larger meeting space with a cooler name. Even though they wouldn't formally meet over summer break, the table groups were free to host their own meetups. For Dana and Josie's table, this included the school yard clean-up project and meeting Yvette's new baby.

They gathered in Matt and Yvette's driveway bearing gifts and dinner for the family. Dana worried they were imposing, and their large group might expose the baby to germs, but Yvette had insisted. Her mom and Matt had gone back to work, so CiCi was dying for some new faces too.

"Dana," shouted CiCi. "Come see my baby sister. Come on." She led Dana by the hand and motioned for the others to follow her. "Dis is Taw-ya."

Dana, Zooey, Kathy, Josie, and Anita Steen all peered into the high-tech bassinette at the sleeping newborn.

"This makes my uterus ache," said Kathy.

CiCi patted Kathy's leg. "You okay?"

The women laughed, and Dana assured her little

companion that Kathy was being silly.

"What's a uterus?" asked Darius. He had come with Zooey and held a bunch of balloons in his good hand.

Anita's eyes widened, and Josie snickered.

"Uh, well, it's the thing that holds a baby when it's growing in the mommy's tummy," explained Zooey. "Don't you have something for CiCi?" She exhaled sharply as he turned his attention from the anatomy lesson to delivering the balloons to the new big sister.

Dana giggled to herself. CiCi and Darius were at such fun ages. Sure, her own kids were fun too, but Nate was at that age where Dana could tell how hard he worked out in athletics by how bad her Tahoe smelled after picking him up from school. And Leah deemed most comments and eye contact from her mother as an act of aggression. The thought of having sweet little babies again made her nostalgic.

She asked Darius about his stitches, and he eagerly showed off his battle wound.

"Not that I can be of much help, but isn't the playground clean-up this Saturday?" asked Yvette.

"Yep," answered Darius before anyone else could speak up. "My school got a new fence, and more swings, and it looks good." He bobbed his head with swagger.

"It sure does," added Josie. "Hunter and his guys replaced the broken gate and repaired all the damaged sections so trespassers will have to take their business elsewhere."

"All it needs now is a clean sweep and some finishing touches," said Anita.

Dana felt a tug on her jeans. CiCi had apparently grown tired of conversation that didn't revolve around her. "Come sit and read me a book."

"Sweetie, Miss Dana isn't here to entertain you today," said Yvette.

Before Dana could say anything, the little girl growled

at her mother and stomped to her room. The slamming of her bedroom door startled the newborn.

"Great," said Yvette. "I'm so sorry. She's not handling big sister life as well as we'd hoped.

Baby Talia wailed, and Yvette winced as she struggled to rise from her seat. She glanced between the hallway to CiCi's room and the newborn, clearly torn between her daughters.

Dana put her hand on her shoulder to stop her from standing. "You stay there. I'll check on CiCi, and Kathy can bring Talia to you." She was momentarily shocked by her own bossiness until she saw relief spread over Yvette's face.

She tapped on CiCi's door before opening it. "Hey, sweet girl. Did you choose a book for me?" There was no point in addressing her jealousy because Dana doubted the little girl even knew what she felt.

CiCi was curled into the fetal position in her bean bag. A wide smile spread across her face. Maybe she realized she wasn't about to get in trouble for slamming her door.

They read a short book together, and Darius appeared with the balloons. "Hey CiCi, you left these in the living room, but they're all yours. I thought you might like to keep them in here." He made a show of placing the weight on the shelf precisely where CiCi instructed him. "Baby sisters can be tough sometimes," he told her. "But when she gets bigger, you're going to have fun with her too. When she's not stealing your toys."

CiCi's eyes grew as she listened to the wisdom of the six-year-old. "Taw-ya can't pway with my toys. You see my doggy?" CiCi plucked a black, white, and brown stuffed animal off her bed and thrust it at Darius. Dis is Haw-vee."

Hobby?" asked Darius.

Dana reached out to touch the plush fur. "I think his name is Harvey. Right, CiCi?"

Dana left the them to play and headed back to the living room where the other women were passing around Baby Talia. She thumbed toward the hallway. "I see y'all got yourselves a Bernese Mountain Dog of your own."

Yvette laughed. "She's been obsessed ever since we came to your house, so Matt ordered her that one online. He's a more manageable size and less work than your Harvey."

Less expensive upkeep too.

Five of the six women from the table group and most of their families had shown up for the work project. Even Matt and CiCi were there. The headmaster thanked everyone for coming and gave a special shout out to Josie for spearheading the effort.

"What about me?" shouted Darius. "She got the idea because I got hurt."

His mother nudged him. "Shush. No one is applauding you for getting hurt."

Josie smiled and ruffled Darius's head. "I wanted to be sure it didn't happen again. And I knew a guy who would work for cheap." She squeezed Hunter's arm.

The headmaster instructed the kids to call for an adult if they saw anything sharp or dangerous. He warned them not to pick up anything with their bare hands.

"What does he think is out there, needles?" asked Will through the side of his mouth. Dana didn't want to think about how close to the truth that might be.

"Yeah, be careful of glass or you'll end up with a scar like mine," Darius interrupted and waved his hand over his head. The sutures had been removed, and now his wound resembled a centipede. It made Dana's stomach twist.

Armed with five-gallon buckets and grabber tools, the

Hardings set about walking through the school playground picking up debris. Dana watched Josie push Peg loaded down with the triplets. She paused periodically and pointed at objects on the ground for Hunter to pick up.

"You sure you don't want me to push the heavy stroller while you use the grabber?" Hunter asked.

"No," Josie panted. "Telling you what to pick up is more fun for me than you being the bossy one."

Dana giggled. She would have a low tolerance for Will pointing out garbage for her to pick up too.

Under the moms' watchful eyes, the group abated the playground of all trash and got to work on the final touches Anita had mentioned. The headmaster had given them permission to install a raised bed where the students would be able to cultivate their own garden. It had been Dana's dad's idea, and Anita implored the retired men at church who did volunteer handyman work to design and build it.

The husbands unloaded the wooden structure from the back of a pickup while Anita guided the kids in fertilizing and planting a border of perennials in a bare area between the building and walkway.

Nate and Adam were far more enthusiastic about digging holes to Anita's specifications than they were about doing yard work at home. Dana had the thought that if kids only got excited about manual labor when someone else benefitted from it, maybe families should trade out children to get their chores done.

"This is so fun!" said Darius. "I can't wait for my friends to get to plant stuff in our new garden."

"Mom, can we build a raised bed and plant a garden at home?" asked Nate.

The question was echoed by Kathy's son and Darius as well. Maybe they were cultivating more than a pretty playground. They were building lasting memories and life skills they would carry with them into adulthood. Dana got chills thinking that a child might even choose a future career, perhaps in botany, thanks their community project.

Chapter 33

Josie

Springtime ushered in the infamous West Texas dirt storms that blanketed the skies in a red haze from March to June. Now the winds were gone, replaced by blistering, oppressive heat.

Connor, Ben, and Olivia were all officially crawlers now, and Olivia and Ben routinely pulled themselves into standing positions on the furniture. They could clear a coffee table faster than the Hardings' dog's tail, and some days Josie regretted the physical therapy that led to their destructive mobility.

They loved being outside, and the mornings were perfect for stroller rides and crawling in the grass. By midafternoon though, the temperature pushed triple digits making the outdoors unsafe for baby skin. The triplets would bang on the door, demanding to be let out, but Josie couldn't keep three tiny humans off the hot concrete by herself.

The doorbell rang. A large box with the distinctive blue smile greeted her, but Josie wasn't expecting a delivery. She must have forgotten about an auto shipment of diapers again.

Inside the box, Josie found a smaller box with a bright photo of children splashing in an inflatable wading pool and an even smaller box with an electric inflator. It was perfect, but she was pretty sure she hadn't ordered either of these things. Maybe Hunter had done it and forgotten to tell her?

She texted Dana. Anyone over there want to help me keep my kids from drowning in a kiddy pool?

Dana's reply was immediate. You got my gift! Adam will. The big kids left for youth camp this morning. It'll give him something to do besides sit at the doctor's office with my dad and me

At least Josie wasn't losing her mind after all. She opened the packages and set up the pool in the living room. The whir of the inflator combined with a giant expanding plastic circle terrified the babies. She took them to their cribs where they continued to cry, but at least it wasn't from fear of being consumed by an inflatable monster.

Once it was blown up, she wrestled the wading pool out the front door and turned on the hose. She was afraid to add more than a couple of inches of water because any deeper, and buoyant baby fat would cause them to topple over. By the time she'd slathered everyone with sunblock and changed them into swim diapers and the sun hats from Emmaline, the water was too warm. She had to add ice cubes to cool it down again.

Josie had two babies on her hips about to unload them in the pool when she realized her error. In the seconds it would take to make a trip inside to get the third kid, the first ones could drown or crawl away. Or one of each. She was staring at the pool about to head back inside when Adam jogged across the street with a bag of bath toys.

The boy was a genius, or his mother was, whoever thought to bring water toys anyway. She sent him inside to grab Ben while she lowered Olivia and Connor into the water. They splashed until Olivia pulled on Connor's hat, causing him to faceplant. Josie lunged for him, but he popped right up and sucked in a breath. She waited to see if he would choke or cry, but he was fine.

Adam gently sat Ben in the water and dumped in the contents of the bag. The babies shrieked and splashed while Adam squirted them with a rubber fish. How had it not occurred to Josie to get a wading pool and a Harding kid sooner?

The mail carrier pulled up in his tiny white jeep and approached Josie rather than putting the mail in the box. "Looks like you're having a party over here," he said.

"Every day's a party with triplets," she replied. "It's like living in a frat house."

"I have no doubt. I had a feeling they were all yours when I saw that triple stroller out here one day."

He handed Josie a stack of mail and pulled a pen out of his shirt pocket and scribbled on a piece of paper. "My daughter has two sets of twins under four. She started a group for moms of multiples that meets at the Methodist church not far from here. I don't want to be a nuisance, but here's her name and number if you're interested. Sometimes it's good to have a community of people who know what you're going through." He tapped the bill of his cap and backed away. "Anyway, have a good day, ma'am. You have a beautiful family, and you should feel honored that God picked you to be their mama."

"Bye, Jack," called Adam.

"See ya tomorrow, Adam."

"You know the mailman?" Josie couldn't have picked him out of a lineup.

"Yep, I talk to him all the time. He's funny. Scared of Harvey though."

Anyone would be terrified of a hundred-pound mass of barking fur taking a running start at them. She flipped through the mail. A credit card application, a Costco ad, a long envelope that was probably another medical bill, and a thick greeting card-sized envelope addressed in calligraphy. This must be Laurel's wedding invitation. She had not expected to even be invited after months of the silent treatment from her sister. Their mother must have sent it.

She asked Adam to run the mail inside and didn't give it another thought.

Chapter 34

Dana

Edward's newfound attachment to the Hardings' sofa was taking a toll on Dana. He mostly napped and watched the news channels, but she hadn't had a moment to herself in weeks. She couldn't concentrate on writing her novel with him in the house. But more importantly, she was worried about him.

Similarly to when her mom passed away, he never wanted to leave the house anymore. Only this time, he was holing up in Will and Dana's house rather than his own. No one could blame him though. He probably pictured Rita having a heart attack in his back yard every time he walked outside. Her family had cleaned out her house and put it on the market. Now the realtor's sign out front was another reminder of her absence. He'd even let the petunias he'd lovingly planted wither in the heat as though he blamed them for what happened to Rita.

With this new onslaught of grief, his mental faculties diminished once again. After making vast improvements between March and May, he now lost track of time, gave up taking care of his appearance, and slept entirely too much. All of which concerned Dr. Leyva as much as it did Dana at his appointment earlier that day.

This time they met in an exam room rather than in her

office.

The doctor's melancholy countenance mirrored Edward's. "As I told you before, Mr. Johnson, brain fog is amplified by depression and not taking care of yourself. You must make a conscious effort to keep a schedule, stay active, and pursue challenges. Prior to Aunt Rita's passing, what activities did you get involved in?"

He and Dana described how he had helped coach Adam's robotics team for a few weeks. Mostly though he had been walking with Rita and gardening. Now he wasn't doing much of anything productive.

Dr. Leyva blinked back tears as she asked Edward how he was responding to the antidepressant and the supplements she had recommended. He admitted that he rarely remembered to take them these days. Rita's nagging had been better than an alarm, and she had made it her mission to make him take his meds and exercise.

For years, Edward avoided Rita, who he thought was a pushy busybody, but the positive changes Dana saw in him the last few months were because of her influence. She had become his friend. Since she'd been gone, he was noticeably worse off, and Dana worried that there would be no easy fixes and prescriptions this time.

"What you *were* doing at my aunt's insistence, do now for your grandkids and your daughter. Aunt Rita would expect you to take care of yourself and be the best version of Edward Johnson you could possibly be. And if you can't do it for them, do it for her."

"Of course, I can do it for my family," he muttered. "They're all I have left."

Dr. Leyva rolled her stool a degree closer to Edward and took his hand. "I can't thank you enough for all you did for my aunt. I know I told you before at the hospital and again at her funeral, but I'm grateful you were there for her, not just at the end, but for the big things before that. You helped her with her yard and that tree that she should have paid someone to cut down years ago. You were a good friend." The doctor hugged him and Dana before giving them a final list of instructions and ending the visit.

After his previous neurology appointment, her dad had grumbled and voiced his opinion on the doctor's advice. But on the ride home today, he remained silent and stared out the side window.

"Dad!" Dana yelled.

"What? I'm sitting two feet away from you."

"I've asked you *twice* what you plan to do for exercise to replace your daily walks with Rita? You can't keep putting it off."

"Huh?"

She resisted the urge to bang her forehead on the steering wheel. There was a good chance it would lead to another fender bender. "Dad, did you hear anything I said?" It was like trying to talk to one of her sons when they were in the middle of a video game.

"Exercise, yeah, yeah. Turn around, would ya? I saw something next to the gas station back there."

There was no telling what her father had seen, or not seen for that matter, but Dana obliged him. She turned onto a side street to make a U-turn and retraced their route.

His arm stretched across her face as he pointed at something beyond the driver's side window. "There! Pull in."

Dana batted his hand down. "I can't see through your arm."

It took a minute to turn left against traffic, and Edward had his seatbelt undone and was ready to bolt the second she pulled into the lot. Was he hallucinating or having a stress-induced episode? As Edward approached the compressed air pump on the side of the building, Dana saw movement in the shadow of the apparatus. A small animal moved toward Edward and allowed him to pick it up.

She waited in the Tahoe while her dad examined what

she could now see was a brown and white puppy.

"Oh no," she said aloud to herself. "This is not going to end well."

He walked to the front of the store, disappeared inside, and returned a moment later with the little thing tucked protectively in his arm. Its fur was caked in dirt and full of who knows what else. He was going to put that flea-riddled thing in her car.

"The store clerk said she didn't know it was there. Probably a stray or dumped," he said as he climbed into the passenger seat.

Dana stared at her dad holding a puppy. In her car. She wasn't even sure what to do or say.

"Why are you just sitting there?" he asked. "Drive home, please."

Obediently, she pulled away from the curb, still dumbfounded. When they turned onto the cul-de-sac, panic began to set in. She couldn't deal with a puppy on top of everything else. Not to mention Will would be furious if she brought home a second dog, even if she blamed it on her ailing father. Besides, the tiny pup might end up a light snack for Harvey.

"Dad, I'm not so sure about this."

He ran his hand down the length of the quivering pup's back. "I'll check the lost dog posts, take it to the vet and see if it has a chip. Unlikely since he's so young. But I'll figure out the next step after the first two. I know what you're thinking, and you can stop."

"What am I thinking, Dad?"

"You're thinking this dog is about to become your problem, but it's not. I've got this under control, sweetheart." His mind-reading skills were rather canny for someone who had just come from a dementia evaluation.

She pulled the Tahoe into the driveway next to her dad's car. "Will you at least take it to your house before my son sees it and gets his hopes up or my dog gets a hold of it?"

Thankfully, Adam was inside the Caraways' house, so his Pops and the puppy made their escape undetected.

If she were a betting woman, Dana's money was on this dog becoming her problem within the next forty-eight hours.

Chapter 35

Josie

That evening, Hunter thumbed through the mail and held up the slip of paper with the phone number on it.

"Hey Jos, who's Taylor?"

How should she know? "You tell me."

"There's a phone number in the stack of mail with the name 'Taylor' on it. Looks like a man's writing."

She laughed. "I forgot about that."

He waited for her to elaborate, but she didn't. "Josie?"

"The mail carrier gave me that when I was outside with the kids. It's his daughter's info. She has two sets of twins. *TWO!*" It would be nice to make some new friends who understood life with multiples. The Wednesday moms were great, but sometimes she still felt like the odd mom out.

Hunter pointed out that she hadn't even opened her sister's wedding invitation, which now sported ink smudges from Adam's wet hands.

"Did your mom warn you about it?" he asked.

Warn her about the invitation? She asked if he meant its arrival in general or was there more?

There was more alright. An embossed card was included with the invitation that stated, "Children are not allowed at the venue, so please plan your childcare needs accordingly."

The bottle Josie was holding slipped from her hand. Was this for real? Laurel knew there was no way they could get a sitter for three babies for an out of state wedding. This was her way of letting them know they were officially invited because it was in poor taste *not* to invite her only sister, but she really didn't want them to come.

She turned to Hunter who had his phone in hand. "Hi, Marie." His free hand was a fist on his hip. "Who sent out Laurel's wedding invitations?" She almost never heard him use that tone, especially directed at her mother. There was a pause. "Laurel sent them herself. And did yours include a supplementary note?"

Josie bit her thumbnail as he took a photo of the card and texted it to Marie.

Hunter flinched and pulled the phone away from his ear. Josie heard her mother curse in Spanish.

"So, this little gem was reserved just for us," he said. "And you had no idea."

Last month Marie came for another weekend visit and talked nonstop about the wedding and how excited she was for the whole family to be together. She even brought matching formal attire for the babies to wear. She obviously hadn't known they wouldn't be invited.

Josie held out her hand to Hunter. "Let me talk to her." He could have put the call on speaker, but he dutifully gave her his phone.

"Mom, I told you, Laurel wants nothing to do with me. I don't know why she even bothered to waste the postage sending us an invitation."

"*Mija!* Don't talk like that. I'll talk to Laurel and straighten this out. You must be there. All of you."

When she hung up, Josie decided to take a walk and clear her head. Storm clouds were rolling in, and thunder rumbled in the distance. A good downpour would be a welcome reprieve from the stifling heat, but she wasn't in the mood to get caught in it. Instead, she walked across the cul-de-sac to drown her sorrows in Harvey's shaggy fur and Dana's sage perspective.

Dana answered the door with a French fry in one hand and a full mouth. "Hey, come on in." She led the way back to the kitchen where Adam was eating chicken nuggets out of a bag and watching a show on a tablet. He looked up and gave Josie a smile and a wave.

"Don't judge me. Will's working, and it's too hot to cook. Thanks again for letting Adam hang out this afternoon, by the way. He had a blast."

"He was a huge help, and his idea to bring water toys saved the day. Will found a job?"

She explained that it was a temporary consulting position to help get a failing restaurant back on track.

"He's happy, and I'm *so* thankful he has something productive to do outside of this house. I was ready to strangle him. The hours aren't great though, so I hope he fixes the restaurant and can walk away from it before school starts."

"What a relief. I was worried I'd have to help you hide his body before long," Josie joked.

"That makes two of us."

Josie reached across the counter and stole a fry. "How did your dad's appointment go?"

She nodded toward Adam and mouthed, "Tell you later."

Josie would have to ask her when Adam wasn't around. Instead, she gave Dana the rundown on the wedding invitation. "Any advice?"

Dana swiped a chicken nugget through ketchup and popped it in her mouth. She chewed thoughtfully, and Josie waited. The thunder rolls grew louder and more frequent, and the room grew dim as the clouds overtook the evening sun.

"What were you planning to do with the babies during

the wedding?" asked Dana. "Sit in the front row with your parents and have everyone entertain a tiny person while the bride walks down the aisle? Because I can see how that might detract from her special moment."

She and Hunter had talked about hiring a sitter to watch the kids in a nursery room during the ceremony. It would be no different than leaving them in the church nursery on Sunday mornings, but the note in Laurel's invitation made it clear that wouldn't be an option. She told Dana as much, but the wisdom she had hoped for never came.

"I'm so sorry. Maybe she'll change her mind."

Harvey rested his head on her lap and looked up at Josie with big eyes as melancholy as her heart. Scratching his ears eased her tension. Between the dog and chatting with Dana about the mundane, the fury that had coursed through Josie when she arrived had now dulled to a low rumble the pit of her belly.

The opposite was true of the storm outside. Thunder clapped, and flashes of lightning illuminated the room.

Josie patted the counter. "I better get back before it starts pouring. Send Adam my way tomorrow. He's the right height to hold the babies' hands while they practice taking steps. I dislocate my spine when I do it." She gave Harvey one more scratch behind his ears and stood.

The first sprinkles of rain were morphing into a steady shower as she jogged home. She shook droplets off her ponytail in the entryway and noticed the babies playing in their saucers while Hunter reclined in his favorite chair.

He motioned for her to come close and pulled her onto his lap. He put a long envelope with the top torn open in her hand. "You need to see this."

She groaned and leaned back against his chest. That medical bill. "How much do we owe this time? Know where I can sell a kidney?"

"You didn't even look at the return address, did you?"

With the babies in the wading pool, she hadn't taken her eyes off them long enough to worry about the mail. The return address was Hunter's family's home in OKC. Josie unfolded a handwritten letter with a very generous personal check. Was it even legal to mail a check this large? Hunter responded to her bewildered expression. "Just read."

Dear Josie,

Our conversation at the craft fair stuck with me. You've inspired me to take up painting and sculpting again, and even Mama has been going with me on her good days. I can't believe I let so much time go by without picking up a brush to do more than cover a wall!

Peter and I believe in you and want you to experience the fullness of following your passion while being a great mother at the same time. We don't want you to put it off until your dream fades again.

Please use this money to enroll in a cosmetology program and to hire childcare while you take classes. There is no rush and NO pressure. This is our gift to you and Hunter for giving us the blessing of those precious grandbabies. Use it in your own time, as you see fit.

Love,

Mom and Dad

She fanned her face to keep from crying. "Huh. This changes things, doesn't it?"

Chapter 36

Josie reread the letter. "Can your parents afford to do this?"

Hunter shrugged. "Dad said he's not planning to retire anytime soon, and they still have most of the money from the sale of their house here. They're helping Stephen get back on his feet, so if they want to do this for us, I don't see why we can't accept it."

He reached across Josie to pick up his phone from the side table. "Look at this." He showed her a program he had looked up where the cosmetology classes only met two days a week and every other Saturday. "The kids could go to Parents' Day Out on those days, and you could have your license in less than two years. It has great reviews too. But you also don't have to decide right now. It's your call."

She rotated to face him in the chair. "You were very busy while I was across the street, weren't you?"

Hunter kissed the side of her head. "Think of all the money we'll save paying for haircuts."

Josie wondered how soon she could apply. The friends she knew with children in Parents' Day Out programs enrolled in early spring for following September. It would be a miracle if the church still had three spots available this late in the game.

A loud clap of thunder rattled the windows and set all

three babies screaming. Josie slid off Hunter's lap and scooped the boys out of their saucers and into their dad's arms and cradled Olivia to her chest. "It's really coming down out there." She worried an intense summer storm might mean hail, or worse, a tornado. "Can you check the weather app?"

"With what hand?" he asked.

Josie shifted Olivia to her hip and picked up her phone from the coffee table. She swiped past a text from her mom urging her to come to the wedding anyway. The weather service showed a tornado watch for their area. "We might have to ride the storm out in the Hardings' basement."

"Then let's get these guys fed and pack the diaper bag just in case."

She texted Dana. This is your heads up that if the watch becomes a warning, we're coming over. Check on your dad

Dana would know what she meant. It was the understood rule in Tornado Alley that the closest available basement became Grand Central Station for the neighborhood during tornado warnings. She turned on the local TV station and buckled Olivia into her highchair. Then she helped Hunter situate Connor and Ben before opening jars of food.

Despite the raging storm, the babies fell asleep soon after dinner. Hail pelted the windows, threatening to shatter the glass. Josie said a silent prayer that it would stop soon and not grow larger. The drumming of ice bombarding the house drown out every other sound.

"How are they sleeping through this?" Hunter shouted.

"They're wiped out from their water fun day." Josie peeked through the blinds in the nursery. "The hail's almost golf ball sized." Easily large enough to crack glass.

Hunter pulled the cribs as far away from the window as possible. They lingered in the room until the hail finally subsided and they were satisfied their children were out of harm's way.

"I'm going to check in with Todd. You should respond to your mom. Besides, you know she keeps better track of our weather reports than we do, so she's probably worried about us," said Hunter.

She threw her head back. "Ugh. Wanna switch?"

"You've got this." He winked and walked to their room to make his call.

Josie sent a text to her mom letting her know that they were in the middle of a hailstorm, but she'd think about the wedding and call her tomorrow. In truth, the only thought she was having about Laurel's wedding was how hurtful that invitation was.

She got a permanent marker out of the junk drawer and wrote "YOUR LOSS" across the no kids allowed card. Instead of checking the "will not attend" box on the RSVP card, she wrote in, "AS IF." Then she snapped a photo of the two cards together and texted it to Laurel.

It was childish. And as soon as Marie Saldana got wind of it, she would get an earful. For the moment though, it gave Josie a small thrill to be mean to her sister.

Moments later, Laurel called, but Josie let it go to voicemail. After all, that's where her own calls to Laurel always ended up.

Josie listened to Laurel's message with white knuckles gripping the edge of the kitchen counter.

"You selfish, entitled brat! If your obnoxious babies can't be center stage at *my* wedding, then you throw a fit. Everything *must* revolve around Josie. Mom flipped about you not coming to my engagement party." Her tone changed to one that Josie recognized as her imitation of their mom. "Oh *mija*. It's not the same without Josefina and my beautiful *nietos."* Her voice returned to her own. "You're always the center of the universe. Excuse me if I want my wedding to be about me for a change."

Josie dredged the recesses of her mind trying to come up with a reason for Laurel's resentment. They had always been close until last year. The pregnancy and new babies had been all-consuming though, and she hadn't kept up with Laurel's life, or anyone's, as well as she could have. It didn't make any sense though that Laurel would be upset with Josie for having kids. They'd talked about it in the first trimester, and Laurel seemed excited to be an aunt.

She got another call, this one from her mother. She debated sending it to voicemail too, but knowing Marie, she would call Hunter when Josie didn't pick up to hear how they were weathering the storm.

She made her way to the living room. "Good evening, Mother."

"Don't 'good evening, Mother' me. Laurel sent me the photo you took. I'm so disappointed in you."

Josie dropped onto the sofa and drew her legs under her. "Are you kidding me right now? The invitation we got was so hurtful. I simply responded with our regrets in the same way it was sent to us." Okay, maybe her response was a tad less dignified. Semantics.

Marie continued to scold her in two languages. "You don't know what kind of year your sister has been through, so you selfishly assume everything revolves around you." How nice that her mom and sister had reached a consensus on her egotism. She was about to ask how her mom felt about Laurel's behavior, but Hunter reappeared rubbing the back of his neck. His phone call must have only gone slightly better than hers.

"Ma, I gotta go. We'll chat soon, okay?" She hung up while Marie was still talking and turned off her phone.

Hunter sat beside her and rested his head against her shoulder.

"That bad, huh?"

"The hail was a lot bigger south of town, so we might be reroofing several houses. At least we didn't put skylights in any of them. What did your mom say?"

She leaned over and grabbed the invitation with the

cards, now graffitied with Josie's regrets. "Oh, she and Laurel both had plenty to say after I sent this."

His jaw dropped. "You didn't!"

She nodded, expecting him to use all four of her names.

"Ah, Jos. You know that's only going to make things worse. It's kind of funny though. I bet your mom flipped."

"Oh yeah. I'm the most self-centered person on the planet." She sniffled and rubbed her nose.

He sat up and looked her in the eye. "That's not true at all. Josie, you're the kindest, most thoughtful woman I've ever met."

"Thanks, babe." She kissed him and excused herself to wash her face. She would have preferred a long shower, but her mother's warning that it was dangerous to shower during lightning was too ingrained in her psyche. Maybe it wasn't even true, but she wouldn't be risking it tonight.

Josie came back to the living room with the damp towel slung over her shoulder. "Why couldn't I have been an only child like Dana?"

"What are you talking about? Siblings are great. They teach you how to eat fast and be tough," Hunter joked. He stood and tugged her hand, leading her to the bedroom. "How about we forget about family drama for a while?" he smiled suggestively.

Josie wasn't really in the mood for sexy time, but she followed him anyway, deciding to forget about Laurel for now. Hunter continued past the bed and into the master bathroom. He sat down on the edge of the tub with his back to her and took the towel off her shoulder draping it around his own shoulders like a cape.

Was she missing something?

"I would like to be your inaugural haircut."

She laughed. "I haven't started lessons. This could go very poorly."

He directed her to the clippers he'd bought back when

he tried to grow a beard. "Just do around my ears and the back where it's getting scruffy. I haven't had time to get a haircut in ages, and I have a meeting with a customer tomorrow. Please, Jos? I'll sweep the hair up afterward."

"What if it looks terrible for your meeting?"

"Then I'll wear a hat."

Twenty minutes later, Josie examined the results. Hunter had less hair now, much shorter, for sure, but at least it seemed fairly even on both sides. The problem was that she kept having to take off more and more to get it that way. Then she had to take some off the top to even out the much shorter sides and back.

"This is why you go to school and get a license to cut hair *before* you actually do it," she said as she wiped loose hair off his neck and shoulders.

Hunter stood up, rather stiffly after sitting on the edge of the tub for so long. "I bet it looks great. And if not, well, that's why hair keeps growing. It's always in a temporary state."

Josie beamed. How did he and his parents have so much confidence in her?

He turned his head both directions and grinned at his reflection. "Jos, you have a gift." He kissed her. "Do you feel like you're making out with a new man now?" His voice was low and seductive.

She kissed his ear lobe and whispered, "Yeah, but there's something else I'd rather this new man do than just kiss me."

He bit his lip and grabbed her waist. "Tell me more."

Josie leaned out of the embrace and pointed at the hair all over the floor. "I want him to get the broom."

FELLOWSHIP OF THE FRAZZLED MOMS

Chapter 37

Dana

Sweat beaded on her upper lip, and blood thumped in her ears. Dana's fingers trembled so much that it was hard to even click on the email from the literary agent to open it. Carlos had helped her write a synopsis of her novel and edit the first chapters. It had been weeks since she'd submitted them to his agent, and she had only checked her inbox every two hours every day since.

"Dear Ms. Harding,

I thoroughly enjoyed reading your short story sent to me by Carlos Ruiz."

Dana jumped up, unable to keep from smiling. She paced a few steps and shook out her limbs before returning to her screen.

"Thank you for entrusting the first chapters of your novel to me. While I liked the character of Kelsey and felt her urgency to save her dying son, I found her gentleness with him to be a contradiction to her cold and calculating demeanor with her victims. I don't think readers will find her to be a believable predator, and therefore, I am passing on your manuscript at this time. Please feel free to send me future submissions."

The rejection letter was so politely worded that she had to read it again to be sure that was in fact what it was. Months of hard work wasted. She could have been doing a thousand other things, none of which she could think of right now. She forwarded the email to Carlos. Whatever favor his agent owed him apparently did not extend to book contracts for his students.

Her chest tightened as though defeat were literally crushing her. She had known rejection was a real possibility, but she hadn't realized how much she had gotten her hopes up until now. Between Will's layoff, Rita's passing, and her dad's relapse, she needed a win for a change.

The kitchen felt like a sauna. She rubbed her upper arm over her face to mop the sweat and tugged the front of her tee shirt away from her chest. Was she having her first hot flash already? She would look up how to tell the difference between hormonal and stress sweat after she adjusted the thermostat.

The digital screen pronounced the indoor temperature was eighty-four degrees. At least that answered her hormone question. A broken air conditioner was better than menopause, but it might be more costly.

Will jogged in from his late morning run and gave her a sweaty peck on the cheek. He'd worked late last night helping an acquaintance get his restaurant out of the red and slept in.

"How can you work out in this heat?" she asked.

"It's the humidity from the storm that's the real torture." He peeled off his tee shirt. "You look upset. And why is it so hot in here?"

She told him about the email and the air conditioner.

"Ah, hon, I'm sorry. You've been working so hard, and I know it's going to be a great book. The right person will recognize your talent soon enough."

Lord, let it be so. Dana forced a smile and tucked an errant strand of hair behind her ear.

"I'll check the unit," he said as he took the stairs two at a time. "It's probably just a dirty filter."

She started to warn him it was more serious than that. She kept a calendar reminder in her phone and a neon Post-it on the unit with the date to change the filter. She changed the air conditioner filters as religiously as Josie made her bed. However, since Will had the energy to sprint up the stairs after his workout, he could see it for himself.

Dana texted Josie and asked her to find out what heating and air company Hunter could recommend. Maybe his professional contacts would afford them speedier service.

As she waited for a reply, she also texted her dad. Did you survive the night?

She'd called him last night and learned that the hail had missed his area completely, and that the puppy was not a fan of baths. He'd hung up abruptly when it started to poop on the rug.

A minute later, she received a poorly taken selfie of her dad and the dog sporting a bone-shaped tag on its collar. Meet Patch Johnson

Sweet mercy, he'd named it.

The three dots indicating her dad was typing stayed on the screen for a full minute. She was starting to wonder if he was writing a dissertation or had set his phone down with the keyboard open when his message finally came through.

Vet said he's been on the street a while, slightly malnourished but otherwise fine. No lost dog posts about him. Got first round of shots and a flea dip this morning. Buying supplies now. Gtg

Who taught the septuagenarian "gtg"? Even worse, who let him get a puppy? "This is bad," she said aloud.

Will lumbered down the stairs without the spring in his step he'd had moments ago. "Something worse than a broken air conditioner in the dead of summer in Texas?"

She clicked on the photo of Patch and held up her phone. "They've already been to the vet and are shopping for 'supplies.'" She made air quotes with her fingers.

"It might be good for your dad to have a pet. It'll keep him active and force him to have a routine. Patch will be his new Rita."

"Except Miss Rita didn't poop in the floor." Whether her dad ever admitted it, his neighbor provided consistency and companionship that kept him healthy. Maybe Will was right, and this literal pet project would help him heal from Rita's loss. Still, she was sure it was only a matter of time before the puppy became too much for him. "Shall we take bets on how long this lasts until the dog becomes *our* problem?"

He waved his hands. "Oh no, either way, that's a

losing bet."

Her phone buzzed in her hand. Josie reminded her that Anita Steen's husband owned a plumbing and air business, and her relationship with Anita might be more helpful than Hunter's contacts.

About that time, Adam stomped into the kitchen, opened the refrigerator, and stared inside for several seconds before closing it and repeating the process with the pantry.

"Looking for something in particular?" she asked.

He shrugged. "There's nothing to do, and I'm hot." Her third child was no good at self-entertaining.

She mopped her brow. They couldn't stay in this four-bedroom oven much longer, but there was a place they could go with central air and a playmate for Adam.

"Hey, buddy. Let's go surprise Pops."

Adam groaned and slumped onto a barstool beside her. "Pops just sleeps in his chair. That's boring."

She swiveled her stool to face him. "I'll make you a deal. If visiting Pops is boring today, then I'll take you to see that new Marvel movie and buy you all the junk food you want."

Adam held out his hand to shake hers. "Deal."

The Tahoe's cold AC restored Adam's good humor, and he persuaded Dana to pick up burgers and milkshakes on the way. She vowed to get a vegetable in him at least once before the older kids returned from camp.

Adam slid out of his seat and accepted the drink carrier of shakes Dana handed him. But when the yapping puppy greeted them in the yard, she had to perform an acrobatic move to grab the cups without dropping the food bag or her purse.

"Pops, you got a dog?" Adam's excitement mirrored the puppy's. After a solid half hour of playing, Patch passed out on the carpet, and Dana convinced Adam to come to the table to eat his cold fries and melted milkshake.

"Adam," said Edward. "I'm gonna need an assistant to help me get this little guy trained. You interested?"

What recently-turned-nine-year-old boy *wouldn't* be interested? His enthusiastic "yes" woke up Patch.

Dana left as Adam coached his grandfather on how to find YouTube videos on dog training.

When she returned home, a work truck bearing the Steen's Plumbing, Heating, and Air logo was blocking her spot in the driveway. She parked along the curb and gave thanks for the mentoring group and the friendships it afforded her. Inside, she found Will rummaging in the pantry like one of their sons.

"Looking for something in particular?" she asked.

He stuck his arm out and waved a granola bar. "This whole thing is full of expired snacks and opened Pop Tarts packages."

"Leave them. At least until we find out if we can afford to buy groceries *and* get the air back on."

"Pretty great though that your friend sent her husband right over. Glad you thought of them."

"We need to thank Josie for that," she said over the doorbell. Will led Harvey out back while Dana greeted Walter Steen who was wiping his hands on a shop towel.

"You want the good news or the bad news first?" he asked.

She was overthinking her options when Will appeared and put his hand on her shoulder. "Hit us with the bad news first, my good man."

"Looks like lightning fried your compressor last night. Pretty common. But the good news is that I can get you a new one installed this afternoon at the friends and family rate."

Hopefully that rate would keep them from having to live on expired granola bars and dried out Pop Tarts.

Chapter 38

Edward's new pet was keeping him on his toes and off Dana's sofa. When she called to remind him to take his medications, he regaled her with Patch's antics, which both worried and delighted her. Perhaps a puppy was more work than he could handle, and he'd get run down. There again, Dana saw a light in his eyes in the last few days that she hadn't seen since before her mom got sick.

Patch was keeping Adam out of the doldrums this week too. He completed his chores as soon as he awoke and begged to be dropped at his Pops' house before Dana could even finish her first cup of coffee. She reminded him he had his own dog to brush and play with to no avail.

On Friday when Dana dropped him off, her dad was slow to answer the door. She was about to use her key to get in when he finally opened it, haggard and still in pajamas.

"Dad, are you feeling alright? You look awful."

"Good morning to you too, sunshine," he said as he planted a kiss on her forehead and handed off a wiggly ball of fluff to Adam. "What I look like is a seventy-four-year-old man with a newborn. I don't get more than two hours of sleep at a time, and my back is killing me from bending over to clean up accidents all day long."

She braced herself believing he was going to ask her to

take the puppy.

"I moved his crate next to my bed, so when he whines, I can comfort him. I just hope he doesn't outgrow it too quickly. Vet thinks he'll be medium-sized, but it's hard to say since he's a mutt." Edward went on to describe how leash training went yesterday, but the request to offload his new acquisition never came. Could it be that Patch was a well-timed gift from Heaven to help a grieving old man move forward with hope?

Adam yelped. "No biting, Patch!"

"You three stay out of trouble, and I'll be back in a couple of hours."

Dana had a long list of to-dos before Leah and Nate got home from camp tomorrow, beginning with a meeting with Carlos.

After she had forwarded the rejection letter to him, he'd texted What does Elise know?

Books, she replied.

He'd asked her to meet for coffee to discuss it further. He was already seated when she arrived at the coffee shop, and he stood as she sat down. "What are you drinking? I'm buying."

She felt awkward letting another man buy her a drink, even if it was just coffee. It was technically his fault she got her hopes up about a book deal, though, so she didn't protest.

"Vanilla skim latte, please." She noticed he had left a book on the table, one he was reading perhaps. She recognized the author as a bestseller. When Carlos returned with their drinks, he pushed the book across the table to her.

She turned it over and glanced at the back cover. "Are you starting a summer book club?"

He steepled his fingers and rested his chin on them. "Elise passed on this book."

Dana didn't understand. She smiled and shook her

head slightly, hoping he would explain.

He tapped the book cover with his index finger. "Six years ago, Hugo Thomas was an unknown writer seeking representation. He sent this manuscript to several agents, including Elise. All of them passed on it. Eventually he self-published and marketed the heck out of it, and as you probably know, it made him a lot of money. So, I'll say it again, what does she know?"

Dana leaned forward with her hands clasped on the table. "Then why would you send her my story and encourage me to write a novel at her suggestion?"

"Elise's an expert, yes. And she has helped me tremendously as a writer. I consider her a trusted friend as well as my agent, but her opinion is not the end all be all. Don't let her disapproval influence your self-worth. I think your instincts about the mother were spot on, and you should finish the novel. Don't give up because of one person's 'no.'"

She leaned back and took a sip of her latte. She'd invested so much of the past five months into writing at the expense of sleep and time with her family. To not finish it after all that would feel like it had been a waste of time. On the other hand, in five months, she had only managed to complete about a third of the novel. At this rate, she would still be working on it when Leah left for college. Not only that, but the sting of rejection was more painful than she had expected, and she wasn't sure she could endure it multiple times.

"I will take that under advisement," she said. "So, no book club, then."

He laughed. "You'll be back in class in the fall, won't you?"

Dana wasn't sure. She couldn't in good conscience spend money on a writing class for herself when the family's financial future was up in the air. "I don't know yet if I'll be able to make it work."

He told her to come to class when she could, and he'd let her audit the class for free without being on the official role if it would help.

"Why are you being so nice to me?" She assumed his motives were pure, but she hadn't seen him offer the same help to other members of the class, so she had to ask.

"No writer left behind. You have a gift, but you're so unwilling to put yourself ahead of anyone else that I'm afraid you'll never realize your true potential without a push. And, when you do make it big in the literary world, you can repay me with a glittering dedication page." He held up his hand gesturing to an invisible marquee. "To the world's greatest creative writing instructor. Without you, none of this would have been possible."

Dana grabbed her purse and pretended to look for a pen. "Hold on, I'm gonna need you to repeat that while I write it down, so I won't forget between now and then."

He was right. Maybe not about her being a gifted writer. She wasn't so sure about that, but he *had* motivated her to dig deep and challenge herself this year in a way she had never taken the time to imagine. Carlos was her Miss Rita.

They spent a few minutes talking about her manuscript and developments and adjustments she could make to the work in progress.

"As a dad, I get Kelsey's struggle between tender affection and fierce protection of her son. I think most parents could consider doing the unthinkable when faced with their child's mortality."

Carlos had a family. The revelation shocked her more than it should have. He was bookish and disheveled, like he wasn't accustomed to taking care of himself, let alone other humans. He never struck her as the father type.

"You're surprised I have kids."

Dana tucked a loose strand of hair behind her ear. "It's not like I thought you lived on campus and didn't have a life outside of teaching, but you've never said otherwise."

He shared that he had gotten divorced last summer, and he was still struggling to find his place as a dad with only part time access to his two young sons who moved to Dallas for their mother's job.

Dana scrawled the web address of her church on a receipt she found in her purse. "I don't know what you're going through, but I can imagine it's not easy. There's a divorce care group that meets at my church, and you can find the details on the website. You should check it out. No one should struggle with something so heavy all alone."

She thought she detected something in his eyes. A sadness that was usually well-masked. He folded the receipt and tucked it into the book.

Dana steered the conversation back to writing. "I wrote another short story that I'd love for you to read." She told him about Rita Brewer's untimely passing and how it had shaken her. "I didn't know her well, but she was important to my dad. He made a passing comment about how she was up in Heaven reporting all his shenanigans to my mom, and it got me thinking about Heaven. I need to believe it's more than floating on clouds in white robes."

Her phone rang with a call from her dad, so Dana thanked Carlos, promising to email the story, and excused herself. She said a quick prayer as she answered that everything was alright with Adam and her dad.

Chapter 39

"Mom!" Adam screeched.

She waited with bated breath. His tone could indicate a DEFCON 1 emergency, or it could be his normal speaking voice.

"Can you ask Josie if the triplets can play out front and meet Patch? Me and Pops are coming to our house so we can get Harvey's old puppy harness."

Dana was pretty sure Harvey was twice Patch's size when he was born, but she didn't say so. "Sweetheart I'm not sure that's a good idea. Let's not take Patch in the house unless..." she heard a thud.

Adam sounded much further away, but loud, nonetheless. "Patch, no. Mom, hold on. The puppy knocked the phone out of my hand."

There was more commotion, and she heard her dad urge him to stay buckled in his seat.

"Dear God, let them get to my house in one piece," she prayed aloud. She had been trying to insist that they wait until she or Will could restrain Harvey before they came over with the puppy, but it was too late now. Her errands would have to wait. The background noise continued, and Dana deduced that the phone was sliding around in the floorboard, where it would hopefully stay until the car was safely in park. She hung up and called

Josie.

"What's up?" asked Josie. "You never call me."

"That's not true, but I'm driving and needed to talk to you before Adam gets there. He and my dad are bringing his new puppy over, and he wants you to bring the babies outside to play with it."

"Ah yes. I heard about the gas station stray." Adam had helped with water playtime in the late afternoons every day this week and must have told her.

"I was going to tell you when you came by Monday night, but I wasn't ready for Adam to find out about the puppy before my dad had even decided if he was going to keep it."

Josie chuckled. "He would have gotten his hopes up if he so much as *thought* he heard the word 'puppy,' I'm sure. What do you think? Is it safe for the babies to be around it?"

Dana was glad Josie couldn't see her face. If it weren't safe for babies to be around small puppies, would she have called in the first place?

"We'll all be there to supervise in case Patch gets too rambunctious, but I don't think you need to worry."

"Can't strays carry diseases like ringworm?"

"It's not a cat, and a vet has already given it a clean bill of health. Also, since when is the woman who forgets to brush her teeth and only bathes her kids when they stink a germophobe?" Josie was acting like Dana let Adam play with a feral, parasite-infested stray, and she felt judged as a mother.

"Touché. I'm not used to being around animals, other than Harvey, okay? My mother wouldn't let us have pets."

Dana wasn't surprised. Marie was too fastidious to tolerate fur and slobber. "How about you think of it like a field trip to the petting zoo? I'm on my way home, but Adam may be at your door before I get there."

Next, she called Will to make sure he was dressed.

Since he wasn't keeping regular business hours anymore, his casual attire had become little more than boxers and a tee shirt. Her call went straight to voicemail. At least she'd tried to warn him.

Will was pacing and talking on the phone when she walked in. It sounded official, and he put up a finger indicating he needed a minute. He was appropriately clothed, so she left him to his all-important call. She crossed the cul-de-sac to where Josie spread a blanket under her lone shade tree.

"Can I help you bring everyone outside?" Dana asked.

"Please. They're too mobile now for me to take my eyes off them even for a second."

Dana lifted Olivia onto her hip and held the door for Josie who had a boy in each arm. "Get used to it. For the next eighteen years, you'll be chasing after them and trying to keep them out of trouble, while they help each other try to get away from you."

Josie groaned.

"The bright side is that you won't have to lug them around like that much longer."

Dana and Josie perched on the edges of the blanket, but keeping the babies on it proved impossible. The triplets were already happily exploring the grass when Edward pulled up to the curb. Adam hopped out as soon as the car stopped. He set Patch on the grass, and the pup clumsily galloped toward the humans.

The look on Josie's face made Dana laugh. Her friend looked like a starry-eyed little girl and a mama bear all at once.

"You have *seen* a puppy up close before, haven't you?"

Josie cut her eyes at her. "I wasn't raised in a bubble. I've just never seen such an adorable little thing taking a run at my kids like they might be his lunch." She put out her hands to keep Patch from pouncing on Olivia. "I don't know what to think."

Edward pulled a folding lawn chair out of his trunk and set it up next to the blanket. His face radiated joy tempered by exhaustion, much like on the day of Adam's robotics competition.

Olivia sucked in a sharp breath and then shrieked in delight as Patch licked her face. Adam grabbed him before he could knock her over and held the squirmy pup in his lap. The babies alternated between fascination and terror. Dana could identify, as few things were as adorable and destructive as puppies.

"I wonder if we should get a pet for the kids," said Josie.

"Do you have a death wish?" Dana shot back.

"You don't think we can handle a puppy with triplets?" asked Josie.

Adam nodded emphatically. "Sure, you can."

Dana scratched Patch behind the ears. "It's not that at all. Puppies are tough to train, and you have tiny people scooting around furniture and learning to walk. You would have to keep them out of dog messes and keep the puppy from chewing up the kids' toys." She didn't understand why Josie would even consider such an undertaking now and wondered if it was a mistake to let Adam bring Patch over.

"I agree," said Edward. "I've about thrown my back out bending over to clean up after this little guy. He shredded my good slippers this morning, and he's not a fan of sleeping when I'm sleeping. If you wait a couple of years, the kids will be big enough to help take care of a dog."

More like a decade. The Hardings got Harvey when Adam was four, and the kids only fed, bathed, and cleaned up after him when they were made to. They were into pet ownership for the cuddles and games of fetch, but the kids weren't much help with the upkeep.

"I'll be happy to bring Patch over for playdates," offered Edward. "Then you get the benefit of exposure to a pet without the burden of responsibility."

"Like my kids' relationship with Harvey," said Dana. She watched Connor use his mom as a climbing apparatus. He clung to her shirt and pulled himself upright. "They're getting so big. They're going to be running around here in no time at all."

Josie put her hand on Connor's back to offer him support. "Tell me about it. All their physical therapy is really paying off, but now I am more tired than I was when they were immobile."

Sometimes Dana longed for those days with her kids, especially when Leah was particularly cutting with her words, but the benefits of having older children outweighed the yearning for little ones. She hoped in a couple of months when Leah got her driver's license that she could get some of her life back that was spent waiting in parking lots. Then maybe she would have time to get more writing done.

"Is ECI still sending the physical therapist, or have they graduated?" she asked.

Josie told her they were still receiving visits twice a month that would end on their birthday. "The physical therapist has been impressed with their progress. He said they're hitting average benchmarks for their age now instead of showing signs of preemie development."

Olivia pulled up on Edward's legs, and he leaned over to hold her hands. He answered her excited jabbers with his own babytalk. Dana thought about how far the babies had come in less than four months. Then she watched Adam stroke Patch's fur until the little dog drifted off to sleep in his lap. He was growing up so fast. All the kids were, and soon Leah would be ready to go off to college. It was a lot of change.

"Oh, guess what?" Josie said. "I forgot to tell you my

big news."

Dana held her breath. Moments ago, Josie considered getting a dog, so there was no telling what was on her mind.

"Hunter's parents want to pay for cosmetology school and childcare for the triplets while I get my license."

"Oh wow! That's been your dream since forever." Dana was happy for her, but she couldn't help worrying that she might regret putting the babies in daycare after being home with them all these months. Staying home was hard, but so was being a working mom.

Becoming a stay-at-home mother had never been on her list of life goals, but the pull to be with Leah and to be the one who witnessed all her firsts was stronger than her desire to pursue her career. When Nate came along, the cost of daycare for the two children would have been more than she'd made working at the library. Sometimes she missed working, but she never regretted being available for her kids or sitting with her mother at chemo treatments. She shook herself out of her reverie and refocused her attention on Josie.

"We're shooting for January enrollment. In the meantime, I talked to a woman who runs a play group for mothers and their multiples, and we are meeting them next week for a park play date. It'll be good to make some friends in our same stage of life."

"Jack's daughter?" asked Adam.

"That's right."

Dana tilted her head and creased her brow as she tried to recall a Jack in Adam's circle of influence. "Are you talking about the mailman?"

He nodded.

"It's a long story," said Josie.

"Jack talked to Josie about his daughter and her twins the other day," explained Adam.

Josie shrugged. "So, not that long after all."

It made Dana happy to see Josie and her dad both moving forward in their lives, even it if included a new animal and more chaos. Now if she could gain some forward momentum in her own life.

She thought of Will's important-sounding phone call earlier and decided to check on him while Adam was occupied. She pushed herself off the ground. "I'll be right back."

"Can you bring me a popsicle?" Adam asked.

Dana found Will in the bedroom donning dress clothes. "This is a look I haven't seen in a while."

He told her he had a job interview with a food distributor. "It's only a senior VP position, but the pay is good, and I wouldn't have to travel much."

She adjusted his tie. "Or work nights and weekends?"

"Probably not."

"Is that what your call was about earlier?"

"No, that was the restaurant manager. He said the new supplier is giving him grief about their account."

"Let me guess, Big Kitchen?"

He tapped the side of his nose. "Bingo. But if I nail this interview, we can put Big Kitchen Supply behind us."

She wished him luck and kissed him goodbye before heading back to Josie's with a handful of popsicles. Progress seemed to be on the horizon for the Hardings after all.

Chapter 40

Leah squeezed a bottle of shampoo onto a plastic tarp from the garage while Nate doused it with the garden hose. They returned from camp yesterday, and all three kids were getting along as if they hadn't seen each other in weeks rather than five days. Dana savored the break from their usual sibling bickering, not even caring if their homemade Slip 'n Slide killed the grass.

She watched them from an Adirondack chair on the patio and propped her feet on the edge of the unlit fire pit, forgetting for a moment that the midday summer sun would have heated the bricks to scorching. She jerked her legs back with a yelp. Nate offered to cool the fire pit with the hose, but she declined. Her clothes would certainly end up wetter than the brick.

Will's interview was two days ago, and Dana had barely seen him since he left for it. He'd worked late at the restaurant Friday and Saturday nights and missed church this morning, which annoyed her. They always attended church together, and the questions from the other parishioners about Will's absence meant she had to explain his career change.

"Mom, you should give it a try," yelled Nate. "It's really fun."

"I know," she replied. "I'm the one who taught you

how to make it extra slippery, but it hurts a lot more to fly across the yard on your belly when you get to be my age."

"Yeah, we can't afford for your poor old mom to break a hip," interjected Will.

She hadn't heard him come outside, but now she squinted up at him in the sunlight and accepted a glass of iced tea he proffered.

He sat in the chair next to her. "Ouch!" he cried as he attempted to prop his feet on the firepit as she had earlier.

Dana raised her glass and took a sip. "Serves you right for calling me old."

He leaned over and kissed her cheek. "I'm sorry, hon. I didn't mean *old* old, but you're not Slip n' Slide young either."

She shot him an icy glare that he would hopefully understand went deeper than his teasing about her age.

The kids commanded, "Watch, Mom. You're not watching. Did you see me slide?"

"Dana, you know I worked 1:00 this morning. I didn't skip church on purpose."

Her tight-lipped smile didn't reach her eyes. "The restaurant closed at 11:00, so I'm having a hard time understanding the two extra hours in the middle of the night." Even if he had a good reason, her emotions were still raw from his secret dealings with Helena Whatshername. "Makes me wonder what you were doing and with whom."

"There were customers until midnight, and we couldn't kick them out. Then I had to help the manager rectify all the tickets for the day. That was after the front and back of the house employees had all gone home."

They both flinched as Adam sprayed the hot patio and splashed them.

"And before you get upset about me being alone with the manager in the middle of the night, *his* name is Dave, just like my brother-in-law. He's an older gentleman who took over managing the place after the last guy was fired for shady dealings that almost bankrupted the owner. This Dave is single with grown kids, so he's never in a hurry to go home to his empty house."

A wave of guilt settled on Dana. Restaurant Dave reminded her of her dad. If Will's consulting gig helped alleviate some of his loneliness, she shouldn't fault her husband for staying late and sleeping in today.

"Mom," shouted Adam. "Can you bring us some more shampoo?"

"Make it dish soap," said Nate.

Will got up to retrieve the soap as Dana watched Nate sling Adam across the tarp by his feet. "Watch his head." she yelled.

"This free Slip n' Slide is going to end up costing a fortune." Will tossed the bottle to Nate.

Will's phone dinged with an incoming text at the same time Dana felt hers vibrate in her pocket. She braced for bad news from her dad.

"It's my sister," said Will. He read the text and paraphrased it. "She wants all of us to meet them at the coast in a couple of weeks."

Even after the friends and family discount on their new air conditioner unit, there wasn't much budget for a family vacation right now.

"She said they got the house for a steal and don't want us to pay anything as their way of thanking us for keeping their boys last March, and Harvey is welcome, too. Would we want to drive that far with the dog?" It sounded like Will had already decided this was a good idea.

Hopefully the invitation meant the Wallaces' marriage was on steadier ground now. She quickly weighed the pros and cons. Will's consultancy job and leaving her dad were the main drawbacks. "Can you get off with that short of notice?"

He ran his hand over his hair. "Restaurant Dave will

be fine on his own. Can you handle a week of Julia and Brother-in-Law Dave?"

"Sure." The beach was a big place. Even if the house got crowded, they'd be outside enjoying the sand and the waves most of the time anyway. She was picturing the surf melting her stress away when she got drenched by the hose.

"Sorry, Mom," yelled Adam. He didn't look sorry at all but rather amused with himself.

"Maybe we could send the kids with Julia and Dave and have the house to ourselves for a week." She went inside to dry off and check in on her dad.

"Hey, sweetie. Get down."

"That's how you answer the phone now, Dad?"

"This dog has more energy than Adam's entire robotics team. What's up?"

She told him about Julia and Dave's invitation and asked how he would feel about them leaving town for a week.

"Sweetheart, I'm a grown man. I don't need a babysitter," he groused.

"True, but I can't go out of town in good conscience unless I know you're going to take care of yourself. I'm also going to call you and make sure you take your pills every day."

"Great, it'll be exactly like you're still here," he said.

"You could come with us." She bit her lip. Julia hadn't included Edward in her invitation, and she was speaking out of turn.

"I don't think so. Patch, no biting. Look, Dana. A long car trip would be stressful for all of us, and Patch is too young to stay in a kennel. He and I will stay here and be just fine. You and Will need a getaway. I've noticed the tension building between you two lately, and you need to refresh without worrying about your old man."

How was he so astute and full of wisdom some of the time and so scattered at others? "Dad, I'm always going to worry about you," she said softly.

"I know, hon. No! Bad dog. I have to go." The call disconnected.

She watched the kids through the window and laughed at their goofiness. How long before Leah was too mature to play in the water with her brothers? After all, she would be off to college in three years. That thought made her stomach roil. The day was coming quickly when they would all be grown, and she would be downsized out of a twenty-five-year career.

Will slipped his arm around her waist and nuzzled her neck. "Are we doing this?" he asked.

"Why not? A beach trip with the in-laws can't possibly be as hard as anything else we've been through this year."

Chapter 41

Josie

The triplets' newfound mobility kept Josie too preoccupied to care that her mom hadn't called in over a week, or that her whole family agreed she was a self-centered brat. Mostly.

The babies would awaken soon from their naps, so she dragged the kiddie pool from the garage into the front yard and began to fill it.

A car she didn't recognize turned onto the cul-de-sac and pulled up to the curb in front of her. As the driver popped the trunk and unloaded luggage, Marie Saldana opened the rear door and waved.

Josie dropped the hose and rushed over. "Mom, what are you doing here?"

Marie pulled Josie's head down and kissed her cheek. "*Mija,* water play is a back yard activity."

"There's no shade in the back."

Her mother wasn't listening. She thrust the handle of a rolling suitcase into Josie's hands and poked her head into the car, commanding another passenger.

Josie couldn't distinguish through the window tint who else was in the car, but she had a feeling. Her palms grew slick, and her jaw tightened.

Laurel dragged herself out of the car and made a

whole production of pulling on her backpack and adjusting the straps. Josie rolled her eyes. *We get it. You're outdoorsy.*

The driver pulled away leaving the three women to their awkward reunion.

"*Mija,* you're flooding the yard."

The pool was overflowing, so Josie left the suitcase and sloshed through the grass to turn off the faucet.

"Girls, take the bags inside. I have a casserole…oh no. I left it in the car."

On cue, the same car turned onto the street again and stopped at the curb. The driver rolled down his window and passed Marie a turquoise insulated casserole carrier.

"Dinner is saved," she announced.

"That remains to be seen," Laurel mumbled.

Josie grabbed the suitcase again and hissed, "What are you doing here?"

"Good question. I went to Albuquerque to work on wedding plans with Mom and the aunts. Next thing I know, we're on a plane to the flatlands, which is felony kidnapping. Living here should be a felony."

That was the most words Josie's big sister had said to her all year, and she used them to insult her town.

As her mother made her way to the front door, a wave of dread filled Josie. Her house was in its usual state of disarray. She said a silent prayer that she wouldn't get scolded for her poor housekeeping in front of Laurel.

The sound of baby chatter filled the silence as Josie and Laurel dropped the luggage in the guest room, careful not to get in each other's path.

"My angels, your *abuelita* is here!" Marie lifted Olivia out of her crib and smothered her in kisses. Josie picked up Ben and held him out for his Abuelita to kiss before reaching for Connor.

Laurel leaned against the door frame with her arms crossed. Her apparent disinterest in her niece and nephews bothered Josie far more than her dig at living in Lubbock and at her months-long radio silence.

"Laur, put Connor in his highchair for a snack," directed her mother.

"Which one is Connor?" Laurel asked as she reluctantly stooped to pick up the only baby on the floor. She lifted him by his waist, and he teetered and arched his back. She had clearly never done this before.

"Don't hurt yourself. I've got him," Josie said. She shifted Ben to her left hip and took Connor with her right arm.

Marie led the way to the kitchen with Olivia, followed by Josie with the boys. Laurel trailed behind them. Once the babies were strapped into highchairs, Josie fired off two texts to Hunter.

SOS!!! Mom and sister just showed up. Mom is barking orders like she runs the place.

I can't with Laurel. Help

He didn't respond right away as she had hoped, but then again, if he was with a client or in the middle of a project, he wouldn't be able to check his phone.

Marie scattered Cheerios on the highchair trays and passed out sippy cups. Josie didn't even bother telling her mother that this was not normal procedure for them. Instead, she cut to the chase.

"Who wants to tell me why you guys descended on my house without so much as a heads up that you were coming? And Ma, you were here like two weeks ago. How can you afford to fly out again so soon? Or take off work in the middle of the week?"

Marie shrugged. "I have points, and it's our slow season."

That may have been true enough. After all, her mother was an accountant, but Josie wasn't buying it. "Right. Well, if you're here just to hang out, then I'm afraid you should have called first. We have plans and won't have much free time." She racked her brain to come up with a plausible event that would allow her to avoid her mom and sister.

"Oh sure," said Laurel. "Didn't you see the pool out front? Josie's hosting a rager this afternoon, and we're cramping her style."

Josie narrowed her eyes at Laurel. A soft knock at the front door kept her from saying something she might regret.

"We came to help you with sunscreen and swim diapers," said Leah.

Adam shook a mesh bag of bath toys and ducked under Josie's arm that held the door open. The older Harding children filed in behind him but stopped short when they saw Marie and Laurel.

"Oops, we didn't know you had company," said Nate.

"It's okay, neither did I," said Josie. "My family showed up without calling first, but water fun is still on. We'll give the babies a minute to eat and then get them ready to go outside."

"Since when do they eat Cheerios for a snack?" asked Leah through the side of her mouth and out of earshot of the women in the kitchen.

"Apparently since my mother arrived," mumbled Josie without moving her lips. The triplets had begun nibbling on finger foods at mealtimes, which helped cut down on their impatience with the unequal adult-to-baby ratio, but they weren't adept enough at their pinching grasp to get many into their mouths. The ritual was more for practice than sustenance.

"Should we go?" whispered Leah.

Josie grasped her arm. "Please don't. They're here to ambush me, but they can't if you guys are here." Josie wondered if she was breaking some code of ethics by using the Harding kids as a buffer between her and Laurel and their mother, but it couldn't be helped. Without them, an all-out war might break out before Hunter got home.

Ben swiped his hand across the highchair tray, clearing

it of all cereal bits and then threw his sippy cup over the side and watched it bounce across the tile.

"I guess that means you're done, buddy." Leah unbuckled Ben and lifted him out of the seat. "Wanna go play in the water?"

Josie followed Leah's lead wishing she'd had the fortitude to intervene and rescue the kids from their grandmother's forced snack time on her own.

"They're not really eating, so let's all go play outside, shall we?" She took Olivia from her seat and handed her off to Nate and then picked up Connor. "Mother, you won't mind dealing with all this will you?" She waved her hand over the highchair trays and retreated from the kitchen with Adam on her heels before Marie could respond.

"You call your mom 'Mother?'" asked Adam when they were in the nursery again.

"Only when she's aggravating me, and today she's super aggravating." As soon as she said it, Josie remembered the baby monitor and cringed.

"Why are you aggravated at your mom?" No one would need a monitor to hear Adam's loud voice across the house.

"Shhh," admonished his sister. "You're being rude."

"Josie said it first."

Leah had already dressed Ben in his swim diaper and sun hat. She massaged sunscreen onto his exposed skin. "Adam, did you tell Josie that you used your own money to buy new water toys?"

"Oh yeah. They're tubes and balls that go through them."

Was changing the subject always that easy with nine-year-olds?

She managed to avoid uncomfortable conversation with her mom and sister for the duration of water play time. Marie knelt beside the pool and splashed with her grandbabies until she was soaked. Laurel stood off to the side, but Josie noticed she took pictures and smiled from time to time.

Hunter still hadn't replied to her texts. She hoped everything was okay at work.

After a while, Marie announced, "I think I'm going to find dry clothes and put the casserole in the oven." She went inside without so much as offering to help get the babies dried off, which seemed weird to Josie. Her mother may have been a bit of a control freak, but she was helpful to a fault.

After the Hardings had gone home, and the babies were dry and happily playing, Josie confronted her family again. "We were interrupted before anyone told me the reason for this surprise visit. Mom, care to explain?"

There was a long pause during which Laurel never looked up from the floor. Finally, Marie answered. "I want you two to sort out whatever is going on between you before it ruins your sister's wedding."

Heat crept up Josie's neck. Before *she* ruined her sister's wedding. "You already know everything. Laurel doesn't want us at her wedding. We aren't going to the wedding. End of discussion. You didn't need to fly out here for that."

Connor pulled up on the coffee table, so she lowered herself to the floor nearby. Ben immediately used her as a climbing structure, which was a great diversion from the intensity of the conversation.

"Mom made me come." Laurel sounded like an eight-year-old child.

Their mom threw up her hands. "Well, I'm just the aggravating mother. What do I know?" She muttered something unrepeatable in Spanish about her spoiled, ungrateful offspring and stomped to the laundry room. That explained why she didn't stay to help get the babies out of the pool.

Josie mentally cursed the baby monitor as the hum of

the garage door announced Hunter's arrival.

He peered around the doorway assessing the room. "Is it safe to come in?"

"Ah, so you did see my texts." Josie could accept if his busy day kept him from his phone, but she didn't appreciate being ignored on purpose.

He grinned and gave her a sheepish shrug. "It seemed like a good idea to let y'all have some time together before I swooped in."

She tried to melt him with the heat of her piercing scowl. "Can I see you in the other room, please?"

He extended his hand and pulled her off the floor. "How's it going?"

Josie led him to their room and closed the door. She pulled him close. "I still don't know why they just showed up," she whispered.

"They can't hear us in here, Jos."

"You underestimate Marie Saldana. She's pouting because of the last thing she overheard me say about her." She accidentally spit. "Sorry."

He wiped his cheek and chuckled. "Your mom dragged Laurel out here to fix whatever's going on between the two of you."

"But that's just it. I don't know what's…" She trailed off as his words finally struck her. "I didn't say Laurel was dragged. You knew they were coming." Her jaw dropped. "I can't believe this."

"Jos, sweetie." Hunter grasped both her hands. "Your mom's really torn up about this thing with your sister. Please let her help." He tilted his head and gave her a crooked smile. "For my sake."

Her forehead wrinkled, and her eyes narrowed. "For your sake. How is any of this a burden on you?"

"When *you're* not talking to your mom, she's talking to *me*, and I need things to go back to normal."

She chuckled. "What's normal?"

He leaned in and kissed her. "It's where your mom calls *you*, and my relationship with her is relegated to reaping the benefits of her cooking when she comes to visit."

Chapter 42

Hunter scooped up Olivia and raised her into the air as he lowered himself into the recliner. "Hey, baby girl. Did you have a good day?"

She grabbed his face and screeched.

"And what about everyone else? Did you ladies have a good flight?"

"Mom left the casserole in our Lyft," said Laurel.

Marie busied herself folding a load of towels Josie had left in the drier. She waved Laurel off. "He came right back. It's fine."

Josie sat on the edge of the sofa with her hands poised on her knees. She couldn't stomach another round of small talk. "You came here to clear the air or whatever, so let's get to it." She addressed Laurel pointedly. "You've barely checked in since the triplets were born because you're too busy living your best hobo life. I told myself it was because you were busy with your hiking trip, and that you didn't have service or battery power, but somehow you managed to keep up with Mom."

She leaned against the arm of the sofa. She knew she should let her family speak, but she couldn't resist one small dig at Laurel. "Also, hiking in winter is like praying for frostbite and starvation. It's ridiculous."

"*Mija!*" She swiped at Josie with a hand towel.

Laurel lowered herself onto the floor with the boys. "It's actually a lot easier to snowshoe in the winter than in the summer." She handed a ball to Connor who slobbered on it and dropped it into her lap. She pinched it with two fingers, looking a little green.

At Marie's prodding, Laurel finally admitted that her Appalachian adventure had come about not because of a sabbatical of her choosing but because she had been placed on administrative leave from the university during an investigation into misconduct allegations by a student.

"I didn't do anything wrong," she explained. "But the court of public opinion had already made up its mind. So, I needed to get away, not just from campus, but from the media and from any place where people believed I had set up a cheating ring for hire to help my students get into law school."

Josie said, "At the risk of sounding like the spoiled brat you've both accused me of being, how does that justify you ghosting me and not wanting my family at your wedding?"

"I figured you'd seen the news story because it's been everywhere since the fall semester. And I didn't want to talk about it. It's humiliating, you know?"

No, she didn't know. She had been a little too busy to watch the news coming out of Austin. Besides, one more college scandal wouldn't have caught her attention. "That's it? *That's* why you've been ignoring me for so long and why you don't want me at your wedding?" Wow, she really did sound self-absorbed.

Laurel didn't say anything for a beat too long, and Marie nudged her with her foot. "Ow! Fine." she continued. "When I called Dad to tell him I got engaged, he wasn't supportive like I thought he would be."

Josie clutched her chest and feigned surprise. Javier Saldana was known for many things, but support wasn't one of them.

Laurel said their father was shocked by her engagement and admitted he had assumed she was gay. "He also told me not to count on his help with the wedding because he was tapped out after setting up trust funds for the triplets and paying their hospital bills. That's when I got mad at you. Dad is never there for me, but he did all that for you."

"Wait, what?" Hunter interjected. "He didn't do any of that."

"I tried to tell her," said Marie. "If your father's assets are tied up in anything, it's his wife's routine maintenance."

"Are you sure that's what he told you?" asked Josie.

Laurel rolled her eyes. "Maybe he was talking about some other triplets, but I'm sure that's what he said."

Josie didn't know who to believe. Her dad had a track record of letting his girls down, so Laurel should have known not to trust him. "Let me get this straight. You decided to hate me based on one conversation with the same man who missed your high school graduation for a court case. You either made up the flimsiest lie ever, or you believed one yourself."

Laurel balled her fists. "Why would Dad lie to me?"

"Why would *I*?"

The babies were beginning to fuss. It was time for their dinner, so they tabled the discussion.

Laurel stood and picked up Connor. This time she lifted him under the arms with more confidence than she had earlier. "I can help. What are we talking, bottle? Puree?"

Josie tried to take him from her. "It's fine. You don't have to help out of guilt. Give me my baby." Connor held onto Laurel's shoulder and turned his face away from his mother. Her son was a traitor.

"He wants his Auntie Laurel. Don't you, Connor. Can you say 'Laurel?'"

"Ls and Rs are the last sounds toddlers learn to say. At best, you might get to be 'Aunt Wah-wah,'" said Josie. She pointed out Connor's highchair.

Hunter and Marie buckled in Ben and Olivia while Josie set out bibs and dished jars of baby food into three divided bowls.

"Have you ever thought about making their food instead of buying jars?" asked Laurel. "You'd save money and prevent a ton of waste, especially since you're feeding three times as many babies as the average family." Leave it to the only adult in the room without children to offer suggestions on how to best care for them.

Josie's lips formed a tight smile. Before she could remind her sister that a couple of hours ago, she didn't even know how to hold a baby, let alone feed one, Hunter intervened.

"Are you volunteering to make baby food for us? That would be amazing since we don't have the time or energy to do it ourselves." He caught Josie's eye and winked at her.

Hunter's support kept her from doing childish things like sticking her tongue out at her sister, which she still kind of wanted to do. Instead, she changed the subject. "So, Laurel, how did you and Jeff...erson meet?" She almost forgot two-thirds of the man's name. That would have *really* put her on Laurel's bad side.

"On a meet up site for outdoor adventurers."

Marie's head swung almost off her shoulders. "*Ay,mija.* That's how predators stalk victims. You told me he taught you how to rappel over the winter break."

"Yeah. I found out about the rappelling class on the website. Then the campus cheating scandal erupted, and I saw that he was leading the Appalachian snowshoeing trip. It was the perfect thing to take my mind off the job."

Josie leaned against the counter. This was the first time since their trip to Oklahoma that she wasn't needed at feeding time. She smirked at Laurel. "I bet it was. Took your mind off your job and put it right on your guide." That earned her a withering stare from her mother.

Laurel tentatively spooned a bite of peas into Connor's mouth. "It wasn't like that."

Their mother used the edge of the spoon to wipe sweet potatoes off Ben's cheek. "What is it like then when you decide to marry a man you have never seen in a real-world environment. You've barely dated. He wants you to move to another state where he has a seasonal job, not a career, and you don't even know if you can still teach. I can see why your father was hesitant to drop several thousand dollars on your wedding."

Josie squirmed. The conversation was less tense when they were fighting about how she was a wedding-ruiner. She edged in between her mom and sister and took the baby food bowl from Laurel. "How 'bout I take over?"

Laurel stood with her hands on her hips. "Mom, stop. Jefferson *owns* a ski shop and a guide business. Extreme kayaking, rafting, snowshoeing."

Josie tried to process what kind of depraved mind produced a person who wanted to take month-long treks in the dead of winter while her sister continued railing at their mother.

"It's not like he's a vagrant. And don't think I didn't notice you and your gossipy sisters making fun of him in Colorado. He's very intelligent and has two college degrees if you must know. As for *my* career, I've already gotten an offer at UC Boulder to teach political science."

Hunter congratulated her on her good news, but Laurel admitted it wasn't all great. Her relocation stipend wouldn't cover the penalties for terminating her contract in the middle of a research grant and getting out of her condo lease early.

"Jefferson and I put a down payment on a house, and we were counting on Dad to help with the wedding like he did Josie's. Since he won't, all we can afford is a tiny, cheap wedding."

"Shouldn't the marriage be more important than the wedding?" asked Hunter. Two sets of eyes shot daggers at him while Josie stifled a giggle. Her mother's family did not mess around when it came to wedding plans.

"Of course," Laurel said. "That doesn't mean I don't deserve the same attention on my big day that Baby Sister got."

Josie wiped Connor's face. "Would you lay off? Dad did not pay for my wedding. Mom and our aunts did all the decorating, and Hunter's family paid for the caterer. Nor did Dad pay off the kids' NICU stays. Our bank account will attest to that. You're bitter about something that has nothing to do with me."

"Ladies, as entertaining as this is, why don't we go to the source?" Hunter pressed something on his phone, prompting the distinct ring of a Facetime call. The women got quiet. He angled his phone so everyone in the kitchen could see Javier's face.

Although it was only 4:30 on the West Coast, he was propped on pillows in bed. He had a grayish pallor despite the sunlight streaming onto the bedspread.

Marie gasped, and Hunter shushed her with a subtle glance.

"Hey Javier, we are embroiled in a family debate over here and hoped you could help us out. There seems to be some confusion about the hospital bills you might have paid." Hunter caught his father-in-law up on Laurel's assertion. "Can you explain for everyone what's really going on?"

Javier laughed weakly and began coughing. "*Hola mis amores.* Laurel got it mostly correct. I did set up trust funds for the babies to pay for part of their education in case I'm not around to help them later. But the medical bills are mine."

Josie's stomach dropped. She didn't talk to her dad very often, but he'd never said anything about being in the hospital. She heard him say "cancer," but her ears began ringing, and she didn't register anything else. She absentmindedly spooned a bite of carrots onto Connor's forehead instead of into his mouth. It snapped her out of her daze. "Oh, my bad, Son." She reached for a wipe on the counter behind her, glad for the distraction from the sobering Facetime conversation.

Everyone said their goodbyes to Javier. Then no one spoke for a long time.

Laurel grabbed Josie up in a hug. "I'm so sorry," she said through sniffles. Josie returned the embrace while she choked back sobs.

Their mother wrapped her arms around them. "Now I feel like a heel for assuming your father missed the engagement party for his wife to get a nip and tuck. I should have checked on them."

Josie wiped her eyes. "Why would he keep such a big thing from us? He'd rather let his kids resent him for not showing up than admit weakness."

No one could explain Javier's motives for keeping his illness a secret. They could only pray for him to make a full recovery. After the babies were fed and bathed, the adults gathered around the table to enjoy Marie's casserole.

Hunter scooped a second helping onto his plate. "This is delicious, Marie. You know who else is turning into an amazing chef?"

Josie kicked him under the table. If her mother knew she had mastered some of her recipes, she might quit stocking their freezer.

"Ow!" He glared at her.

"Who, sweetie?" asked Marie.

"Um, Will. Our neighbor across the cul-de-sac." He shoveled another bite into his mouth.

Josie snickered. He hadn't even lied.

"How refreshing," Marie said. She shook her head, and Josie figured her mom didn't know what else to say in response to Hunter's random announcement.

"Hunter, if my dad can't make it, will you walk me down the aisle?" Laurel's eyes shone with tears.

Josie thought she'd had all the surprises she could handle today, but this one made her grin. Hunter would hate having to walk her sister down the aisle, but he would do it out of love.

"Okay, Aunt Wah-wah," he said. "And we can help cover the wedding expenses and take some pressure off of you and Jefferson."

Laurel adamantly shook her head. "No, I can't let you do that."

"Sure, you can. My father-in-law has already called dibs on paying for the triplets' education," he joked.

"Me too," Marie said, "You should have let me help in the first place instead of being stubborn like your father. Now tell us all about this cheap and tiny wedding that you tried to hide from your mother."

"I was planning to tell you in Albuquerque, but we left." Laurel described the corners they'd cut to limit the cost. To Josie, it sounded lovely and intimate. Fairy lights in the church courtyard, no dinner or assigned tables that make guests feel uncomfortable. She wished she had gone the simple route instead of letting her mother and aunts plan her over-the-top wedding extravaganza. But she thought it best to keep her regrets to herself and be a supportive sister.

"So, Denver huh?" asked Hunter when they were finally lying in bed later that night.

"Denver. More stops than driving to Oklahoma and no kitchen or help from your parents when we get there."

Hunter rolled on his side to face her. "But we won't have to sleep in bunk beds." There was that.

Reconciling with Laurel today had been a gift. She

wanted to savor it before worrying about travel plans again. "You know this is all your fault. If you had just answered my texts and kicked them out this afternoon, we wouldn't have to drive to Denver."

"You're not mad at me for inviting them here, are you?"

"You *invited* them?" She elbowed him in the ribs. "I thought Mom strong-armed you and swore you to secrecy. But you were the devious mastermind of the whole operation."

He tried to snuggle her. "I just don't like to see you unhappy, and I wanted y'all to clear the air and make up so you could get excited about cosmetology school."

She melted into his embrace. He knew her heart better than even she did sometimes. "Yeah well, you remember that when we're in the middle of nowhere halfway to Denver with three screamers and a bag of dirty diapers. Can you believe all this drama was over such a little misunderstanding?"

"Right? You were sure quick to forgive your sister when she blamed you for everything between her and your dad."

"I guess I could see why she would have a grudge under the circumstances."

Hunter asked if she was worried about her dad. How could she not be? He had always been an island, separated from the rest of her family, but he was still her dad.

"You, sir, are my hero. You fixed everything by bringing my mom and sister here. Thank you." She kissed him.

"Well not everything. We still have to drive to Denver with three babies."

"I think you mean 'we *get* to.'" Josie pulled the blanket up to her chin and fell asleep happy. She had so much to look forward to, and she couldn't wait to get to it.

STEPHANIE PAIGE KING

Chapter 43

Dana

"Put your phone away. We're at the beach, for crying out loud," admonished Julia.

Dana hadn't heard from her dad yet today. "I'm waiting for confirmation Dad's taken his pills and hasn't chased that puppy of his off a cliff or something."

"You live in the flattest place in Texas. I don't think you have to worry about cliffs."

Will and Dave finished setting up the shade canopy, and Will plunked into a chair next to Dana. "You don't know her dad very well then. Mischief has a way of finding him."

Will's phone chimed in the beach bag next to him. He ignored it until Dana poked him in the rib.

"Check it in case it's my dad." She gave him time to scan his screen. "Well? Is everything okay?"

Will let out a whoop. "It's fantastic. The food distributor offered me the job, and the compensation package is comparable to what I was making before. I haven't had time to look over the benefits, but this is what we've been praying for, Dana."

She leaned over to kiss him. "That's great news. I'm so proud of you."

"Celebratory dinner on us tonight," Will announced.

Julia congratulated her brother and trotted down the beach to take pictures of the kids skim boarding on the surf, and Dana checked her phone again. "I'm giving him ten more minutes, and then I'm sending Hunter over to check on Dad."

"Did you track his phone?"

"Yeah, it was at the park. Do you think he left it there?"

"I think he took the dog to the park. Maybe they made friends. Maybe he went to that Tai Chi class you've been hounding him about."

Doubtful. She checked the time.

"Mom, come look." yelled Nate. He and Adam were bent over something fascinating at the water's edge. Dana walked toward them.

"Don't pop it. Are you crazy?" yelled Nate.

At that, her pace quickened, and she saw the oblong blue balloon resting on the sand. It was a man-of-war.

"The top won't sting you," said Adam. Nate and Dana both swiped his hand away before he could test his theory.

"We do *not* take marine safety advice from Disney movies. Assume the whole thing will sting you. Always. It's fascinating though."

Tentacles trailed behind the polyp. As she snapped a photo of the creature, she thought to herself that there must be a biblical lesson in its beauty concealing its toxicity. If a blood curdling scream hadn't emanated from Leah, she might have mulled over the analogy.

A singular word pierced her thoughts. *Shark!* Terror paralyzed her momentarily before her maternal instincts kicked in, and she sprinted into the water to rescue Leah from danger. When she reached her daughter, Leah was standing in knee-deep water, and there was no blood in sight. Dana looked around for the predator that had attacked her, but she saw only Leah, unharmed.

"What happened?" Dana asked between gasps for air.

"Something touched my foot!"

That was a real possibility. After all, Texas beaches were not known for their crystal-clear waters. Any number of creatures could have swum by.

"Are you hurt?" asked Dana.

Leah shook her head. She was fine, only spooked.

"Thank goodness. But maybe reserve that scream for life-or-death matters, would ya?" Dana started back to shore and put her hands on her hips while she caught her breath. That's when she realized she didn't have her phone in her hand. She retraced her steps to where the boys were still examining the man-of-war.

"Boys, do you see my phone anywhere? I think I dropped it when I went to save your sister."

They shook their heads. "What did you save her from?"

"Don't ask, Nate. Just keep looking."

They scoured the beach until Nate exclaimed, "Found it!" He held up the dripping phone triumphantly.

Dana dropped her head. What were the odds that a sand and sea-soaked phone would work?

As though he could read her thoughts, he said, "You can put it in rice."

She already knew there was no rice in the rental house. She held her phone out in front of her, shaking as much excess sand and water out of the port as possible, and jogged back to the shade tent to slip on her flip flops.

"Where are you going?" asked Will.

She explained her predicament and trotted toward the long boardwalk that led to the house. "Try to call my dad," she called over her shoulder.

Dana examined her phone under the range light in the kitchen. It felt sticky from the salt water, so she rinsed it under the tap. At this point, what could it hurt? Then she rummaged through the cabinets looking for something that would dry it out.

"What are you looking for?" Will asked, startling her.

Dana jumped and hit her head on the open upper cabinet. She pursed her lips to stifle a swear word and clamped both hands on the top of her head. When the pain subsided enough for her to speak, she chastised Will for sneaking up on her. "Are you trying to kill me? Good luck starting that new job when you have to raise our kids on your own."

He wrapped a handful of ice cubes in a dish towel and gently pulled back her hands, replacing them with the towel. "I wasn't trying to sneak up on you. What were you looking for?"

"Something to dry out my phone."

"Your phone is water resistant. Maybe it's okay. Let's check."

They both peered down at the phone sitting on a paper towel next to the sink. Dana tapped the screen, but it was black. Keeping one hand on her head to hold the ice in place, she picked up her phone and held down the button on the side and waited. Nothing happened.

"Let's give it time to dry out and try again. We have the insurance plan though, so if it's dead, it won't break the bank to replace it," Will assured her.

She lowered the ice pack and tilted her head toward Will. "Any blood?"

He touched the spot. "You have a knot, but no blood. You're safe to go back in the water."

A giggle erupted in her throat and morphed into an all-out guffaw.

"What's so funny?" He used his thumbs and forefingers to pry up her eyelids. "This might be the sign of a concussion."

She batted his hands away. "I'm laughing at the irony. Your daughter was screaming like she was being attacked. I *literally* thought a shark bit our child. At first, I couldn't move, but the panic in her voice made me run to her, and that's when I must've let go of the phone. Now you're assuring me my wound won't make me shark bait. It's all so absurd. Like something that would happen to Dad." She had forgotten about him for a moment. "Oh no, now I can't even call him, and I don't know if he's okay."

Will put his arms around her. "I'm sure everything's fine, but even if it isn't, God's got it. We trust Him."

She did, mostly. It was a funny thing to be a control freak in charge of other humans without having any actual control. Trusting that things would work out for the best was all she could do.

"Let's go back to the beach and relax. Teach the kids how to build a proper sandcastle," Will suggested.

Building a sandcastle sounded more like a chore than a way to relax, but she gave her defunct phone a backward glance and followed Will outside.

When they reached the boardwalk, she took his hand. "Are you excited about this new job? I'm really happy for you, and I'm sorry if I was too distracted to make that clear."

He squeezed her hand. "Thank you. I *am* excited. It's been a fun challenge to help Restaurant Dave get the place back on its feet, and I am looking forward to another new challenge. I didn't realize I was getting complacent in my old job until I lost it."

"I guess this means I can sign up for the fall semester of creative writing?" After her conversation with Carlos at the coffee shop, she decided to stop wasting time, wondering if she had what it took to be a writer. She already was one and needed to act like it. Her very sanity might depend on it.

"Of course. You've always been a talented writer, and Carl was right that you should finish your book. And when you do get it published, you should send an autographed copy to that lady who rejected it."

They had reached the beach. Dana scanned the area

and saw Adam, their nephews, and Leah building together in the sand, but Nate was nowhere in sight. A sense of urgency washed over her once again.

She grabbed Will's arm and shook it. "Nate's missing. Will, we have to find Nate." She tried to take off running, frantic to find her missing child, who by now could have drifted out to sea, but her arm was tethered at the wrist. And why weren't his aunt and uncle keeping an eye on him?

Will pulled her to his side and pointed at the kids playing in the sand. "Look closer."

Dana followed his gaze and realized the four of them were not building a sandcastle at all but were burying Nate. They must have scooped out a hole, first because there wasn't even a body-shaped mound of sand, only his face peeking up through the earth, surrounded by his siblings and cousins.

She took a deep breath and let it out in a whoosh. "I guess that explains why your sister and Dave are sitting there calmly instead of trying to save our lost boy."

He laughed and ruffled her hair.

"Ow! Careful, sir." The bump on her head throbbed.

He hugged her against him. "I'm sorry. I didn't think. You're going to have to lighten up though, or you're going to have a heart..." He clamped his mouth shut.

"A heart attack like Rita Brewer?" Dana knew she needed to get a grip. He was right, but she didn't tell him so. She only smiled. "I'm going to need another vacation after this."

Julia walked toward them holding out Will's phone. "It's Edward."

Dana snatched it from her hand and swiped the screen. "Dad!"

"Will, your voice sounds so feminine. It must be the humid sea air," Edward joked.

"Very funny. Why haven't you called me back? Where

have you been? What happened?" Her questions spilled out so rapidly there was no way he could answer any of them.

"First of all, I did try to call you, but it went straight to voicemail. Second, I'm fine. *You*, on the other hand, need to learn to relax."

"So I've been told. Did you take your pills this morning?"

He assured her he had and that there was little chance of forgetting them with the alarms she put on his phone and her constant calls and texts. He went on to explain why he hadn't responded this morning in a timely manner. He and Patch walked to the park, and the puppy escaped his collar and took off after some ducks.

"It was probably the same ducks that tore up my flower bed last winter."

Dana's mind flashed back to the underwear and mailbox debacle, and she shuddered.

"That rotten dog ran straight into the pond, and I thought he would drown before I could get him out. Might make a fine hunting dog one day though."

Dana pinched the bridge of her nose and closed her eyes. "Dad, you don't hunt. Did you really get in the water? Because you know dogs can swim."

"Well, he got stuck in the mud. It was a whole thing. So, I took off my shoes and put my phone and keys in one of them and waded out to get him. Anyway, Patch and I were such a mess when I finally wrestled him back into his collar and tightened that thing so he couldn't wiggle out again that I just walked back home barefoot and hosed us both off in the front yard before we went inside."

He seemed lucid and competent, even if his circumstances were outlandish. "Let me guess, you left the shoes on the porch with your phone." That's probably what she would have done herself.

"Bingo. See? You have nothing to worry about."

When they ended the call, she felt relatively confident

that he was going to be alright on his own for the week. God had everything under control all along. She handed Will his phone and recounted the story to the adults, much to everyone's amusement.

"Your dad is such a fun guy," said Dave. "Who else coaches junior robotics and rescues strays at his age?"

Dana smiled. She hadn't thought of his antics so much as fun, but rather annoying and exhausting. Now though, she pictured her dad wading through pond sludge and laughed.

"You're right, he's a handful for sure, but my dad is pretty great." He would probably continue to struggle with dementia, but for now his condition was stable, and he was embracing life.

She sat in the sand with the kids and helped them sculpt a mermaid tail for Nate, resolving to embrace her own life more fully.

"Mom, take my picture," he said.

"Sorry, Son, I think my phone sleeps with the fishes now." She inhaled a deep breath of salty air and took in her sand-coated family with their tangled hair and sun kissed cheeks. Dana felt at peace. Happy even. Maybe she wouldn't become a renowned author, but she was hopeful for the future. God had her family in the palm of His hand, and she vowed to embrace all the callings He'd placed on her-wife, mother, daughter, friend, and writer.

Epilogue

Dana nervously paced the bookstore looking for a familiar face. It was the release party for an anthology of short stories, and "The Last Day" was one of them. It was the story she'd written after Rita's death. She had finally completed the novel version of "Dying to Donate," and was in the process of editing it. Now that Leah could drive and her dad was more independent again, she had more time to focus on writing.

Patch turned out to be just what the doctor ordered. The puppy forced Edward to stick to a schedule and exercise daily, which kept the brain fog at bay. Miss Simms had enlisted him to help with robotics club again, and Adam's team came in second place in the district competition.

Dana spotted Yvette and CiCi first and rushed to hug them. "Thank you so much for coming."

"Of course," said Yvette. "We wouldn't miss your big debut. I also saw the Steens and Kathy coming in."

It meant so much to Dana that her table group showed up to support her. In the year since its experimental inception, the mentor group had grown to over fifty mothers helping one another survive the pitfalls of raising kids and celebrating each other's successes. A permanent banner in the church foyer announced, "Embracing Grace for Motherhood," and Serena was championing the church leadership to expand their program into an outreach ministry for new mothers in the community.

Josie waved from the doorway and rushed over to hug Dana. She wore a ruffled V-neck dress that accentuated her long legs. Her hair was shoulder length now and styled into soft waves. Cosmetology school looked good on her.

"Thank you," said Dana. "Not just for being here, but for being my village. Thanks for always having my back and helping me be the best version of myself."

"It's mutual. I couldn't raise all my kids without you and your family."

"Where are the babies?" asked Dana.

"With a sitter. A college girl who works at their Parents' Day Out."

Dana commented that she was impressed that they only hired one babysitter. Usually, they hired Leah and a friend to babysit together.

"They're slightly less work than they were as infants," Josie said.

"Yeah right," countered Hunter. "They run in opposite directions and get into everything now. I miss plopping them down in their bouncy seats or saucers. Oh, and they're big into hitting now, so that's a treat."

"Okay fine," said Josie. "Since our usual sitter and her friends were coming here tonight, this new girl was the only one we could find."

Dana pointed to her family walking in behind them. "Speaking of…I was beginning to think you guys weren't going to make it."

Will kissed her and shook Hunter's hand. "There was a little snafu with Patch when we went to pick up your dad."

"Yeah," said Adam in a far quieter inside voice than he used to sport. "He ran out the door, and we had to drive down the block to catch him. Then he jumped in the car, and he would *not* get out when we got back to Pops' house."

"I think we're going to go back to that obedience school for another round," said Edward.

Nate hugged his mom. He was taller than she was now, which stung her heart a little. "I would ask you to autograph your book for me," he said, "but I already have your signature on tons of school papers. When you get famous, I can sell them on the internet."

She ruffled his unruly hair. "I'm counting on it."

Stephanie King writes humorous contemporary Christian fiction and nonfiction articles about God refining chaos into connection. She and her husband have raised three children in Texas, where they currently live with the youngest and an opinionated German Shepherd.